Waking the Sleeping Soul

The Immortal Fate Book 2

For

Those we lost these past few years; among them my husband's
grandmother, Nanny Hession
and
my grandfather, Jack Anderson.
Your memories will live on through us
and our children, and you will
remain forever a part of us.

❧ **1** ❧

I felt I was falling. Falling through blackness with an image burning in my mind. The image was of a familiar woman with long, wavy brown hair and blue eyes. The eyes stuck with me: so full of hatred and accusation. I was astonished by the remembrance of the woman, but I was beginning to forget why. Why was it so important that I'd seen her? Why did I feel an overwhelming sense that I'd been betrayed by someone close to me?

"Elizabeth? Are you feeling well, darling? Elizabeth, please wake up," a familiar voice called from far away as if from another room.

My eyes fluttered open and were met by the stinging burn of sunlight. I sat up abruptly, my heart beating in fear, but from what I couldn't say. I looked around at my surroundings, confused about where I was and how I'd gotten there. Hadn't I just been in a hall? Hadn't I been trying to escape from something or someone? I was sure the sun had only just been coming up moments ago, but here I was in full afternoon daylight. I looked up frightened by the glaring sun, knowing deep down I didn't belong in this place; I didn't belong in the light.

I was lying on a blanket spread across the ground, in what looked like a park. There was a book beside me, placed down as if to hold the spot where I'd left off reading. *The Moonstone* was typed in gold lettering across the linen binding. That seemed fairly familiar, but I was hazy as to why. I struggled to sit up, the tight confines of my gown making it an awkward movement.

Suddenly a gentleman, that I'd failed to see sitting across from me on the blanket, offered his hand and helped me to sit up. He was dressed strangely, much too formal for what looked like a picnic. He was eyeing me with a troubled look on his face, but why he was so worried about me I couldn't guess. My head felt muddled. Something about the sunlight on my skin didn't seem right, as if I were half expecting it to burn me, to hurt me, but I couldn't remember why.

"Elizabeth?" the gentleman questioned again with more concern in his voice.

I looked at him, sitting there so expectantly, waiting for me to give him some answer. I felt sure I recognized him, but for some reason my mind would not recall his name. His bright blue-green eyes sparkled with tender worry, and I almost felt guilty to not be able to remember who he was. He obviously knew me, and by the tender concern he showed I guessed we knew each other very well. More than feeling guilt, though, I felt frightened that something was wrong with me. Perhaps I had gone mad; why couldn't I remember anything? I took a deep breath and pushed the thought away hoping the familiar gentleman would be able to help somehow.

"I believe I am well. I must have fallen asleep, and I confess I do feel more than just a little confused about what is going on," I admitted, still trying to decide if I did indeed know the man I was speaking to. His name seemed to be just on the tip of my tongue, but I was unable to utter it.

"Are you quite sure, darling? You seemed to go very pale, and then you fainted away," the gentleman recounted for me.

Why was he speaking so formally? Why had I answered him so formally? Something seemed so out of place, but I couldn't quite put my finger on what it was. I stared at the man's carefully side-parted blonde hair and his pouting salmon-colored lips. I could tell our relationship was intimate, though in a formal kind of way, but beyond that I had no knowledge. I looked down, suddenly preoccupied with smoothing out the bottom of my forget-me-not hued dress, making sure it hadn't pulled up past my ankles. Even as I did it I wasn't sure why it would matter if my dress had pulled up a little. Certainly it wouldn't be completely shocking if I'd shown a bit of skin, but despite what my mind was thinking my hands felt it necessary to protect the honor of my boot-laced ankles. I looked up to see the gentleman staring at me, still waiting for me to explain my behavior.

I pursed my lips, trying to decide how to ease this concerned man's mind, as I suggested, "My mind seems a bit muddled at the moment. Perhaps if you told me what we were speaking of just before I fainted it might help break this strange spell I seem to be under."

"Surely you haven't forgotten my proposal?" the gentleman asked in earnest, gesturing to my left hand.

I spread my hand, looking at the delicate silver filigree ring there, and was startled to realize, "Moonstone!"

I wasn't even sure how I knew that it was moonstone, but it seemed so familiar and important. For some reason my hand shot to my neck as if I expected a necklace to be there, but I wasn't wearing one and it only confused me further. I felt certain I'd been wearing a necklace with a moonstone pendant that I rubbed when I thought of…someone; I couldn't remember who. My mind was screaming at me that this all seemed wrong, like it had happened before, but then why couldn't I remember it. I felt a kind of foreboding looking at the beautiful white-clear stone that reflected back many different colors in its center. I felt a very sad attachment to the ring even though I didn't even remember receiving it.

The gentleman straightened up, seeming to mistake my inspection of the lovely gem for disappointment as he explained, "You have always said they were your favorite, but if you find it an improper engagement ring I will replace it, of course. I know that most ladies are fond of diamonds and pearls, perhaps that would be more suitable."

"No, I love moonstone and the setting is beautiful. Moonstone is supposed to be good luck for lovers." *How did I know that?* "It just seems so strange...I feel this has all happened before." I paused, trying to decide if a proposal would have caused me to faint. *Was I really that ridiculously delicate?* "Did we speak of anything else after you proposed, and...I obviously said yes?"

The gentleman beamed delightedly and asked, "Your memory is restored?"

I lowered my eyes apologetically, answering, "No, I have no memory of that moment, but as I have the ring upon my finger I assume I accepted your proposal. Was there nothing else that might have caused my current malady?"

Wow, did I just say malady? I couldn't be sure, but I didn't think that was a word I used very often. I looked down at my purple-blue dress again. The tight bodice met with the puckered folds of the skirt and though I could see that I was dressed properly by the way the gentleman was dressed, it felt wrong. I felt out of place, but strangely I felt familiarly attached to the man I was looking at in his trim-cut, gray tweed suit. I felt attached to him, but I simply could not remember the extent of that attachment.

The gentleman was shaking his head as if at a loss for my memory problems, but decided to tell me, "After you accepted my proposal you snatched up my copy of Byron." He gestured to a book lying beside him and continued, "You read a poem to me. I don't think that would cause you any distress, though. We often read poetry together."

"What was the poem?" I asked, looking for anything that would explain my foggy brain.

"The poem was "Darkness"," the gentleman answered, waiting to see if it sparked anything, and then he repeated from memory, "I had a dream, which was not all a dream. / The bright sun was extinguish'd, and the stars / Did wander darkling in the eternal space, /Rayless, and pathless, and the icy earth / Swung blind and blackening in the moonless air; / Morn came and went- -and came, and brought no day..."

I stared at him, caught in the beauty of his voice and the poem, and then remembering myself I looked down and commented, "That was lovely, sad, but lovely. I'm sure that could not have caused me anything but pleasure to have read. Was there anything after that? Did we speak of nothing else?"

He tapped his lip with his forefinger in thought. "You said you couldn't understand how such a wicked man could write such beautiful verses," the gentleman paused, lost in thought and then added, "I then asked if you would join my family this evening for dinner, to celebrate our engagement. I don't see why that would cause you any distress; you know that my parents adore you."

I sighed loudly, more in aggravation at the limitation of my own mind than that I was worried that there was something wrong with me. I was fairly certain I wasn't crazy; I felt as though my powers of reason were intact, and I didn't feel as though I had endured any kind of injury to my head. So what was clouding my memory? I looked around the park in which we were picnicking, hoping I would happen upon a familiar sight. Off in the distance I saw a great manor house cloaked in ivy just beyond a long, narrow tree-lined drive.

"This is Cuckfield Park!" I exclaimed in excitement, recognizing the dark but romantic looking house.

"Yes, darling, you remember," the gentleman gushed, moving closer to me to tenderly take my hand.

I didn't want to disappoint him, but I had to explain, "I recognize this place, but it seems different than what I remember." I shook my head in frustration. "I'm not sure why I know this place, but it does seem so familiar, as if I saw it in a dream once. Please, continue telling me all that we spoke of before I fainted, I believe it is helping."

The gentleman looked down at our entwined hands and continued recounting, "I then explained that my mother has an engagement party prepared for us this evening-"

"Already?" I asked in surprise, looking down at the ring the gentleman had only recently offered as he asked for my hand. "What if I had said no?"

"I don't know," he answered nervously, wringing his hands. "I've been hinting at it for weeks and you seemed to light up each time. In truth, I had planned to ask you almost a month ago. I spoke to your father and my own parents about it then, and my mother started making plans immediately. It's my fault for unnecessarily delaying. I was so terribly anxious that you might refuse me; I put it off for much too long. I suppose you could say I find you quite intimidating at times. I know that I need you more than you need me, and I feared you might hold that against me. You didn't seem upset by my procrastination, though. You actually laughed and teased me about it. I then went on to apologize that a stranger would be in attendance tonight. I spoke harshly of the man...perhaps my course words were what caused your agitation."

"I doubt you could have said anything so shocking that it would have caused me to faint. Who is the gentleman? Do I know him? Is it possible he's someone I dislike greatly and wish to not come into contact with?" I asked on a whim.

This was becoming too much. It was one thing to be confused about who I was, where I was, and with whom I was with, but it was quite another to have to endure listening to myself speak as if I were some upper-class Victorian. I looked down at my dress again in wonder. Was I an upper-class Victorian? This was Cuckfield Park in West Sussex, England. I was sitting with a gentleman on the front lawns of a great manor house, a private manor house that would surely not allow anyone access to its grounds. It would make sense from my clothing and that of the gentleman's, not to mention the reserved manner in which we were speaking to each other. I decided to keep my mind open to the possibility that I was not only confused about who I was, but when I was. The main problem with keeping my mind open, though, was at that moment my mind was not exactly working properly.

The gentleman's face took on a harsh sneer as he said, "No, you would not know this man. He is a foreigner. I was just explaining to you that the man seemed to believe he is related to my ancestors, the Hunyadis."

I looked at him, startled by the name he'd mentioned. "Hunyadi. I know that name somehow. From Romania, are they not?"

"Indeed," the gentleman answered delightedly, "you are beginning to remember."

I didn't want to get his hopes up. "No, I'm not sure if I remember anything. That name just sounds familiar. Please go on, tell me what else you said to me. I think it is helping to hear the conversation we were having before I fainted."

The gentleman smiled warmly at me and continued, "I

6

was telling you how this Romanian claimed he was distantly related to my family through the Hunyadis. He claims that my father's great, great grandmother was sister to his great, great grandfather, or some such nonsense. We know that there was a split between a brother and sister in our past and the Hunyadis, the male line, renounced the family legacy. My father, Lord Sergison," he paused momentarily to see if I recognized the name, but went on when I made no answer, "invited the man to dine with us this evening, but I don't trust the man. I believe he is a charlatan, trying to tie himself to an old, wealthy family. I'm sure he's hiding something."

"Do you really believe that? You truly think the man is being dishonest?" I asked genuinely intrigued by his assertion.

The gentleman seemed distracted, but answered, "Yes, I believe he is not what he seems, but my father doesn't wish to accuse the man without proof. I am sorry that he'll be joining us on such a special evening, but I promise to not let my annoyance ruin our celebration."

I smiled shyly at the gentleman, feeling not only tenderness for him and his reserved attentions to me but also an undeniable attraction. He was an uncommonly handsome man; his eyes alone were mesmerizing, like looking out over a tropical sea. His lithe but strong body moved so elegantly, just the movement of his hands as he spoke made me wonder how skilled they were at other things. I looked down, hoping the gentleman didn't notice my face suddenly reddening, and tried to focus on what we had been speaking about.

Calmly I asked, "Was that when I fainted? Just after you had explained that this mysterious man would be attending our dinner party?"

The gentleman thought a moment before stating, "No, it was just after that. You asked me the man's name, and when I said it you fainted."

I waited anxiously for him to say the name, but he seemed to need prompting. Was he afraid the mention of the man's name would affect me again? How could something as simple as a person's name have caused me to faint? I was behaving strangely, even in my own opinion, but surely I wasn't so frail as to faint at the mere mention of the name of a man I didn't even know. I had to admit I didn't feel like myself and everything that was happening seemed so foreign to me, and yet somehow familiar; it was entirely possible something as benign as a name could have caused me to faint. I didn't even have much control over what was coming out of my mouth or how reserved I was behaving, and yet my thoughts seemed to be my own and not ludicrously dripping with proper English.

Finally, as the gentleman wasn't offering any more information, I questioned him sternly, "What was it? What was the man's name?"

The gentleman seemed hesitant to say it again, biting his lip in thought, but he eventually said softly, "Samothrace….Dardanos Samothrace."

"Your highness, is everything all right?" a man asked from behind me.

I turned, confused about my surroundings, to see a blonde haired man dressed in a short, simple chiton carrying a tray with fruit and a cup on it. As he came closer I saw his eyes were a beautiful blue-green. He set the tray on one of the tables in the vast tiled room.

"Have you been crying again?" he asked quietly.

"Yes, Xanthós, My father wishes to send me away, and I have no hope of changing his mind," I explained, wiping at my eyes.

Xanthós looked to the door to make sure no one was there before putting his hands on my shoulders. "Have you prayed to Athena for help?"

As a eunuch Xanthós was permitted certain liberties in the palace. Slaves were only to speak when spoken to and were never permitted to touch those above them unless expressly instructed, but because he'd been a eunuch from such a young age his intimacy with my family was allowed. Though, he was only a slave I considered him my friend; he listened when the rest of my family scoffed at me or ignored me entirely.

"Go to the temple. Pray to Athena," Xanthós instructed smiling. "All will be well."

I nodded, feeling a little less hopeless. "Will you go with me?" I asked him, knowing his presence would give me courage.

"Of course, your highness, I would do anything you asked of me," he answered eagerly.

"Elizabeth?! Darling, please wake up!" pleaded a voice, but I couldn't see its owner.

Once again I found myself opening my eyes to the blinding brightness of the afternoon sun. I was still in a park, during the day, and wearing the same forget-me-not gown. The gentleman was still sitting across from me, though he'd moved a bit closer. I could feel the warmth coming off of him as he helped me to sit up. I wasn't used to being trapped in such confining garments, maneuvering seemed to be a little tricky, especially after fainting...twice.

I felt confused looking at the gentleman as I was sure we'd just been in a palace, and he'd been dressed as a slave, but the memory was slipping away. "What happened?" I asked, feeling keenly aware of the gentleman's hands still resting in mine.

"You fainted again, darling," the man said, brushing a strand of burgundy hair out my eyes. "I think, perhaps, I should escort you home. Rest may be all that you require."

I looked down at our entwined hands, focusing on the moonstone ring, and suddenly my head seemed to clear. "Gabriel!" I exclaimed, pushing the strange dream of the eunuch from my mind.

Gabriel ran his fingers through his perfectly parted sandy blonde hair and sighed in relief, "Thank God, your memory is restored. You really frightened me. How was I going to marry a woman with a broken head?" he joked.

I laughed lightly and shook my head playfully as if I were angry. "I suppose it would have been a perfect match. A woman with a broken head and a man born without a brain," I teased.

Gabriel grabbed my hand happily and kissed it before he busied himself clearing our picnic away. I looked out at the great estate of Cuckfield Park, now remembering every detail of it.

From the familiar tree-lined drive to the various gardens which encircled statues at their center, and to the large pond at the back of the property. Gabriel and I spent many hours either strolling through the gardens or fishing in the pond, Gabriel teasing me that fishing wasn't a proper activity for a young Lady. I knew he actually found my interest in such things amusing. He had told me on more than one occasion that he found most women dull, and that they should take interest in more things that men are interested in. My response back, though I did in fact agree with him to a point, was that perhaps men should take more interest in educating their daughters to not marry men with too many "interests".

Even as the son of an earl, Gabriel didn't hold strictly to the rigid, conservative traditionalism that society dictated a man of his status should exhibit. He was very open and easy with people, of all stations, and it was the main reason I had fallen in love with him. His parents, Lord John Sergison and Lady Cynthia Sergison, were just as easy mannered, and didn't shock easily. They had accepted me immediately as Gabriel's love interest even though my father was only Lord Sergison's lawyer. My family wasn't poor by a long-shot, we were actually very well off, but nothing close to the Sergisons who held a title along with unthinkable wealth.

Gabriel would one day inherit his father's title of Earl of Lewes, and would also one day become master of Cuckfield Park. I smiled to myself, remembering that I had just agreed to be Gabriel's wife. The title didn't excite me; I knew my family would be proud that I was a countess, but what really made me happy was to know that one day I would be mistress of Cuckfield Park. I had always felt I was connected to it somehow, and now I truly was.

I had actually fallen in love with Cuckfield Park before I'd even been acquainted with Gabriel Sergison. My family had been invited to a ball at Cuckfield Park by Lord and Lady Sergison. My father had connections to the Sergisons by way of his exclusive handling of their estate and other holdings; he was a well-respected lawyer of above average wealth, and owed much of his success to the Sergisons. In addition, he and Lord Sergison had been great friends for most of their lives, but for some reason our two families had never been acquainted. That is, until the night of the ball at Cuckfield Park when I fell in love with the grounds and darkly beautiful manor house.

I never understood why my father and Lord Sergison had never introduced our families, especially because they had been friends well before either man was even married. I had my suspicions that Lord Sergison was an overly proud man that did not wish to mingle his high-born family with our moderately wealthy and notably title-less family, but I was proved wrong upon our first encounter. Not only was Lord Sergison not cold and indifferent to our introduction, he actually treated us as family he had long heard about but never met. He was full of smiles and laughter, and shared several stories my father had told him about us. Even Lady Sergison, who, I have to admit, I was a little nervous to meet, was kind and gracious. The stories we had all heard, probably most people heard, about her painted her as a dark, melancholy enchantress, but she talked with my mother, sister, and me as if we'd known each other for years. She even invited us to have tea the following week, which was a special honor; not only because she had only just met us and she was of a much higher social rank than we were, but because Lady Sergison in general did not invite many visitors to her home except for parties.

Then there was Gabriel Sergison. Tall and slim with a smile that made my knees weak. When we were introduced I forgot momentarily how to speak, as I was entranced by his beautiful aquamarine eyes, and only stared as his soft salmon-toned lips parted to greet me. He was much more delicate looking than most men I'd been around, with his perfectly parted sandy-blonde hair and soft facial features, but he moved with such elegance and determination that the strength of his body was undeniable. When words finally found their way into my mouth I sputtered something about the beauty of the Park. Whatever nonsense I had uttered in my nervousness made Gabriel laugh and ask if he might escort me into the ballroom.

It was strange how easy it had been: to fall in love with Gabriel, for him to fall in love with me. It felt as if someone had planned the whole thing without either of us knowing. Gabriel had confessed to me that had we of met without so many eyes upon us and without the scrutiny of his and my parents' watchful eyes, he would have proposed the moment we met. I thought he was just trying to make himself sound more spontaneous, because I teased him constantly about his need for planning. Whether it had been planned by someone or was just a happy accident our love affair had reached its pinnacle that day, the day Gabriel had finally worked up the courage to ask me to be his wife, and no matter how strange the circumstances seemed I could never entertain the idea that any of it was fate.

"Elizabeth, don't forget your book," Gabriel reminded me, waking me from my daydreaming, pointing to the little green book still folded open beside me. "Let me take you home. You should rest. I think perhaps you've had too much sun today."

I scooped up *The Moonstone* fondly remembering how Gabriel had chosen it because of my love of moonstones, and because one of the main characters was named Gabriel. He was disappointed when I told him the story was actually about a yellow diamond called the moonstone because of its association with an Indian moon god, and that the character Gabriel was actually a well-aged and delightfully peculiar house steward. I knew he had meant it to be a thoughtful gift, though he had taken little time to actually examine the book, but I assured him continuously that I was quite enthralled by the story. It was a clever, twisting plot about the disappearance of the title gem, and I now remembered how we spent many a lazy afternoon together. I would read sections of the book to Gabriel that I had already read on my own and we would then discuss it. Much like we had done earlier in the day, before he'd proposed, and before I had fainted. I smiled at the simple, pleasant time we shared together.

Gabriel took my hands to help me to my feet and as I looked up I realized I had stepped forward too far; I could actually feel his breath on my lips as I agreed lightly, "Yes, I think you may be right. I should rest. I feel a bit unbalanced still."

I laid my hands on his forearms to steady myself, but I couldn't look away from those sea-swept eyes. Without so much as a glance to make sure no one would see, Gabriel plunged forward, covering my mouth with his as he wrapped his arms around me. Of course we had kissed before, but it was always quick, before anyone could see us, and usually at some party in which we would have to find a dark corner to hide in for a moment. This was nothing like what we had shared before; I was very nearly ready to suggest we sneak off somewhere more secluded, but then reprimanded myself for such thoughts. We weren't married yet; we hadn't even officially announced our engagement.

Thankfully Gabriel had the sense to pull away, giving me a devious smile as he commented, "Yes, I see how unbalanced you are, but I must say I can't complain. I should leave you out in the sun more often."

I gave him a sour smile as I took his arm, but his words reminded me of my earlier feelings. "In all seriousness I actually had this strange thought after I'd fainted the first time that the sun was going to harm me. I almost felt I remembered being someone else, it was so odd. Then I had the strangest dream after fainting the second time. You were in it, but it wasn't exactly you. You were dressed differently and you kept calling me highness."

As we started our walk back toward the manor house Gabriel teased, "Perhaps you were remembering a past life."

I narrowed my eyes playfully, retorting, "Mr. Sergison, you know I don't go in for all of that nonsense. I am sure you haven't forgotten the ridiculous spectacle I had to endure at Lady Sergison's last séance party."

Gabriel laughed and admitted, "I will never forget it. I do apologize for convincing you to attend, but I must say it was the most interesting séance I've ever been forced to attend."

I huffed in mock annoyance, chiding, "That is only because it has fueled you with endless opportunities to taunt me."

"Well, how could I resist? Honestly, if you were in my place you would tease me as well. Not only did the woman claim you were a princess, but that you were descended from beings that once ruled the earth; how absurd! Why do mediums always seem to conjure up important figures from the past? Surely they must realize we would more readily believe them if they said they had conjured a common merchant or that you had been a butcher's wife in your past life."

I smirked, knowing Gabriel wouldn't believe anything a medium told him even if it weren't so ridiculous, as I said sarcastically, "Oh yes, I can see you being very happy to be told that you were nothing more than a fish monger in your past life. It's all a show; you know that. Mediums and so called mystics merely tell their wealthy employers what they want to hear. Can you imagine if a medium actually told the truth at a séance? They'd be out of the job; no one would book them for parties."

As we approached the front of the great manor house, the ivy-encased facade shaking gently in the breeze, Gabriel motioned to the coachman to pull the carriage around, and then turned back to me and joked, "Well, I see that I shall have a cynic for a wife."

"Not at all," I answered lightly, "I simply don't believe in past lives, especially ones that involve me being some tragic princess descended from gods."

Gabriel offered his hand and helped me into the maroon and black carriage. The coachman was used to driving us about unchaperoned, but Gabriel made it a point to always have the top folded down on the extravagant Landau carriage. I climbed into the forest green felt seats as Gabriel asked the coachman to take us to my home.

"So your highness, should I assume then that you believe nothing in destiny, in fate?" Gabriel asked playfully, sitting across from me.

I narrowed my eyes at him, regretting telling him about my dream. "I don't believe that we have no control over our own destinies; if that's what you mean," I retorted.

"So you don't think fate had any hand in our being brought together?" Gabriel questioned, though now in a serious tone.

I shook my head, unsure if I should continue as Gabriel seemed to be getting upset, but I explained plainly, "No, I do not think fate had anything do with it. I think it was mere coincidence that our fathers knew each other and introduced us. Further than that..." I paused and gave him a sly smile, "how could I not love you? We were simply two people with a mutual attraction and similar bizarre humor."

Gabriel huffed as if in outrage, but I could see a trace of a smile on his lips. "Well, that is quite likely the most unromantic explanation for love I have ever heard."

I snickered, glad he wasn't angry with me, and asked, "What would you have me say then?"

Gabriel tapped his finger on his lips as if in thought and offered, "I would say there is no such thing as coincidence; we were destined to meet and fall in love. I would say destiny had a specific plan for us."

The coachman opened the door, but before I took his hand I proclaimed firmly, "I control my own fate."

&2∞

As I entered the foyer of my home my mother came bustling out of the main drawing room with a gawking smile on her face. I did my best to put on a serene smile, but it was obvious; she and my father already knew the news. My mother grabbed my hand, pulling me along behind her drab gray taffeta dress, her high collar giving her a severe look as if she were more annoyed by my good fortune than truly happy about it. I followed obediently into the drawing room to see my father lounging casually on the maroon sofa. He very rarely sat in the drawing room, unless he had matters to discuss with my mother, my sister, or with me. It was yet another sign that my parents had known of the engagement before I had. My father was clearly waiting in the drawing room where he rarely sat to pepper me with questions.

"Ah, Lizzy, you're back so soon? How was your picnic?" my father asked innocently.

I sat in the large upholstered chair to the right of him, steadying myself for questions which, apparently, my father already knew the answer to. He put his book down clumsily, not even noting the page number, and ran his hand through his black hair that had just begun to show traces of gray at the top. His bright green eyes, so similar to mine, sparkled with excitement waiting for my response.

"Well, are you going to tell us anything?" he prodded.

I laughed at his childish enthusiasm and countered, "Why should I tell you a thing? You obviously know what has happened so I won't waste my breath telling you the details."

My mother sat in the matching chair to mine, just across from me, and pursed her lips impatiently. She didn't play the game my father played, knowing something and pretending not to, trying to get me to admit everything. My father enjoyed knowing things before I did and finding out how I would describe it to him. Most of the time I found it to be a pleasant attention from my father, but just then I was a little annoyed that such an important decision had been known before I'd even agreed to anything.

I sighed loudly and glared at my father, "Oh, if you must have me say it…Gabriel has asked me to marry him."

My father bit his lip as he smiled like a fool. "And…and," he prompted, waiving his hand at me to get it all out.

I clasped my hands together and looked down at my book resting on my lap. I wanted to be over-joyed, my father was, but something was nagging at me. The strange feeling I'd had after I'd fainted, the anticlimactic realization that I was engaged before I could even remember who Gabriel was, and the feeling that things were too perfect, too planned were still swirling in my brain. I worried that a trap had been set and I was the prey; only I was too ignorant to know that I was in a trap. It was weighing on me, dulling my heart, and not allowing me to feel any happiness.

Finally I relented, "I have accepted him. Here is the ring," I said, holding my hand out dutifully to my mother.

"Of course you have," my father said simply as my mother very nearly jumped out of her seat to examine the ring.

"What is that?" she asked, knitting her eyebrows as she squinted at the stone.

I knew my mother wouldn't approve. She was too wrapped up in the customary fashions, and would have expected a pearl surrounded by diamonds or an exorbitantly large diamond. She was probably disappointed that she wouldn't be able to brag to her friends about the enormous ring Gabriel had bought me. After all, her only interest in Gabriel was that he came from a wealthy family with a title, and she expected everything connected with him to be extravagant, including the engagement ring he'd bought. I could see her mentally calculating how to put a positive spin on this unforeseen predicament.

"It's moonstone, mother...my favorite gemstone. Obviously Gabriel pays attention to my likes and dislikes, and decided to give me a ring that would make me happy, instead of giving me a ring that everyone else would expect," I explained a little harshly.

My father rose from the sofa, as if to inspect the ring that I could tell he had already seen before, and gushed, "It is lovely, isn't it Mary? Simply lovely. You have fine taste, Lizzy, and don't let anyone tell you differently." He kissed me on the head and then left the room.

I smiled a little triumphantly to myself, knowing he'd directed the comment at my mother, who seemed to always worry what others thought of her or us. It wasn't that I disliked my mother, I loved her very much, but we were very different in our ideas about life. I was stubborn like my father: I liked what I liked because I liked it and didn't let other people's likes or dislikes influence me. My sister, Emma, she was more like my mother. Telling the latest gossip, wearing the latest fashion, and grooming herself to one day become...well, my mother. That is until recently.

I excused myself from the drawing room, telling my mother I had to start getting ready for the engagement dinner that evening. My mother feigned surprise at having to attend dinner at the Sergison's house that evening, and did her best to fuss about what she would wear on such short notice. Before I left the room she made a comment about Emma having disappeared again, and I could see that she was more worried about my sister's absence than she was delighted about my engagement.

I went to my room thinking about Emma. Where was she now? Would she make it home in time to attend the engagement dinner? I hadn't even thought about Emma all day, yet it was a subject that was daily on my mind. A few months back, not quite a year ago, Emma had started to disappear without any explanation. At first she would only be gone an hour or so here and there; it wasn't every day, just a few times a week. Then as time progressed she would disappear for longer and longer, and when we would question where she'd been she would fly into a fit of rage, only to be consoled by our mother. I would hear them whispering to each other and I believed that my mother knew more than she was letting on, but she swore she didn't. Lately, when Emma disappeared it would be days before she returned home, sometimes so exhausted she would sleep for a few days and need to be nursed back to health. Other times she would stop in for clothes and a quick argument and be off again with no hint of where she'd been or where she was going.

I closed the door to my room, carelessly tossing my book onto my bed and inadvertently onto a gown laid out on the bed. I stared at the gown; my mother's choice, apparently. At some point she had ordered a dress for me for this particular evening, an evening that she had just pretended she knew nothing about. She and my father had known Gabriel would propose for a long time and that we would be attending a celebratory engagement dinner on this particular date, but no one let a word of it be known to me. They must have had at least a few weeks' notice about the dinner for the dress to have been ordered and delivered, and yet I had had no hint that anything was going on. Everything had been planned, including my supposed yes, behind my back by everyone around me. My life seemed to be laid before me, and it felt as if I had very little say in any of it.

I glared at the dress laid on my bed, angry at everyone's presumption that I would do what they wanted me to. The dress was typical for an evening party. It was pale pink with ivory lace; all romantic innocence, but I didn't feel like a blushing bride-to-be. I felt troubled, I felt dark. I ignored the dress and went to my armoire. I knew exactly what dress I would wear, even though when I'd bought it I thought I would never wear it. I pulled the enchanting sage colored dress up, slipping my arms through the straps bedecked with light and dark sage-colored flowers. The dress itself was a light sage color with dark sage damask designs all over, and the dress front was pulled tightly into a slight bustle at the back with more of the light and dark green flowers gathered there. The hem of the dress was scalloped with a wide green satin trim just above the bottom. I placed the opera gloves that I would wear on the bed; they were the same shade of green as the satin trim on the dress and went past my elbows.

I sat down triumphantly at my vanity, smiling at the open defiance I was committing by not only refusing to wear the dress my mother had chosen, but also to wear a gown that was not traditionally worn by an engaged woman. I stared at my reflection trying to decide what to do with my hair when my maid, Ann, knocked lightly and entered. I could tell by her insistent apologies that my mother had sent her to look after my appearance. Her first statement was a light reminder that my mother had expected me to wear the pink and ivory gown, but when I stood from the vanity to face her she stopped.

"Oh, Miss, you look beautiful. Like a princess, you are," Ann said, coming toward me to sit me back at the vanity. "I know exactly what we should do with your hair."

I watched in the mirror as Ann curled my already softly curling burgundy hair further and then pulled it up and back, leaving a part down the middle. She fastened most of my hair at the crown of my head and let long ringlets fall down the back. After disappearing from the room for a few moments she returned with white and green flowers to place in my hair.

After Ann left the room I applied a touch of beeswax with dye in it to my lips to make them a light plum shade, lined my top and bottom lid with a small amount of soot, and rubbed beet juice on my cheeks to give them some pale color. Every woman I knew used cosmetics on her face, but no woman I knew would ever admit to it. It was one of those strange games we played in society; only poor, common women would "paint" themselves, not high upstanding ladies like my mother or Lady Sergison, but they did. We just never spoke of it. The last thing I did was place a few drops of belladonna into each eye; I didn't use it often because it did sting a bit, but I liked the effect of making my eyes look larger. I usually only used it for balls or fancy dinner parties. My mother had used it much of her life and now complained of blurred vision. She would never admit to the use of belladonna now, but when we were younger she shared all her beauty secrets with Emma and me. I had a sneaking suspicion that her overuse of belladonna was the cause of her eye problems, and so I used it sparingly to avoid such problems myself. I placed all of my secret beauty items back under the false bottom in a drawer in my vanity.

I stared at my now blurry image in the mirror, waiting for the fuzziness and stinging to subside in my eyes. I fixed a few pieces of hair that had started to slide out of place, and I wondered if I had made the right decision in accepting Gabriel's proposal. My bright green eyes finally came back into focus, but they held no answer for me. I loved Gabriel, that was easy, but something felt forced in our relationship. I almost felt I was being tricked into loving Gabriel. It made no sense; I had no reason to think that, nor any reason to not be completely happy about being the future Mrs. Sergison, and then of course one day Lady Sergison. I needed to clear my head, calm my suspicions before Gabriel sent the carriage for me.

Without drawing any attention to myself or telling anyone where I was going I quietly walked out the back door and entered our private walled-in garden at the back of our property. I pushed the wrought iron gates open, fastening them shut behind myself and followed the path of flagstones scattered across the sparse grass toward the center of the modestly sized garden. In the center there was a simple three-tiered fountain which the flagstones encircled and branched off into other directions of the garden. It was late spring so nearly everything was in bloom in the garden; the waist-high spires of white and bluish-purple bellflowers, coordinating blooms of columbines, friendly clusters of bright white daisies, purple and pink spires of both delphinium and the bell-shaped flowers of foxglove, fragrant lavender, and the impressively tall spires of red, purple, and yellow hollyhocks. Just the smells of the garden were enough to put me at ease, but the flowers were not my reason for seeking the solitude of the quiet space. I followed the flagstones to the right of the fountain and found myself standing in front of one of several stone benches that were scattered throughout the garden. This bench, however, was my favorite, because of its placement just in front of my favorite statue.

Since I was a child the garden had been my hiding place, my means of escape from the bland, strict world I was surrounded by. I had dubbed the place my fairy garden, as it was the most magical place I'd ever been, and the statue that I now stared at: she was the fairy queen of the garden. I'm not even sure why the statue had caught my eye, it wasn't particularly impressive or beautiful. It was wooden, unlike all the other statues that were made of stone, and it was shorter than I was by nearly a foot. Most statues were bigger, grander, but this statue had some kind of magic. I had felt it as a child and I still felt it when I sat before her.

The statue was my reason for sneaking into the garden. It seemed to calm me, make me feel safe, and I often found myself sitting on the stone bench facing the statue when I was troubled. I wasn't sure if it was the story surrounding the statue or just the idea that it had existed for so long, but something about it was different than any other statue I had ever seen. It was my father's prized possession, dating back, supposedly, before Christ, and much sought after by those that knew what it was. The statue was The Palladium of Greek myth.

The Palladium was thought to be made of olive wood, standing about four and a half feet tall, and portrayed the standing figure of a woman. The woman was Pallas, daughter of Triton, herald of the sea-god Poseidon. Pallas grew up with the goddess Athena, as Triton had agreed to raise her, and the two were like sisters. During a practice fighting match Zeus held up the Aegis, a terrifying shield with the image of Medusa upon it, distracting Pallas as Athena was striking a blow. Athena's accidental attack killed Pallas and in her guilt and sorrow she created The Palladium to honor her friend. Many years later the statue was credited with giving a sign to the founder of the great city of Troy, showing him where he should build the city, and until it was stolen by the Greeks the statue not only protected Troy, but blessed it with peace and bounty.

"Something is bothering you," my father's voice came from behind me.

Startled, I turned around to see my father's bright green eyes staring down at me as I protested, "Not at all, why would you say that?"

My father walked around the bench to sit beside me. "Lizzy, you wouldn't have stolen from the house so secretly in your fine clothes to sit in front of The Palladium unless you were troubled by something. Is it about Gabriel?"

"No," I answered a little too quickly, but seeing the knowing look on my father's face I admitted, "Well, maybe. I'm not sure what is wrong. I've felt strange all day, as if someone else were inside me, trying to tell me how to feel about everything...it's confusing. I know I should feel absolute joy, but I have this nagging thought that something terrible is going to happen and this is the catalyst. It seems so perfect, but it scares me that I may just be accepting the life put before me and in the end I will pay a price for my complacency."

My father placed his hand over mine and comforted, "I'm sure it's just nerves. Making a decision about the rest of your life can seem daunting, especially when that life comes with many responsibilities that you are not used to having. I'm sure I don't have to tell you what an honorable man Gabriel Sergison is, and I know that he will do everything in his power to make you happy for the rest of your life."

I smiled at the simplicity of my father's explanation; I wished it was only nerves, but it was more than that. I felt this strange foreboding that something bad was going to follow this path, should I choose to take it. Just the idea that a single decision was going to affect a certain outcome felt uncharacteristic to me. I had never believed in such things as destiny and fate, of sensing impending doom or causing bad luck with one seemingly joyous decision. Although I took after my father in most things, I had, unfortunately, developed my mother's cynicism for never believing in anything that I couldn't see with my own eyes or touch with my own hands. I looked back at The Palladium, now thinking it odd that I had always been drawn to it, like a lucky talisman, and had believed I could actually feel magic coming from it. How had my cynical nature not caused me to overlook Pallas; how had my very cynical and practical brain created a fairy story surrounding Pallas?

"I know," I admitted to my father, "I should be nothing but ecstatic and I truly couldn't be happier to have Gabriel's affections. I just have this feeling that things are too perfect, and perhaps there are secrets that have been kept from me that will change everything."

My father shifted uneasily and cleared his throat before answering, "That is nonsense, Lizzy. You're just letting your imagination get the better of you."

"Perhaps," I said distractedly, and then seeing the concern on my father's face I added, "I fainted this afternoon just after Gabriel proposed. He suggested I had probably gotten too much sun; that's most likely the cause of my feeling out of sorts. All of these strange feelings began after I fainted, and I felt as though I were having memories that were not my own. I'm sure it was too much sun, that's all. I am happy, father. I don't mean to worry you."

My father rose from the bench, kissing me on the head, offering softly, "You know that you can tell me anything, Lizzy, no matter how trivial or troubling it may seem."

"Yes, I know," I said beaming, "Maybe that is the real reason I feel unnerved. Once I'm married I won't have you there every day to confide in. Who will listen to my ramblings?"

"Well then, I will have to ease your nerves," he boomed delightedly, grabbing my hand, "I shall have to give you a gift to take away your fears." He paused as if scanning the gardens for something. "Perhaps...The Palladium?"

My eyes shot wide in disbelief. "But, father, it's your prized possession!"

He laughed gently as he lifted my chin with his hand. "There are things I prize more, and I know what she means to you. When you and Gabriel are wed you may take The Palladium with you to Cuckfield Park."

I jumped up, forgetting my fears and hugged him. "Thank you, father! You don't know what it means to me."

"There now," My father said as he pulled back to look at me, "there's the smile I've been hoping to see all day." He paused and looking down at my gown remarked, "Am I to believe that my wife's tastes have changed or is that a gown of your own choosing?"

I blushed at my father's knowing comment. "I found this to be more to my liking, more...me," I added.

My father smiled as if he could already foresee the annoyance my mother would exhibit when she saw me. "Well, you look lovely, my Lizzy."

After my father left I sat back down to look upon my wedding present. The Palladium, the statue of Pallas, she was mine. She would accompany me to Cuckfield Park and protect me and my new family. I pushed the silly feelings I'd had all day aside, and was able to rejoice in the pleasant events of the day finally. Everything was going to be fine, and the idea that there were any imperfections in my life were all in my mind.

"Should I be concerned that you've taken refuge in front of your fairy queen?" Gabriel questioned playfully from the end of the path, just a few steps from the fountain.

I turned and gave him a superior smirk. "Actually I'm just admiring our wedding gift."

Gabriel sat down beside me and sighed exaggeratedly, "Please don't tell me your father is really giving you that antiquated replica as a gift?"

I laughed at his playful attempt at annoyance and reprimanded, "How could you say such a thing about The Palladium? You know my father truly believes she is the original, and she has always protected my family."

"Hmmm, and you find my mother's obsession with the afterlife bizarre? You, who thinks the statue that stands before you in your fairy garden was created by a goddess and is imbued with magical protective properties?" He asked teasingly, raising his eyebrows.

I lightly smacked his arm and objected, "I don't believe any of that and you know it. I simply think she's lucky."

"Well, I can't argue with that," Gabriel said as he offered his hand, "after all, I have been lucky enough to not only find my fiancée sitting before her, but also looking more radiant than any goddess in history."

I accepted his hand, letting him lead me out of the garden. I left him waiting momentarily in the foyer while I quickly went back to my room to fetch my small silver mesh reticule in which I'd already placed a handkerchief, a fan, and a scent bottle. I put on my satin opera gloves and, as it wasn't particularly cold, I decided to wear my embroidered black velvet elbow-length cape instead of a heavier cloak.

Gabriel led me out to his grand Landau carriage, but unlike earlier that day the top was up. His footman was holding the door open for us to get in. I hesitated a moment, not sure if it was prudent to enter the private confines of the carriage as we were not even officially engaged, and even then it would seem rash to be so secluded with a man I wasn't married to. I looked at Gabriel, who seemed to be nervously fiddling with his buttons, obviously aware of the position he was putting me in. Then I thought about the kiss we'd shared in the park earlier. Perhaps that prolonged moment of passion had been Gabriel's motivation to escort me to our engagement dinner enclosed in his carriage where no prying eyes could find us. I by no means sought to cause others to gossip about my behavior, but nor was I so prudish to think it wrong to spend a few intimate moments with the man I planned to spend the rest of my life with. With my heart beating anxiously I got into the carriage.

Gabriel climbed onto the seat beside me, turning to me with a nervous look on his face as he apologized, "I know an unmarried young lady would not usually consent to an unchaperoned ride in a closed carriage, but there are things I feel I should explain before we make our engagement public."

Now my heart was thudding fiercely, not from nervous excitement that Gabriel might take me in his arms any moment, but from dread. That feeling was coming back to me; the feeling I'd had all day that things seemed wrong. The feeling that my seemingly perfect world was going to come tumbling down, and my adoring future husband had secrets that would send me spiraling into a world of confusion and hopelessness. I thought back to what my father had said: Gabriel was an honorable man and he would do anything to make me happy. I decided to push all the nonsense floating around in my head aside and give Gabriel the benefit of the doubt. Knowing Gabriel, his deep dark secret was probably that he had to go out of town with his father or that our engagement would have to be prolonged.

I forced a smile and assured him, "Gabriel, you can tell me anything. I promise I won't be angry."

He was gazing distractedly out the window as he sputtered, "I forgot to ask…how are you feeling?"

"I feel perfectly well now," I answered smoothly, knowing he was stalling.

Gabriel turned his sea-swept eyes toward me and asked earnestly, "Your memory has fully returned then? You no longer have the strange feeling of being someone else?"

I pursed my lips nervously not wanting to admit the bizarre thoughts that had been swirling in my head. "I remember everything perfectly," I said hesitantly, "and the strange feelings I had seemed to have passed. I feel perfectly myself except…" I paused, giving Gabriel a forlorn look and then added, "…except that you're making me nervous. What is it that you wish tell me?"

"Well, you see, my family…we…we're…" Gabriel turned away once more to gaze out the window, and putting his fist to his mouth he tried once more to explain, "my family…we…there is a secret…"

He faced me again as if he expected I would guess what he was trying to say, but I shook my head lightly at a loss as to what he was alluding.

The blank look on my face prompted him to say dejectedly, "You're going to leave me."

"Gabriel," I said in anguished confusion, "why would you say that? I love you and there is nothing you could say that would change that." I wasn't so sure that was true, but I needed to know what was upsetting him. "Please tell me what's wrong."

I could see tears forming in his eyes as he admitted, "It's

a great secret. Not even my mother knows. It could put you in danger....your connection to me alone puts you in danger, may even put your whole family in danger."

My head was telling me to try to change the subject, not to let him reveal his secret, because I was starting to believe it might just be bad enough to cause me to call off the engagement. I looked down at the moonstone ring on my left hand. Moonstones were supposed to give their wearer clarity and enlightenment, but as much as I'd thought something secretive was going on I now decided it would be better to not know. Maybe there were times when ignorance was bliss and being in the dark was a fortunate place to be. I had always prided myself in my belief that honesty was always the best choice, even at the expense of it causing some hurt, but at that moment I wanted desperately for Gabriel to lie to me. I wanted him to simply take me in his arms, laughing, and tell me it was all a ruse. I made a silent promise to myself that I would pretend to believe him implicitly and never bring the subject up again; if only he'd make up a lie.

Gabriel noticed my distressed glances at the ring and muttered sadly, "You're already considering leaving me."

"No, I'm not, truly," I lied, taking his hand. "You're just scaring me. If you would tell me what's wrong we could figure it out together."

I pleaded with my eyes, but he seemed hesitant still to reveal his secret. The book I'd been reading, *The Moonstone*, suddenly popped into my head; the strange occurrences all seemingly connected and the sudden disappearance of the stone causing an investigation by a clever detective. I wondered what the renowned Sergeant Cuff would have surmised from Gabriel's behavior. Would he have found all this strange: my fainting and feeling odd earlier, an engagement settled before I'd given my consent, a party planned with an unwanted guest in attendance, and the desperation with which Gabriel now wished to impart a family secret to me? I reasoned the mystery of the moonstone was child's play compared to my own mystery, but I didn't have the cunning mind of Sergeant Cuff to help me solve it. I would have to do it on my own; if only I could persuade Gabriel to give me some hint as to what he wanted to tell me.

The carriage was slowing to a stop. I hadn't even noticed we'd gone up the tree-lined drive leading to the manor house of

Cuckfield Park. I knew this would probably be the last time Gabriel and I would have a chance to speak alone; unless I could persuade him to escort me home later. The carriage was stopped and I could hear the attendant approaching the door. I thought momentarily of a poem by William Blake*: Cruelty has a human heart, / And Jealousy a human face; / Terror the human form divine, / And Secrecy the human dress*. I had never seen such displeasing things in Gabriel, but whatever the secret he held inside it showed horrible on his face.

I looked pleadingly at Gabriel. "Please, trust in me."

He hung his head and stated rigidly, "My family, we are part of a secret order-"

Before he could finish the door to the carriage had swung open and I was being forcefully pulled from my seat by Gabriel's ecstatic mother, Lady Cynthia Sergison.

ℰᴑ3ᴑℬ

"My dear, I am beside myself. Finally you are to be my daughter, and you will come to Cuckfield Park, of course, so I can have your company every day," Lady Sergison gushed as she led me into the front hall.

"You know, Mother, I may want to spend time with my future wife as well...every day," Gabriel tried to tease his mother, but it came out sounding sad as if he knew it was never to be.

Lady Sergison just waved her hand dismissively at him as she asked me, "Now, did Gabriel explain about the foreign gentleman joining us this evening?" Before I was able to answer she continued explaining, "The man claims to be related to my husband by way of his Romanian ancestry, but Lord Sergison is hesitant to believe him. However, we must try to be polite and forgive any strangeness of character as he is a foreigner. I myself have yet to meet the man, and perhaps we shall be lucky enough to have him unable to attend this evening. I'm sure you must feel quite imposed upon to have a stranger at our little celebration-"

I just smiled, knowing that one more person was not going to make a difference. I was sure Lady Sergison had not only invited all of her relations within the area, but most likely dozens of upper class friends of hers and Lord Sergison's that I wouldn't know. My own parents would be there later, hopefully with Emma, but as she was missing again not likely. There would, no doubt, also be business associates of both Lord Sergison's and my father's attending of whom I had perhaps met once or twice. It struck me once more that an entire elaborate party had been arranged for Gabriel and me before I'd even said yes. Large parties like this would have taken weeks if not months to plan, and they had done it all quietly without my knowledge before I had even consented to marry Gabriel. I wondered what they would have done if I'd declined. I wondered if declining was ever even an option for me.

"Mother, at least let Elizabeth sit down before you begin

talking incessantly," Gabriel teased again as we entered the massive dining room.

I wanted to laugh at the easy affection between Gabriel and his mother, but I was distracted by the urgent confession Gabriel had tried to impart on the short carriage ride. The only clue I had to his confession were the hurried words about belonging to a secret order. I knew there were all kinds of men's clubs and secret organizations attended by the wealthy, but I didn't think that was what he meant. The way he had behaved it seemed to be something darker. It certainly sounded more sinister than simply a group of extravagantly rich men with nothing better to do than meet secretly to play cards and billiards. I could tell by Gabriel's concerned glances that he was uncomfortable about the cryptic message he'd given me; he must have realized he had only told me enough to set my curiosity on fire with outrageous ideas. I knew he wasn't going to even hint at our strange conversation in front of his mother; he'd said she knew nothing about it, and so I did my best to hide my discomfort from her.

Lady Cynthia Sergison was a beautiful but fragile woman, and I did not want to be the cause of an emotional or psychological breakdown. I didn't blame her for her sensitive mental state; she certainly had reason enough. Lady Sergison was not yet forty, but her husband Lord John Sergison was quite a bit older at fifty-two. They certainly seemed to be truly in love with each other, despite their difference in age, but I'm sure Lady Sergison's age had a lot to do with her mental faculties. When Lady Sergison had married she had been shockingly young, only sixteen years old and had her first son, Edward, a year later. She then gave birth to Gabriel the following year after that, and she told me many times both she and Gabriel were lucky to have survived. Added to that the Sergisons had been struck by unspeakable tragedy.

The elder son, Edward, who should have inherited everything and become the next Earl of Lewes had died in a bizarre murder just four years ago. I had only been acquainted with the Sergisons for a little over a year so I knew very little about the eldest son except what my father would tell me, which was little, and whatever pieces of gossip I would hear in town or at parties. I was certain that the death of Edward had drastically affected Lady Sergison. Most accounts of her were that she always seemed to be daydreaming, living in her own little world, but she had a charm that was infectious and she always made a show of outward happiness. Although I felt she was one of the most charming people I'd ever met I could honestly say that happiness seemed to have been ripped from her; even when she said she was happy there was a sadness behind it as if she felt guilty to even pretend to feel happiness again. I was also quite certain that her obsessive hobbies of séances and anything to do with the afterlife were due to Edward's death. She seemed unable to accept the resulting investigation that her son had simply been in the wrong place at the wrong time, and had most likely been killed for his money. Still Lady Sergison sought meaning in his death with mediums and mystics, but every time she got answers from these supposed psychics she became depressed and would retreat to her room for days. As much as she made her enthusiasm for such things known it was obvious she knew they had no answers for her and simply told her what she wanted to hear.

I studied Lady Sergison as she paused to allow Gabriel to open the doors to the dining room. She wore black, still mourning the loss of her son, and since I had known her I'd never seen her wear any other color. That evening she was dressed in a somewhat loose fitting Grecian-style gown, which would have shocked anyone that wasn't used to Lady Sergison's eccentricities. Usually she left her hip-length dark brown hair down, but that night she had her hair braided in a kind of crown on top of her head with the excess spilling down the center of her back. Despite spending many hours of her day crying in her depression and being frightfully pale from her confinement to the manor house, Lady Sergison still retained a soft, youthful appearance. When she added a bit of color to her lips and cheeks, as she had that night, she could pass for a woman almost ten years younger.

I couldn't help but compliment her, "You look well tonight, Lady Sergison. I think you will outshine me this night."

Lady Sergison plunged forward to embrace me, and said with tears in her eyes, "My brightened appearance is only the result of the great joy you have brought this family. It seems like an eternity since I have felt so happy and it is all because I know that you will soon be my daughter-in-law." She turned slightly to see if Gabriel was listening and added, "Don't worry about anything. You and Gabriel were meant to be together, and I know you will make him very happy."

I entered the dining room feeling guilty about my suspicions about Gabriel. Lady Sergison had obviously sensed something was wrong between us, and I worried she would not make it through dinner without breaking down in tears. I realized that this engagement was about more than just Gabriel and me; it was about our families and society. My connection with the Sergisons would not only elevate my family's fortune but would allow my sister better prospects in marriage. No doubt my mother and father would be welcome into more prominent circles as in-laws to the Sergisons and my father's position with Lord Sergison would be cemented for the rest of his life.

Then there was Lady Sergison. What would it do to her if I broke off the engagement? She had already endured so much misery over losing her eldest son; how would she react to her only living son having his heart broken? Gabriel and Lady Sergison had a very close relationship despite Gabriel's admittance of some great secret that was being kept from even her. Actually I had always admired the tenderness and open affection the Sergisons showed each other. I was very close to my father and at one time to Emma, but my mother was beyond my comprehension. She had always seemed cold and over-calculating, no warmth or simple affection. I felt more genuine tenderness from Lady Sergison, who up until that day was only the mother of the man courting me, than I ever had from my own mother. I didn't want to cause Lady Sergison any distress, but more than that I didn't want to lose her affection.

"Will your lovely sister be joining us tonight?" Lady Sergison asked gently, pulling me out of my thoughts.

That was a good question, but I didn't know the answer so I admitted, "I'm not sure. My parents will of course be here, but I have yet to see Emma...today. I had so wished to tell her the news myself of our engagement."

Lady Sergison didn't answer, but looked down as if deep in thought. I had a guess at what she was thinking as I had on a few occasions expressed my concerns about Emma, and my father had acquainted Lord Sergison of our predicament. Lady

Sergison seemed to slip into a dark mood whenever Emma's name came up. She, on more than one occasion, had likened Emma's behavior to that of her eldest son's before he'd been murdered. I was fairly certain Lady Sergison's thoughts were turning with the stories of Emma's disappearances and she was reminded all too much of her lost son.

Emma had taken to going off on her own more and more lately and no one knew where she was going. She wouldn't even tell me, and we had always been so close...until about a year ago. Even in the beginning Emma would confide nothing of where she'd been to me. She was always exhausted and irritable, and looked at me as if I had caused her some affliction. After some prodding she would simply shrug and say she had been visiting with friends. The only problem was we had the same friends; being so close in age we'd always stayed close and socialized in the same circles. I questioned everyone I knew as discreetly as possible. Not only did they not know where she was spending her time, but they admitted to not being able to remember the last time they had even seen Emma. Obviously if Emma was visiting with friends they were people not of my acquaintance, and based on her secrecy on the matter they must have either been disreputable or she was having an inappropriate relationship with someone.

“Why don't you sit, Elizabeth? I'll fetch you a glass of wine,” Gabriel offered, probably trying to escape a possible slip of his secret on my part, and as he bent to kiss my cheek he whispered, “Please don't trouble yourself about Emma. We will find an answer.”

As Gabriel walked off Lady Sergison and I sat on one of the many ornate settees scattered around the perimeter of the enormous dining room. I wanted to feel hope at Gabriel's words about Emma, but I wasn't sure anyone could find the answer to what had changed Emma. My own father had devoted many long hours trying to discover where she was going and with whom, but so far all he had found was a wrathful temper from Emma when she realized he had been trying to following her. My father was at a loss of what to do next. He was trying to be discreet in his investigation, just in case Emma had fallen in with an undesirable crowd. We were desperate to keep Emma's reputation intact, even if she had compromised herself. Only the Sergisons knew besides us, and that was only because Lord Sergison was such an old friend of my father's and insisted on helping him with his inquiries.

Lady Sergison touched my arm and lamented, "You know it's a strange coincidence, Edward had been disappearing more and more just before he was mur..." Lady Sergison pursed her lips uncomfortably.

I usually tried to steer clear of mentioning Emma around Lady Sergison as she had on previous occasions compared my sister's behavior with Edward's just before he had died. Any other time I would have shrugged off her words, attributing it to her obsession to dwell on the subject that had caused her life to be tormented by sadness. She seemed to have latched on to that one moment and looked for ways to fit it into everyday conversation. It was like she missed her misery if she didn't remind herself of it at least a few times a day. Normally I would have considered her comments in the same light as her obsession with séances; it was her coping mechanism, but that evening her words actually gave me pause. I was seriously considering there might be some convincing similarities between Edward's behavior before he had died and Emma's current behavior. Would Emma meet the same fate? Was she perhaps caught up with the same kind of dangerous people Edward had gotten mixed up with? Was she putting us all in danger?

Lady Sergison must have noticed the wide-eyed look of desperation on my face, and changed the subject, "Well, dear, what do you think of the table setting?"

I looked blankly at the monstrously long, oak dining table which could seat up to sixty guests. The entire table was strewn with an ivory linen, gold accented designs along its scalloped edges. The table was set with close to forty settings of white porcelain dishes and crystal glasses. There were spaces marked with cards where the food would go; Lady Sergison liked to serve dinner in the buffet style where food was brought to the table course by course and each guest could choose what to put on their plates. Down the center of the table she had impressively large crystal vases filled to over-flowing with white calla lilies and tall spires of some purplish-blue flower. Though Lady Sergison was in general a sad, depressed woman she always took great care with her party decorations.

"Your flower arrangements are always so lovely. What are the tall purplish flowers?" I asked still distracted by thoughts of Emma.

Lady Sergison smiled to herself at my compliment and responded matter-of-factly, "They are wolfs bane. Oh, but you probably know it as monkshood."

My eyes widened in shock as I stuttered, "Monkshood? Aren't they poisonous?"

Lady Sergison waved her hand in the air as if that were a preposterous notion. "Only if ingested or handled improperly. I have even heard of people taking some types of it medicinally to relieve body aches. The only real danger is if you handle the plant with your bare hands or you eat it, and I'm sure my excellent dinner will keep the guests from partaking of the floral arrangements."

I stared at the dangerous clusters of flowers remembering what monkshood symbolized; every flower had a meaning and I knew Lady Sergison was very attentive to such things. She had several copies of *The Language of Flowers* in her home so that even the servants would be knowledgeable about such trends of the upper-class. For some reason I had committed most of the book to memory. White lilies, naturally, symbolized purity and a calla lily specifically symbolized beauty. A very appropriate choice for an engagement dinner, but then there was the monkshood. Monkshood was meant to be a warning, it literally meant beware. I thought about Lady Sergison's comment about Emma. Was she worried that whatever troubles Emma had gotten into would affect me, and through me Gabriel? Was she sending a secret message to Gabriel that he should beware tying himself to my family? Or had Lady Sergison, without consciously knowing it, chosen the flowers as a warning to me of her own family's dark secrets?

"Elizabeth, is everything all right?" Gabriel asked, standing in front of me holding out a glass of wine.

As I looked up to take the glass from him I felt a tear roll down my cheek.

"Oh, Mother, what have you said now?" Gabriel berated lightly.

I wiped at the tear and objected, "No, no, it wasn't anything Lady Sergison said. I'm just so worried about Emma, and...of all days for her to have chosen to stay hidden from us...I had hoped to have her here tonight."

Gabriel opened his mouth as if he wanted to tell me something, but as his eyes lingered to Lady Sergison he seemed to change his mind. I wondered if it had to do with what he was trying to tell me in the carriage. He had said his mother knew nothing of the secret he kept and he obviously was not keen to reveal it to her now. Could this secret order have something to do with Emma? Had Gabriel, through his connections, found something out about Emma? I desperately wished at that moment that Lady Sergison would leave the room so I might be alone with Gabriel again.

As if she had heard my thoughts, Lady Sergison rose abruptly and apologized, "Please excuse me, Elizabeth dear, I must check on the fish. We had to send out for it and I need to give instruction when it should be served if they have been able to get it."

I watched her hurry from the room, knowing she always planned her parties perfectly, checking and rechecking everything hours before, and she would never have sent out for fish at the last moment. If they didn't have fish she would have changed the entire order of the courses to accommodate the lack of it, but I had gotten my wish; she had left the room. Now it was only Gabriel and me in the room, and a few servants in and out putting on the finishing touches. Gabriel sat down beside me, and I thought this was the moment I would have my answers.

He must have noticed my anxious looks as he stated sadly, "I have so much I want to explain to you, but I can't do it here. Please, don't give up on me." He took my hand boldly and pleaded, "I love you more than I can say. I just want you to beware the dangers involved."

There it was again, that word: beware. Maybe Lady Sergison was trying to send me a secret message with her flower arrangements. Maybe she did know Gabriel's secret, unbeknownst to him, and she worried for my safety. I pushed the thought from my mind, deciding it was too far-fetched. Instead I let my eyes wander, passing over the elaborate table and strange choice of flowers. Upward my eyes drifted until they rested on my least favorite part of Cuckfield Park.

It was the great centerpiece of the ceiling, a large reproduction of a famous painting that resided on the ceiling of the Louvre in France. Lord Sergison was prodigiously proud of the painting that he had had commissioned only a few years after the original had been completed at the Louvre. The painting was called "Apollo Slays Python" by a French romantic painter by the name of Delacroix. I found most of Delacroix's work darkly attractive, some of it astonishingly sensual, but this particular painting gave me a chill.

"It's beautiful, isn't it?" Gabriel asked seeing that I was transfixed by the painting. "It is a perfect depiction of what is right and good, and what should be destroyed."

I didn't turn to look at him, but I found his words startling. "What do you mean?"

"Well, look at the way the light surrounds Apollo...the hero, full of virtue and bravery, and then look at Python, shrouded in darkness," He explained, sweeping his hand up toward the painting. "Monsters have no place in this world...they must be stamped out before they can destroy what little beauty and goodness is left."

I turned to him, but he was still glaring at the painting as if he had personally met Python and knew his evil. It was a side of Gabriel I'd never noticed before. A dark, violent side that brought back thoughts of his secret life. I wondered how well I really knew Gabriel. Had he masked this other dangerous self by pretending to be the kind, gentle man I always thought him to be?

"I have always felt this menacing feeling that Apollo was

watching me in this room," I admitted, "That painting has always made me uncomfortable, but not because of Python...I almost feel sorry for Python being hunted so."

Gabriel swung his eyes almost fiercely toward me. "How could you feel sorry for that beast? It's a hideous, killing monster. A monster that would kill you without a thought."

For a moment I didn't recognize him; he'd never spoken so harshly to me, nor had his eyes ever seemed so savage.

I shrank from his wild eyes and explained quietly, "I've read one version of the story of Apollo and Python in which Apollo attacks Python merely because Python is the oracle of Delphi and Apollo wishes to have his own oracle there. I don't know why, but I have always thought of Apollo as a greedy, self-centered god that can't seem to abide the thought of anyone else having attentions that could be his. Whenever I see this painting it reminds me that seemingly good, beautiful people can be false and do horrible things."

Gabriel seemed to relax and forced a light laugh, "You read too much, but when you look at the painting with that story in mind I suppose I could see what you mean." Gabriel paused and took my hand to his lips. "I'm sorry that I was so severe; I've had a taxing week. I shouldn't have taken it out on you; my nerves are just raw. Please forgive me."

I was just about to tell Gabriel there was nothing to forgive, I understood he was taking on more responsibilities and it must have been quite stressful, but I was halted by the opening of the dining room doors.

"Elizabeth, my dear," Lord Sergison gushed, addressing me the same way Lady Sergison always did, as he crossed the room to take my hand. "I'm sorry if I'm interrupting any declarations of love," he teased, winking at me, "I am just so overcome. You can't imagine how terribly happy I am that Gabriel has finally worked up the courage to ask you."

I smiled in spite of my worry for Emma. Gabriel seemed to look down as his cheeks reddened a bit. It was hard to feel unhappy or anxious around Lord Sergison; he always had a smile on his face and a way of speaking to people that made everyone feel they had known him for years. It was easy to see why Lady

Sergison had fallen in love with Lord Sergison despite an almost thirteen year age difference. Though Lord Sergison was fifty-two he was a very athletic-looking man, and had proved many times that his energy could match even that of his twenty-one year old son. He was tall and trim like Gabriel with vibrant blue eyes, but his sparsely gray hair was a much lighter blonde than Gabriel's. To all of that he also exuded a genuine love and devotion for his family. Even when Lady Sergison was in one of her dark moods he never raised a word against her, but attempted to pull her out of it with his tender teasing and constant attentions. Gabriel mostly took after Lord Sergison in his easy manners, but from time to time he also exhibited a sadness much like Lady Sergison.

"So...you will come to Cuckfield Park, will you not?" Lord Sergison asked excitedly, "Lady Sergison and I are so happy you will reside here."

"Father, we haven't even announced our engagement yet, and you already have Elizabeth moving in," Gabriel chastised, though I could see it put him at ease to hear others speak of our engagement so finally.

Normally I would have teased Gabriel, proving that I did not shock easily at such talk, and said something to elicit a laugh from Lord Sergison, but I wasn't sure if a joke would have made Gabriel uneasy. Instead I just smiled politely at them, unable to think of anything to say. I was saved by the opening of the dining room doors. A servant entered quietly and propped the double doors open. It must have been time for the party to begin. A moment later a man entered, pausing at the doors to scan the room. I very nearly dropped my glass as I found I recognized the man, though I couldn't say how.

In shock I mouthed the word, "Dardanos."

❦4❧

The man's eyes turned abruptly to me as if he'd heard my puzzled whisper. He stood in the doorway, his hand grasping an ornate ivory-handled cane, as he pretended to be scanning the room. He wore a gray and gold brocade frock coat that went half-way to his knees over a white waistcoat, dress shirt, and dark gray trousers. Instead of the usual stiff bow-tie he wore an alluring white cravat tied about his collar. He turned suddenly to hand his black silk top hat and his cane to the servant waiting at his side. As the man turned to do this I caught a glimpse of his long, glossy black hair tied at the base of his neck, spilling half-way down his back. His dark features, from his full ebony eyebrows to the tauntingly seductive traces of shadowy stubble faintly covering his jaw and circling his mouth made his icy blue eyes stand out like beams of light from across the room.

I actually shivered from the cold intensity of the man's gaze. I tried to look away as polite decorum dictated, but I was unable to turn my eyes from the entrancing man. Gabriel and Lord Sergison seemed to notice my discomfort and turned toward the door to see the source of it. Apparently they hadn't seen the gentleman enter, and must have only noticed the servant propping the doors open. I felt a strange flutter in my heart, but seeing the quizzical look on Gabriel's face I smiled reassuringly to show that I was not troubled.

Lord Sergison gave me a tight grin as he turned to welcome the man. "Mr. Samothrace, how are you, sir?" he said as he approached the man with his hand extended.

I expected to hear Dardanos answer coldly back, but was surprised to see a handsome and gentle smile spread across his face as he took Lord Sergison's hand to shake. "My friend, I am delighted to see you again. Allow me to congratulate you on the engagement of your son."

Lord Sergison ushered the man to where Gabriel and I

were standing. Gabriel smiled politely, though I could see it was forced, but he was very good at showing friendly restraint in public. For my part I forgot myself and stared curiously at the man, then realizing my rude behavior I looked down uneasily, trying to command my heart to stop from beating out of my chest.

"May I present Mr. Dardanos Samothrace," Lord Sergison announced cheerily to us, and then as if suddenly remembering asked, "or is it General Samothrace? You did say you were a general? What war was it that you fought in?"

Dardanos shifted uneasily on his feet and admitted, "That was long ago. I have not been addressed that way in many years." Shaking his head he added, "The war is not even worth mentioning; it is long forgotten now."

Lord Sergison nodded politely and then gestured to Gabriel and me, "This is my son, Mr. Gabriel Sergison, and his fiancée, Miss Elizabeth Cranford."

I politely nodded my head but tried to keep my eyes down as Gabriel shook the man's hand. Lord Sergison excused himself in order to find Lady Sergison to let her know there were guests to be greeted.

Dardanos noticed my cold response and apologized, "Miss Cranford, I hope you will forgive my intrusion upon such an important occasion. I only recently discovered my connection to the Sergisons and as my own beloved family have left me alone in this world I thought it might ease my loneliness to acquaint myself with my distant relations. You see I am not so fortunate as to be surrounded by family, but I hope in time you will all be able to consider me at least...your distant relation."

He said it in such a genuinely sad tone that I couldn't help but feel sorry for him; even as my thoughts were whispering cautions I felt impelled to put him at ease. "Of course, General, you are welcome here, no matter the occasion. I can't imagine how lonely it must be to be without any family. My own family should be here shortly and I would be honored if you would allow me to introduce you," I responded softly, not really knowing why I had said so much or why I suddenly felt the need to be kind to the man.

Gabriel knit his eyebrows and gave me a confused look. He knew I wasn't in the habit of pretending fondness for anyone I disliked, and I certainly never put on a show of sympathy unless I truly felt it. I wasn't sure what had made me soften my opinion of Dardanos; I had, since Gabriel had said his name to me earlier, felt as though I should absolutely loathe the man when I met him. Maybe I was just sensitive to the sadness he had conveyed over losing his family as I was dealing with my worry over losing a member of my own family.

Gabriel was still giving me a scrutinizing look so I explained lamentably, "It must be very difficult to lose those you love, don't you think?"

"Allow me to offer my condolences," Dardanos said low, but when I looked back at him his eyes were turned toward Gabriel, "I heard about the unfortunate circumstances surrounding your brother's death. I cannot claim to know that particular loss, but I did lose both my parents quite cruelly. I can only imagine how you must have craved vengeance against his attacker. Pity they never discovered the murderer."

I pursed my lips nervously, waiting for Gabriel, who I could see was caught off-guard by this comment, to snap harshly at Dardanos. Looking at Dardanos I saw that his face was like stone; he had given the words but not the feeling behind them. He seemed to be also waiting for Gabriel's angry reply, and I wondered if he had said it purposely to get a rise out of Gabriel. I wasn't sure why he would even want to do such a thing as he seemed to be trying to get into our good graces, not make us despise him. His eyes flickered to me and seemed to hide a touch of guilt in them, but when he looked back at Gabriel he smirked tauntingly.

Finally Gabriel answered bitingly, "Thank you, sir, for your...kind words. Please excuse me." He quickly nodded to Dardanos, bowed to me, and walked away.

It was very unlike Gabriel to allow his emotions to get the better of him in front of strangers, or to even be concerned by what a stranger had to say to him in the first place. Had Dardanos's words really upset him so much? I had heard others offer their condolences in much the same way, but he had never been upset by it. Perhaps he was just angry that Dardanos, a stranger claiming to be linked by blood to his family, had brought up a dark occurrence in his families past on a night that should be filled with happiness and laughter. Perhaps his anger had nothing to do with Dardanos, but with the secret he wanted to reveal. Was Edward's death somehow connected to this dangerous secret?

"Perhaps I have overstepped my boundaries. I should not have mentioned his brother's death; it was...tactless of me," Dardanos apologized, his brilliant blue eyes fixing me with a look of curiosity once again.

I swallowed nervously, feeling a little uncomfortable to be stared at so openly, and muttered, "I'm sure Gabriel is not really angry, General, he just has a lot on his mind today."

"Of course," Dardanos answered automatically, but seemed to stop in surprise. "You called me General again. I have not been called that for a very long time."

"Oh yes, you did say that didn't you," I muttered, my cheeks growing hot in embarrassment as I added, "I don't know why, but I felt as though I should call you General for some reason. Perhaps I've too much on my mind today as well."

Dardanos's face lit with warmth. "That is a very charming thing to say. I would be honored if you would call me General; it sounds quite comforting coming from you. And please, let me once again apologize for my intrusion. Perhaps my appearance on this particular evening was not the best idea. I am sure I have only added to Mr. Sergison's anxiety of the evening."

I gave Dardanos a blank look before realizing that he thought the source of Gabriel's uneasiness was our engagement dinner, which made sense, but I confess because my thoughts were still preoccupied by the secret he had as of yet to tell me and with Emma's disappearances I had attributed Gabriel's uneasiness to those same things.

"Yes, I'm sure he's just anxious that everything goes well tonight," I agreed.

I took a sip of claret to fill the silence; I wasn't sure what else to say to the man. My thoughts were full of secrets and unpleasantness that were unfit to share with a stranger. It seemed funny to me at that moment that just as I had started to relax and laugh and forget a little of my worries Dardanos had walked in. I couldn't say that I despised him as I had thought I would, but he had certainly had an effect on my mood. He seemed to have a shadow of sadness trailing behind him, following him wherever he went, and it had settled itself over me. The room itself seemed darker since he'd entered, even the bright innocent lilies on the table seemed to have dulled. For all his darkness I felt a need to be near him and a desire to comfort him, to ease the tragedies that had touched his life.

"I see Lord Sergison has a love of myths," Dardanos said, filling the uncomfortable silence.

I looked at him puzzled by why he would say such a thing, but then he pointed to the ceiling explaining, "The painting there. It is Apollo slaying Python, is it not?"

"Oh, yes," I answered.

"You do not like it?" He guessed, scrutinizing me with those hypnotic eyes.

I wondered how he could know that, but admitted, "It makes me uncomfortable. Apollo, he's...well, I get the feeling he's not what people think he is."

Dardanos seemed to find what I said amusing, and he prompted, "You mean that he is not a golden hero, brave and true?"

"Something like that," I agreed. "I suppose he seems more like a villain to me...a villain dressed in angelic clothing."

Dardanos laughed out loud, nodding his head in amusement. "You are not far from the truth."

I didn't understand what he meant by that, but at that moment I saw out of the corner of my eye my parents entering the dining room just behind some of Lady Sergison's relatives. I felt relief to have someone else in the room with Dardanos and me, but my relief melted away when I realized they were alone. Emma was not with them, and I could see my mother was uneasy to be out among our society without the presence of her elder daughter. Lord Sergison came in behind my parents, quickly shaking my father's hand and whispering something in his ear, and then escorted Lady Sergison's relations toward the refreshments. Dardanos must have noticed the look on my face as he followed my gaze to the open doors.

"Do not be anxious about your sister. I am sure she is perfectly safe. If I may be so bold as to offer my assistance I can promise you I will find her out, and return her to you," Dardanos whispered, and then seeing the shocked look on my face he excused himself.

I watched him walk away, unnerved by his knowledge not only of my sister, but of my very thoughts. Had Lord Sergison told him about my sister's recent behavior? I didn't think Lord Sergison would have done such a thing, but how else would Dardanos have known? I never even mentioned I had a sister. I watched with curiosity as Lord Sergison beckoned Dardanos over to introduce him to Lady Sergison's relations, all smiles and politeness. I could see that Dardanos had an effect on the ladies in the group; they all seemed to blush as he bowed to them. He turned momentarily to look at me, giving me a weak smile as if he understood he had upset me. Without planning to do so I smiled back.

"Who is that, Elizabeth?" my mother asked, startling me; I hadn't noticed her and my father approaching. "And what are you wearing?"

When I turned to face them my father gave a slight shake of his head, as if to say don't even ask about Emma. I understood. He didn't want my mother to get upset, especially in front of others. As difficult and alarming as Emma's behavior was to all of us my mother seemed to take it much harder. Her moods were becoming more and more like Lady Sergison's by the day. I knew Emma was her favorite. It didn't bother me because I also knew that I was my father's favorite, not to mention that my mother and I very rarely saw eye to eye. She was a strange creature that I couldn't understand and found frustrating to interact with on a daily basis, and similarly I think she saw me as some bizarre new specimen under a microscope that no one had found a name for yet. Emma knew how to talk to my mother and how to play to her wants and vanities in a way that I was never able to. I was sure that if it had been me, not Emma, disappearing and behaving oddly my mother would not be quite so bothered by it.

I heeded my father's silent warning to not mention Emma, answering my mother's first question and ignoring the second, "That is Mr. Dardanos Samothrace from Romania. He is apparently related to Lord Sergison by way of his Romanian ancestors, the Hunyadis."

"How exciting, a foreigner in our company," my mother remarked in her clever tone, giving Dardanos a curious look, and then turning a sour glance at me inquired, "What happened to the dress that was laid out for you?"

My father seemed to scrutinize Dardanos for a moment before turning his back to where Dardanos now stood across the room. "So that is the man? I dare say Sergison is being overly generous with the fellow."

"Father," I reprimanded softly, "Mr. Samothrace has no family. He is alone in the world and is simply trying to reconnect with his distant relations. We should pity his loneliness, not suspect him of insincerity."

My father huffed at my scolding, but my mother would not be ignored, "Elizabeth, I had a perfectly lovely gown ordered for tonight and you chose to wear that?"

"Yes, yes, she does look handsome," my father remarked absently and then commented with a smirk, "Well, ladies, allow me to retrieve you refreshments. You both look parched."

I looked down at my glass, noticing it was still more than half full, but before I could say anything my father had walked away. He was heading toward the drink table at the other end of the room, just past where Dardanos stood with the now present Lady Sergison and her relations. He was walking conspicuously slowly past the group when Lady Sergison called him over.

"For once in your life why couldn't you accept that I know what is expected in society? The gown I chose was a perfect example of what a young, engaged lady should wear," my mother reprimanded.

I knew her anger was intensified because of Emma's absence so I attempted to answer back calmly, "I know what is expected, Mother, but what I don't know is why everyone thought it perfectly acceptable to assume that I would say yes to Gabriel? You must have ordered that dress quite some time ago, before even a hint of Gabriel's intentions, and yet you decided there was no other choice for me but to accept his proposal."

My mother opened her fan and fanned herself agitatedly, "Well, I...I mean...we were sure...you seemed so....You needed an appropriate dress should such an occasion arise."

I drank deeply from my glass before answering, "And I found an appropriate dress of my own choosing. You must excuse me, Mother, but I believe I am a better judge of my own tastes."

My mother's fanning slowed as she raised her head proudly. "I fear Emma is being targeted, because of our connection to the Sergisons," she whispered almost accusingly.

I turned to her, caught off guard by her statement, and a little hurt by her insinuation. "Has father found something?" I managed to ask.

My mother shook her head, looking down at the floor as if she couldn't bring herself to look in my eyes. "I've just been thinking about everything leading up to this, and it seems to me that Emma's behavior really started changing a little less than a year ago. Just after the ball, just after you and Gabriel started spending so much time together."

My mouth dropped open in shock; I couldn't believe my mother was indirectly blaming me for Emma's behavior. She still wouldn't look at me, but she didn't seem angry any longer. She seemed sad, hopeless. I wondered if she had told my father her assumption, and he had perhaps scolded her on the subject. I was stunned she had even mentioned it to me, especially on the night of my engagement dinner. Now I knew why she was chastising me in public about not wearing the gown she'd purchased. She had formed a notion in her mind that I had caused Emma's behavior in some way, and she couldn't openly accuse me in public without someone taking notice.

"Do you think it's my fault?" I asked in disbelief.

"What's your fault, Lizzy?" my father asked, walking up beside me with two glasses of wine.

I turned my angry face away a moment in thought and lied, "That Gabriel isn't here to receive you. I sent him off to tell Lady Sergison that guests had begun to arrive. I can't imagine what happened to him."

My father handed a glass of wine to my mother and took a sip from the other glass, obviously forgetting he had gotten it for me. "Oh, we've seen Gabriel; he's at the front door greeting everyone as they arrive," he said, looking at my mother in confusion.

I could see my father had seen through my lie, but before he could say anything I excused myself. I exited the dining room into the wide open main hall, and turned left toward the front entrance to find Gabriel. It seemed the majority of Lady Sergison's guests had arrived on time, that is to say half an hour or more past the designated time, and Gabriel was busy shaking hands and smiling sternly as the last groups were entering.

"Gabriel, is everything all right? You never returned."

Gabriel's blue-green eyes seemed ablaze with annoyance. "I needed some fresh air, and then I noticed my mother wasn't here to receive anyone."

"She's in the dining room talking…with guests," I

explained, taking care not to mention Dardanos.

There were no longer guests arriving as Gabriel turned to me angrily, "Yes, and I'm sure I can guess which guest she is speaking with. They all seem to be quite taken with Mr. Samothrace...even you."

"Gabriel, how could you say such a thing?" I demanded, feeling the anger rising inside of me.

Gabriel seemed to falter, lowering his eyes in shame. "I know it isn't your fault. Even demons have the gift of charm, but I can't bear to watch it. I can't bear to see your usually sharp eyes softening to him. I'm going to fix this, but you must excuse me for now." With that he stomped out the front door leaving me standing alone in the hall.

I was at a loss as to why he was behaving so vehemently. I considered following after him to beg that he explain his temper. Even if he was angry at me for being civil to Dardanos I might at least convince him to reveal his secret to me. I knew there was a very minimal chance that we would have another opportunity to be alone that night. Most likely my parents would insist I accompany them home at such a late hour. I decided I had better go after Gabriel; dinner would begin soon and it would be a bit awkward to attend our engagement dinner without the man I was engaged to. Plus, I thought I might at least be able to calm him down before he came back into the house; I worried he was beyond the point of rational thought and might end up saying something shocking to Dardanos in front of everyone. I was just walking over the threshold when I heard someone call my name. I froze, as the voice was low and rich like a man's, and I thought there was something in it that I had no choice but to acknowledge.

Dardanos stood a few feet away, gazing at me with those sad, pale blue eyes. "Miss Cranford, I am grieved to see that I have caused you unhappiness."

I opened my mouth to answer, but I was unsure what he was referring to. Then I realized he had heard what Gabriel had said. My cheeks flushed, embarrassed not only by Gabriel's rudeness toward Dardanos, but also his inference that I was showing particular interest in the man.

"I do not mean to discomfit you. I have never been very good at pretending to have not heard something, but I will make no further mention of it to please you. I was seeking out Mr.

Sergison. I wanted to apologize to him," Dardanos paused, and looking down added shyly, "Forgive me for saying so, but I feel we have met before."

I shifted uneasily, unnerved by his frosty blue eyes, and making sure no one was in the hall to hear, I replied, "It is strange, I had a feeling even before we met that I knew you from somewhere, but I can't imagine how that could be. I know it isn't proper to say so, but something about your face and your voice...it's like remembering a faded dream."

Dardanos stared at me, his eyes betraying a look of longing and heat. "Would you allow me to escort you back to the dining room? I believe they will be looking for us if we do not return."

I took his arm and let him lead me back to the dining room, but he paused just before entering. "Perhaps we did know each other once...in another life. Some believe that two souls that knew each other in another existence might recognize each other. Sometimes the soul remembers what the body has tried to lock away."

ℬ**5**ℭ

The next morning I dressed quickly, without the help of my maid, which took some doing with a corset, bustle, underskirts and a petticoat besides the actual dress: a light blue taffeta that seemed much too cheery for my present mood. I was anxious to check on Emma; to see if she had finally returned home. After the disastrous events of the night before I needed some good news, and I hoped to confess my strange feelings for Dardanos and my worry for my relationship with Gabriel. Surely, my sister would have words of comfort for me. I took *The Moonstone* along with me, not only did it comfort me to hold the book Gabriel had given me, but it also afforded me an alternate companion should Emma be unwilling to share her time with me. I opened Emma's door without knocking and stood disappointed in the open doorway.

"Miss, she returned last night."

I turned to see our maid, Ann, standing behind me with a pitcher of water, most likely for me.

"She was here last night? When did she leave?" I asked eagerly, "What did she do while she was here?"

Ann shifted uneasily as if she wasn't sure she should tell me, after all she was Emma's lady's maid as well and she didn't like to cause disturbances between us. "She asked that I tell no one I saw her, but I'm so worried for her, Miss. She didn't look like herself, she seemed so thin, and the only thing she did was take some clothes and sit in front of your statue."

That surprised me. Emma had never cared for The Palladium. "My statue, The Palladium you mean?" I asked to be sure.

"Yes, Miss, she sat in front of it for a while and then...she touched it. I hid so she wouldn't know I was watching, but I worried she was going to break the statue. I know how much it means to Mr. Cranford and to you. I wouldn't have let her harm it, but she seemed to be looking for something."

My curiosity was overcoming my worry for Emma. "What do you think she was looking for?"

Ann shook her head unhappily. "I don't know, Miss, but I think she found it. She was particularly interested in the base of the statue and when she looked up she was smiling. It seemed strange to see her so happy as I can't even remember the last time I had seen her smile. That was when she spotted me. I thought she would fly into one of her fits of rage, but she continued smiling and told me not to mention she'd been home. That was it. She walked straight out the door…with that strange smile on her lips."

"Thank you, Ann," I muttered distractedly as I walked away.

Why would Emma suddenly be interested in The Palladium, and what was she looking for? I had a horrible thought that, just as Ann had thought, Emma had meant to break or destroy my statue. If she knew that my father was giving it to me she might have tried to damage it out of jealousy. Although I didn't want to admit it my mother had been right. Emma's bizarre behavior had taken a turn just after Gabriel and I had met and he had started taking a serious interest in me. Was she jealous of my involvement with Gabriel and the fortune that I would have as his wife? Was she jealous that I might one day have a title while she would only be the sister of a countess? Maybe it really was my fault, indirectly, as my mother had hinted.

I decided to attempt an investigation of the statue myself to see if I could figure out what Emma had been looking for. I had been planning to visit the statue of Pallas anyway after the horrible night I'd had. I knew she couldn't make any of my troubles disappear, but I always felt my mind was more at ease sitting before her. She was my fairy queen that I could whisper my fears to and she would use her magic to make them dissolve. She was my temple that I could visit any time for consolation. She was my link to an ineffable power that could quiet the part of me that always seemed to be at odds with my life.

As I descended the stairs to the main floor my mother emerged from the drawing room to the left. Her face was like stone. She seemed to be walking determinately toward me, and I worried she was going to blame me once again for Emma's disappearances. Perhaps she too thought my behavior from the night before had been inappropriate and wished to reprimand me for it. I paused, momentarily contemplating turning back up the stairs and pretending I hadn't even seen her, but my resolve to see The Palladium was set and I wouldn't let any harsh words from my mother stand in my way.

Instead she waved an envelope in the air and exclaimed, "We have been invited to one of Lady Sergison's very fashionable parties!"

"Ummm, fashionable parties?" I asked confused and then I realized my mother was indeed taking on more of Lady Sergison's moods. "Are you talking about a séance? Mother, why on earth are you excited about a séance?"

Her face once again turned harsh, as if I should have known why she wanted to go to a séance, and she admonished, "We've tried everything else, short of involving the police. The next logical step is to consult those beyond our realm for help."

I was too shocked to answer. I wanted to protest that interrogating spirits by way of a performance artist was actually the opposite of logical, but my mother didn't even sound like herself. Any other time my mother would have scoffed at such an invitation from Lady Sergison, and made her excuses for not attending. I had my suspicions that my mother was secretly jealous of Lady Sergison and so tried her best to avoid her without obviously insulting her, but suddenly she was excited to attend Lady Sergison's party. I worried that Emma's behavior was having much more of an effect on my mother's heart and mind than I had thought, and now looking at her I could see it was having an effect on her appearance as well. I noticed for the first time just how much weight she'd lost and her eyes were red and ringed in bluish-black as if she hadn't slept.

"Lady Sergison is hosting the party in honor of that foreign man-"

"Mr. Samothrace?" I cut in.

"Yes, that's it," she answered back, pointing the envelope at me. "I can never remember how to say his name. I will write back to say we will be attending."

"What?" I asked, surprised by my mother's sudden interest in the supernatural. "I thought you despised such nonsensical things."

My mother straightened her back and lifted her chin. "I have never said anything of the sort. I simply never had a reason to attend a séance before; now I do. You must accompany me. We must both have a reading. Please...for Emma's sake. We must find some clue as to what is happening to her," she pleaded, her eyes tearing up dramatically.

How could I say no; I could see this meant a lot to her. "Very well, but promise me one thing. Don't be disappointed if the medium has no answers for us. She may well be just another charlatan preying on Lady Sergison's money."

"Of course. I will not be taken in. You know how I pride myself on being level-headed at all times," she said, a triumphant smile creeping over her lips as she walked away.

"Wonderful. I can't wait," I muttered sarcastically to myself, continuing my mission to inspect The Palladium.

When I entered the garden I could see that my father had needed the comfort of Pallas as well. I entered quietly, watching him as he whispered fervently to the statue, his hands clasped in anguish. A twig snapped under my boot as I crossed the path toward The Palladium. My father swung his head around, startled.

"Ah, Lizzy, it's just you," he said wearily.

I wondered if his whispered pleas to Pallas had been about Emma. Had he asked Pallas to deliver her home safely? Was that disappointment on his face because it was only me standing there and not Emma?

"Father, you look tired," I commented, sitting next to him on the stone bench.

He waved his hand dismissively, as if that wasn't important. "How are you, my Lizzy?"

I knew what he was asking without coming right out and asking it. He didn't mean how was I holding up with Emma's disappearances; he meant how was I after the night before. After the confusingly tense, almost embarrassing engagement dinner. Perhaps I had been wrong about his pleas to Pallas; perhaps they were for me and not Emma.

I didn't look at him, but instead studied The Palladium, trying to figure out what Emma could have been looking for, and why had she been so happy once she had found it. I didn't want to think about the night before; it was easier to preoccupy my mind with this new mystery. Of course, my father knew something had been wrong the night before; everyone must have known. Once everyone had sat to dinner Gabriel hadn't even seated himself next to me, but instead situated himself directly across from Dardanos. He proceeded to glare at Dardanos through the first two courses, and then suddenly during the third course he jumped to his feet as if he'd just remembered something. He whispered hurriedly in Lord Sergison's ear, and though I could see Lord Sergison trying to persuade him to sit back down he hurried from the room. Lord Sergison tried to cover for Gabriel's behavior by making up some story about urgent business, but everyone knew that wasn't true.

My father took my hand and said encouragingly, "I'm sure everything is fine, Lizzy, you'll see; Gabriel will show up with a bouquet of flowers and an apology. Lord Sergison assured me that Gabriel had just been informed by one of the servants that a large investment was on the verge of being lost. You understand Lord Sergison is turning all financial decisions over to Gabriel so it is his responsibility to handle such things."

I wasn't sure if I was even worried about what had happened the night before between Gabriel and I; my feelings had been so mixed up to begin with, but I didn't accept my father's explanation either. "That doesn't make any sense, father. If it had to do with an investment then why didn't you go as well, or even go in place of Gabriel all together? Isn't that precisely what your position to the Sergisons entails?"

My father stood abruptly as if I'd said something horribly

rude and rebuked, "Elizabeth, it is extremely complicated; you would not understand. Please do not embarrass me by repeating such absurd ideas to Gabriel. He loves you and that is all that matters." With that he left the garden, leaving me with an uneasy feeling that my life had slowly started to slip away from me in the past day.

I sat there confused about what had just happened. My father had never treated me like an ignorant girl before, but that was exactly what he'd just implied: my female mind was too simple to understand men's complicated financial burdens. He'd never spoken to me so condescendingly. If I didn't understand something he always took time to explain it to me, and he on more than one occasion expressed his delight at my hunger for knowledge, even those things which women in general did not take interest in. Maybe he blamed me for what had happened the night before. Had I shown too much attention to Dardanos? Had I made Gabriel jealous to the point that he stormed out of the house? I had only meant to be kind, but maybe my kindness had been misinterpreted.

I huffed as I looked at The Palladium, "I thought you were supposed to protect me, protect all of us? Emma is in some kind of trouble, my mother blames me and expects me to attend another dismal séance to make it up to her, Gabriel left me with a cryptic message about some secret and then conspicuously walked out on our engagement dinner, and my father...he blames me for something...and it is plain to see he expects me to forgive Gabriel for his behavior last night, no matter what his reasons or excuses were for his behavior. Maybe last night was a sign, if I believed in such things, that Gabriel and I should not be married. I love him, but something feels forced, and now that this man showed up…Dardanos. No, I can't blame him. I felt uneasy ever since I fainted. I felt as if I had two people inside my head, but neither one of them will make up their mind about anything. Maybe I'm just looking for problems where there are none. Oh, Pallas, can't you just tell me, should Gabriel and I marry? Is his secret so terrible I won't be able to look at him the same?"

I waited for Pallas to come to life and speak to me as I had pretended she had so many times as a child. She didn't, but I could feel some strange sadness coming from her, as if she knew the future and it was not going to be good. I glanced around the garden making sure I was completely alone, placed my book down on the bench, and then gently lowered myself to the ground in front of the statue. If Emma had risked coming home just to inspect The Palladium it must have been important. I searched the base as Ann had said Emma had done. On the right side close to the bottom I saw etched into the wood what looked like small pictures or hieroglyphs, but I was fairly sure it wasn't Egyptian as I knew the statue was supposed to be much older. I ran my fingers along the characters feeling I had seen them somewhere before.

"They say it's Cassandra's prayer."

I turned nervously, feeling I had been caught doing something wrong, to see Gabriel standing behind the bench watching me, a bouquet of flowers in his hand. I glanced back at the little pictograms, repeating the thought, *Cassandra's prayer*. That seemed so familiar.

Without a word Gabriel extended his hand to help me up as I asked, "What is Cassandra's prayer?"

He dropped down onto the stone bench, looking defeated, and replied wearily, "Why is it important?"

I stared at him a moment, biting my lip, trying to decide if I should even explain to him. He had been so strange the night before, and I thought perhaps he was starting to think that marrying me would be a mistake as well. I was already causing a problem to his family's reputation by way of my sister's behavior, and then there was my conduct towards Dardanos which had obviously been perceived as inappropriate. I hadn't meant to show so much interest in the man, but something about him had seemed so familiar and excitingly mysterious.

"Elizabeth? You're daydreaming again," Gabriel mentioned distractedly, calling me back from my thoughts, "Why is The Palladium so important? How did you find the prayer?"

"Emma," I finally admitted, "she was here last night. My maid saw her, and she said she seemed to be looking for something at the base of the statue. Whatever she found made her uncommonly happy. I assume it was that writing. I don't know why it's important, but it is. If Emma came here just to see that, then it must be very important. Can you read it?"

Gabriel didn't raise his eyes to meet mine, but answered, "No, I don't think there is anyone that can. It is an ancient, forgotten language."

I regarded Gabriel a moment, determining how he would react to anything I had to say. He seemed tired, not just from lack of sleep which his eyes betrayed, but his body looked weary as if he'd kept it active since I'd last seen him. He was so melancholy I was sure he had come to break our engagement, but I wasn't really worried about that right then. I wanted to know more about the prayer, but I feared Gabriel might lie or change the subject out of anger towards me.

I decided I had to try; my curiosity would not let the subject be and so I asked as sweetly as I could muster, "Do you know what Cassandra's prayer was?"

Gabriel sighed as he seemed to be deciding if he was going to tell me. "Do you know who Cassandra was?" Gabriel asked sadly.

I looked at The Palladium, remembering there was a Cassandra connected to the statue. "Do you mean Cassandra of Troy? She was a prophetess, was she not?"

Gabriel finally raised his eyes to look at me, surprised that I knew, and nodded his head. "Yes, that is who I mean."

"But..." I looked at him puzzled. "I thought the Trojans spoke Greek. Shouldn't Cassandra's prayer be in Greek?"

"It is thought that the Trojans spoke a language called Luwian, which was written as symbols and hieroglyphs. They probably knew Greek or something similar as they had many dealings with the Greeks, but the prayer is thought to be in their native Luwian."

I waited for him to explain further, but he didn't go on so I prompted him, "Cassandra was some kind of priestess, was she not? In the temple of Athena where The Palladium was kept?"

Gabriel again gave me a surprised look and finally conceded, "Very well, I'll tell you what I know, but your father will not be happy. Please don't tell him I told you." Gabriel paused, checking to see if anyone else was in the garden, and then continued, "Cassandra was a priestess in the temple in Troy dedicated to the worship of Athena. She had made a vow to the god Apollo, who I'm sure you already know was in love with her, that she would serve as a virgin priestess in the temple for the rest of her life rather than allow any man to be master of her. You see Apollo wanted her for himself, but she didn't trust the god; he had a tendency for falling in love and then right back out of love once he had his prize. So Cassandra made her vow to convince the god that she was not slighting him, she was simply giving herself over to the life of a celibate priestess, but of course in time the day came when her vow was put to the test."

I was enthralled. I, of course, knew the story of Cassandra, but the way Gabriel explained it made me remember how mesmerizing he could be. I asked excitedly, "And...what happened?"

Gabriel flashed his blue-green eyes at me and answered sadly, "She fell in love."

He said it as if he were speaking about me, and my guilt for my behavior the night before welled up as I commented, "I assume Apollo wasn't happy."

Gabriel shook his head. "No, not that it mattered much; all the gods were taking sides at that time. Cassandra's betrayal just pushed Apollo to finally make up his mind about what side he was going to take in the war."

"The war?" I asked and then realized, "You mean the Trojan war?"

"Yes, it was the beginning of the end for the gods. They took too much interest in human affairs and it started to unravel them."

I looked at The Palladium, the protector of the city of Troy, wondering how much of the story was true and how much had been invented to teach mortals a valuable lesson: never go against a god. I still couldn't see why Emma would care about anything that had to do with The Palladium. Unless she thought it was worth a great deal of money if she could prove it was the true Palladium. Perhaps in her episodes of absence she had met some scrupulous people that would be all too willing to steal a priceless artifact like The Palladium and help her sell it, but why would she consider doing such a thing? Maybe I was wrong and her interest had to do with Cassandra's prayer.

"Do you know what Cassandra's prayer was supposed to have been?" I asked quietly not expecting an answer.

Gabriel cleared his throat and explained, "She prayed to the statue of Pallas, to Athena who had created the statue, to release her from her vow and protect her from Apollo. She prayed that she and her love could be together."

I was sure I knew the answer, but I asked anyway, "And did Athena protect her?"

"The statue was stolen by the Greeks before the prayer reached Athena's ears. Apollo, in his wrath, allowed the Greeks to enter the temple and have their way with Cassandra."

I remembered that horrific part from my reading of *The Iliad*; Ajax the lesser had raped Cassandra and after the city had been sacked and destroyed Agamemnon took Cassandra back with him to be his lover, but his wife murdered both of them soon after they arrived.

Then I remembered what the prayer was about: Cassandra's lover. "What about the man Cassandra was in love with, what happened to him?"

Gabriel seemed to shift uneasily before answering, "He was no man. He was a god. A minor god, but a god all the same. He was cursed by Hecuba, Cassandra's mother."

I didn't understand how a mortal could curse an immortal, minor god or not. "How could Hecuba curse a god?"

Gabriel smiled at my question and stated smartly, "Because she was a god herself. Hecuba was a goddess living a mortal existence. Her real name was Hecate."

"The goddess of magic!" I exclaimed. "So she cursed this minor god for causing her daughter's ruin? What was his curse?"

Gabriel gulped nervously. "He was cursed to walk forever in darkness and feed on the humans he loved so well."

I gave him a perplexed look and inquired, "Like a vampire?"

Gabriel stood abruptly, thrusting the bouquet of flowers

out to me. "I have to go, Elizabeth. Please forgive me for my rude behavior last night." He looked longingly at me as if he wanted to say more, but merely uttered, "I'll explain everything later. There is something I must do first. We should have protected you better, but I'm going to make everything right, I promise." He grabbed my hand and lingeringly kissed where the moonstone ring rested before rushing away.

I didn't understand what he meant, but my mind was still on the story of Cassandra and before he walked past the fountain I asked him earnestly, "Who was the god, the one Cassandra fell in love with? What was his name?"

Gabriel turned and looked at me a long while before he stammered, "His name? It was...I don't...I don't remember."

∞**6**α

"Mrs. Cranford, Elizabeth dear, I am so happy you both could attend. Don't you look lovely tonight, Elizabeth," Lady Sergison gushed, grasping our hands as we entered.

"Thank you," I said, smiling awkwardly as I looked down at my gown. "I hope Gabriel will approve."

Along with allowing my mother to guilt me into attending the séance I had also given in to another of her requests. In my frustrating confusion about what was going on between Gabriel and me my mother had pointed out that perhaps my choice of the sage gown on the night of the engagement dinner had not been quite so lucky for me, and she entreated me to wear the lacy, pale pink gown she'd purchased. It was common for engaged ladies to attend functions wearing gowns of pale pink or ivory until their wedding day, but I felt a little defeated to have given in to my mother. It wasn't that the dress was unattractive in any way, admittedly it was quite beautiful with its pale pink lining and extravagantly detailed lace overlay, but it didn't reflect how I felt. I felt lost, confused, and eerily somber, and the cheerful dress simply made me uncomfortable.

"Oh, he didn't tell you?" Lady Sergison frowned. "I'm afraid Gabriel had business to attend to elsewhere; he won't be here for the séance. Nor will Lord Sergison be attending, he is preoccupied in his study with urgent business as well, but never you mind that. We will have a wonderfully diverting evening!"

Lady Sergison seemed particularly animated, almost chipper. I eyed her in suspicion, but tried to hide my uneasiness. She seemed not herself. Her normally pale face was lit with blushing excitement, and her eyes for once showed no sign of redness or sleeplessness. I was also surprised to see her long, brown hair pulled up in a massive chignon; I had only ever seen her with her hair partially up or left loose all together. Even her dress was different. She so often wore silk or some other flimsy material in a loose-fitting, exotic style, but tonight she wore a traditional tight bodice and a skirt with a modest bustle. Her clothing was still black from head to toe, but her clothing was so different from her usual attire I felt I was looking at a complete stranger. I was so taken aback, in fact, that I forgot to speak as Lady Sergison took my hand.

"Are you all right, dear?" Lady Sergison asked, a puzzled look on her face.

"Yes, of course, I'm fine. I just...I was surprised by...your appearance," I admitted.

"Elizabeth!" my mother admonished under her breath.

Lady Sergison smiled and held her hand up to my mother. "That's quite all right, Mrs. Cranford. Elizabeth and I are great friends and always say what is on our minds." Then turning to me she answered uncertainly, "I thought it was time for a change...time to stop living in the past. Everything changes eventually; now is my time."

I was just about to tell her that there was no reason for her to change; no one that knew her could say that she was lacking in anything, and obviously she was liked despite her eccentricities. I wondered if she thought the trouble with Gabriel and me had to do with her. Did she think she had to start behaving like everyone else for our sakes, for the sake of our marriage?

Before I could say anything more Lady Sergison continued, "Refreshments are in the hall, and the table is set in the West parlor as usual." Her hand suddenly shot to the sides of her head, checking that her hair was still in place. "Oh, Elizabeth dear, Mr. Samothrace is attending tonight, as I'm sure you already know from the invitation. Will you help me to make him feel at ease? I don't believe he is acquainted with anyone, and I think it's his first séance. You seem to have such an easy way with him though he's a foreigner. You'll help me won't you?"

I was surprised by Dardanos's involvement in the evening's festivities, but I managed to agree to Lady Sergison's request even though my heart began to annoyingly beat faster. "Of course, I will certainly help you with Mr. Samothrace."

I led my mother further down the hall to the refreshment table. Lady Sergison always served punch at her séance parties, making it feel like we should be at a country dance in the middle of summer instead of a dark room communing with the dead. The servant behind the table offered me a cup of punch which I gestured away and instead asked for claret. If I was going to be subjected to petty theatrics I wanted to at least have a few mind-numbing glasses of wine first.

My mother took the punch I had not wanted and a piece of sweet cake. I could see she was eager to go to the West parlor to see where we would be conducting our séance. All of the other attendees were headed to the West parlor as well, taking their drinks and deserts with them, but I had another destination in mind. I had decided if I was going to be forced to endure another painfully faked séance that I should at least get something out of it. I had made up my mind to question Lord Sergison about Cassandra's prayer; if he didn't know anything about it he might at least be able to point me toward a few helpful books. Normally I would have gone to my father, but as Gabriel had mentioned he would be angry at my knowing about Cassandra's prayer (though I didn't see why he would be angry) I decided to try to keep it from my father for Gabriel's sake.

"Mother, why don't you go on to the West parlor. I'd like to talk to Lord Sergison...about the other night," I lied, pushing her forward.

My mother seemed to scrutinize me for a moment before agreeing, "Yes, of course, I understand. I'm sure Lord Sergison will be able to put your mind right at ease about Gabriel...but do hurry back."

I smiled weakly and made a reminder to myself to actually ask Lord Sergison about Gabriel to make my lie more believable. I assumed if Lord Sergison was home he would be in his study on the second floor, and thankfully Lady Sergison had confirmed my assumption. I had never actually been in Lord Sergison's study, but Gabriel had pointed it out once when we'd passed by it to get to the library.

I quietly climbed the grand staircase to the second floor, glancing down every few seconds to make sure Lady Sergison didn't noticed me going upstairs. I kept an eye out for Gabriel as well should he arrive home earlier than expected. I simply didn't want to have to lie to him or Lady Sergison about what I was doing. Lady Sergison would probably see through my lie any way and ask more questions; Lady Sergison always seemed to be able to pick up on what was really on my mind.

Once I reached the top landing of the staircase I spied the door to Lord Sergison's study only two doors down the hall on the right. I was a little relieved to see the door was slightly ajar. Perhaps he was expecting someone and I could ask quickly for the information I needed and then excuse myself, giving Lord Sergison little time to inquire as to why I wished to know such things. As I approached the door I realized Lord Sergison was not expecting someone; they had already arrived and had forgotten to close the door all the way.

"I think she's becoming suspicious," a man's voice said.

"How do you mean?" Lord Sergison questioned uneasily.

"She's been acting strange ever since Gabriel proposed, and she isn't ignorant like most young ladies. She picks up on things quite easily," the man stated brusquely.

My heart began to thud as I realized they were speaking about me. I couldn't hear the man's voice distinctly through the door, but I felt sure it must have been my father's. I had often heard my father speak of my intellect in such a way; almost angry that others underestimated me. Although it was flattering to hear my father recommend me so highly I couldn't understand why he would be telling Lord Sergison about my suspicions or how he would even know about them himself. Obviously my father knew much more than I thought, about me and perhaps even about Gabriel's secret.

"Do you think she has discovered anything?" Lord Sergison asked anxiously.

"No, no, I don't believe so," my father answered, "but I

think Emma may have found something out."

"How? How would she be able to...unless you..." Lord Sergison said angrily, but did not finish.

My father didn't respond back as loudly as Lord Sergison, "I have only just been told by Mary that she discussed Edward with Emma. She was angry that Gabriel took a liking to Elizabeth instead of Emma and out of anger she told her about Edward. Apparently she told Emma about Edward shortly after your ball."

"And is that why Emma has been disappearing?" Lord Sergison asked calmly.

"I believe it is. I think she was trying to find out more; investigate the matter on her own as it were," my father admitted wearily, "I only pray that she does not meet the same fate as Edward. I don't think I could do it."

"Well, let's not think on that right now. Whatever she thinks she's discovered it can't be remotely close to the truth. Who would believe it? Any rational person would think it ridiculous superstitions and lies. No, we must focus on finding her out before she is beyond saving," Lord Sergison stated resolutely.

What could that have meant? What couldn't my father do and what did it mean if Emma was beyond saving? I wondered if what Lord Sergison spoke of was the same as Gabriel's secret, something a rational person wouldn't even believe. I decided I had heard enough. I was fairly certain their conversation was nearly at an end anyway, and I didn't want to be caught eavesdropping. I tiptoed quickly and quietly away from the door, holding my frustratingly noisy gown up so as to make less noise, and hurried down the stairs.

I was standing at the refreshment table in a daze waiting for another glass of claret when I felt someone standing next to me. I could feel eyes on me, though no words had been spoken, at least I hadn't heard any. My thoughts were so muddled with conspiracies and secrets concerning my family and the Sergisons that I was quite in my own little world. I turned to see Dardanos staring at me as if he were waiting for me to answer some question he had asked.

"Are you feeling well, Miss Cranford?" he asked, knitting his eyebrows in concern. "You look strange. Is there something I can do to help?"

I smiled involuntarily. "General," I said softly, feeling a calm wash over me as I looked into his face. "I...yes...I'm well. I...I've just...I heard something that has me distracted; that's all. I'll be fine in a moment; there's no need to fuss over me," I stuttered, noticing again how bright and clear his blue eyes were; they almost glowed white with their brightness.

He regarded me a moment and whispered, "You look quite lovely tonight."

I felt the heat rise in my cheeks as I confusedly looked down at myself. I nervously adjusted the neckline of the dress which hung just off my shoulders, and smoothed out the lace that I had rumpled in my escape from the study. I didn't feel lovely. I felt awkward and miserable, and I was fairly certain it showed on my face. I stared at Dardanos trying to decide if he was just being polite by complementing me, or if there was intent behind his words. I gave him great liberty in his manners due to his being foreign, but surely he knew showing such attentions to an engaged woman was considered shocking.

I clumsily took the glass of claret from the servant behind the table and mumbled nervously that my mother was waiting for me. I didn't wish to seem rude, but I worried that I had been gazing too long at Dardanos again. I also worried that if he pressed the matter I would most likely tell him everything that was bothering me. How could a complete stranger have such an effect on me? I thought back to what Dardanos had said a few nights before: *Perhaps we had known each other in another life...Sometimes the soul remembers.* Was my soul recognizing his; was that why I felt so drawn to him? No, that was ridiculous, and I didn't believe in such things anyway. Nothing influenced my destiny but my own thoughts. I was in control of my feelings and my fate.

I entered the West parlor and found my mother talking animatedly with another of Lady Sergison's favorite séance guests. I stood beside my mother nodding politely to the woman, Mrs. Lucas I believed was her name, and I listened to her testimony of the miraculous occurrences at past séances. As I listened to the woman recount strange happenings and the dead loved ones she had been able to contact I realized in order for my mother to try to get the answers she desired she would have to explain, at least some of, Emma's behavior.

We had been so careful through all of this that Emma's reputation wouldn't be compromised. That was the whole reason we hadn't contacted the police yet. Now my mother seemed ready to put Emma's reputation, and indeed our whole family's reputation, out in the open for an entire roomful of people from the Sergison's and our social circles. I wasn't sure if my mother had completely thought this through, but this could not only ruin Emma, but shed disgrace on our family and anyone connected with us. It could affect our relationship with the Sergisons, who of course knew our troubles, but were not concerned because it was still unknown to others. It would certainly add more complications to my already complicated relationship with Gabriel. It could possibly be the thing that convinced Gabriel to cut ties with me; I could lose him forever.

My mother and Mrs. Lucas were staring at me.

"Excuse me, what was it you asked?" I questioned, smiling weakly and hoping the reason they were staring was because one of them had asked me a question.

Mrs. Lucas answered excitedly, "I was just telling your mother about your reading at the last séance. It was so interesting, and rather exciting. When you fainted I thought we were going to have to call a doctor, but you awoke muttering something. I think it was he knows, he knows." I looked at her strangely, not remembering that had happened, but she continued before I could ask about it, "You'll be happy to know Lady Sergison has engaged the same medium to come back. I don't know how she did it; I know she is well sought after. Oh, what was her name?"

I tried to keep the annoyance out of my voice as I answered, "Gibson, if I'm not mistaken, Mrs. Mariah Gibson."

"Oh, yes!" Mrs. Lucas exclaimed, clapping her hands together, "that's it, Mrs. Gibson. Such a memory you have, but I suppose after that amazing revelation about your past life how could you not remember her?"

I proceeded to busy myself with draining my wine glass in a very unladylike manner as Mrs. Lucas recounted down to the tiniest detail my reading from the previous séance. I wanted to ask her about my fainting and what I said after coming round, but Mrs. Lucas was only interested in prattling away. I could see my mother was completely enthralled by Mrs. Lucas's story, which I found strange as my mother was untrusting and cynical by nature, but she kept looking at me with interest as if she were just seeing me for the first time. Before the narrative came to an end I excused myself to get another glass of claret, but as I turned I found myself face to face with Dardanos.

"Miss Cranford, please allow me to get you another refreshment," Dardanos entreated, gesturing for me to take a seat on the other side of the room where there were a few empty leather armchairs. I felt awkward to accept his request, but my only goal had been to escape the conversation between my mother and Mrs. Lucas so I couldn't complain.

"Thank you, General," I answered shakily as my heart began to annoyingly beat faster, "that's very kind of you."

Dardanos returned a few moments later with two glasses of claret; he handed one to me and sat in the overstuffed, leather chair facing me.

"That was a very interesting story the lady speaking with your mother was telling. You believe in such things, Miss Cranford? Past lives I mean," Dardanos asked eagerly, turning his eyes down sadly for a moment.

"No," I stated firmly, "actually I think it's all complete nonsense. I think séances are nothing but a show."

"Hmmm," he laughed, gesturing toward me, "and yet here you are."

I smiled at his reaction; most men would have been appalled by my harsh opinion. I decided to explain, "Well, I was coerced into attending tonight. You could say I'm here against my own will."

"Surely it's not all bad," Dardanos commented, raising

his glass, "at least the company is worth having. I must confess one of the only reasons I accepted Lady Sergison's invitation was because I thought I might see you again. You have enchanted me."

I pursed my lips nervously, looking down at my lacy gown, and reminded him, "You understand that I'm engaged? It isn't proper to say such things to an engaged woman. I will marry Gabriel," I insisted, more to myself than to him.

"Of course, you must think me so uncouth. I understand my manners are a bit unconventional and I let my imagination run away with me sometimes. I understand your situation...but it does not make me want to be in your company less. I am a man that is used to speaking his mind and I should like for you to know my thoughts...no matter how improper they may be." He paused sliding forward in his chair and said quietly, "I really did find your story about your last séance interesting. We do not have parties like this where I come from, only ancient traditions and superstitions. Would you tell me what the medium told you? I am quite captivated by what I believe she was trying to tell you."

❧ 7 ☙

I shifted uneasily in my chair, under the bright attentive gaze of Dardanos. The way he stared at me both frightened and exhilarated me. It was as if I'd been sleeping my whole life and he was watching anxiously for the precise moment I would wake up.

Although I disliked giving any credence to mediums and psychics, I felt impelled to tell Dardanos what he wished to know. "I attended Lady Sergison's last séance quite against my better judgment," I wanted it to be made known. "I only attended out of respect for Lady Sergison; she has always been so kind to me, and to accompany Gabriel; he finds such gatherings as tedious as I do and wished to have a diversion." I paused, taking a sip of wine as I decided I should explain séances in general to Dardanos as he seemed unfamiliar with them. "Usually séances are conducted strictly to contact the dead, whether it's a particular person that someone wishes to contact or just any random spirit with knowledge of the afterlife. Some mediums have become known for the new novelty of being able to tell people who they were in a past life. Many mediums don't bother with such theatrics as it adds an element of improvisation and unpredictability to their normal routine. You see most mediums claim to have a familiar, a spirit guide that appears at their beckon call and aides them in contacting the other side. So you see all a medium has to do is find out what the hostess's wishes are and do a practiced routine involving her so-called familiar and add a few personal experiences for the wealthy or favorite attendees. It is obviously nothing more than a pre-orchestrated show, and therefore it is completely irrelevant what this medium told me."

I felt sure Dardanos would find my bold opinions

appalling and would look for an excuse to be out of my company. Perhaps that was for the best; if he stopped showing so much interest in me then perhaps I wouldn't indulge him with my attentions. Instead of being offended, though, he seemed to be beaming with interest and seemed in no way shocked by what I had said or likely to leave our conversation. He looked at me in very much the way Gabriel had looked at me the first time we'd spoken, a mixture of surprised intrigue and desire.

"Well, Miss Cranford, now I know your stance on mysticism," Dardanos quipped, a smile still on his generously full lips, "but I am most interested in what was said to you. Your particular experience is what I wish to know. I have reason to believe it is directly connected to the very pursuit of my entire existence."

I knit my eyebrows, curious how some meaningless reading from a medium could be connected at all to this mysterious, yet entrancing man. He sat back in his chair, placing his arms on either side of the armrests as if he were opening himself up to my examination. I was sure if anyone were paying attention to our behavior toward each other I would be the cause of much whispering, but I couldn't help accepting his silent invitation to study his entire person freely. Something about his easy and honest manners inspired a sense of familiarity in me; I felt I knew him while he was yet a mystery.

For a moment I felt the room disappear and all I could see was Dardanos. My breath came heavy and I swallowed hard feeling a strange attraction to Dardanos's darkly exotic features. The thought entered my mind that I wanted to go to him, cross the space between us, and lean down to put my lips to his. It felt like a memory or a thought put there by someone else, and I did my best to shake it off. I glanced uneasily from side to side to make sure no one was watching us, but the other guests were so caught up in their own gossip we might as well have been invisible. I turned back to Dardanos and those penetrating blue eyes, telling myself to look away to do anything but get caught in those icy pools. Instead I took a large, shaky drink from my glass to calm my nerves.

I set my drink down and pretended to be irritated, "You're as infuriating as Sergeant Cuff."

"Who?" Dardanos asked with a snicker.

I forgot that I wasn't with Gabriel; the familiar way in

which Dardanos spoke made me forget myself and mention the book Gabriel had given me. "I'm reading a book titled *The Moonstone*. The first narrator is an elderly steward in a great house assisting Sergeant Cuff to find the lost stone. He is outsmarted continuously by Cuff into helping him, though it might disgrace his revered Mistress and her family. Still, the steward cannot help but be curious and impressed with the Sergeant's cunning mind," I explained, blushing.

"I shall take it as a compliment then," Dardanos replied, fixing me with his piercing eyes once again. "It would be the most appreciative favor if you would indulge me with the story of your last experience with the medium. I should be in your debt; it is that important to me."

I bit my lip nervously, but finally assented, "Very well. I'll tell you what the medium said to me, even though I don't see why it's so important."

"It is important to me," Dardanos whispered, looking deep into my eyes as if he'd seen my private thoughts.

I grabbed my glass once more, sipping deep and for longer than I should have so as to tear my gaze away from Dardanos and his hypnotizing eyes. "The medium, Mrs. Gibson, said she felt a particularly strong soul among us. She said it was different than anything she had ever felt before. She made a big show of putting her hand over everyone's heads and closing her eyes. When she got to me she declared I was different; I had a very old and powerful soul. She said I had had no less than three incarnations before this one and that one of those was as a princess and priestess thousands of years ago, but of course she couldn't give an exact time period or even a name...it was cloudy, I believe was her excuse," I said sarcastically. "Then she said that I had not always been mortal; my soul still remembered being more than human. She claimed that my blood had traces of the immortals; I was descended from gods."

Dardanos's smile had widened so much he almost looked wild, and his eyes had a faraway look to them as he said softly, "Is that all? Did she say anything else to you? A warning perhaps?"

I was surprised by his question. I had never told anyone more than that, but the medium had told me more.

I sipped nervously from my glass, wondering how he would know there was more. "When everyone was preparing to leave Mrs. Gibson took me aside. She begged me to believe what she had said, although her so-called sight wasn't always as particular as she would like, it was accurate. She cautioned me to be wary of my past; my soul had a tendency to attract darkness and death. She said I had the power to cause unparalleled destruction."

Dardanos's face was lit with near manic joy. "Incredible, she must have been drawn to you...or you to her," he mumbled distractedly.

I didn't understand what he meant, but I laughed, "I can assure you I was in no way drawn to the medium. I make it a point to try to steer clear of such charlatans."

Dardanos looked up surprised, obviously not realizing that I had heard him, and explained simply, "I wasn't talking about you and Mrs. Gibson. I believe your prayer may soon be answered."

A chill went down my spine, but I wasn't sure why. I was just about to ask him what he meant when Lady Sergison clapped her hands and called for everyone to sit at the enormous round table in the center of the room. Dardanos rose from his chair, smiling warmly, and made a move as if he were going to brush his hand across my cheek.

He pulled his hand back abruptly as Lady Sergison walked up and entreated, "Mr. Samothrace, as my honored guest I'd like to have you sit next to me." Then she noticed Dardanos looking down at me and added, "Oh, Elizabeth, there you are. Come, dear, I want you to sit beside me as well. I cannot wait to see what Mrs. Gibson tells you this time."

"Nor can I," Dardanos said under his breath.

I let Lady Sergison lead me to the séance table which had been dramatically covered with a silky black cloth. Dardanos followed close behind and I thought I could actually feel the heat coming from him, but that seemed unlikely as the man's hands, even through my gloves, always felt cold as death. Lady Sergison, thankfully, did not seat us next to each other, but put me on her right and Dardanos on her left.

I looked around the table, seeing a few familiar faces from the previous séance. Mrs. Gibson had not taken her seat yet; she was still talking with a few attendees, but I was sure she would take the empty seat directly across from Lady Sergison.

While everyone found their seats and chatted animatedly I found myself absently counting the seats. I remembered Mrs. Gibson insisting that a séance circle should be made up of an even number of people to protect the circle from being open to malicious spirits. I was surprised to find our number to be seventeen. Surely Lady Sergison hadn't forgotten such a detail. Even if other mediums she'd employed did not mention this point I recalled how adamant Mrs. Gibson had been about the importance of an even number. I didn't believe in such superstitions; I didn't even believe in séances, but my conversation with Dardanos had put me on edge. Best to play it safe...in case I was mistaken in not believing in the spirit world.

"Lady Sergison," I whispered, "We have an odd number. Mrs. Gibson may ask someone to leave the circle." I was ready to volunteer myself.

Lady Sergison turned from her conversation with Dardanos. "I know. In all honesty I did not think your dear mother would accept the invitation. I assumed she disliked such gatherings, but I don't think Mrs. Gibson has noticed. I'm sure it will be fine," she said lightly, patting my hand reassuringly.

That was strange to hear Lady Sergison talk so nonchalantly about an ominous warning from one of her psychics; she was the most superstitious person I knew. I watched her out of the corner of my eye as she laughed and joked and blushed; she seemed so enlivened, so full of joy, so not like herself. My heart fell as I considered it might have been all my fault, this new behavior of hers. Was she having a breakdown because of what was going on between Gabriel and me? Had Gabriel confessed something to her? Perhaps he had already told her that our engagement was off, but then why would she sit me beside her? I wasn't even sure what was going on between Gabriel and me. He had been so strange when he'd brought me the bouquet of flowers, but he hadn't said anything about calling off the engagement. He had apologized, even if it had sounded forced and distracted, but then what had caused such a change in Lady Sergison?

"...some of you may remember me from Lady Sergison's last séance, but for any new seekers of knowledge here I am Mrs. Mariah Gibson."

I looked up, unaware that the séance had begun.

74

Everyone had taken their seats and were staring fixedly at Mrs. Gibson. She stood with her hands on the table in front of her with a look that challenged anyone to disagree with her. She was a bit younger than most mediums in popular demand; my guess was that she was near thirty. Tonight she had her long, blonde hair braided down her back with black ribbon wrapped around the braid and tied at the end, letting long cuts of ribbon dangle past her hips. As she had been the last time I'd seen her, she was wearing a black evening gown of silk and lace, a black shawl with red poppies tied around her waist. She wore long, dangling jewelry and rings on most of her fingers.

Like an actress dressing for her part, I thought looking at her costume.

Mrs. Gibson's dark eyes flashed momentarily at me as she continued explaining, "In a moment I will light the candle in the center of the table and have the rest of the lamps and candles in the room extinguished. At that time I will ask everyone to take hold of the hands of the people sitting to your right and left. The servants will then leave the room; only those within the safe confines of our circle may remain in the room. We will attempt to call on my familiar, the spirit that aides me in discovering the secrets of the afterlife. My familiar, as some of you may know, is my late husband, deceased these past five years. Once we have succeeded in calling him he will help me to contact anyone you wish from the other side. It is very important that we keep our hands clasped, keep the circle closed. At the very least breaking the circle will break our bond with the other side, but at worst it can allow something to get through."

"Will you do any past life readings?" the question came from Dardanos, though I couldn't see him on the other side of Lady Sergison.

Again Mrs. Gibson's eyes flickered to me, but then shot rigidly at Dardanos, contemplating him for a moment before replying, "Yes, I believe I shall do a few readings...if the spirits cooperate."

I felt a shiver as she agreed, knowing Dardanos hoped to unveil more of my supposed past life. I was curious if Mrs. Gibson had noticed Dardanos and me sitting together and perhaps that was why she had looked at us so keenly. I had a feeling she was already devising a plot to ensnare Dardanos and myself into some fabricated storyline. I closed my eyes wishing the evening was already over.

Mrs. Gibson turned and nodded to one of the servants behind her, and like a great wave of darkness folding over the room each light was systematically snuffed out. Leaving only the lone candle in the center of the séance table, and the single candles the servants were using to light their way out of the room. Every distinguishable face seemed pale and gaunt with empty voids where their eyes should have been. The room was a wall of imposing darkness in which I thought I could hear whispers. My eyes darted around the table in genuine discomfort; I didn't remember feeling this unnerved at the last séance. This time, though, something felt different. The very air in the room felt heavier, more tangible.

"I ask you all to join hands, close the circle, the most perfect configuration on earth. Let us bind our intentions together and beg that the darkness will offer us a guide. Focus on the flame of the candle. It is our beacon, it is our heart's desire. Come, oh spirit, come into the light that you crave. My dear husband come forth...Mr. Henry Gibson, I call you, I beseech you, come forth." Mrs. Gibson lowered her voice and entreated, "Everyone focus your minds on the flame and repeat silently the thought...Henry Gibson, Henry Gibson. Keep repeating his name in your thoughts."

I looked at Lady Sergison; she was staring fixedly at the candle and moving her lips as if she were speaking, but no sound came out. My eyes scanned the table for my mother's face, but the table was so large and the room so dark I couldn't be sure where she was seated. Mrs. Gibson was still muttering her husband's name, leading the rest of us to repeat his name in our minds. Finally I gave up on resisting to be part of the séance and I focused on the candle and repeated the name Henry Gibson in my head. I was so focused on what I was doing that I slipped and said his name aloud at the same moment Mrs. Gibson repeated it aloud.

A great gust of wind swept through the room, carrying with it what sounded like a man's voice. "Beware!" boomed around us.

My initial thoughts were that that word seemed to be popping up often over the past few days. Once I got over the fright of so loud a voice crying out I tried to convince myself that Mrs. Gibson must have had someone hiding beneath the table. It was merely part of her theatrics. I looked up at Mrs. Gibson's face and for a moment our eyes locked, fear written on her face, just before the candle was blown out by the mighty gust still swirling in the room.

The other guests seemed to panic as I heard women shriek in fear and a few shouts about feeling something brush against them. Lady Sergison was calling for a servant, but they were outside of the room and not much could be heard over the chaotic chatter and intermittent screams any way. Suddenly the table started shaking and I heard a few men shout for everyone to back away from the table.

"She brings death; she brings the end. Beware, beware," a man's voice sang out wildly, and I thought it sounded as if it were coming from the center of the table.

I pushed my chair away from the table, but was unsure of where I should go. It was so dark in the room that not even outlines of people or furniture were distinguishable. Even as I told myself this was all a show, nothing more, I felt my heart fluttering in panic. I was more afraid of the chaos going on around me; surely people would get hurt trying to rush from the table in pitch blackness. I didn't want to admit it, but I was just the tiniest bit frightened by the disembodied voice which had followed the unlikely appearance of a strong wind within a closed room. I could feel something in the room, some presence that didn't seem to belong.

"Elizabeth, come with me," Dardanos whispered in my ear so closely that his lips momentarily brushed my ear.

His hand slid down my arm until he found my hand, enclosing it in his. "This way. I can see a little in this wretched darkness. I will take you someplace safe."

I closed my hand around his nervously and asked with a quiver in my voice, "What about the others? I'm afraid there will be a panic. Should we not stay where we are? If everyone tries to flee the table at once people might get trampled."

Dardanos took hold of my other hand, finding it easily in the dark, and pulled me to my feet. "I will not allow any harm to come to you, but my fear is that you will get injured if I do not lead you away. Everyone seems to be fumbling about, but I can find a safe place where you will not be harmed by anyone trying to get away in fear." His face was close enough to mine to feel his breath on my lips as he spoke.

I didn't answer but merely nodded my head. He immediately pulled me forward, leading me away from the table as if he had seen my assent perfectly in the pitch blackness. It felt as though he were leading me toward the large leather chairs we had been sitting in just before the séance had begun, but I was unable to really get my bearings, frightened as I was by the peculiar occurrences. Furthermore I was distracted by the giddy excitement I had just from being so close to Dardanos.

"This should be safe," Dardanos said turning me around and pushing me back against a wall. "Please do not be alarmed. We are in the far corner of the room; no one should happen upon us here. We will simply wait here until the candles are lit once more."

I felt my skin tingling with excitement knowing that we were so far removed from the rest of the company in this impenetrable darkness. Everyone was still chattering loudly and screams erupted now and then from the ladies. Dardanos and I could speak of anything and no one would hear us. I imagined that was probably the reason Dardanos had led me so far from the others.

His hand was still resting protectively on my arm as he moved closer and in a hushed voice apologized, "I have been hoping to be able to speak with you without the inconvenience of other listeners so that I might tell you I am sorry."

He was so close I could feel the cold coming off of him like wind billowing off an icy sea. Even his fingers radiated a chill through my gloved arm, but where his thumb rubbed lightly on my bare skin just above the line of my glove I felt warmth spreading from his frigid touch. I felt my breath catching as I imagined him sliding his hand up my bare arm, to my shoulders, and cradling my neck to pull me forward into a stolen kiss. Where were these thoughts coming from? It was true Dardanos was an undeniably attractive man, but I was already engaged to a beautiful and charming man. It must all be a result of my uncertainties about Gabriel and the bizarre situation I now found myself in.

I steadied my voice and tried to calm my nervous breathing in order to ask, "What do you have to be sorry for? You have done nothing wrong to me." *Unless you count showing up on the day of my engagement and causing me to second-guess my feelings for Gabriel.*

Dardanos let go of my arm, answering guiltily, "I wish to apologize for my behavior the other night, at your engagement dinner. I have caused a rift between you and Mr. Sergison, and it was most unintentional."

I was a little disappointed by his remark, feeling a twinge of excitement that he had found me as alluring as I had found him, but then I silently reprimanded myself for such a thought. "Not at all," I said a little coldly, "It had nothing to do with you, I assure you."

"Whether anything happened because of me or not, I am at fault. I am guilty of thinking things I should not have thought," he explained with a sigh.

My cheeks flushed, imagining what he meant and I knew I shouldn't ask, but I couldn't help myself, "And...and what is it that you should not have thought?"

For a moment it seemed his cool, blue eyes flashed wantonly at me, illuminating in the dark as he admitted heartbreakingly, "From the moment I walked into Lord and Lady Sergison's dining room my thoughts have been full of you."

He reached through the darkness, cupping my cheek in his cold hand, but I felt as though a flame had been held close to my skin. I forgot for a moment where we were, longing with my whole body that he would put his lips to mine. I wanted to know how it would feel to kiss him passionately in this forgiving darkness. I wanted to know how different his kiss was to Gabriel's. I tried to convince myself that if only he would kiss me these feelings would end and I would stop wanting to feel his touch. I would realize he was nothing but an alluring man and all the silly fantasies in my head would end. I would tell him how meaningless and wrong it had been to indulge his flirtations, but that I was in love with Gabriel and I would marry Gabriel. I felt it was true; if only he would kiss me all these feelings would disappear.

I felt his body lightly brushing mine as he leaned forward, nestling his cheek against my free cheek and pressing his lips close to my ear to whisper, "I am not worthy to have such thoughts of you and I know you do not think of me so, but I hope to change that."

"General," I breathed heavily, expecting his lips to touch mine.

"I will never steal your affections; I hope I shall one day

earn them. I cannot bare to even imagine going the rest of my life without touching you," he paused, pulling away to rub his thumb along my bottom lip, "without kissing you."

❧8❧

The room seemed eerily quiet. Dardanos grabbed my hand without a word and pulled me forward, back toward the séance table. He put his hand on my shoulder to stop me, still saying nothing. My heart sank as I realized our stolen moment was over. There was no chance to quench the infuriating desire building within me. Dardanos hadn't sought to satisfy some carnal yearning; he sought to convince me of his unyielding affections, and explain the hope that I might one day return those same feelings. I wanted the darkness to remain indefinitely. It was how I felt: in the dark. Did I only long for Dardanos's touch or did I want his love? How could I claim to love Gabriel if my mind and my body both craved Dardanos?

Suddenly the candle in the center of the table was lit by a servant carrying a candelabra. In the dim light of the servant's candle and the one on the table I could see everyone huddled against the far wall on the opposite side of the table, looks of fear or confusion etched on most faces. I noticed that I was standing just behind my chair which was pulled a few feet back from the table. I turned abruptly from right to left, feeling the absence of Dardanos's body from my side. He was standing directly behind his chair as if he had never moved. When I glanced over at him he turned slightly toward me, a small smile on his lips as he raised his left hand up to his mouth and kissed his thumb. The thumb that moments earlier had swept across my lip.

"Elizabeth, I was so worried," my mother called from across the table, rushing to me, "You must have been so frightened all by yourself."

I glanced momentarily at Dardanos, sharing a conspiratory grin as I assured her, "Yes, it was frightening to be alone, but I was able to calm myself. I imagined I was somewhere safe…with someone to protect me."

Lady Sergison had the servants lighting the oil lamps

along the walls and on the scattered side tables, and she asked another servant to fetch refreshments for the guests. Apparently our evening of communing with the dead was over before it had even begun. I could see the women that had attended with their husbands were still shaky and noticeably pale as they were held up. The others seemed to be settling at the table, waiting for a drink to stiffen their resolve. My eyes suddenly locked again with Mrs. Gibson; she was still standing in the same spot she'd been standing when the candle had gone out. She was staring openly at me, a strange look of accusation and curiosity on her face. Lady Sergison whispered something to her and she broke her stony gaze.

"Yes, that's fine," Mrs. Gibson said to Lady Sergison.

"Mrs. Gibson has agreed to do readings for anyone that would like one. In light of the foreboding message we heard Mrs. Gibson and I both agree tonight may be an inauspicious time to call on the dead," Lady Sergison lamented, giving a weak smile.

A few of the couples in attendance made their apologies to Lady Sergison, but it seemed many of the ladies were still frightened or feeling faint. While some eight to ten people took their leave Mrs. Lucas excitedly sat down next to Mrs. Gibson, obviously exhilarated by the events of the evening and ready to have her reading. Mrs. Gibson's eyes flitted to me and then quickly to Dardanos as if she had expected one of us to jump at the opportunity; for my part I was planning no such thing. I was beginning to worry that Mrs. Gibson had seen some kind of familiarity between Dardanos and me and would announce it to the room in order to prove her superior skills.

Everyone left was now seated at the table as the servants went around handing out drinks. When it was my turn I asked for port; it was a bit out of the ordinary for a woman to drink, especially in public, but I knew it would calm my uneasiness more quickly than the claret. My mother was seated to the left of Mrs. Lucas, looking on with uncharacteristic interest. I was sure she meant to go next. It would certainly be better now that most of the guests had gone, leaving only Mrs. Gibson, Mrs. Lucas, Lady Sergison, my mother, Dardanos, and myself. I would feel less on edge if Mrs. Lucas and Dardanos would leave before my mother mentioned anything about Emma, though I suppose Dardanos's presence didn't matter as much as he seemed to know something about Emma's disappearances. I had a sudden brilliant idea how to prevent my mother from revealing anything shocking in front of Mrs. Lucas.

I lightly tapped my mother on the shoulder and lent close to whisper in her ear, "When Mrs. Lucas's reading is complete ask her to accompany you in the hall for a drink so you might discuss what Mrs. Gibson told her." My mother started to turn toward me, about to ask why, but I continued, "I will have a reading from Mrs. Gibson and I will ask about Emma so that you don't have to."

My mother smiled and for the first time I noticed how nervous she had been. Her face relaxed as she waited patiently for Mrs. Lucas to be finished. For my mother gossiping with another lady was easy, no matter what the topic; speaking to a clairvoyant about her daughter's shocking behavior, not so much. She played her part perfectly, expressing her excitement and interest in Mrs. Lucas's reading, ushering her out of the room before Mrs. Gibson could even ask who would like to be next.

I immediately jumped up from my seat and slid into the seat previously occupied by Mrs. Lucas, doing my utmost to give Mrs. Gibson a winning smile.

"Miss Cranford, I am glad you decided to attend tonight. I have been very agitated since our last meeting. I hope your life has been...untouched... by what we spoke of," Mrs. Gibson said low so that only I could hear.

"If you mean to ask if I have attracted darkness and death since we last met, I have not," I replied back smartly.

Mrs. Gibson narrowed her eyes as if she were trying to see into my soul, but simply said, "I see you would like to have a reading."

I bitingly agreed, "Yes, I would very much like to have a reading, but I wanted to ask a particular favor in my reading."

Mrs. Gibson eyed me carefully, turning her eyes nervously to Dardanos, but finally agreed, "Very well, but first we must make a connection and then you may make your request. Give me your hands; lay them over mine."

I never got the chance to ask her about Emma. As our hands touched I felt a shock and my head felt as if I'd had a bolt of lightning enter straight through my forehead. My vision exploded in a blinding light. I saw myself, my hair wild and curling, my long dress loose as a nightdress, flailing at the base of The Palladium. Tears were streaming down my face as I seemed to be pleading with the statue. Then the scene changed and I was in a wide open building with a man; only he was like no man I'd ever seen. He had vibrant blue eyes that seemed to swirl and change with the light and his hair was so golden blonde it seemed to glow with the brilliance of sunlight. He seemed familiar. I'd seen his face somewhere, but something about his appearance looked wrong, as if he had changed something about himself that I couldn't quite place. He was caressing me, kissing my arm, and moving toward my lips. Although he was the most beautiful man I'd ever seen, what I would imagine an angel would look like, something about him scared me. I was trying to pull away from him, but I feared angering him. It was as if I were watching myself perform a pantomime; every movement seemed exaggerated, but there was not a sound to be heard.

The man seemed to be offering me something, but without being able to hear I had no idea what it was. I was under the impression that he was in love with me; perhaps he was asking for my hand, but I was too cautious of him. I felt I couldn't trust him.

Then my vision faded again and I was in what looked like a dark temple, the smell of wax and flowers overpowering. The walls were of a pale yellow sand and the only light came from flickering candles. I was placing a bowl of flower petals on an altar, bowing my head, and muttering something. It must have been a prayer, but again I could hear nothing.

Once again my vision dimmed; this time no new scene revealed itself. Everything was dark and I felt I was falling down a swirling pit of blackness. Voices were calling my name from somewhere. I felt something cool on my face and a piercingly strong odor filled my nostrils. My eyes shot open and I found I was surrounded by my mother, Lady Sergison, and Mrs. Gibson. I was slumped in one of the large leather chairs, but I was fairly certain I hadn't gotten there on my own.

My mother was dabbing my face with a cool cloth. "She's coming round. How do you feel, Elizabeth?"

I looked around me, still trying to decide if I was me or if I was dreaming. "I feel...confused...I guess. What happened?"

"I'm not exactly sure," my mother answered, looking to Mrs. Gibson to explain.

Mrs. Gibson looked uneasily at Dardanos and said simply, "You seemed to be able to see what I saw, of your past, and then...I assume you fainted from the mental exertion."

Great, I fainted...again. This was becoming a very embarrassing habit, not that most women didn't at some point in their lives succumb to fainting spells. We were in the age of fragility after all, women I mean, and between over-tight corsets, societal pressures for modest eating habits, the occasional or even daily doses of laudanum, and the perpetual consumption of wine and brandy we had made it almost an art-form. One could be sized up in society by the soft, ladylike grace of one's swoon. I had a feeling my marks on this occasion were probably not in my favor. Knowing my luck I had most likely pitched forward, banged some part of my head into the table, and let little streams of drool escape down my chin.

"It was strange," I explained as I quickly swept my hand across my mouth, just in case, and gingerly ran my fingers around my head looking for a sore spot. "I saw myself-"

"You should rest," Mrs. Gibson interrupted me, "Sometimes speaking about it so soon after it happens can cause another lapse." Mrs. Gibson paused, turning to Dardanos she said, "Mr. Samothrace, would you be so kind as to bring Miss Cranford a brandy? I think it will help calm her."

Lady Sergison walked away with Dardanos and my mother followed close behind them to fetch our cloaks. I guessed that Mrs. Gibson had purposely sent Dardanos out of the room, but she seemed pleased that the others left as well, leaving us completely alone. She watched them leave before she turned back to me.

"Miss Cranford, I know you don't put much stock in my abilities, but I believe you may have some psychic abilities yourself." She turned her head to see if anyone was coming back. "I believe that is why the spirits warned us earlier to beware, and I believe that is why you were able to see into your own past."

"Did you see it too?" I asked carefully.

Mrs. Gibson nodded her head. "May I beg an audience with you tomorrow afternoon? I can come to your home. I must speak to you about something urgent, but it is for your ears only," Mrs. Gibson said in a rush.

I was surprised by her request, but assented, "Of course, Mrs. Gibson, if you believe it to be so dire."

"I do," Mrs. Gibson answered, rubbing a pendant that hung amongst dozens of others around her neck, "I believe that dark days are ahead for you, and it may be all my fault. There are things we must discover if you are going to stop them from happening...*if* you can stop them from happening."

"I don't understand," I whispered as my mother entered the room.

Mrs. Gibson reproached herself, "I woke your soul up, but some souls are better left sleeping."

❧9☙

I was in an alley. A pristine, cobbled alley. It was miserably dark, but that was what I wanted. I had the hood of my cloak up and made certain to keep my head down, lest anyone should recognize me. Most anyone would know my face, and wonder why I was sneaking about the city alone. I heard footsteps echo. Swinging my head round I discerned the man I had been waiting for down the street. No matter how close he came I was unable to make out his features, but I knew it was him...I could feel him. I could feel the power pulsating from him and I knew by the determinate way he walked toward me, bright, blue eyes flickering in the night.

"I am frightened. He will find out," I whispered, though the man was still some ten paces away.

"I will protect you, my love, do not be uneasy," came his cool reply.

My eyes seemed to close as I relaxed a bit, but when I opened them I was somewhere else. I was in what looked to be a library, but it had the feeling of a cave. It was dim, save a few candles lit in front of me, and the air hung heavy and damp. I had papers spread out before me with strange pictures and a language I didn't recognize, yet I was reading it.

"Yes, it must be part of her spell. It must be why I was drawn here."

I looked up at the strange sandy walls and closed my eyes with a smile on my face. I had discovered a clue that I had been looking for; a hint that I was following the correct path. I silently thanked the goddess for I knew it must have been she that led me to the information I was seeking.

My eyes opened and once more I was somewhere else; I was someone else. Now I was in a small room, a bedroom, but I didn't recognize it. I walked around trying to figure out how I had been in an alley one moment, a library the next, and then in this unfamiliar bedroom. I saw a desk on the far wall in front of a window. The window seemed like a good place to start; perhaps I would recognize what was outside and be able to figure out where I was. As I walked past the end of the bed my foot caught on something. I nearly fell straight into the desk.

I steadied myself and turned to inspect what my foot had caught on. To my horror I discovered a body lying face down on the floor. My foot had caught on the end of a foot belonging to the body of a woman. I didn't need to lift her head to see that she was dead and not merely passed out. There was a small pool of blood around her head and soaking into her blonde hair; far too much blood to not be fatal.

I put my hand to my mouth to keep from being sick. I wanted to run from the room screaming, but I knew that I was in an awkward position. I didn't even know where I was, let alone how I'd gotten there, and I just happened to stumble upon a dead body. I was fairly certain that no one would accept that explanation least of all the police, no matter how well connected and respected my father was. I was just forming a plan when I heard someone calling my name. The whole room seemed to shake as my name was called again.

My eyes shot open and were met by the familiar white canopy of my bed. I sat up confused, realizing I was still in bed, in my bed, in my bedroom. I could still hear someone calling my name and finally knew it to be my mother. It had all been a dream. I hadn't met some mysterious lover in an alley, I hadn't been reading some bizarre language on ancient looking pages in a humid library, and I hadn't discovered a dead woman in an unknown bedroom.

"Elizabeth, you will scarce believe what has happened!" my mother was half yelling as she entered my room without knocking. She paused a moment, seeing me still in bed. "Are you well? You look quite pale."

"Yes, Mother," I assured her, "I had some troubling dreams, that's all."

"How can you speak of such trifles as bad dreams when there are real worries to be had," my mother gushed excitedly as she plopped onto my bed, obviously excited about some new gossip she'd heard, and with Emma still missing I was the only one for her to tell it to.

I yawned in annoyance, "Are you going to tell me what has happened or shall I guess?"

My mother's face was still lit with excitement even after my unenthusiastic response. "It's Mrs. Gibson!"

I was about to explain that it was no great gossip that Mrs. Gibson was planning to pay me a visit, as I thought that was what my mother was hinting at. Instead my tongue froze as the image of Mrs. Gibson in her black dress and long blonde hair were suddenly present in my mind. *Blonde hair...*

"What about Mrs. Gibson? What has happened?" I asked nervously.

"Murdered," my mother whispered dramatically, raising her eyebrows and giving me a strange smirk as if she were merely mentioning the unflattering cut of someone's dress.

I gulped, feeling panic rising in me. "How? When?"

My mother folded her hands in her lap as she explained, "From what anyone has found out it must have been sometime last night. She was found in her room...her neck punctured open oddly, as if an animal had got at her. They said though, no animal could have done it. What animal would gouge her neck so precisely, attacking her nowhere else on her body, and then quietly let itself out without causing any damage to furniture or such? No...it must be murder. Oh, I wish Emma were here so I could tell her. To think we were just in Mrs. Gibson's company last night...I should probably ready tea and cake; I'm sure I'll have quite a few curious visitors today." With that she left the room as quickly as she had entered.

I huffed in annoyance at my mother's excitement at being the center of attention because of someone's death, but even more than that I was troubled by the strange dreams I'd had. Mrs.

Gibson was murdered in her bedroom with strange punctures on her neck. Had I seen her in my dream? Had I dreamed of Mrs. Gibson's death before it had even happened, or worse, had I actually been in that room somehow? It had felt so real; I could still feel where my foot had struck her boot. No, that was ridiculous. How could I have been there and gotten home without knowing it? Still, the idea of dreaming something before it had happened seemed even more ridiculous. Yet what had Mrs. Gibson said to me the night before...that I must have some psychic ability, that she had awoken my soul? What exactly did she awaken in my soul?

I dressed in a daze, taking no time to put my hair up. I simply needed space to think, and fresh air, and I needed it immediately. Surely this was a situation that required the comforting solitude of The Palladium. I grabbed my book, my only means of escape from the strange world I now found myself in, and headed to The Palladium. Unfortunately I was thwarted in my plans and instead was called into the breakfast room, though I argued that I had no appetite at the moment. I found that my eating habits were not the reason for my being summoned into the room.

My father sat at the head of the table eating his customary porridge and sausages, but when I entered he stopped eating and stabbed his spoon in the direction of a man sitting to his left (my seat, by the way), "Lizzy, this is Inspector Coghill. He's investigating this horrid business to do with Mrs. Gibson."

"Oh," I answered, giving him a quizzical look, "how do you do, Inspector?" I said as pleasantly as I could muster, remembering the deviously clever Sergeant Cuff from my book, and hoping Inspector Coghill would be equally as diligent in his investigations as the fictional policeman.

"Miss," Inspector Coghill said, reaching to tip his hat which had already been removed from his head.

Inspector Coghill was dressed in the style of the London constables with navy tunic and trousers, the silver buttons on the front of his tunic shone as if he'd just polished them, and the silver chain of his whistle was tucked into his left breast pocket. Although the inspector was very neat and seemed to take great pride in his appearance he was ordinary looking. His black hair was tidily combed over to one side, his black mustache was trimmed perfectly to a point on both sides, and even his fingernails were pristine as if they'd never seen a day's hard work.

Inspector Coghill was smiling smugly at me, noticing my inspection of him. "Nothing to worry about, Miss. Just a formality...got to question the last people to see the lady alive."

"Of course, I understand," I replied somewhat annoyed by his presumption that I found anything about him worth looking at. I took the seat directly across from him; the seat usually left for Emma. "You said it's just a formality? May I ask, Inspector, do you already have a suspect?" I thought anxiously about my dream, hoping it had been just that, and that the inspector hadn't found some evidence that I'd been in Mrs. Gibson's room.

Inspector Coghill gave me a puzzled look and then explained, "No, Miss, not a particular suspect, but it's always the same with these women."

"What do you mean?" I asked as the color rose in my cheeks, appalled by the off-hand remark, and realizing the man was certainly no Sergeant Cuff.

Inspector Coghill looked to my father, who seemed to wave his hand giving the inspector permission to explain what he meant. "Well, Miss, I don't expect a fine young lady..." he paused to wink at me "...of your station to know much about how these wayward women live. Some of 'em are no better than prostitutes."

"How so, Inspector?" I demanded through gritted teeth, my cheeks burning, not in shock of his words, but in anger that he was not only flirting with me but that he could speak so of a woman that had been murdered.

"Well most of these so-called mystics are nothing more than actresses, you see, and they're usually working for a man," Inspector Coghill rambled, oblivious to the anger rising in my face, "and this man, well, Miss Cranford, he isn't her husband, if you get my meaning. These men usually control the whole operation and collect the money. I know you can't understand, Miss, but that's how most of those women live, and somewhere down the line they want out of the dishonest life they'd been leading and those awful men I mentioned, well they have no conscious, and they kill the lady to keep her quiet," he concluded with a smile on his face, obviously proud of his cleverness, and expecting me to praise his superior intellect.

I took a deep breath and looked to my father to answer the inspector as I felt my temper rising to a fever pitch, but my father merely took up his paper, smirking behind it as if he knew what was coming next.

"What I don't understand, Inspector, is how a brainless dolt such as yourself has risen to your current position. It seems to me that you have asserted your own prejudiced ideas onto a case which you have yet to even investigate. Perhaps you should collect your evidence before you go around slandering the name of an innocent woman!" Now I was on my feet and my mother had entered the room, apparently hearing me getting louder and louder. "I think a dog would do a better job sniffing out clues than you, but as you are so incompetent in your interviewing let me offer you a few points of interest that you might not have thought to ask me about. Mrs. Gibson was a highly sought after clairvoyant, and she was paid very well by many affluent members of our community. She was always dressed in luxurious material; hardly something a woman that was pressed upon by a bad man would do. She always arrived alone and performed her séances alone; using only the guests to help her. Her manners were so genteel that she was not only invited to stay in a room at a reputable house in town, but she was also invited to all the fashionable parties given by both middle and upper-class families. Hardly the marks of a fallen woman. Also, last night there was a disturbance at the séance. Most of the attendees were frightened out of their wits by a warning from Mrs. Gibson's late husband. A warning which caused her to cut the séance short and several couples to leave early. Perhaps you should speak with all of these attendees before you close your case! Furthermore Mrs. Gibson made an appointment to meet with me this afternoon to discuss something that she described as dire, and she was adamant that we speak alone. Perhaps whatever she had wanted to warn me about is the reason she is not with us today! You, sir, are no Sergeant Cuff!" I yelled, waving my book in front of his face. "You are a sorry excuse for a police officer and I am severely offended by your unsolicited flirting! To think I should be impressed by a fool like you," I huffed at him before stomping out of the room.

"Elizabeth...Elizabeth? Lizzy?" my mother called after me, reverting to the nickname only my father and Emma ever used.

I ran straight to The Palladium, tears rolling down my face. I wasn't even sure why I was crying. Were they tears for Mrs. Gibson, had I upset myself in my unladylike tirade against the inspector, or was I starting to feel some unknown darkness closing in around me? The voice from the night before still echoed in my mind: *Beware!*

I flung myself at the foot of Pallas, much like I had in my dream from the night before. I ran my fingers along the base of the statue until they found the carved letterings of Cassandra's prayer. Cassandra had asked for protection, but none had been given. What hope then did I have of asking Pallas to protect me and those around me? My fairy queen was not as magical as I had always believed her to be; she was no great talisman that warded off evil. Something had changed. I could feel it, as if something dark had moved close to me, and Pallas didn't seem to be able to stop it.

I pushed myself up away from The Palladium, brushing off my skirts as I sat on the stone bench. I stared hard at Pallas's face, and I thought I heard a whisper. A low, familiar woman's voice whispering to me: *Beware*. It brought to mind Mrs. Gibson's urgent looks from last night, and her insistence that we meet in private. She had given me a warning as well: *I believe dark days are ahead for you.*

I thought over everything that had happened the night before. I remembered the many troubled looks on Mrs. Gibson's face, and her suggestion to not speak about what I'd seen during my reading. Then our conversation held in private urging me to allow her to visit me alone. Had she seen something in my reading that she needed to warn me about? Was I in danger, or perhaps someone close to me? Was Mrs. Gibson's death a result of this warning that she wished to impart to me alone on this very day?

"Mr. Samothrace to see you," our house maid announced to my mother and me while we sat quietly in the drawing room.

I was trying to get absorbed in the mystery of *The Moonstone* to take my mind off of Mrs. Gibson. Reading *The Moonstone* always reminded me of Gabriel, and I needed some familiar memories to comfort me. My feelings for Gabriel seemed all mixed up since his odd behavior, but I felt an endearing connection to the book he'd made me a gift of and it made me think of the things I loved best about him. I was having a difficult time of letting myself enjoy my book as a new narrator had been introduced and her overly pious and superior beliefs made me feel even more depressed. I found myself despising the angelic man she put on a pedestal and liking those that she denounced as living imperfect lives. It made me think of the differences in Gabriel and Dardanos. Gabriel was very much like the all-too-good Godfrey Ablewhite in that he has always seemed so perfect: handsome, from a good family, impeccable manners, and a light, easy personality. Dardanos seemed very much like Franklin Blake, a worldly and interesting man with some bad habits which make him even more endearing. For all the preaching of the lady narrator I was inclined to think ill of her favorite, the seemingly perfect Godfrey and felt drawn to the mysterious and attractive Franklin Blake.

"Mr. Samothrace," the maid announced once again.

At the mention of Dardanos's name I pulled my book closer to prove his appearance had no effect on me. He entered the room with soft grace, bowing to my mother first and then to me. I glanced up momentarily out of polite acknowledgment, and found Dardanos's eyes full of an unsettling look of yearning. He sat in the chair to the right of the sofa where I was seated. My mother made an excited fuss about Mrs. Gibson's death as if Dardanos would not have heard the news yet. Although Cuckfield was nothing to the grand size of London we were not a tiny country town; many neighboring towns actually ventured to Cuckfield for its variety of amusements and shopping. Still, we behaved like a small town, many of the inhabitants were either acquainted with each other or had at least heard of the family, and so news traveled quite fast. Especially provocative news such as a mysterious death.

"Yes, quite disturbing," Dardanos answered smoothly, "I would never have thought such a thing would happen in this charming town. It is strange to think we were just with her last night and now...she is no more."

"I know exactly what you mean," my mother gushed, obviously susceptible to Dardanos's captivating looks and manners. "Why Elizabeth was supposed to have met with Mrs. Gibson this very day."

"How curious," Dardanos said turning to me, "What do you think she wanted to discuss with you?"

I was just about to open my mouth to answer when my mother interjected, "It is very strange that she sought a private audience with my Elizabeth." *(Now I was her Elizabeth?)* "I believe she must have had some warning for us."

"Indeed," Dardanos commented in mock interest, but quickly winked at me to show he was merely humoring my mother, "I wonder then why she was attacked? Do you think it had to do with this secret warning she had for Miss Cranford?"

I had been thinking that very thing, but hearing it mockingly presented by Dardanos I realized how absurd it sounded. My visions hadn't been particularly shocking; I hadn't noticed anything that would seem to imply that I was in any danger. I couldn't think what it was that Mrs. Gibson had seen in my visions that had worried her. I thought back to the visions, picturing everything again in my mind, trying to remember if there was something that I had missed. Perhaps it was something in the background that I hadn't seen the first time.

Suddenly I was once again in the great wide open building where I'd seen the inhumanly beautiful man. My back was pressed against a massive white pillar, my fingers crawling their way back around the pillar until they just grazed another fingertip.

"He will see us here," I whispered sadly.

From the other side of the pillar came a deep, comforting

voice, "I will find a way to release you from your promise. I will free you from his desires...somehow."

I closed my eyes as they filled with tears. "I cannot go against him. He will destroy us both."

"I do not care what the consequence! I will not go on without you!"

"Elizabeth," a man's voice whispered near my ear.

I opened my eyes lethargically, in confusion I managed to utter, "General...what happened?"

My eyes focused on the entrancingly frosty eyes of Dardanos. I was lying on my side on the sofa as if I'd fallen to the right when my vision had struck. Dardanos was kneeling in front of me, his head tilted to the side to look me straight in the eye. His right hand cupped my cheek and his left held my hand that had fallen to dangle over the edge of the sofa. When I realized where I was and how inappropriate our proximity to each other was I sat up, pushing Dardanos lightly away.

He didn't move, but placed his hand over mine where they rested on my leg. "You must not be embarrassed. Your mother has gone to fetch a bottle of salts and a glass of claret for you."

I tried not to look at him, feeling my cheeks warming, but I couldn't stop myself. "You must think me intolerably weak to have fainted yet again."

"Not at all," he answered intimately, "I believe you are a remarkably strong and intelligent woman. I also believe your recent bouts of fainting, as you call them, are really memories your soul is trying to show you. It can be difficult to control at first, but it will get better in time."

"I don't understand. What do you mean?" I asked suspiciously; it sounded very similar to what Mrs. Gibson had said, about waking the soul.

Dardanos seemed to bend his head slightly as if he were listening for something, and then said, "We will have to speak later. Your mother is returning."

"How do you..."I began as he quickly took his seat moments before my mother entered.

"Well, good, you've awoken," my mother stated glumly, handing me the glass of wine, and obviously annoyed that I had interrupted her gossip about Mrs. Gibson.

Dardanos rose, announcing, "I must be on my way. Thank you, Mrs. Cranford, for your hospitality. Miss Cranford I hope you are feeling better."

My mother and I stood to take leave of Dardanos as he left the room, but I had a sudden anxious need to speak to him before he left the house. What he had said about my fainting really being memories puzzled me, and I couldn't allow the opportunity to question him about it slip away.

I turned to my mother and explained softly, "Mother, excuse me, I should thank Mr. Samothrace for his kindness. I forgot myself and I'm afraid he will think me rude."

My mother had already sat back down and taken up her embroidery. She didn't look up, but just nodded her head and made a little noise of agreement. I rushed from the room, hoping I had not missed Dardanos, and saw as I entered the main hall the front door just closing. I pulled the door open in hopes of finding Dardanos had not gone far but was surprised to find him still there. He stood just outside the door, the gas lamp on the house illuminating his expectant face.

I closed the door behind me, feeling a little embarrassed to have sought him out, but I could see by the look on his face he had hoped I would follow him. He boldly took my hand and led me away from the eye of the burning lamp, into the darkened drive where his carriage waited.

"I need to know what you meant by what you just said," I hurriedly demanded, self-consciously smoothing out my dress.

Dardanos seemed to pull himself away with some effort as he said in a hushed voice, "Not now. Not here. It will take time what I have to tell you. You must meet me somewhere."

My heart was pounding as I imagined meeting Dardanos somewhere secluded. "I can't imagine where we could meet that we wouldn't be discovered."

Dardanos took both my hands in his and whispered, "The Palladium. Tonight. Meet me there after everyone is asleep."

"Yes," I said without hesitation, "Yes, The Palladium."

As I walked back to the house it struck me that I had never mentioned The Palladium to Dardanos. I thought it strange that he should even know about it and even stranger that he should choose it as a meeting place. The one place in the world that was my sanctuary and he had divined it to be the perfect place for us to meet in secret. I couldn't deny it felt only natural to have a mysteriously concealed encounter with Dardanos before the statue of Pallas and I was anxious for the time to come. Had Pallas brought Dardanos to me, to fill the strange emptiness that seemed to be filling me? Were these strange occurrences linked and perhaps why I felt so withdrawn from Gabriel?

Just before midnight I slipped out of my room, carrying my small bedroom candle to light my way. I passed by my parents room to be sure I would not be happened upon trying to sneak out of the house. My father had retired soon after my mother and there was now no hint of light peeking beneath their door. The house was eerily quiet and dark, which could only mean that the servants had all gone to bed as well. Satisfied that I was not going to be found out in my secret mission I proceeded to the garden.

Once I stepped foot outside I realized the night was not as warm as I had anticipated. I hugged my thin, ivory robe closer, pulling at the lacy collar and sleeves to try to cover more bare skin. The garden gate was conspicuously standing ajar, the latch having been lifted and the gate pulled open just wide enough for a person to slip through. My heart beat quickened knowing that Dardanos was most likely already waiting within, and I confess I was more excited by the thought of being alone with him in the silent darkness than I was to find out why I was having strange visions and fainting spells.

I slowly made my way along the path toward the fountain in the center, taking care not to trip and in so doing either injure myself or soil my night clothes. I turned right, following the flagstones toward the stone bench and The Palladium just beyond. I stopped at the bench, turning the moonstone ring Gabriel had given me in trepidation, considering that my actions were not those of a woman engaged. What would Gabriel say if he found out I had met Dardanos secretly in the middle of the night? My heart beating wildly I held my candle high to illuminate the area, but there was no trace of Dardanos. I went closer to The Palladium, bringing the candle closer to her face. I thought I heard that whisper again: *Beware*, but I knew how the dark could play tricks on one's mind. I turned back toward the bench but found my long hair, which I had failed to tie back, had caught on a thorny vine swinging from the tree to the left of The Palladium.

I cursed lightly under my breath to have gotten myself stuck in such an awkward position.

"Do not move," Dardanos's voice lilted as he appeared just a few paces in front of me, "I will untangle you."

Surprised by his sudden appearance I breathed nervously, "General."

He smiled softly. "I do so enjoy hearing you call me that; someone I knew long ago called me that, even before I went to war. She said I was her champion, her warrior." Dardanos shook his head sadly as if trying to shake the memory from his mind. "I thought you should know; I don't want you to feel you have to call me that."

"It just seems less fierce than Dardanos, not to say that I don't like your name. General just seems to suit you," I stammered, my cheeks flushing as I tried desperately to untangle my hair on my own. "I'm so clumsy. I should have known not to get so close to that tree," I huffed.

Dardanos walked closer until his face was inches from mine, and then he put his arms around me, tugging lightly at the strands of hair that were caught. "You are not clumsy, you are enchanting, and you have given me the opportunity to come to your rescue. Every man likes to feel like a hero now and then."

I could smell sweet musk coming from him, engulfing me. My body trembled, but I no longer felt the chill in the air. I was focused on Dardanos's icy blue eyes, and as much as I felt I should look away, I was unable to. I felt my hair released from the vine, but Dardanos did not pull away.

He put his fingers in my hair and studied my face closely as if comparing it to someone else's as he whispered, "The night is darkening round me, / The wild winds coldly blow; / But a tyrant spell has bound me, / And I cannot, cannot go."

"But nothing drear can move me; / I cannot, will not go," I recited, gulping nervously, my eyes locked to his. "I'm not hurt. There is no need to fuss over me," I finally stammered in a hushed voice.

Dardanos smiled, almost adoringly, and for the first time I noticed he had strangely sharp eye teeth. "I know you are not hurt. To tell you plainly I find myself unable to look away from you. I believe you have cast a spell over me and that our futures are destined to be entwined."

He was staring into my eyes as I fought hard not to let the building emotions spill from them. I knew I shouldn't have been there, alone with him. I knew I shouldn't have had thoughts of his lips touching mine. I knew I should have had feelings only for Gabriel, but something deep inside of me was tearing at me to get out. I felt the very core of my being longing for Dardanos, longing for that dark mystery surrounding him.

With my eyes still locked on his frozen pools and my body still trembling in excitement my secret wish was finally granted. Dardanos softly pressed his lips to mine, gently pushing my mouth open with his tongue. I forgot myself, dropping my candle to the ground and causing the light to be extinguished, as I forced my own lips deeper into his. He had pulled open my robe to run his hands over the gauzy prison of my nightdress. As our lips hungrily devoured one another I was slowly pushed backward until my back was pressed against the front of The Palladium. Dardanos's lips were now moving to my throat and I was consumed with the thought that Gabriel had never awakened such passion in me. Then my guilt found me.

"Forgive me, Pallas," I whimpered.

Dardanos pulled away, concern in his voice, "You have nothing to ask forgiveness for. It is I that am at fault. I told you that I would win your affections, and here I am stealing them from you like a monster.”

I can't deny that I wanted to plunge back into his lips as he absolved my guilt, but I worked to calm the heat that had built up inside of me. “We are both at fault. I will forgive you, General, if you will forgive me.”

“That is generous of you, but there is nothing for me to forgive. You have never been any less than perfect in my mind. I, on the other hand, owe you everything that I am. I do not deserve your forgiveness, I know, but I shall strive for it none the less...for the rest of time.”

౮10ౚ

I pulled my robe tighter and tied it once again before I found my way clumsily to the bench to sit. I hoped Dardanos's keen eyes couldn't make out the shuddering that his passion had caused; I barely felt the cold any longer, only excited desire that his body had been so close to mine. Dardanos had somehow found my discarded candle on the ground and lit it.

My eyes were finally able to discern his face in the flickering light of the candle. "How did you know about my visions?" I inquired, trying to ignore my obstinate yearning.

Dardanos handed me the candle and turned back toward The Palladium as he answered, "I know about your visions because I too have experienced them...though long ago."

"But how could you-" I began.

Dardanos turned toward me, his form in shadows, and raised his hands to stop me. "You must forgive my hesitation, but I have waited a very long time to find you and explain everything...and I will. I am just...well...I am nervous that you will not believe me."

"If it will help me to control these visions I'm willing to hear anything you have to say with an open mind," I entreated, staring down at the little flicker of flame from my candle.

I watched Dardanos's dark form turn away and gently caress the face of the statue. "Some of what I must tell you will seem impossible, and yet I must persuade you to believe or all I have worked for is lost. I am not sure where exactly I should begin. I have repeated it so many times in my head, but now with you here before me I falter in nervous fear."

"Perhaps if you started with the origin of your own

visions," I offered.

"Yes," he said, nodding thoughtfully, "that may be easiest to explain. My story will most likely raise even more questions in your mind, but for now I need you to know my own experience. Please try to gain knowledge of my own visions and disregard the rest for now." He paused, gulping nervously, and began again with a great release of breath, "I was a prince, son of a queen and king, long ago, in a land full of ancient customs. I was raised to believe that our sovereignty was ordained by the gods, that our blood was connected to them, quite literally that we were descendants of the gods. I believed this so completely that in my early twenties I became obsessed with finding the link, the proof of lineage, between my ancestors and the gods. I poured over manuscripts and scrolls...I visited temples and spoke with priests and priestesses, but I found nothing beyond legends and foolish rituals. Then in my early thirties I entered a temple devoted to Isis. Presiding over this temple was a small group of priestesses that were taught the old ways of the goddess. Most of them were well aged and all had promised their bodies and souls to the worship of the goddess, but one was quite young. Her name was Amunet. She held all of the answers I had ever wanted to find and revealed to me a great destiny that I had no idea was even possible."

"Isis?" I interrupted, "Isn't she an Egyptian goddess?"

Dardanos stepped closer and I could see the surprise in his eyes. "You have heard of her?"

"Of course," I said with a light laugh, brushing my long hair back from my face, "I should think most of England has heard the name Isis. Egypt has been a very popular subject for quite some time, but...you...are you...were you...an Egyptian prince?"

"Yes," he answered, regarding me as if he were waiting for me to recognize him, "I was a prince of Egypt, and I would have been king one day if not for the misfortune that befell me and my family. That is not important right now though. I want to tell you about my own experience with visions."

"You said the priestess, Amunet, had answers for you," I prompted him.

I could see the shadowy outline of his head nod in agreement. "She was tending the altar, placing burning perfumes and bowls of flower petals along its length as she recited their daily prayers. When I entered the sanctuary the other priestesses knelt to honor me, but her back was to me. When she did finally turn she did not kneel like the others had, but stared at me with recognition in her eyes. She did not hesitate to announce to me, 'You have come. I was beginning to think that my visions were wrong.' I found it surprising that she should have expected me as I never announced my visits beforehand to any sight. I was intrigued and felt sure it was dire that I speak with this young priestess, but as I got closer I was again astounded. She was not only young but uncommonly beautiful. I had never seen a woman with red hair before, though, I had heard there were Israelites with such hair. And those eyes," he paused, pulling my chin up and looking into my eyes, "those piercing green eyes stopped my breath and caused me to lose my will to speak."

I was reminded of my dream, in which I'd been in a dark, quiet room and I was placing a bowl of petals on an altar. I had never told anyone about my dream and I was fairly certain Mrs. Gibson hadn't either, but how could Dardanos describe something so similar? I decided to keep it to myself for the time being. When I looked back up at Dardanos he was still staring at me, studying my features as if he were making sure they hadn't changed since last he looked at me.

"Do I look very much like Amunet?" I whispered sadly.

"Identical," he commented with hurt in his voice, letting go of my chin, "only your skin is a bit paler, but that is to be expected in this confining English environment."

"Were you in love with her?" I questioned softly.

"Completely," Dardanos answered, "and so she was with me." He looked at me for a moment as if deciding what to say next. "Let me continue...from the beginning. Once I laid eyes on Amunet I had an indescribable feeling of familiarity, as if we had met before, though I knew that was unlikely. She told me that I had spoken to her, in a dream, that I had revealed to her my plan to visit the temple. The head priestess asked me to excuse Amunet's peculiar ideas as she had been learning the old ways; I think she feared that I would think the girl's familiar way of speaking with me was rude or inappropriate. 'You are the prince?!' Amunet exclaimed in surprise. I thought that strange as she had said I told her I was coming, but before I could find out what she meant she asked that we speak in private. She took me to a kind of library in which the priestesses studied their ancient writings and transcribed fading teachings onto new papyrus. It was not a large room, but it was cool and quiet and I was assured we would not be interrupted.

"The young priestess asked me a strange question as we sat. 'You admit you do not know exactly why you are here?' I simply nodded my head and explained to her my obsession with finding a link between my family and the gods, and how that obsession had finally led me to the temple. She told me that she was learning the old ways of worship from when Isis was known as the goddess of magic, the three-faced goddess of earth, sky, and underworld, but she hadn't been studying very long. She was new to the temple. She had just arrived at the end of Akhet, a season marked by the rising water of the Nile, which would have made it roughly six months, and ever since her arrival she had been having visions and dreams. Most of her visions were of herself in an ancient temple of white stone and sometimes I was there...and sometimes another man."

"A brilliant man with golden hair?" I interrupted with a shudder.

Dardanos didn't seem surprised by my outburst as he assented, "Yes, I believe you and she have had similar, if not the exact same visions, and before I am done I will tell you why.

"Amunet told me that precisely one month earlier she had a vision in which I told her I would come to her before the next new moon. I asked if she knew why I was there and she said she had a guess based on her visions. She said I had obviously been drawn to the temple because of her presence, or rather the presence of her awakened soul, and I was most likely drawn to a certain artifact which had also drawn her to the temple. "

Before I could stop myself I burst out, "Mrs. Gibson told me that she believed she had awakened my soul. She also said some souls are better left asleep," I said thoughtfully and then added, "Did Amunet ever tell you how her soul was awakened?"

"Yes," Dardanos answered, sitting down beside me,

"shortly after she arrived at the temple the eldest priestess, who still practiced the old rituals which tied Isis to an ancient Greek goddess of magic-"

"Not Hecate?" I interjected excitedly, remembering the story Gabriel had told me about Cassandra of Troy being the daughter of the mortal incarnation of Hecate.

Dardanos turned to me slowly, shock in his eyes. "How could you know who Hecate is?"

I could see from the look on his face that this was important to his story, but I didn't want to reveal how much I knew just yet. "I've read about both Greek and Egyptian mythologies. I don't claim to be an expert but I believe I possess at least a general knowledge of both, and I came across some stories linking the two."

"Of course," Dardanos said smiling warmly, "you must have been drawn to those stories just as you were drawn to The Palladium." He paused, looking down and clasping his hands in thought. "You are correct. Many of the older priests and priestesses remembered a time when Isis was worshiped as the tri-fold goddess, like Hecate: goddess of sky, earth, and the underworld. In the old days she was worshiped through rituals performed using magic. The old priestess knew immediately that Amunet had been sent there by the goddess, and she knew she had to help her find out why.

"The old priestess brought Amunet to a seer, another who practiced the old rituals. When the seer put her hands on Amunet they both experienced a vision and Amunet lost consciousness for a few moments just as you had with Mrs. Gibson. Amunet told me that from that moment on she would fade in and out of visions against her will. You see the seer unlocked a door that had been locked inside of her, and when the door was opened everything within fought to rush out at once. She returned to the seer a few months later as her visions were becoming more frequent and she was unable to stop the inevitable fainting and weariness that followed.

"The seer told her that her visions were becoming more frequent and intense because her destiny was fast approaching. The seer taught her how to push the visions back so they would not affect her mind so much or to ignore them completely, but she warned that the visions were occurring for a reason and it was in her best interest to find out their meaning.

"I didn't understand what Amunet's visions could have to do with me, but then she proceeded to tell me each of her visions and I was stunned to discover I was in nearly all of them. These visions I am about to describe may seem familiar, they may even be identical to ones you have had. If I am correct your visions, just like Amunet's, are of your past life; a past existence in which you and I knew each other...and loved each other."

I raised my eyes to his, searching for the truth of what he was saying. He had told me once that souls could recognize each other, even when we ourselves did not. Was that why I couldn't control my undeniable attraction for him? Was my very soul longing to be reunited with him?

"What were her visions?" I asked, looking down at the candle flame once more so that I wouldn't have to look into Dardanos's hypnotizing eyes.

He looked at me thoughtfully for a moment and then asked, "Have you heard of the Trojan war?"

"Of course," I answered shortly.

"Do you know who Cassandra was?"

There it was again. That reference to Cassandra. "Yes, I know who she was."

Dardanos studied me once again, as if reassuring himself that he was right about me. "Amunet's visions were of Cassandra, of herself, in a past life. Many of her visions were nothing more than seeing herself in a great white temple, or standing before The Palladium, which interestingly enough was a relic within the temple of Isis."

"The Palladium was in Egypt?" I asked in surprise, forgetting that I didn't completely believe Dardanos's story.

"Yes, how it got there I do not know, but it seems a great coincidence that it should be in the exact place that Amunet was drawn to, and stranger still that it should come to be here in your home," he said.

"My father found it before I was born; when I was a child

he told me it would protect me. Why is that important that The Palladium is here; if it's even the true Palladium?" I asked smartly. "What does The Palladium have to do with any of this?"

"Have you not guessed? Can you not see the clues before you?" Dardanos questioned, grabbing at my hand anxiously.

I knew what he was hinting at, but it was so far-fetched I couldn't allow myself to acknowledge that the thought had even crossed my mind. "I don't know what you mean," I lied. "I don't believe in magic, or fate, or gods. I believe in facts and what I can see with my own eyes. I believe that I am in control of my own destiny, not some invisible mystical force."

He ignored my argument and said exactly the strange, unbelievable thing that had momentarily been in my thoughts, "It is plainly evident you were Amunet in a past life; you were Cassandra of Troy in a past life. The fact is you still are Amunet and Cassandra, and the paths they followed in their lifetime have led to you; what they have set in motion is affecting your life right now."

I couldn't look at him. It was too ridiculous a thing to agree with, but the memories of my visions were creeping back. How could I explain them? How could I explain that this other woman had had the same visions?

"You do not deny it is possible?" Dardanos almost begged, "I know it is hard to accept, but the evidence is too overwhelming to believe otherwise."

"It must be some kind of trick," I tried reasoning, jumping to my feet and taking a step toward The Palladium. "Maybe Mrs. Gibson hypnotized me. Maybe that was how she made people believe she could do what they thought she could."

Dardanos followed my lead and stood, placing his hands on my shoulders from behind. "You were not hypnotized, and if you were how can you explain the visions Amunet had? How could I describe visions so similar to yours?"

I stared at the statue of Pallas as I answered him sadly, "I don't know...it's not possible. None of it seems possible." I put my right hand over his left, needing to feel his skin against mine. "Who is the golden haired man I've seen? I was so frightened of him."

Dardanos pulled his hand free and turned me to face him. "You have seen him? He is the reason we were separated...both times we were separated."

"But who was he? Why am I so frightened of him in my visions?" I asked anxiously.

"Can you not guess who he was? You know the myths, you know the story of Cassandra," he pushed.

I closed my eyes and felt the darkness completely invade my mind. There was nothing to see, and try as I might my eyes would not open. It was quiet, so peacefully quiet, and then a voice echoed in my ears.

The sweetest, tinkling voice, a man's voice, whispered tenderly, "Cassandra...Caaassaanndraaa. I have a gift for you, my beauty."

I opened my eyes, my head resting on hard marble floor. I sat up confused, my eyes scanning until they rested on The Palladium standing over me. Now I remembered: I was in the temple of Athena again, seeking refuge from my family, and the life that my father and brothers were trying to force on me. I often wandered to the temple to cry before the statue of Pallas, and beg Athena to intervene and help me.

My father and my two elder brothers wished to send me away to be married off to a new ally. They believed by marring me to this new, unpredictable friend of Troy that it would keep him loyal. I was appalled by the very idea of being sent away from my home to marry a stranger, a stranger that was nearly thirty years older than me.

I pulled myself onto my knees once more, clasping my hands together I pleaded, "Athena, wisest of gods, protector of women, you must see the injustice of what my family is trying to do. How can I be forced to marry a man I do not love? How shall I bear to be sent so far from my home? Please, help me, Athena."

"You have always been one of my favorites, Cassandra," a smooth voice sang into my ear. "So lovely, so intense."

109

Startled I swung my head around to find the origin of the voice. A beautiful man with glowing blonde hair, the color of sunlight, was kneeling beside me, his smile as bright as his hair. He was turning his head from side to side, studying me as if he'd never seen anything so interesting.

"My lord Apollo?" I questioned, surprised by his appearance in the temple. "Have you been listening to my prayers?"

"Of course I have. What else do you think we gods do? Humans are the greatest source of entertainment," he stated, brushing my hair behind my ears. "I have a gift for you."

"A gift for me?" I asked incredulously. "What have I done to deserve a gift from the great Apollo?"

"I have been watching you for a long time, and I must say that alone is enough, but there is something more about you. You have a strength...perhaps it's because of your mother's powers coursing through you, but you exude the presence of a god. There have been a few before of course that had this same essence about them; they were all destined to become gods."

I shook my head. "No, my lord, I am not meant to become a god. I am being sent away to marry an old man in a strange land," I explained, tears rolling down my cheeks.

Apollo smiled broadly and wiped the tears from my face. "That is where you are wrong. You will marry no one. I told you, I have a gift for you, and it will change your destiny."

"What is it?" I dared to whisper.

Apollo leaned forward, a hissing sound filling the silence, and ran his tongue along the outside of my ear. He brushed his cheek against mine until his lips fell softly over my mouth. Lightning filled the temple with blinding light, and I found myself falling helplessly into Apollo's arms.

Apollo's laughter echoed in my ears, "Uh, oh, father doesn't approve. You must be important, and now you have the power to see what will be. You will have the ability to change the future before it happens, or, I should say, you'll have the ability to try."

I blinked and found myself in the garden staring at The Palladium. "Apollo," I answered, remembering the question Dardanos had put to me before I'd drifted into another vision. "The god Apollo."

"Precisely. Apollo, god of the sun and light," Dardanos said in disgust.

"But," I protested, "that's not possible. Apollo wasn't real; he was just a legend created to explain the rising and setting of the sun," I argued more to convince myself that what I'd just seen was nothing more than a dream, a fantasy. "He was created because people had no understanding of the way the world worked."

"Hmmm, you mean like a story in which an all-powerful being creates an entire world from nothingness," Dardanos answered, smirking.

"That is completely different," I objected indignantly. "Belief in the one true God was a result of man's observation and recordings of his interactions with that higher being."

"So the mythologies, the stories that were told and retold and eventually recorded over thousands of years, do not hold any similarities to your belief in a God who's story was merely told and retold until someone finally wrote it down or claimed to witness it?" he scoffed, "Then you would probably be thoroughly shocked to find out that your one true God was once part of the stories you find so absurd, the stories of the many gods."

"You can't say that!" I stated in shock, thinking how my parents would react to such talk, how Gabriel would react. "People would call it blasphemy."

"I can say that," Dardanos said simply, "because I have seen the truth. What was it that you said? You believe in what your eyes can see. Well, I have seen. I know the tainted history of this world. I know how men's lives have been manipulated by nothing more than the sheer boredom of the gods. I know what punishments there are for angering the gods, and I know how it all came to an end...until there was only one god left."

"Are you saying," I hesitated, "the god that we worship

today is...was once...the king of the Greek gods? Zeus?"

"Yes, well, that was one of his names anyway. He has been called many different names by different peoples, but yes, at one time your God was called Zeus," Dardanos said sternly, almost daring me to contradict him.

I wanted to tell him he was out of his mind, but for the sake of finding out more information I bit my tongue. "Very well, that part aside, what does any of this have to do with me, or with my having been Cassandra in a past life?"

Dardanos brushed my cheek lightly as he answered, "It has to do with the war that ensued after what happened to Cassandra."

I shook my head severely and disagreed, "No, the war had already ended when Cassandra met her fate."

"I am not talking about the war of men at the city of Troy." he countered, "I am talking about the war between the gods."

"Why would the gods care about what happened to Cassandra?" I asked, echoing the spiritual separation felt by humans to their deity.

"Because of who she was and what she was. Cassandra was half-goddess and her mother was a powerful goddess with many allies. She was also a devoted priestess to Athena, a goddess that watched over women and took the protection of her priestesses very seriously. Furthermore Cassandra was loved by a minor-god; he was not particularly powerful, but he also had many allies and he was willing to do anything for her," Dardanos said the last sadly.

"Oh yes, the cursed god," I remembered, "I was told about him. He was cursed by Hecate for the fate of her daughter."

"Where did you hear that?" Dardanos asked angrily, but cooled his tone, "It was not Hecate that cursed him; she tried to help him. It was Apollo in his jealousy that cursed him. Apollo, god of the sun, cursed him to hide in darkness, cursed him to be burned by the dazzling rays of the sun."

I was still confused about what any of that had to do with

my visions. Based on what I'd seen it could be argued that my visions in the white temple could have been visions of Cassandra, and the visions of the dark, candlelit room with the altar could have been visions of Amunet. Beyond that, what did Dardanos expect me to believe? That I was his long, lost priestess Amunet; that I was also the reincarnated prophetess Cassandra; that he was the cursed god that loved Cassandra, and that these things proved we were meant to be together? I could admit there was an unexplainable connection between us, and I might even admit I had been looking for some reason for my uncontrollable attraction to Dardanos. Having a soul-attachment between two lifetimes would certainly be a convenient excuse for my infidelity to Gabriel.

"So why do you think The Palladium ended up here, even before I was born? Do you think it's drawn to Cassandra's soul simply because she was a priestess in the temple where it was housed?" I asked almost mockingly.

"I believe the statue and Cassandra's soul, your soul, are bound to each other," he answered, ignoring my tone.

"But why are they bound?" I demanded.

Dardanos bent down to stroke the base of the statue. "Because of this. The prayer...it was never answered. It reached Athena's ears too late and she was truly anguished by it. I believe the statue and Cassandra's soul will continue to be drawn to one another until the prayer is fulfilled."

I stared at Pallas's face, feeling as if Dardanos had put the weight of the prayer on my shoulders. It was now up to me to make sure the prayer was fulfilled. I had to accept everything as true and give my love and my life to Dardanos, or we would be doomed to try to find one another again in another life, presumably never finding our true happiness until such a time.

"There are a few things I want to know," I said finally. "Firstly, you have spoken about your time in Egypt and Amunet as if they were in your past, not your past-life, but that would be impossible. Based on the age you were at the time you met Amunet and the age you are now...there isn't enough time passed for Amunet to have died, for me to have been born and lived nineteen years. It simply doesn't make sense. Also this minor god that Cassandra supposedly fell in love with: what was his name, who was he, why was their story not recorded?"

I could see my questions had made him uneasy. I was sure I had him; he would have to admit at least part of his story was a lie. I sat down triumphantly on the stone bench, over-dramatically resting my chin in my hand and resting my elbow on my crossed leg.

"You are correct," he began slowly, "I have talked of my time in Egypt as if it were a part of my not so distant past. That is partially true. In this lifetime, and by that I mean an existence uninterrupted by death, I was an Egyptian prince and I did meet and fall in love with a priestess name Amunet. I am not ready to explain how that is possible to you yet, but I will...in time, I promise. For now I want you to consider what I have told you, and consider the chance, no matter how small it may seem, that I have told you the truth." With that he walked past the bench as if he were leaving.

"Wait," I protested, jumping up and nearly running into him, "you didn't tell me about the minor god."

Dardanos huffed as if he had hoped I'd forgotten. Once more he gently pushed his lips against mine, slowly and languidly lapping at my mouth as he brushed my hair back from my face.

I thought that was his way of silencing me, and I was more than willing to accept it, but after he pulled away and took a few steps he said sadly, "His name was Dardanos. I took his name after I learned the soul I possessed was his. There are still bits of information available, nothing too in depth, and most of it so vague it could be about anyone. His story, his true story, was lost because of his curse. It was thought so abominable that his involvement in the Trojan War and everything after was effactually erased from history."

❧11❧

"Do not allow him to go to Sparta!" I screamed, twisting the folds of my silk gown in my fists.

"That is not your decision," my father fumed. "He will go with his brothers. It is time he takes his place as a prince of Troy and learns to keep up our relationships with our allies."

I stomped my foot angrily. "I have seen-"

"I do not care what it is you think you have seen. He will go and you will respect my word," he demanded. "I have allowed you too much freedom. You go where you wish. You spend more time than is necessary at the temple. You go about claiming you can see things that have yet to happen. I allowed you to refuse the marriage I had planned for you, and I allow you to be present when we discuss the future of this kingdom, but do not think that entitles you to tell me how to rule. I will not budge on this, daughter. That is all."

I opened my mouth to argue, tears filling my eyes, but I could see my father would not be moved. I hid my face in my hands and ran from the room. Like so many of my visions, this one too, would be ignored. I knew there was trouble stirring; the gods were irritable. Something had happened to rouse their interest and anger for mortals, and it had something to do with my brother.

"Princess, are you all right?" Xanthós, the house servant and my friend, asked from down the hall.

I lifted my eyes to him, wiping at the still streaming tears. "I have seen another vision, but my father will not listen."

Xanthós checked to see if anyone were coming and then put his strong but lithe arms around me. "What have you seen? Is there something I could do to help?"

I pulled away gently and searched his blue-green eyes for an answer, but shook my head. "I do not think there is anything to be done. My brother will start a war if he goes to Sparta, but I do not know how or why. The only way to prevent it is to keep him from going."

Xanthós smiled reassuringly. "What if I went as well? At least I could try to prevent something from happening, and if I cannot then at least I will know how it has happened and bring the news back to you."

I looked at him in disbelief. "You would do that for me?"

"Of course," he said, blushing, "I would do anything for you."

I smiled sadly at him, knowing his feelings for me ran deeper than friendship. "I must go to the temple and pray to Athena for help. The gods are angry and I must see if there is a way to appease them. Go to my father and ask to be allowed to go to Sparta. He will listen to you; he trusts you above all the servants."

Xanthós nodded and headed resolutely toward my father's room. I broke into a run, running out of the palace, out of the gate, down the stone paved roads to the temple.

The wind was picking up and the sky was darkening as I raced up the steps. It felt as if the very temple were quaking in anger. As if Athena herself were in a rage. I'd been feeling this for days now. The electricity in the air; the excitement and anger throbbing from up above. I lowered myself in front of The Palladium to beg Athena's advice.

"She won't listen," purred a familiar voice from behind.

I turned to see Apollo leaning against the pillar behind me. "My lord?"

Apollo pushed off the pillar, walking toward me like a lion in sight of its prey. "She's angry. I wouldn't even bother asking for her help," he scoffed, offering his hand to help me up.

I accepted his hand, avoiding the ravenous look in his eyes. "Why is she angry? Have I done something to offend her?"

Apollo laughed, throwing his head back, as he lead me to a nearby bench. "Cassandra, how could you offend anyone? You, who have the grace and temperance of a queen. No, you must have a guess who is to blame. Have you not been using my gift; have you not had any visions?" He asked running his fingers along my cheek.

"I have had a vision. I did not understand what it meant exactly, but I am sure it has to do with my brother. I think he is going to do something while he is in Sparta that will put us all in danger." I ventured a glance at Apollo. "Why would that anger Athena? It has not happened yet."

Apollo pulled my chin forward and placed a light kiss on my lips. "That is not what she is angry about. She is angry because your brother declared Aphrodite to be the most beautiful goddess, even compared to Hera and Athena. Hera isn't very happy with him either for that matter. You of all people know that you should never compliment a god by slighting another."

"Why would my brother do something so careless? And to have offended Athena," I whispered, shaking my head.

Apollo was still tracing his fingers around my face when he answered, "Your brother is only mortal. He was made an offer by Aphrodite that he couldn't refuse. It really wasn't fair, but we gods don't always play fair," he whispered the last as if it were a great joke.

I gulped nervously at Apollo's increasingly uncomfortable caresses. "What did she offer him?"

"Love," he said, smiling strangely at me. "The love of a beautiful woman."

Before I could ask more Apollo plunged forward, pushing his mouth aggressively into mine. His hands grasped the back of my head so firmly I couldn't escape his violent kisses. I felt panic rising in me. How could I refuse him? How could I escape his wanton desire without angering him? His hands on my body were like stings from a whip, a punishment for believing his interest in me was anything noble.

"No," I managed to whisper.

"No!" he screamed, pulling away from me. "Surely you

117

would not refuse me. I have done nothing but help you. I have worshiped you, respectfully, waiting for you to be ready to receive my affections."

I clasped my hands and begged, "Please, Lord Apollo, I mean no disrespect. It is only that...that...I..."

"She wishes to be my priestess," a woman boomed,

I turned to see a tall, regal woman in a flowing gold tunic standing next to The Palladium. I immediately fell to my knees recognizing the goddess, a shining helmet on her head and an owl circling about her.

"Athena," I muttered, looking down to the ground. "Please forgive my brother for his ignorance. I am ashamed of his actions toward you."

"You need not apologize for others, my daughter," Athena announced and then turning to Apollo she chided, "You, Apollo, should know better than to defile my temple with your sorted hobbies. Cassandra is not one of your empty-headed playthings. She is part goddess, a woman of reasoning and strong intellect, and she wishes to bind herself to my worship."

I looked up to see Apollo's face turn to stone, his eyes narrowing, but he merely flouted, "Sister, I know more of Cassandra's qualities than you give me credit for. I have foreseen a great destiny for her...but I shall not interfere with her being your priestess." He bowed, smirking.

"Very good...brother," Athena sneered the last, and then turning to me said, "Cassandra, you are welcome to be a priestess in my temple for as long as you like. I know the virginal life of a priestess is not for everyone, and I will understand if you should change your mind one day."

Before I could say a word she vanished.

"Just know that should you change your mind you belong to me," Apollo stated cruelly, "Promise me. Promise me you shall never love another. You will never give yourself to another."

My lip quivered, but I assented, "I promise...I shall never love another."

I opened my eyes. I was no longer in the temple but on a dark road. There was a faint light coming from the lone flickering street lamp. I heard a crash behind me and whirled about to see its origin. There were two men in a scuffle. A few feet away there was what looked like a short, curved sword on the ground. One of the men pushed the other against the wall of a building and suddenly I was running toward them shouting.

"Stop! You're hurting him!" I shouted, running to intercede.

The man up against the wall crumbled to the ground though I couldn't see anything that the other man had that could have injured him. I stopped short, frightened by what the man would do to me. The attacker turned abruptly toward me, but his face didn't look human. It looked more like a wild animal. His eyes glinted in the darkness and his mouth was curved in a ferocious snarl.

"No!" I screamed, throwing my hands out in front of me to protect myself.

Instead of fending off some fierce monster I found myself sitting up in my bed, my body damp with sweat. It took me a moment to realize I was safe and it had all been a dream...again. I put my head in my hands, steadying myself, and trying to decide if what I'd seen were actual visions or just a product of the very late conversation I'd had with Dardanos.

"Hello, Lizzy," a voice said softly from the doorway.

I turned, surprised to see Emma standing there, looking at me with a strange mix of anger and sadness. I stared at her a moment disbelieving she was really there; perhaps I was still dreaming. She looked as if she'd been ill, her face was thinner and all the color was gone out of her lips and cheeks. Her long, curly black hair hung loose down her back and her usually bright blue eyes were dull with tears. Then I discovered why she looked so pale and gaunt; she was dressed all in black crepe. A dress that should have been reserved for deep mourning.

"Emma, are you well? You look ill," I said distressed at her appearance, getting out of bed and pulling my robe on.

"I am as well as can be expected," she answered cryptically, "you should come downstairs at once."

I thought for a moment that I must surely still be dreaming. I couldn't believe that Emma was really home, and even stranger she was treating me as if I'd done something wrong to her. She was the one that had risked not only our family reputation but her own health and safety these past months. Still, the darkness in her eyes worried me and motivated me to dress quickly to find out its meaning.

I found both my parents and Emma sitting eerily still and quiet in the drawing room, my mother holding Emma's hand as if to comfort her. When I entered my father's eyes shot wide as if he'd forgotten I still existed. He seemed to deflate in his chair, making me feel as if my presence were a burden to him, but he soon recovered and pulled himself up. He looked at my mother and Emma, deciding what he should do.

"Lizzy, take a walk with me in the garden," my father said sadly, gesturing for me to lead the way.

I knew it must be serious if he was taking me to The Palladium to tell me something. For a moment I considered that he had found out about my late night rendezvous with Dardanos, but then I reasoned Emma would have had no reason to be upset about that. She had looked as if she had been crying. I thought it must be about Emma. She must have done something to compromise us all. She was wearing a mourning dress and looked as if her heart had been broken. Wild thoughts filled my head; thoughts of a secret marriage, of an improper pregnancy, thoughts of a death involved in one or both of the previous thoughts. Instead my father said the last thing I ever expected.

"I have to tell you something, Lizzy, and I am frightened to do so," my father said barely whispering as he wrung his hands in agitation, "I'm afraid your plans for the future will not come to pass. All our grand hopes for you are...are..."

"It's Gabriel," I interrupted, feeling a pang of guilt, but calmly asking, "he will not marry me, will he? Has Emma's behavior been exposed? Has she done something worse than what we already know?" I asked agitatedly, walking through the wrought iron gate into the garden.

My father stopped and smiled weakly at me. "It isn't that, my dear. Gabriel has not called off your engagement," he explained sadly as we continued walking toward The Palladium, "as for Emma, we are as surprised by her appearance this morning as you are, and she has been too distraught to get any explanations out of her."

We walked the rest of the way to The Palladium in silence. I sat on the stone bench, feeling my heart pulling apart, though I wasn't sure why. Something was wrong, terribly wrong, and I had the feeling my father's hesitation was due to his reluctance to have to witness my reaction to his news.

My father didn't sit down but stood behind me, finally letting the horrible truth fall like heavy stones from his lips, "Gabriel is dead."

My breath caught in my chest, though I didn't notice that I had ceased to breathe as I searched the face of The Palladium for a confirmation. I felt my eyes filling with tears, but I was sure I hadn't heard my father correctly. I spun around anxiously to ask him what he had said, believing my imagination had produced the words I'd heard.

He was gone.

I could hear far-off footsteps retreating away from me. Then it struck me. The truth of what my father had said was proven by the absence of his comforting presence. He couldn't bear to see my reaction; the pain of losing Gabriel and seeing how it tore me apart was too much for him. The tears rolled down my face as I still tried to think of an excuse that would explain away my father's words. Perhaps Gabriel really had broken off our engagement and my father had meant it metaphorically; as if to say after what he has done he is dead to me. Perhaps he wanted to save me from the embarrassment of being denied and thought it better that I believed Gabriel was dead instead.

"He really is dead," Emma's voice said matter-of-factly behind me. She sat down beside me, looking straight ahead. "I think Father was more distraught to have to tell you than he was about Gabriel's death. As if it were all about you," she said the last in disdain.

My tears were running like a river now as I said defensively, "Why are you so angry with me? I have done nothing but worry about you."

Emma turned her black-rimmed eyes toward me in disgust. "You seem to always be in the way of my happiness."

"I don't know what you mean," I rebuked, "I have never wanted anything but for you to be happy." Then I broke down, almost unable to form my next outburst, "I don't understand how my fiancé's death has hindered your happiness or why you seem to be implying his death was somehow my fault!"

Emma didn't take her eyes from The Palladium as she answered, "You are so naïve. You think our lives have been a series of random occurrences; you couldn't be more wrong. We have been caught in the middle of a deadly game that has shaped our fate. Do you really think Lord Sergison would be happy that his sons should marry the daughters of a mere lawyer?"

That sparked my memory. "Wait, is that why you were investigating Gabriel's brother's death? Were you meant to marry Edward?"

This time Emma faced me, her eyes hard with un-shed tears. "Yes, that was their plan, our father's and his. They hoped to keep their secret within our families. Then Edward was killed, but not by some common thief. Their plan had to be altered; they decided to promise Gabriel and me to one another. Gabriel knew of their wishes, but after you seduced him into liking you he persuaded his father to allow him to marry you. So you see, you have taken my happiness. If you hadn't taken Gabriel away he would be married to me and he wouldn't be dead now. I wouldn't have found out so many awful things, but it always has to be about you. You always have to be prettier and more clever; you always have to have all the attention and all the compliments. I'm tired of living in your shadow."

Emma jumped to her feet and stomped away, leaving me alone and dispirited.

"Gabriel!" I broke out loudly as my tears and sobs gushed forth uncontrollably, "Alas! that all we lov'd of him should be, /

But for our grief, as if it had not been, / And grief itself be mortal! Woe is me! / Whence are we, and why are we?"

I found myself laying my head on the base of The Palladium, feeling guilty somehow for Gabriel's death. It was more than Emma's hurtful words that caused my guilt. I knew it was really guilt for my feelings for Dardanos, for the rift that had come between Gabriel and me these past days. I had this illogical idea that if Gabriel had only told me his secret he would still be alive. If I had ignored my feelings for Dardanos and kept Gabriel close I could have changed the course of the past few days and he would still be here. I knew it was all nonsense; there was nothing I could have done that would have changed anything. The very thing that my rational mind had been railing against for so long seemed to be true: our destiny, our fate, was set before us, and there was no fighting it.

My hair was long and loose, and much curlier than I remembered it. The wind was catching it and pushing it back from my face. Even my plain white cotton dress was plastered against my body due to the unrelenting and strangely cold wind. I was on a high balcony looking out over a pristinely beautiful sand-colored city.

"A storm is coming," I said agitatedly, turning away from the balcony, "A storm of swords and fire."

When I looked back into the room I could see several people lounging on sofas eating and drinking as if nothing were wrong. The servant, Xanthós, was waiting on them. He looked up and gave me a weak smile, knowing how I despised the pompous attitudes of my family, and perhaps feeling guilty for not having stopped all this from happening in Sparta.

One of the younger men, seated next to the most beautiful woman I'd ever seen, stood and mocked, "You always think there are signs in the clouds. Why don't you just say what is really on your mind? You blame me for bringing a war to our doors!"

The beautiful woman pushed her long, golden hair back

over her shoulder as she moved languidly on the sofa, her bright blue eyes sparkled menacingly from across the room and I couldn't help but think I knew her from somewhere else. "I am sure she must blame me, but for my part I could not help but fall in love...it was altogether beyond my control," her voice tinkled merrily.

The others seemed to smirk at each other, as if our argument was an amusing past time for them. Even the beautiful woman had a mocking smile on her face, waiting for me to challenge her, and I should have as it could be argued that this was all her fault. I glared at her in hatred a moment, wishing I could break the spell she had over the others. My hatred of her had nothing to do with her beauty or even her being the cause of the war. If she was truly in love with my brother I would have praised their courage to fight to be together, but she seemed indifferent to it all. It was apparent, to me at least, that she acted out of pure boredom and not love. She had been amused by the youth and beauty of my brother, very much the opposite of her old and burly husband, and allowed herself to pretend to be in love. It certainly helped that besides being intensely loyal and attentive to her, my brother was the son of a king. I wondered what her real plan was, or if she had even thought past having an affair with an attractive, young prince. Since she'd been brought to the palace it had been obvious she cared for nothing and no one, but she cared very much for attention and being admired by all around her.

I finally answered my brother's accusation, "Paris, I am not blaming you for bringing an army to our gates; I am only stating what I see. I know your heart has been moved to do what you have done." *Poor boy!* "I only stated my prophecy that we may be prepared for it when it comes."

Everyone in the room seemed to grow bored with our conversation. I felt out of place among them though they were my family, my blood. They lounged about in their fine clothing, drinking and eating their fine food, and having their amusements while the rest of the city scrambled about in a panic. The city was running out of supplies, but the palace was over-abundantly stocked for the royal family and they viewed the daily battles outside the walls as just another amusement. I longed to go back to the temple; I longed to sneak away from this strange world and find my love.

I turned back to the balcony. "The storm is being pulled like a great chariot by a treacherous horse."

I closed my eyes, trying to think of a way to convince my mother, the only one that listened to anything I had to say, that the temple was just as safe as the palace. I was growing restless pacing the halls and listening to my brothers talk of clever assaults they would execute the next day. Then there was the tiresome company of the woman that had caused all of our troubles. I could see through her tricks, as a daughter of Zeus she was not only beautiful and imbued with godly charms, but a gift given to her by Aphrodite caused her words to be laced with magic. Most everyone that listened to her became enchanted with her and would agree to anything she said. Even my father was taken with her and encouraged my brother in his fight to keep her. My mother seemed to always be busy somewhere else when the woman was around and kept her opinions to herself on the matter, but I knew she felt as I did. Only Xanthós and myself seemed immune to the woman's charms; he was the only reason I could bear the palace at all.

"Perhaps, you wish this war was all about you," the woman teased, "It must be so dull to spend your days in a temple; I understand why you might want to be me."

I opened my mouth in outrage, but found words would not be enough. I steadied myself, clenching my fists at my sides to keep from striking the self-centered witch. The others merely laughed as if it were the cleverest joke they'd ever heard. Xanthós gave me an anguished look, and though I could see he wished to say something in my defense my brothers would have punished him for such a thing. I motioned with my hand for him to stay silent and turned toward the coming storm, silently begged that it brought misery to the woman.

"Elizabeth...Elizabeth dear, wake up."

I opened my eyes, confused as to why my pillow felt hard as stone and why my hand was gritty as if covered with dirt. I sat up blinking the afternoon sunlight out of my eyes and discovered

I was actually on the ground. I had fallen asleep with my head resting against the base of The Palladium.

"Elizabeth."

I turned lethargically toward the stone bench and was surprised to see Lady Sergison sitting there. She was in black as usual, but she had reverted back to her previous style of a loose-fitting, exotic looking gown. Her hair once more hung long down her back. The relentless sadness had returned to her face which was streaked with damp trails of unending tears.

"Lady Sergison," I began, not even attempting to pull myself up from the ground, but I was only able to mutter, "I don't know what to say."

"I know how you feel," she commiserated, "I had this feeling that I must speak with you. I know it won't change anything; I know I am grasping at a false hope that something might make me able to accept what has happened. When we lost Edward in such a vicious way I thought nothing would ever make me feel more hopeless." She looked hard at me, fighting herself to keep from breaking down. "This is far worse. I know I have let my anguish for Edward affect my mind and I am terrified that if I can't discover some logical explanation for Gabriel's death that I will go completely mad."

I was weeping again, but I had no idea what kind of answers Lady Sergison expected from me. I sat silently, tears still falling as I fiddled with the moonstone ring uncomfortably, waiting for her questions to begin.

She shifted uneasily as she looked at the ground in front of her, mumbling softly, "I know there was a...disagreement...between you and Gabriel..." Lady Sergison's face seemed to contort as she said apologetically, "I don't mean that I think this was in any way your fault. I simply wish to know every possible thought that could have gone through Gabriel's mind before last night."

I didn't want to look at her, not because I suspected she was trying to accuse me of anything, but because I had already been feeling guilt over the disconnect between Gabriel and me and it seemed others had noticed it as well. I wasn't sure exactly what to tell her. Had our disagreement begun because of

Dardanos? Had it begun before that, with the secret he had never imparted? The evening of our engagement dinner was something of a blur now; so much seemed to have happened in these short few days, and the particular moment that sparked a disagreement seemed a bit hazy. I assumed Gabriel had been angry with Dardanos, and perhaps annoyed with me for being polite to the man, but I had never really had the chance to find out for sure. I didn't want to bring up Dardanos to Lady Sergison; I was sure I would betray some feeling for him and I was ashamed of what she might think of me. Her next question saved me from mentioning Dardanos and renewed my own suspicions.

"Did Gabriel perhaps tell you something in private, a secret perhaps that weighed heavy on him?" she prompted.

"Yes," I recalled in surprise, looking up at her at last, "yes, he did have a secret. He was so distressed. He wished for me to know before we were officially engaged; he said I probably wouldn't want to marry him once I knew."

"What was it?" Lady Sergison half-shouted, moving to the edge of the bench.

I opened my mouth, wishing I had an answer for her, but lamented, "He never told me. He was so hesitant to tell me in the carriage, then we were here before he realized it. We were surrounded most of the night, and, of course, he later became agitated and left without explaining why. I saw him the following day; he seemed...distracted, and still very much agitated."

"You spoke of nothing else?" Lady Sergison was now nearly off the bench.

"Nothing that seems of any importance," I answered, shaking my head, but recalled, "Actually we did speak of The Palladium. Emma had been home the night of the dinner and she had been very interested in the base of the statue. I found writing there and Gabriel knew about it. He told me a story about a cursed god and a doomed princess. I don't know what it has to do with any of this but it was connected to Emma's disappearances and it seems to be connected to what Mrs. Gibson told me-" I stopped, knitting my eyebrows as I thought about the strange coincidence of Mrs. Gibson having been killed as well.

Lady Sergison seemed enthralled, "What did Mrs. Gibson tell you?"

"She saw my past life, or claimed to, and I myself have had visions I can't explain. I have reason to suspect that this past life that she has opened up for me is that of Cassandra of Troy; daughter of the king, dishonored prophetess, and priestess in the temple of Athena." I knew it sounded ridiculous as I said it aloud, but I had to tell Lady Sergison something.

"Do you think any of that was linked to what happened to Gabriel?" Lady Sergison asked in all seriousness.

"I don't know," I said at a loss, amazed at her willingness to consider it, "it was simply the last thing we spoke of; the story of Cassandra and the cursed god. I was surprised he knew so much about the story even though it seems to have never made it into any book, nor been passed down even as a legend. He was...hesitant to tell me the story; he said my father would be angry with him for telling me. I don't know if that means anything."

We sat silent, pondering these things that seemed connected but were too fantastical to be believed. I could see Lady Sergison was trying to make some kind of sense of what I had told her. Suddenly her eyes lit with a harsh kind of realization, lighting in savage determination like torches lit in battle.

"Edward spoke of a secret," she mumbled as if to herself, "he said there were things in this world I couldn't even imagine, terrible things...wondrously terrible things." She seemed to remember I was still there and asked gently, "What do you think he meant by that?"

I shook my head, wondering to myself if Edward's murder was indeed connected to what was happening now. "I have come across so many strange ideas in the past days I'm starting to forget what is possible and what is not. I've been asked to believe in ancient stories and gods, in curses and magic, and reincarnation and fate. It's all so overwhelming, as if the bright flowering world has turned dark with decay all at once. How can Edward's death be connected to Gabriel's...but then, how can it not be?" I was rambling in anguish as the tears started again.

Lady Sergison jumped to her feet, motherly concern on her face as she helped me to my feet. "Elizabeth dear, I've upset you even more. Come, let me take you inside where you can be looked after."

I let her lead me through the garden, my feet barely lifting off the ground but dragging as if they were weighed down.

Before we left the garden Lady Sergison stopped and asked one last question, "Did Gabriel say anything else about this secret? Does anyone else know about it?"

I pursed my lips, admitting, "He said it was a family secret, that it was dangerous, and that you knew nothing about it. He seemed to want to keep it that way. I assume that meant that Lord Sergison knew about it, but I can't be sure."

She nodded her head, setting a determined scowl on her face. I wanted to ask what she planned to do, but I had the feeling it might be best to not know. It seemed clear she had an idea of what to do next. I just hoped whatever it was would bring her peace and not send her further into madness.

As we approached the back of the house I stopped and felt my heart had stopped as well, blurting out, "I don't even know how Gabriel died!" I stared at Lady Sergison wide-eyed and admitted shamefully, "No one told me how he died. How could I have been so thoughtless not to ask? Why would no one tell me?"

Lady Sergison gave me a weak smile and wrapped her arm around my shoulders. "I am so sorry, Elizabeth. I would have told you immediately if I'd known. I assumed your family would have told you, but perhaps they thought it would upset you more to hear the particulars. I know you are strong, and you and I have no secrets."

While she composed herself I felt a pang of guilt, because I did have secrets. There were a great many things I had never told Lady Sergison, either out of politeness for her delicate mental state or because it was not proper to speak of. In the past few days, though, the secrets I was keeping seemed to have grown exponentially, and I feared what she would think of me if she knew them.

"It seems Gabriel was walking last night and he was

attacked. The police believe it was another case of a theft gone wrong. They believe someone tried to rob him and he resisted."

"You don't seem convinced," I said, picking up on her sarcasm.

She shook her head as she explained, "They only said he was robbed because of the area he was found in...and he had been badly bruised. They said it seemed as though he'd gotten into a scuffle with perhaps more than one man, and the only reason they could come up with was theft."

I felt light-headed and fell slightly into Lady Sergison. "Where was he found?" I managed to ask.

"He was found in Northern Cuckfield, near Ardingly. The police say they have trouble there often, because of the unfortunate creatures that are forced to take residence there at the workhouse. Elizabeth, are you well? You've gone very pale?"

I closed my eyes, fearing my dream from the night before had actually been another vision. "Did he...was there a sword found near him? A short, curved sword?"

"Yes," Lady Sergison answered, eyeing me cautiously, "but he wasn't killed with the sword. The police were inclined to think it was his, though I've never seen it before, and it was a strange looking sword…foreign looking. That wasn't the strangest thing. Remember the story going about that Mrs. Gibson had been attached by a wild animal because she had strange marks on her neck? Well, Gabriel too was found with strange marks on his neck. They had no explanation for them. That is why I don't believe this was some random act of thievery. I believe whomever was responsible for Mrs. Gibson's death may also be responsible for Gabriel's. And in my heart I know that it has some connection to my beloved Edward's death."

ℬ12ℭ

That night my father asked if I would consider spending the next few weeks at Cuckfield Park. He seemed unable to look me in the eyes as he asked, and I wondered if he wanted me to go so that he might not have to watch me grieve. The Sergisons were going to begin the wake for Gabriel the following day and Lady Sergison asked especially for me to be sent to keep her company. What could I say but yes. After all, Gabriel had been my fiancé; it was my duty to grieve as a widow would, or at least somewhat like a widow would, and I wanted to make up for some of my shameful behavior by tending to Lady Sergison's needs.

The following morning the Sergison's carriage came to retrieve me and my belongings for an indefinite period of time. Most likely I would stay the three days of the wake, followed by the funeral and formal dinner on the fourth day, and then...I wasn't sure how long Lady Sergison would want me to stay. I guessed that she would need a companion for at least a few weeks following, but neither she nor Lord Sergison had really specified a length of time. My father seemed mysteriously vague about the matter, but I fortified my spirits with the thought that I would be doing a great service to Lady Sergison by being there. It would be difficult to find comfort for myself without The Palladium there to escape to, but I would have the magnificent gardens of Cuckfield Park to get lost in when I needed to be alone. I felt so disconnected from everyone that I figured it didn't matter where I was, my grief would go with me, and at least I might do some good to Lady Sergison.

The carriage that had been sent was not the same one Gabriel had often used, but it felt surreal to be stepping up into the cabin without his helpful hand, dressed in my widow's

weeds. I caught myself staring distractedly at the moonstone ring
on my left hand as I pulled myself into the carriage, the footman
pulled his hand away from my right hand, waking me from my
daze. Gabriel had always sent his carriage to fetch me for picnics
and parties, usually coming along to escort me, but now the
carriage had been sent to collect me to mourn with his family and
witness his funeral proceedings.

     I should have been full of nothing but overwhelming
grief and resentment at the twist my fate had taken in depriving
me of my future husband, but instead my thoughts were full of
Dardanos. I hadn't seen him since the night in the garden. I had
felt sure he was going to pay his respects at my home the day
before; surely he had found out about Gabriel's death as all of
Cuckfield must have. Perhaps he was also feeling guilty. We had
selfishly revealed our feelings for each other without thought of
how it would hurt Gabriel...and now he was dead. We had
wronged him and now there was no way to make amends to him.
It mattered not that he knew nothing of my betrayal; I knew...and
it weighed heavy on me. I wondered if the weight of that guilt
was what had kept Dardanos from me, or had his feelings
changed for me in light of what happened to Gabriel?

     I knew in my heart the duty I felt obliged to undertake on
Lady Sergison's behalf had to do more with my guilt and my
need to make amends somehow than that I felt a true obligation
to mourn Gabriel as his previous bride-to-be. I would do my best
to mourn as was expected, but my feelings for Gabriel were still
so mixed up that I knew my heart was already beating for
another. I swore to myself, no matter my confused feelings, that I
would do everything within my power to help Lady Sergison and
keep her from dwelling incessantly on her sad situation. Before
stepping out of the carriage I hardened myself to stay strong for
Lady Sergison's sake and to be ready for any manner of
eccentricities.

     My first surprise came as I exited the carriage and was
not met by Lord or Lady Sergison. The footman said he would
bring my trunk in for me and then signaled the coachman to
bring the carriage around the side of the house where the carriage
house was located. I was left in the drive alone and for the first
time ever in my acquaintance with the Sergisons I had to ring the

bell at the front door.

I stared at the laurel wreath wrapped in crape hanging on the door as I waited for someone to answer. A moment later the door swung open and I readied myself to embrace one or both of the Sergisons, but again they were absent and the door was held open by one of the house maids dressed in mourning black. Obviously Lady Sergison had made sure her servants were provided with mourning garments, otherwise they would not have been able to afford them.

The maid's eyes were rimmed red as she sniffled, "Miss Cranford, let me offer you my deepest condolences. I'll take you straightaway to Lord and Lady Sergison."

I made no sound but followed in a daze as if I'd just stepped upon the stage of an eerily somber theatrical play. I was led, bizarrely enough, to the West parlor where the séance had been held just days ago. The double doors were thrown open, but I could see that the room was engulfed in darkness. Although the sun didn't shine directly into the windows of the room in the morning it should have been high enough in the sky to illuminate the room a little. Once I entered I could see the source of the uncharacteristic darkness. The large Westward facing windows were usually, at this time of day, unobstructed by the thick curtains that now covered them. Black cloth had been draped not only over the already heavy curtains but also over all the portraits and mirrors in the room. The room's only source of light came from three massive, free-standing candelabras placed at the head, foot, and a few paces in front of the open casket which stood off to the right.

I quickly averted my eyes away from the casket, prolonging the inevitable shock of grief I knew would come upon seeing the lifeless body of my former love. It was difficult to make out distinguishable forms in the miserly flicker of candlelight, but I thought in addition to Lord and Lady Sergison that I could almost make out three or four others seated. Probably Lady Sergison's relatives was my guess. There were two servants standing against the wall to the right of the doors, but they hadn't noticed me enter as they were both dabbing their eyes. The woman, whom I took for Lady Sergison's personal maid, noticed me a moment later and ushered me over to where the Sergisons sat.

Lady Sergison sprang from her seat and threw her arms around me, caring nothing for decorum. "You have come. I worried it would be too frightening for you and you wouldn't come, my dearest friend. Oh, but it must be morning you're here," Lady Sergison rambled in a kind of delirium. "Have the lamps lit. We must have a little more light now it's day."

I could now see a little better that my eyes were adjusting and I discovered that I was not the first visitor of the morning, though Lady Sergison seemed under the impression that I was. Lady Sergison's family were seated behind her, quietly watching the casket as they fought the random tears that fell with a quick wipe of their handkerchiefs.

My eyes darted momentarily to the two ladies and one gentleman seated behind the Sergisons, and I gave them a quick smile of acknowledgment. Lady Sergison followed my gaze as if she had no guess to what I was looking at. When her eyes fell upon her two sisters and brother-in-law she seemed startled for a moment, but attempted to cover her surprise by inviting them into the other room to breakfast. While she was preoccupied I took the opportunity to address Lord Sergison.

Lord Sergison stood and I took a step forward to embrace him. "I still don't believe it. I keep waiting for someone to say it was all some awful mistake," I whispered confidentially.

Lord Sergison took me by the shoulders, nodding his head. "I know, I know," he muttered, pausing to wipe at his eyes. "I'm so glad you're here. It may be difficult at times, but I am going to depend on you to help me to see to Lady Sergison. Already she has not slept nor eaten. You will help me look after her, won't you?"

"Of course," I answered soothingly, "I had hoped I would be of some use to you both. That's why I came."

Lord Sergison seemed to brighten, and then as if suddenly remembering said, "Lady Sergison and I have something we'd like to speak with you about. Later...perhaps after dinner."

I nodded, not able to even venture a guess as to what they would wish to speak to me about. I had a fleeting fear that they had found out about Dardanos and me, but I reasoned that they would hardly speak of such a topic with me, even if they did know. They would have discussed the matter with my father and he would have said something; unless that was why he had been so withdrawn toward me. Perhaps he did know, but didn't know how to ask me about it or deferred asking me until I had mourned for Gabriel. Lord Sergison, meanwhile, had turned to Lady Sergison and her relatives, trying to convince Lady Sergison of something.

Lord Sergison had apparently gotten the response he'd hoped for as he turned to me with a weak smile. "My dear, I know you would like your time alone with Gabriel," pausing he put his arm around Lady Sergison and stated with a wink, "Lady Sergison and I are going to breakfast with our family."

As they followed Lady Sergison's family out of the room Lady Sergison seemed to remember something, and put her hand on my arm to get my attention. "Please...don't leave him alone," she whispered. "The monsters...I'm afraid they'll come back for him."

"I won't leave him alone; I promise," I assured hurriedly.

I gulped nervously, nodding my head encouragingly as I pursed my lips to keep the calm in my face. I wasn't sure what she meant by monsters, but the note of panic in her voice worried me. Was she already succumbing to madness? Was she worried that the men that had killed Gabriel would come back for his body, or was she truly frightened that some evil monster would take Gabriel away? I tried telling myself Lady Sergison had simply gone through a very trying night. She must not have slept, but stayed awake staring at the body of her dead son in the impenetrable darkness while strange shadows danced about the room. Surely her imagination had been overcome with dark, evil thoughts through such a sleepless night.

I couldn't seem to look her in the eyes and so focused my eyes on her hand resting on my arm. About her wrist was a narrow, braided bracelet, and I knew what it must have been. Many people took hair from their dead loved ones for lockets, or to make wearable jewelry or hair accessories. Lady Sergison had had Gabriel's hair made into a bracelet. I watched her turn back to go, a manic smile on her face. Then it hit me. I was being left utterly alone, in an eerily dim room, with the corpse of the man I should have been marrying.

I wasn't usually prone to superstitious thoughts, but my guilt overwhelmed me. My imagination swam with all manner of supernatural punishments for being unfaithful to Gabriel; first of which was that he would rise from the dead and seek some revenge on me. I bit my lip unnerved at how easily one's mind could be ruled by such fantastically wicked thoughts, and felt I understood a little how Lady Sergison could allow such madness to permeate her life. I squeezed my eyes shut and with a great sigh I convinced myself I was being silly; this was Gabriel. Sweet, loving, understanding Gabriel. Then I realized I actually wished he would come back as some remnant, some animated corpse that I might speak to. I was saying a little prayer that it were possible that I might ask his forgiveness, and my heart ached not only with the wrong I'd done to him but the love that was once so unquestioning inside of me.

My heart raced and my eyes felt like the portholes of a submarine holding back the rush of the ocean, but I forced myself to finally approach the casket. I couldn't bring myself to raise my eyes as I commanded my feet to transport me to Gabriel's side. I nearly knocked into the massive candelabra in front of the casket, but I managed to steady it without having to look up. I stared a few moments at the side of the casket; my form casting a dark, flickering shadow over it. I let out a loud sigh and finally lifted my eyes.

There could be no thought any more of this being a mistake. I could no longer cling to my fantasy of Gabriel suddenly appearing and saying, "You took that wretch to be me. See I am here, I'm perfectly fine." Nor could I harbor the idea that he would somehow come back from the dead to hear my apologies. No, this deathly vacant tomb that once was home to a brilliant soul...was empty. It was no longer Gabriel...and yet it was. It was his hair, his eyes, his body, even the expression on his face was his, but the horrible trick of it was that he was no longer master of any of these things.

The most heartrending vision to behold was that of his eyes.

Someone had decided to leave his once sea-swept eyes wide open. Now the sea was all out of them; they were left dull and clouded. That was when I could no longer hold back that ocean of sorrow. Looking at those dead, frosted eyes broke the barrier that I had fought so hard to maintain. I clutched the edge of the casket, trying to steady my quaking body. The result was a disturbing movement within the casket which caused me to break down further.

"I'm sorry, Gabriel," I whispered through raucous sobs, "I am so sorry. I should have been more sensitive to your mood. I should have made everything right...before it was too late."

I had to stop speaking as I erupted in an uncontrollable storm of tears and clapped my hand over my mouth to silence the whimpering. I was reminded of the poem "Tears, Idle Tears" by Alfred, Lord Tennyson: *Dear as remembered kisses after death, / And sweet as those by hopeless fancy feigned / On lips that are for others; deep as love, / Deep as first love, and wild with all regret; / O Death in Life, the days that are no more!*

I could never have back yesterday; I could never change the wrong I had done. All I could do was live with my regret, and remember the sweetness of our once innocent love. The world had grown darker since Dardanos swept into my life, but for all my regret I couldn't deny my inexplicable connection to him. Perhaps I was simply an indecent woman deep down; perhaps it was better that Gabriel had never discovered my inconsistencies. How it would have destroyed him.

Once I had control of my power of speech I entreated in a yet louder whisper, as if he might hear me beyond this realm if I said it loud enough, "Please forgive me. I didn't mean to Gabriel...I didn't mean to fall in love with Dardanos."

I spent the remainder of the day seated next to Lady Sergison, staring numbly at the casket, and feeling the guilt continuing to build within me. Lord Sergison convinced Lady Sergison to take some time from her mourning watch to dine with us. Throughout the day visitors had come and gone so that there was never a time when we weren't surrounded by whispered condolences and sniffles. In this continued outpouring from the community was Lord Sergison able to convince Lady

Sergison that there would be a never-ending flow of mourners to sit by Gabriel, and Lady Sergison's own maid swore she would not allow Gabriel to be alone if she had to stay there herself for days. It was the first peculiar eccentricity I noted in her; she was adamant that Gabriel not be left alone.

Even my own parents sat for the better part of the afternoon. Emma, too, was there, but she sat as far back from the rest of us as she could. I didn't attempt to speak with her; the words she had spoken the day before still stung like fresh whip lashes, and I feared another outburst from her. In my current capacity of trying to lessen Lady Sergison's burden I thought it prudent to avoid my sister's temper, but I knew I would have to acknowledge her eventually as she and my parents had been invited to dine at Cuckfield Park as well.

The dinner went much better than I had predicted, withstanding my discomfort of feeling as if Apollo were watching my every move from his hard-to-ignore place on the ceiling. I had to force myself to look down at my food for fear that I might see that golden face turn toward me with his menacing bow. Somehow I felt he must know my betrayal; somehow Apollo knew how wicked I was and he was just biding his time to punish me. Then I would silently chastise myself for such silliness; paintings couldn't come alive and punish someone...not even paintings of gods. It was the guilt. It had to be. The guilt was driving me mad.

My sister and I were seated far enough away from each other that only a few polite words were necessary. My father and Lord Sergison seemed suspiciously quiet toward one another, as if they had important matters to discuss, but matters that could not be uttered in front of the rest of us. Lady Sergison continuously pulled away from Lord Sergison, both physically and mentally, another peculiarity that I noted, as if she saw something repulsive in him. I assumed she felt a bit of the blame for Gabriel's death rested with Lord Sergison, but for what reason I couldn't guess. The only really strange occurrence to be noted was when dinner was very nearly at an end. My mother was commenting on the similarities in Mrs. Gibson's and Gabriel's deaths and she mentioned something she had overheard at one of her teas.

"It never did enter my mind before, but then I heard a lady make mention of vampires-"my mother said loud enough for the whole table to hear.

Almost in unison my father, Lord Sergison, and Emma exclaimed, "What?!"

The pitch with which they had exclaimed bothered me. I took notice of my father and Lord Sergison giving each other troubled looks, and Emma looking down as if she'd been caught doing something wrong. A moment later Emma stared at our father and Lord Sergison with a mischievous smile as if she knew what they were thinking. There was an uncomfortable silence in which I could see my mother fretting over whether she'd said something wrong.

I felt I should say something to save her from the awkward silence. "Hmm, yes," I forced a laugh, "I wish it were so easy to blame some evil wraith, but alas the world is unjustly home to a great many dangerous humans. I believe killers and madmen far outweigh our worries over vampires."

My mother gave an uneasy laugh, "I quite agree, Elizabeth. Some people simply let their imaginations run wild."

Emma suddenly perked up with a sly smile and asked over-sweetly, "Lord Sergison, did the coroner discover what the marks on Mr. Sergison's neck were?"

My father moved uneasily in his chair as he looked to Lord Sergison anxiously. "Emma, perhaps now is not the proper time for such conversations."

"No, no, that's all right, Cranford," Lord Sergison said softly, holding up his hand, "The coroner had no explanation for the wounds, Miss Cranford. His official report simply noted a small, sharp object had been used."

Emma didn't stop there. "What about the blood loss? I heard rumors that he had been completely drained."

"Emma!" I burst out, worrying that her words would upset Lady Sergison. "We are still mourning. His body is still lying in the other room for God's sake."

I knew my outburst would be seen as more improper than Emma's questions, but I had sworn to myself to protect Lady

Sergison from such cruel thoughts. She had said nothing, but I could see by the vacant look on her face that her mind was actively pondering these ideas. I put my hand protectively over hers to call her out of her thoughts. She started as if I'd woken her from a bad dream.

"I'm all right, Elizabeth," Lady Sergison whispered, giving me a forced smile.

"Well," Lord Sergison said, rising from his chair, "I believe it's time we left you ladies to your conversation. Please help yourself to tea or wine, if you'd like." Then he kissed Lady Sergison on the head and announced, "Cranford, Elizabeth, would you please join me in my study?"

I looked to my father with surprise, a question in my eyes. "Of course," I answered, rising from my chair nervously.

I remembered Lord Sergison telling me that he and Lady Sergison wished to speak to me about something particular, but why would my father need to be present? Lady Sergison was also rising from the table, excusing herself from my mother and Emma, but she headed back to the parlor instead of following us. I trailed behind Lord Sergison and my father up the stairs to the study, all the while searching my mind for a reason for this meeting.

Lord Sergison seated himself behind the large desk as if he were preparing to do business; my father and I sat in the two plain wooden chairs facing him.

"Elizabeth," Lord Sergison began, "I know you can hardly guess why I have asked to speak to you, but in light of what has happened I must plan for the future. I have already discussed this with your father and he has agreed to allow me to put the proposition to you."

I swallowed hard, but managed to utter, "Of course, sir, I will happily hear whatever it is you have to ask of me."

"You're a good girl. I always knew you were of strong character. In light of both of my sons, my heirs, dying before both Lady Sergison and me..." he stopped to lightly wipe at his eye. "I have no close family and Lady Sergison's family are all well taken care of and...I would like...I very much wish for my legacy to continue. There are things...important things that your father and I do and I had hoped my sons would carry on our work, but as that is not the case I would like to pass on my work to someone else." He reached his hand across the desk and I put my hand in his as he entreated, "Elizabeth dear, we would like to name you our heir. We want you to take over Cuckfield Park and all attached holdings and fortune at the time of our deaths, and I would like to, with your father's help, teach you everything you must know to carry on our important work."

My father put his hand on my arm, calling me out of my shock. "Lizzy, there is no one else. It is imperative that we have someone to take over, and your training needs to begin immediately."

My eyes felt as though they would pop from my head as I opened my mouth to say something, but nothing came out. I simply looked from my father to Lord Sergison, not believing what they had just told me. I kept opening my mouth to speak and then immediately pursing my lips together at a loss.

Lord Sergison cut in before I could find any words to say, "Of course, it is entirely your decision, my dear. It will be a great responsibility and of great mental and physical fatigue, but I am convinced that you are not only intelligent enough but fortified enough to take this on. Please think about it. There's no need to answer just yet; I know you've already had a trying few days. I have already had the will written; it only awaits my signature witnessed by your father." He stood, showing the discussion to be over, but before we exited he added, "I do believe this is the best course of action and it would greatly relieve us of a great deal of anxiety."

I walked silently back to the parlor to resume my watch with Lady Sergison. I was overwhelmed by this proposition; it felt as if a great burden had been added to the pile that was beginning to weigh upon my mind. It was true I had always loved Cuckfield Park. I had often imagined myself happily roaming the halls and gardens, but now at what cost? My father's words chilled me, *there is no one else...your training needs to begin immediately.* What kind of important work did they do, and what kind of training would I have to endure? A fleeting thought entered my mind about the secret Gabriel had attempted to reveal to me. Was this important work related to Gabriel's secret? A secret that may have gotten him killed?

"He asked you?" Lady Sergison suddenly asked.

I turned, surprised to find I had already entered the parlor and sat down. "I...I don't have an answer. I don't know what to say."

Lady Sergison thought I was showing modesty for their having chosen me. "Oh, dear, it is as it should be. You were meant to have Cuckfield Park, anyone could see that. It's your destiny. Plus, I should very much like having you here."

I turned slightly to see who else was in the room and lowered my voice, "What do you mean having me here?"

Lady Sergison scrunched her eyes and exclaimed, "He didn't ask you!" She huffed, "We would like for you to reside here. We would like for you to become not only our heir but our ward. Please for my sake...consider it."

How could I say no? Hadn't I sworn to myself that I would do whatever it took to help Lady Sergison? "Of course, I will give it my full consideration."

Lady Sergison took my hand and turned it so that my palm faced up. "I want you to have this," she said as she placed a smooth, round item into my hand, "I had given this to Gabriel's brother, Edward when a close friend of his died young, and I had always meant to give it to Gabriel. I should have given it to him when Edward died, but...well, I suppose I couldn't part with it right then. My father gave it to me when my mother died. He said it had been passed down in our family for many generations. He claimed it dated back to the Roman Empire. I want you to have it."

I looked down into my open hand where a jet broach the size of my palm rested. The relief cut into the jet was that of a crescent moon entwined by a serpent. It was a beautiful piece of jewelry even though it was worn for the sole purpose of mourning. I pinned it to my dress just below my throat, feeling uneasy to have taken a family heirloom and personal keepsake from Lady Sergison.

"Thank you...it's so lovely," I managed to stutter.

I turned round in my chair, feeling a strong presence, and locked eyes with Emma. She was glaring at me and her previous words echoed in my ears, *it's always about you*. I wondered if my father's enthusiastic push to accept Lord Sergison's offer had anything to do with wanting to distance me from Emma. I turned back toward the casket wondering what Gabriel would have thought about all of these bizarre circumstances. He probably would have laughed and said "just think, one day they'll put it all in a book, like *The Moonstone*; it will be a great mystery and you'll be greatly pitied for having been forced to be at the center of it all."

ಬ13ಚ

"Elizabeth, dear, why don't you go on to bed?"

My eyes shot open and I heard a loud bang as my book slipped off my lap onto the floor. "What is it?!"

"You should go on to bed, dear; I will stay with Gabriel," Lady Sergison whispered.

"Gabriel!" I half shouted, sitting up in confusion.

I was still sitting beside Lady Sergison in the parlor. Well, I should say I was now sitting, as moments earlier I had actually been slumped sideways in my chair. The room was once again shudderingly dark with only the three massive candelabras near the casket still lit. The face that was lit by those tapers now showed less of the man it had once belonged to. The cheeks and eyes were further sunken and the shade of white had deepened so as to almost appear gray in the gloom. I shook my head from these images and instead looked about the room. No one was left save a lone servant by the doors.

"It's all right, dear, I will stay with him. You are too young yet to be surrounding yourself continuously with death," Lady Sergison said matter-of-factly. "Go, get some sleep."

I started to argue, but she insisted I get my rest. Reluctantly I nodded my head, feeling inept in my endeavor to be of use to Lady Sergison. I scooped my book up from the floor, stood with some difficulty, and began my stumbling, half-sleep walk from the room. I wasn't sure if it was all in my imagination, but I felt the smell of death clinging to me. I tried to remind myself to place bunches of flowers in my skirts the next day to help overpower the smell, but my exhaustion was so prevalent I knew I would most likely forget.

I would have to endure at least one more day like that as the burial was set for the day after next, but I didn't trust my stamina to hold. I felt something building up inside of me, a kind of welling up of hopelessness that scared me. I felt I was beginning to long for a life in which I didn't have to do what was expected of me, a life in which I was free to do anything, not just what women did. My weary brain turned these thoughts over as I walked to the back of the house, toward a back staircase that led almost directly to my room, but I was halted by the sound of my name.

I searched the partial darkness where my candlelight didn't quite reach. "Elizabeth," it was Dardanos repeating my name in anguish as he stepped forward into the light.

I pursed my lips, feeling a surge of emotion rising, but I was able to restrain my tears. "General," I breathed.

He wordlessly blew out the candle and enveloped me, and then he led me out a back door which led to the courtyard. I let him lead me out into the wide night, taking comfort in his strong arms and soft, musky scent. He walked me through the cobbled courtyard and beyond, where the lawn opened up and sloped down toward the large pond at the back of the property.

The dark was so enclosing we could have been in a small closet for all I could see, but I had no fear. My thoughts were full of relief to finally have Dardanos before me, and full of guilt for feeling as I did. His arms around me were enough to melt the cold tomb that had been growing around my body throughout the day.

"I'm sorry," he whispered, kissing my head, "I should have come to you sooner. I worried that you would despise me for revealing my feelings to you just as he was..." he didn't finish. "I felt so low to have wronged Gabriel...I didn't know how to face you."

I wished I could make out his countenance, but it was too dark. "I felt the very same thing. Guilt and disappointment for my actions against someone that I can't even attempt to make amends to." I let a little sob go before admitting, "It wouldn't have made a difference, it wasn't something I ever planned, but I feel I am inexplicably tied to you. I don't even know if I believe your story of our past connections, but there is a connection. I feel an uncontrollable pull toward you; I don't think I could fight it if I tried. I don't think I can go on without you in my life," the last I whispered almost against my own will.

Dardanos slid his hands around my face and pulled me into a violently passionate kiss. My emotions were too raw to be shocked or full of guilt for kissing him. I needed his mouth, his taste, anything he would give me in that moment. I put my hands over his broad, cool chest, wanting more of him than his lips. He pulled away suddenly as if he feared losing control, and I thought his hand went up to cover his mouth. If he was trying to shield something from my eyes it was not necessary; the dark was so encompassing I could only guess his movements because I had my hand on him, but I could see nothing.

He took a few steps away from me, asking as if to distract me, "Have you thought about what I have told you so far? Have you considered that it is possible all I have said is true?"

"I confess, I didn't think on it much. So many things happened since that night. My thoughts were more engaged with the strange position I've found myself in...and longing for you," I explained sadly.

"There is so much more I have to tell you, so much more for you to understand," he said almost to himself, "and some of it has to do with a great evil, that I fear, has followed me to Cuckfield."

I thought I heard a touch of guilty inference in his voice and asked, "Do you think this evil has anything to do with Gabriel's death?"

He seemed to hesitate, but finally admitted, "Yes...and perhaps your Mrs. Gibson's as well. I fear it is this very evil that Mrs. Gibson hoped to warn you of, and that may be why she was targeted."

"But," I protested, "Gabriel had nothing to do with that; he didn't even know about what Mrs. Gibson had told me."

"I do not think I am the proper person to explain it to you, but Gabriel had a secret which put him in danger. The creature that followed me here must have discovered Gabriel's secret, and decided he needed to be gotten out of the way. This secret was actually the driving force behind my selfish whim to become acquainted with the Sergisons."

"Uhh," I huffed, "everyone keeps talking about this secret, but no one will tell me what it is. Gabriel told me he had a terrible secret, but he never had the chance to finish telling me. Now it seems I may finally learn this secret...and you say it is the very thing that has brought you here…this secret that seems to putting us all in danger."

"How would you learn this secret?" Dardanos asked, ignoring the worry in my voice.

I bit my lip in hesitation. I wasn't sure how much I should reveal to Dardanos. My feelings for him excited a need for complete openness with him, but my rational mind (which I'd been ignoring lately) told me I still knew so little about him. Plus he had just admitted his arrival was somehow linked to Gabriel's secret...which might be linked to Gabriel's death.

My feelings won out, along with my dislike for lying, as I explained, "It is a private matter and I beg that you repeat this to no one...I have been made an offer to inherit Cuckfield Park."

"But that is," Dardanos started slowly and then broke out excitedly, "that is wonderful! Why should you sound so weary; are you not pleased?"

"I love Cuckfield Park, but..." I shook my head forgetting the blinding darkness. "My father and Lord Sergison spoke of some important work that they wish for me to take over. I know it has something to do with how Cuckfield Park is run, but I can't see how that could be so dire. All estates are basically the same; I don't understand why Cuckfield Park's operations should be a great secret. If it is something they have kept hidden from everyone, something which Gabriel felt sure I would never marry him for, and something that may be tied to both his and Mrs. Gibson's deaths...how can I not view this offer with unmitigated dread?"

Dardanos was quiet a moment but then said gently, "What if I said you would not have to face whatever it is alone? What if I told you that my greatest wish is to partake in that life, do that important work, as Lord Sergison called it, with you?"

"I...I guess...I" I stammered, unsure in what capacity Dardanos meant to share in this life. "I guess I wouldn't be quite as frightened if I knew I'd have someone helping me...standing beside me," I stated the last part, but I really meant it as a question.

Dardanos caught me in his arms unexpectedly, entreating, "Elizabeth, you must know I mean more than to just help you. I am in love with you, my life is tethered to yours. I mean to have you by my side, to take on the world together."

I felt relief that he still wanted me, that he still wanted to be with me. "I don't know about taking on the world, but if I'm with you it might just be possible."

He kissed my lips and gushed, "It is possible. It is our destiny. The world will never be the same; we shall make it magical once again. I know that as long as I have your love the world can be ours."

"I wish my mother would end this war," I said wistfully, looking out over the sea. "I know that it is within her power."

"Then why does she not?" asked the man sitting by my side.

I turned, smiling at him, happy to have this brief, stolen moment with him. I knew he was not like other men, his skin almost shone with brilliance, but we never really spoke about it. I knew he was like my mother; he was like Apollo, who had bound me to a vow that I dared not break. He wasn't as powerful as those two, but I knew he was a god, and I was desperately in love with him.

He brushed his long, ebony hair from his face, pushing the pin-straight strands behind his shoulders as he fixed me with his icy blue gaze. "Have you asked her to intervene?" he persisted.

"No," I said simply, laying my head back against his firm chest, "she refuses to break the laws of mortality. She said if she interferes as a goddess her mortal life will end and she will be confined to heaven until her descendants are no more. Zeus wills it to be so, she claims. There are rules, she says, even for immortals."

"Yes, I know," he said thoughtfully. "Sometimes I think mortals have it easier. They are not bound by promises and vows the way we are. They are only punished if it is found out that they've broken a law. The universe knows when we break a law."

"Yes, well, at least you may hide from one another," I huffed, "us mortals must bow and scrape to you gods." I sat forward, lamenting "There is no escape for us, should a god fix his eye upon us; we have no will, no life of our own."

He wrapped his arms lovingly around me and whispered, "I believe I did my share of bowing and scraping to you last night."

My cheeks warmed at the mention of our intimate evening together. "You know what I mean. Our lives are not ours to control; they are the playthings of the gods."

"I know," he commented sadly, "that is what this war has become about. I think before the end we will all be forced to take a side...even your mother."

"Yes, I have seen as much," I answered, looking behind us, checking that we had not been found out. "Though, it will require a catalyst. Gods are stubborn. They will not all join the fight unless they have no other choice."

We sat in silence, listening to the sound of waves crashing below, as I watched the distant hills that led back toward the city. We had often spent secret afternoons sprawled on a bit of cloth on the edge of a cliff that dropped off to a sandy beach below. The beach was reachable only by a narrow and rocky path, and we did sometimes venture down to frolic in the waves, but this spot afforded us a view of oncoming danger. As an ancestor of the founder of the city, my love knew all of the city's secrets, including tunnels that no one, not even other gods, knew about. It was laughingly easy to sneak in and out of the city while on the far side of the island the Greeks were desperately seeking entrance.

This had become our refuge; the only place we could truly be alone without fear of being caught. The vow which bound me to Apollo kept me in constant fear of being found out, but I couldn't deny my love. The prophecies I'd seen looked grim, for not only myself, but for nearly everyone else involved in the war. As troubling as my visions of the future were I had decided to live for the precious time I could spend with my love. I tried to pretend the future didn't exist and I held out hope that I had misinterpreted my visions.

Suddenly a form appeared, running toward us. "Someone is coming," I warned, my heart beating wildly.

My love turned calmly to look behind. "It is only Xanthós. Something must have happened," he said, rising and helping me to my feet.

We met Xanthós half-way. I worried the Greeks had finally broken through our defenses and Xanthós had come to warn us to not return to the city, but the war was not what his news was about.

Panting he said, "Lord Apollo is looking for you. He found me in the garden and demanded to know where you were."

"What did you tell him?" I asked shakily.

"I only said that I did not know. That I would tell you that he was looking for you when next I saw you. I fear he is becoming suspicious, Princess. You must be careful," Xanthós pleaded.

"You should probably get back," my love stated, and then clapping Xanthós on the shoulder he said, "You are a good friend, Xanthós. I know I can count on you to watch over Cassandra. Will you take her back to the city and make sure she stays safe?"

"Of course," Xanthós answered automatically, "I would do anything for the princess."

I turned to my love to embrace him and inquire, "I will see you tonight, will I not?"

"I will not be able to visit you this night," he whispered in my ear.

I pulled away abruptly and demanded, "Why not?"

He looked at me gravely and admitted, "I told you I was trying to appeal to Zeus. All of this meddling in mortal lives needs to stop. I have managed to gather a group of immortals that agree; we are to have an audience with Zeus tonight."

I gulped nervously, "Will *he* be there?"

"No," he said firmly, "Apollo has made it very clear that he enjoys using mortals like toys for his greedy hands. I am going to try to speak with Zeus alone, to appeal to him on your behalf. I will beg him if I must to have you released from your vow."

I could see his eyes had filled with tears before he looked away. For my part, I was unable to keep the tears from falling. Everything he was doing...was for me. I had always believed fate had been unduly cruel to me; first for receiving the so-called gift of prophecy from Apollo, then for being cursed to never be believed because I did not accept Apollo's advances, and then to be bound to a vow to never love another if I would not love Apollo. For all of that, I realized I was lucky. The love and devotion I received were things most, mortals and immortals alike, would never experience. I had something that not even Zeus, the greatest of all gods, could claim to have. I knew my life would end soon, but I pushed that thought away and instead willed myself to believe that our love was strong enough to find each other again. Perhaps in my next lifetime, and maybe things wouldn't be so difficult. I clung to the idea that there had to be a happy ending for us...somewhere in time.

I opened my eyes to an unfamiliar room. I sat up in frustration; angry that I had no control over these visions. I looked around, wondering what bizarre thing I was going to see this time. I hesitated getting out of bed, remembering the last time I had ended up in a strange bedroom. Was I going to have another premonition about someone's death?

A knock came at the door, followed by, "Lizzy, are you awake?"

It took me a moment to shake the sleep completely from my head, but I finally recognized the voice as Emma's. I looked around once more, now seeing that the room was actually mine. Well, mine at least while I stayed at Cuckfield Park. The night before came back to me; most of which had been spent with Dardanos by the pond. I couldn't even remember walking to my room, and hoped nothing else had happened that I couldn't remember.

"Lizzy?!" Emma's voice rang out again.

"Yes," I croaked, "Yes, I'm here."

Emma burst into the room, a look of concern on her face. She rushed to my bedside, flinging her arms around me. I was a little shocked at first and didn't know what I should do, but finally I put my arms around her as well.

"Is everything all right?" I asked hesitantly, "Has something happened?"

Emma pulled away from me, nodding her head as a tear slid down her cheek. "I am so sorry."

My heart pounded, expecting the worse. "What is it? What has happened?"

Emma hung her head and said softly, "I have behaved terribly toward you. I know that you are grieving and instead of trying to console you I've added to your grief."

I would have been less shocked if she had told me that Gabriel had miraculously come back to life. I couldn't answer her more than making a sound to fill the silence.

"I know how horrible I've been to you, especially since I haven't been around much, and then I showed up and started piling all of these issues on top of your misery," she said in a rush as if saying it fast made it easier. "I want you to know how very sorry I am...and I want...I would very much like to go back to the way things were."

My mind was still caught between the world of my vision and this one as I listened to Emma. Could I believe this sudden need for forgiveness from her? Was she truly sorry for everything: the disappearing, potentially ruining our family reputation, and the venomous words she spat at me? I looked at her, deciding if there was anything left of my lighthearted sister, my best friend, still there? I couldn't make up my mind, but I wanted so much to believe her.

"There is nothing to forgive," I said, trying to keep the sarcasm out of my voice. "We have all been hit hard by this tragedy, and we are sisters. Who can we vent our emotions to, if not to each other?"

She plunged forward again, embracing me tightly as she broke into sobs, "I was so scared you wouldn't forgive me. I didn't think you would even speak to me."

"I was...angry...and upset," I admitted, "but I was more worried about you, about what could have happened to you to cause you to say such terrible things. I worried...I worried that you were beyond our love and help."

Emma seemed to have slipped back into her dark mood as I spoke, but then she looked up and forced herself to brighten. "How kind of you to worry about me when I had acted so inexcusably. Do you think we could try...and I promise to do my best...could we try going back to the way we were before we met the Sergisons?"

I wanted to agree immediately, but then I remembered Lord Sergison's proposal and I worried Emma would be angry when she found out. "There is something I want to tell you. Please, don't be angry with me; it was a great surprise to me and really it will benefit our whole family. I'm not even sure I'm going to accept."

Emma kept her calm, almost forced smile as she said smoothly, "Of course, Lizzy, you can tell me anything."

I didn't trust Emma's docile exterior but I reasoned it would be better she hear it from me now than from someone else later. "Lord and Lady Sergison wish to name me their heir. They want me to live at Cuckfield Park and learn how to run it," I said it quickly, wincing as I waited for her reaction.

Emma seemed to grit her teeth, but answered sweetly, "Oh, Lizzy, that's wonderful. It's a wonderful prospect for you, and I'm sure you will be helping Lord and Lady Sergison immensely by accepting."

I stared at her, stunned again by her happy and positive reaction. It almost sounded like she was trying to convince me that I should accept. Of course if I were the heir to the Sergison fortune that would put Emma in a much better position to marry well. Somehow I didn't think her calm behavior and forced cheerfulness had anything to do with hopes of better marriage prospects.

"Are you well, Lizzy? You look a bit dark around the eyes," Emma commented, having time to examine me as I sat in stunned silence.

I turned to her, finally finding my voice, "I didn't sleep well last night. I'm just tired."

"Oh," Emma said, trying to hide a smirk, "is that why you went out for a walk last night?"

I felt my eyes about to burst from their sockets. "How did you..." I didn't finish.

Emma stood up, still wearing a mocking smile. "Your boots," she said, pointing to the floor beside my bed, "they're covered in mud, and I know they weren't when I saw you last night in the parlor. Also..." she added, tossing a book onto the bed, "I found this out by the pond."

I smiled weakly, picking up *The Moonstone* to examine the traces of dirt on its linen cover, and stuttered, "I thought the fresh air would do me some good. I suppose I was so exhausted I dropped my book without even realizing it."

"Just be careful walking about at night. You never know what you'll stumble upon, or what might stumble upon you. Remember there's a murderer lingering about. I wouldn't want to have to mourn you as well." She gave me a forced smiled. "Well, I'll wait for you downstairs," Emma said, rising to leave, but stopped in the doorway. "Lizzy, you will accept the Sergison's proposal, won't you?"

I thought I had made my mind up the night before when I'd spoken to Dardanos. The news had lit an excitement in him which I didn't want to extinguish. I had this naïve dream of a future in which Dardanos and I would marry and live happily ever after at Cuckfield Park. Hearing Emma so enthusiastic about my prospect made me second-guess myself. Did she have some ulterior motive for wanting me to take over Cuckfield Park? Was she really happy for me, or was she planning some devious plot to punish me for supposedly stealing her happiness? I didn't want to think such things about my sister, but she was so different. She seemed to be calculating every word she spoke as if she were playing a game, only no one else knew we were playing it along with her.

"Lizzy," she called again, still standing in the doorway. "Will you accept?"

"I believe I will," I admitted grudgingly, not really wanting to commit to a decision just yet, but what harm was there in letting my sister know? "Are you sure it's the right..." I stopped, noticing Emma had already left the room, leaving me questioning if I was making the right decision.

ɛɔ14ɕʒ

Soon after Emma left me sitting there in confusion the lady's maid Sallie entered to help me dress. I had not brought my own maid along as she was not only Emma's maid but also had other duties in our house to attend to. My family was well-off but not so well-off that we could afford personal maids and house maids, but Lady Sergison had many servants and always made sure her guests were cared for by one of them. Sallie was a little taller than me with a strong and sturdy body. I envied her white-blonde hair and blue eyes. She must have been at least twenty five, but she carried herself as if she had seen it all. I liked her immediately. She spoke to me as her equal, which I suppose might have offended most, but I found it comforting to at least have someone I could confide in that was near my age.

"Oh, Lizzy, these'll have to go through a wash. Were you out trampling through mud in the middle of the night?" Sallie asked lifting my dirty boots from under the bed.

"I felt so confined yesterday. I needed to get out of the house," I explained, swinging myself out of bed. "Please don't tell anyone I was out of doors so late. They'll only worry."

Sallie nodded. "Of course, I understand. I can't imagine what you must be going through, losing your sweetheart so young, and in such a strange way."

As Sallie helped me into my corset and began lacing the back I wondered aloud, "It was strange, wasn't it? I keep thinking that I could have prevented this, but I know that doesn't make sense. I'm beginning to think we don't have as much control over our lives as I always believed. Maybe there is such a thing as fate."

"There's nothing anyone could have done, Lizzy. God has his plan. Who are we to question it?" She asked rhetorically, picking up the black skirt and bodice my mother had sent over the evening before.

"What if there was something that could upset God's plan? What if there were some other power out there strong enough to change fate?" I rambled, looking down at the moonstone ring on my finger.

Sallie eyed me strangely and answered, "Don't trouble yourself with such thoughts, Lizzy. Let us just pray that they catch the madman that did it. If it was a man at all that did it," Sallie said as if trying to see what I knew.

I stepped into the skirt Sallie was holding out for me. "Do you think it could have been an animal?" I asked curiously.

Sallie adjusted the skirt over the bustle as she answered cryptically, "There's been strange stories going about. Stories I dare not repeat." She seemed to be considering telling me as she helped me into the top of the gown, fastening the buttons at the back. "Please be careful. If the thing people are speaking of is out there...well, then we are all in great danger." Sallie quickly bowed and left the room before I could question her further.

I was left to pin my hair up on my own, and decided against applying any color to my face from my secret toiletry box. It didn't seem right to add color to my pale and emotionally drained face, not when I would have to stare at the ever decaying features of Gabriel all day. Instead I went to the armoire and opened the door to look at my reflection, and to see how extravagantly dressed I was. The sheen of the black taffeta seemed too fancy for sitting in front of a coffin all day, and the ruffles below the gathered skirt of taffeta spilled down in seductive black lace. There was even a bit of black lace at the rounded neckline and draping at the three quarter sleeves. I huffed as I pinned the broach Lady Sergison had given me just below the neckline of the dress, and I hoped Lady Sergison wouldn't find my attire too garish.

I knew my mother had spent much more than my father would have agreed to on such a frilly garment, and I was sure she had purposely picked out such an ornate mourning dress to show off. She wanted the other mourners to see how well dressed I was; she wanted to prove to society that we were as elegant and refined as the Sergisons. The only problem was I was the fiancée of the deceased, and decorum dictated that I shouldn't wear such decorative clothing. I usually wouldn't have cared what society thought of me, but my current emotional state made me want to turn invisible not be the center of attention. If I had had another dress to change into I would have, but I only had one black dress which I'd already worn and which had already been taken away to be cleaned. I cringed to think what dress my mother would send over for the actual funeral the following day.

I went first to the breakfast room, needing some nourishment to give me strength for the trying day ahead. I quickly breakfasted alone, (Emma was nowhere to be found) and then I forced my feet to carry my emotionally numb body back to the West parlor. I again sat beside Lady Sergison, giving her a comforting smile.

She patted my leg excitedly and gushed, "I'm so pleased. Lord Sergison wishes to see you in his study."

I looked at her puzzled, but rose to do as she asked. I noticed Emma sitting behind us as I turned to go; she must have slipped in just after I had. When I looked at her shrugging my shoulders in confusion she nodded and gave me a knowing smile. I wondered how Emma could know what Lord Sergison wanted to talk to me about as I walked to his study.

This time, though the door was ajar, I knocked quickly hoping to avoid over-hearing another strange conversation. "Lord Sergison?"

"Come in, Elizabeth."

I entered to find my father sitting with Lord Sergison, apparently waiting for me as well. I immediately knew why Lord Sergison wanted to see me; it must have been about naming me heir, but I wasn't ready to give my answer. I thought he would give me more than just one night to consider the idea.

"Elizabeth, I am so relieved you have accepted my proposal," Lord Sergison said, beaming.

I sat down, looking confusedly from him to my father. "I don't understand. I didn't say-"

My father cut me off, seeing my puzzlement, "Emma told us you had made up your mind. She was so happy for you she couldn't hide it from us."

"Really?" I asked incredulously.

"You haven't changed your mind?" Lord Sergison inquired, his shoulders drooping a bit. "Emma told us she had just spoken to you and you assured her you would accept."

I wanted to explain that I had only agreed with Emma

because I had been so confused by her affectionate behavior toward me. I wanted to tell them the only reason I was even thinking of accepting was because it had made Dardanos so happy and I was in love with him. I wanted to tell them that I needed more time to make sure I was making the right decisions. I looked from Lord Sergison's anxious face to my father's pleading face and found myself unable to go against their wishes. Everyone seemed to want me to accept: Lord and Lady Sergison, my father, surely my mother would find the elevation in society pleasing, now Emma seemed adamant for me to accept, and most especially Dardanos. I didn't want to let anyone down, but mostly I kept the perfect image of sharing a life filled with unending love with Dardanos in mind...and he wanted to be part of Cuckfield Park.

"I will do what is expected of me," I answered flatly, keeping my indecision to myself, "anything to help my family...and the Sergisons, of course."

All that was left to do was finalize a few documents. My father instructed Lord Sergison where he should sign, and they had written up a provisional document that I had to sign as well. The document made it very clear that I had to agree to be properly trained in order to take over Cuckfield Park by Lord Sergison and my father. In the event of my training not being completed before both died a secured box of documents would be released to me by my father's law firm; I was to follow the instructions enclosed explicitly, no matter how strange they seemed. My father and I both left the study at the same time, he to bring the legal documents to his law firm and I to resume my "death watch".

Before we parted in the main hall my father turned and embraced me. "I am so proud of you. I understand what a difficult decision this was for you; you expected to live at Cuckfield Park under very different circumstances. I know that it worries you to not know what burdens will be yours, but I think once you learn the truth you will see how important this decision was."

I felt a shiver roll through my body as he walked away. I still had no guess at what this great secret was, yet I was about to become part of it. I silently reprimanded myself for not forcing Dardanos to reveal everything to me the night before, though I reasoned that I would have eventually accepted the Sergison's proposal anyway, if for no other reason than to please Dardanos. I still couldn't understand why Emma had been so happy for me, and further why she would tell my father and Lord Sergison I had made up my mind. I didn't want to think so ill of my sister, but I wasn't convinced that her new affectionate and penitent attitude was real.

That day moved so slowly and was far more dull than the day before causing me to spend most of the day reading bits and pieces of *The Moonstone* and nodding off in my seat. Lady Sergison had once again ordered the room lit when morning arrived, but without the sun's rays to warm the room the chill of the night never quite left it. I also found the flickering of the candles and gas lamps strangely hypnotic; it was easier to focus on those dancing flames than the ever deteriorating form of Gabriel.

I continuously heard Gabriel's voice reciting a poem by Lord Byron in my head, *I had a dream, which was not all a dream. / The bright sun was extinguish'd, and the stars / Did wander darkling in the eternal space, / Rayless, and pathless, and the icy earth / Swung blind and blackening in the moonless air; / Morn came and went–and came, and brought no day*

It was how I felt. The sun, the light, had gone away, and though the sun seemed to come every morning the darkness never seemed to leave. The cold was ever present. I was aware of people coming and going, offering their condolences, commenting how lovely I looked, but it was as if I were watching it from far away...as if in a dream.

I remembered the evening Gabriel had read the poem to me, in this very house, before a warm fire, his body turned toward me on the sofa. Afterward he laughingly said he could understand my attraction to such pretty lines, but for the life of him he couldn't forget the poet's sinful life. I answered him that a man may have beauty in his heart even while depravity is in his head. I preferred to enjoy the beauty that Byron left behind, and pity his struggles with morality. Gabriel merely grabbed my hand, kissing it slowly and said he would pity the poet for my sake, and thank him for his own sake. When I asked what he would thank the poet for he told me for the passion that he so appreciatively lit in my soul.

I shook my head with these remembrances, wiping the tears I hadn't even realized had begun to fall. Lady Sergison patted my hand and sent me to bed, and this time I put up no resistance. I followed my feet up the back staircase and into my room. I was so exhausted I threw off my mourning dress, top petticoat, and bustle, leaving my combination undergarment, corset, and second petticoat on as I climbed into bed.

"She has changed. Something happened to her ten years ago and she will not tell us what. Ramose, you remember how it was," the man behind me commented addressing his servant. "We thought she would die, but she did not; she only changed."

"I remember, Sire. The attacks were horrible," Ramose answered.

I turned around regarding both men curiously. Setepamun, future king of Egypt with his long, jet black hair and hypnotizing blue eyes, and Ramose, his faithful servant with light brown hair and blue-green eyes. They were both striking men, even Ramose who was only a servant, had a graceful attraction with his soft features and long, lean body. Setepamun trusted Ramose implicitly with all his deepest secrets, and so I too came to trust him and consider him a friend.

I returned to what I was doing, pulling rolls of papyrus down from embedded stone shelves. I wasn't sure I knew what I was looking for, but I had this determined thought that I would know it when I laid eyes upon it. Though there were many scrolls to go through I handled each one gently and with patience. My training had taught me to respect the writings of the past, even if they were not the particular writings I was looking for.

Setepamun continued even though I hadn't answered, "My brother believes she has been infected by something. He believes she is dying. She sleeps all day and emerges only once the sun is no more. I would agree with my brother that she was sick except once she is awake she seems stronger than ever and nothing fatigues her. I cannot be sure, but I would swear she has not aged these past ten years."

Finally I turned to answer him. "That is strange. The scroll I spoke of described something like that having happened to the god Dardanos. He could only move about at night; it had to do with some curse called The Immortal Fate. In my visions his name was never spoken, and I only saw images from before he was cursed. Oh, if only I had known his name before I would have paid more attention to that scroll!" I reprimanded myself as I turned back to the shelves.

"You think what has happened to my mother is connected to our destinies?" he asked in surprise.

"I don't know," I answered, shuffling newer scrolls aside, "it seems a great coincidence and-"

Both he and Ramose cut me off, "And there is no such thing as coincidence."

"Precisely," I said, laughing lightly at them and pulling an armful of scrolls down and placing them on the table. "It should be one of these or...or someone has removed it."

I sat down as Setepamun began unrolling one of the scrolls, but he seemed distracted. I pretended not to notice, handing a scroll to Ramose. I opened a scroll and read over it quickly before discarding it to the side; Ramose too was setting his scroll aside. As I reached for a second scroll I noticed Setepamun was still holding the same scroll, staring down at the table.

"Setepamun, what is it?" I asked, seeing the faraway look on his face.

His pale blue eyes shifted up to my face as he stated, "This could be the link I have been looking for. What if my mother has begun the transformation into a goddess?"

"She has the undeniable beauty and strength of a goddess," Ramose commented, looking up from his third scroll.

I swallowed and cautioned, "Yes, but the god that walked the night was cursed. If your mother has become like him...then she too must be cursed."

"Perhaps that is the only way we can become gods once more," he muttered dreamily, "by becoming cursed." He swung his bright blue eyes up to mine suddenly asking, "Would you risk it?"

My eyes darted momentarily to Ramose; his eyes were full of questions. He, too, wondered what I would risk. Ramose had already pledged himself to both Setepamun and myself; he swore to serve and protect us no matter what course we took. His loyalty gave me strength, and I smiled appreciatively.

I reached my hand across the table to take Setepamun's

hand. "If it means being with you I would face an eternity cursed."

My heart caught in my chest as I sat bolt upright in bed. My entire body was moist with sweat, though the room itself wasn't hot. It was the dream causing my anxiety. The tremors that racked my body at the mention of a curse scared me. Could this curse be real? Could it be following me over the great expanse of time? Was my very soul cursed?

I now knew the man with the black hair I continued to see in these dreams and visions was Dardanos, and the servant from Cassandra's time and Amunet's time was Gabriel. I still couldn't give in to the belief that what I was seeing in these visions was in fact the past. For one thing I found it strange that Dardanos had never mentioned Gabriel when he spoke of the visions; if it was all true why hadn't he spoke of Gabriel as not only being my trusted servant in the past but also his? More likely my dreams and so-called visions were nothing more than a result of the stories Dardanos and Gabriel had told me combined with a great deal of stress. I wiped at my damp brow, telling myself none of this was real; it was all a product of my imagination.

My heart was still beating fiercely and my combination undergarment beneath my corset and petticoat clung uncomfortably to my moist skin. I put my head back onto my pillow, unable to push the images from my dream away. With a huff I lit my bedroom candle and tugged on my robe. Lighting my way quietly through the house I found my way to the back door and the courtyard beyond. I disregarded Emma's and Sallie's warnings about being careful and decided a walk in the gardens in the cool night air might help stop the feverish sweat and help me get back to sleep.

After a few circles of the courtyard I still felt anxious and knew I wouldn't be getting to sleep any time soon. I ventured out of the courtyard and into the hedgerows. I enjoyed the close proximity of the hedges and the fresh, leafy scent given off as I dragged my hand along the sides as I walked. My thoughts turned to Dardanos, to the inexplicable longing I felt for him, to the shame of wanting him on the eve of my fiancé's burial. I was wandering through the maze of hedges without really seeing where I was, and in my detachment my robe caught on the wing

of a cherub statue in one of the alcoves. It caught me so
surprisingly that as my robe was tugged backward and I was still
moving forward the unexpected jerk caused me to drop my
candle, snuffing out the light and leaving me in the center of the
hedgerows in pitch blackness.

My first instinct was to scream for help. I was
immediately filled with a panic that some ravenous creature
would attack me, thanks to Sallie's strange warning, and I
wouldn't even know which way to run. I took a few calming
breaths and gingerly walked forward with my hands waiving in
front of me so I wouldn't run into anything. I stopped short after
just a moment of walking; I could have sworn I'd heard
something. I held my breath, straining to hear. I thought I could
make out what sounded like delicate crunching, as if something
were walking carefully in fallen leaves, very near to where I
stood. I didn't move a muscle, waiting, trying to convince myself
it was only my imagination playing tricks on me, but then I heard
a voice.

"Have you done what he asked?" It was a man, but he
didn't sound familiar.

"Yes," a woman answered; it sounded as if they were on
the other side of the hedge.

"He wishes for you to stay close. Make sure everything
goes as planned."

"But what about what I've been promised?" I recognized
the voice as Emma's. "I have done everything he has asked of
me, when will I get what I want?"

"Patience...there is still more to be done," the man
soothed and then to my surprise he asked, "How is your sister?"

There was a long pause before Emma answered bitingly,
"Why do you care? Don't tell me you're in love with her as
well?"

"You might want to keep that jealousy in check," the man
said calmly, "it might get you into trouble one day. I can't say I
blame you all together though. It's obvious where your jealousy
stems from; she is very beautiful, and from what I've seen she
has a much sweeter disposition. It must be difficult for you to
have such a radiant creature for your sister, always outshining
you."

"Is that all?" Emma grumbled.

"No, it isn't," the man answered almost laughing, but then

dropped his voice to a grim whisper, "There is another of our kind lurking about. He is very powerful and very dangerous; keep your eyes open. If this man tries to disrupt our plans...if he attacks...Well, let's just say there is no one that can stop him."

"Can't *HE* stop him? I thought he was very old and powerful?" Emma asked sarcastically.

"This one...is older, much older," the man said, all joking out of his voice, "this one...I have never even heard of one so powerful. It's rumored he can't be killed; it's rumored he may be the very oldest of our kind."

Our kind? What did he mean by that and why was my sister meeting secretly with this man? What was it that my sister was going to get out of whatever deal she'd made? If I hadn't felt so wide awake I would have been sure this was just another one of my bizarre dreams, but I felt none of the confusing detachment that was so prevalent in my visions and dreams. I let my breath out slowly, not realizing I had been holding it while I listened to the conversation. I readjusted my feet and leaned in closer to the hedge, hoping to hear more.

Emma huffed, "So what does this all-powerful being look like, and what do I do if I see him?"

"He has short black hair, graying on the sides, and his eyes are a strange gray, almost silver I would say. You will recognize him as one of us by his pallid complexion and the unusual glint of his hair and eyes. He shouldn't be difficult to spot; I have never seen another of my fate so aged. He looks to be past forty, a few thin wrinkles are visible, but other than that his skin is as smooth as a new born babe's. As for what you should do if you see him," the man paused dramatically, "run. Take your sister and run, and pray that he doesn't follow."

"Oh, yes, let's not forget about her," Emma said tartly.

"Yes, let us not," the man stated sternly, "remember if anything happens to her the deal is off. You'll have to find some other way of getting what you want. That is if he doesn't punish you for letting something happen to her."

I swallowed hard, feeling anxious about all of this talk having to do with me. I forced a breath of air out, steadying my nerves, but found that the sound cut through the empty silence. It hadn't been very loud, but in the dead silence I felt as though I'd screamed, *here I am!*

"Shhh, I heard something," the man whispered.

I backed away from the hedge slowly until my body was pressed up against the far side, hoping they had no light with which to see by. I held my breath and did my best not to move. Suddenly a hand shot through the wall of leaves. I jumped slightly, but kept my mouth from opening in a squeal by clamping my hand over it. The hand swept side to side as if it expected its prey to be right there. I realized if I hadn't moved that hand would have shot out right at the level of my throat.

"What is it?" Emma whispered.

The hand pulled back. "It must have been an animal. We've stayed too long anyway; you should return to the house before anyone notices you're gone."

I heard the light footsteps as Emma retreated to the house. I waited, listening for the man's footsteps, but they never came. Slowly I approached the small gap in the hedge left by the man's arm. I bent slightly to look through the hole. To my horror a bright, swirling blue eye was staring back at me. A swirling blue eye that I was sure I'd seen somewhere before; an eye that filled me with fear.

"Ahhh, there you are, little queen," the man purred.

I didn't wait to see what he would do next. I ran. I ran without pausing to look behind me, and I rushed into the house slamming the door behind me. It was loud enough to wake the whole house, but I didn't care. I didn't wait to see if I'd roused anyone. I only stood there long enough to lock the door behind me before dashing to my room.

❧15☙

I was kneeling in front of The Palladium, whispering frantically in hushed tones, begging for her help. I could feel the shift of the war; many gods had been angry at Dardanos's demand that they stop interfering with humans. As a result a great number of gods were now aiding the Greeks, trying to prove to Zeus that the gods needed to be involved in human affairs. Their power came from the human's belief in them, and how better to cement belief than to cause the destruction of an entire civilization.

"Where were you?" A voice rang out behind me.

A chill ran down my spine as I recognized the voice. "Apollo," I whispered fearfully as I turned on my knees to look up at him. "Please, this war must end."

His hair gleamed brilliantly in the sun and his eyes seemed to reflect the sky with its many hues of blue. "You have already seen its end, my little serpent. You know it is almost over, all of it."

I gulped nervously. "Yes, I have seen its end, but there must be a way to stop it. Please, Apollo, do not allow my kingdom to be destroyed because of your hatred for me."

He stooped down to put his hand at my cheek and said sweetly, "I do not hate you, Cassandra. I love you, but you continue to betray me and I cannot have that. So tell me, where were you?"

I shook my head. "I do not know what you mean. I have been in the temple, begging Athena to intervene."

Apollo placed his fingertip under my chin and lifted me up until I was dangling at his eye level. "Perhaps today that is where you have been, but what of last evening? What of the evening before? What of the many times I questioned your servant, Xanthós? Curious that a faithful servant that has been your close companion all your life never knows where you are, or was he simply protecting you? Was he lying for you because he knew you were breaking your vow to me? "

He knew. My lips trembled to think of an answer, but none would come.

He released his finger from under my chin but I still levitated before him. "Did you think I would not notice?" Apollo asked, running his finger down my neck along the curve of the top of my dress. "You have been sneaking out of the temple at night. You return in the early hours of morning, and...you stink of him."

"Please," I managed to utter.

Apollo moved closer and said bitingly, "You can stand to have his hands upon you, but not mine?! There are consequences for betraying a god!" He forced his mouth over mine, roughly pushing his tongue into my mouth.

There was nothing I could do. I was powerless to his advances. Tears fell feebly from my eyes as he moved his hands over my body. I screamed inside for Athena to help, and a sudden quaking of the temple seemed to be my release.

Apollo pulled away and looking to the ceiling shouted, "Yes, yes, I heard you." Then turning back to me he lowered his voice threateningly, "I may not be able to touch you in Athena's temple, but I will have you...or everyone and everything you love will be destroyed."

The next morning I was awoken once more by Emma calling my name as she entered my room. I was still dreaming about that haunting blue eye shining at me through the hole in the hedge, and a hand reaching out to grasp my throat. The night had been full of distressing dreams and I was glad to see the morning light peeking from behind the curtains. I rolled over in relief, opening my eyes to see Emma standing beside my bed with something draped over her arm. My relief soon turned to cautious scrutiny as I remembered the conversation I'd overheard the night before. Was Emma only putting on an act with me, because someone else was forcing her to? In exchange for something she wanted?

"Mother sent this over for you," she explained, oblivious to my searching glare, as she laid what appeared to be a dress at the end of the bed. "Today is an important day; Mother knew you'd want to look your best. It's time to put away the past and make a new start."

I studied her as she spoke, looking for some hint of what she'd said the night before. Some touch of that jealousy that I had heard so openly spoken to a stranger with swirling blue eyes. She gave me a curious grin before gesturing to the gown on the bed and remarking how late it was getting, and that Sallie should have known better than to have let me sleep. I couldn't decide if she was being sarcastic or if she truly cared about helping me get through the difficult day.

As Emma was pulling the door closed she muttered, "I will watch over you. No matter what happens...I won't let anything bad happen to you."

It seemed like a sweet sisterly thing to say, but I now knew there was some other force prompting her to watch over me, to pretend to be my friend. Some selfish goal that could only be achieved if I was kept safe, but from what? And why did the stranger with the blue swirling eyes even care if I was safe or not? Did it have something to do with my visions; were the demons of my past life coming back to claim me? Was I fated to meet the same tragic ends I had in past lives? I wasn't sure what had happened to Amunet in Egypt, but I did know the story of Cassandra. Raped multiple times before being taken prisoner by a king, and finally being poisoned by the king's wife.

As I was about to lift the gown Emma had brought I made a note to myself that I really should ask Dardanos more about Amunet. Just in case everything turned out to be true...I should know more about my past so that I might keep from repeating it.

I stopped, a low gasp escaping my lips. The gown laying on my bed was the very same I had worn the night of the engagement dinner, the night I had met Dardanos. It was the beautiful sage green gown I so loved...only it had been dyed black. Of all the gowns she could have chosen why would my mother choose that one? It didn't seem like something she would do. My mother was more likely to use the occasion as an excuse to buy us all new black gowns to show society that we were so well-off that we could purchase clothes just for mourning, and didn't need to simply dye old gowns like everyone else.

I might have cried if I had any tears left, but as it was I knew I needed to save whatever moisture was left in me for the dismal day ahead. I felt a wave of dread staring down at my once vibrant gown. If I believed in such things I would have thought it an omen, a dark portent of things to come. Since the night of the engagement dinner it had seemed as if some great black cloth had been draped over my life. It saddened me further to think that the night when so much darkness entered my life was the very same night I had first met Dardanos.

I wanted to hide the dress and wear something else. I wanted to reject the symbolic image the dress now represented to me: a once fresh, spring-like thing withered to a black, dead thing. I wanted to wear something else, but in reality I had no choice. I had only one black gown which I'd been wearing since Gabriel's death and the extravagant gown my mother had purchased I'd worn the day before. Both had still not come back from being cleaned, and neither were exactly appropriate. One being far too simple and the other being far too showy with excessive ornamentation. This was all I had, this horrid dress that my mother wished me to wear. I had no choice but to wear it...unless I chose to not wear black, but the gossip that would incur would be disrespectful not only to my own family but to the Sergisons. I silently cursed myself for allowing the maid to take my only other black gowns for the wash.

"Oh, damn!" I huffed angrily, snatching up the gown.

Immediately my eyes were filled with a blinding light and I was no longer in my room holding the wretched mourning gown. I was floating, looking down on a man weeping over a casket. I thought the man must have been Dardanos with the long, black hair tied in back, and I assumed he must have been mourning Gabriel. It touched me to see how wholeheartedly he wept that, though I didn't want to interrupt him, I felt a desire to comfort him. Somehow I willed myself closer, to lay my hand on Dardanos's shoulder, and I whispered to him that I was there. If he heard or felt me he gave no hint of it, but he did finally raise his head.

"Why must you continue to torment me?! Why must you always take her from me?!" He shouted angrily toward the heavens.

Her? I turned my head back to the casket. It was not Gabriel in the casket...it was me. I stared in horror at my own body laid within the casket, looking the same as I did when I'd awoken that morning, only that my head didn't seem positioned correctly, and I was wearing the dyed engagement gown. I felt a wave of nausea flooding me, but as I had no body I suppose it was literally all in my head.

"I'm here! General, I'm right here!" I bellowed in terror, praying he could still hear me.

Again, he made no hint of being able to hear me, but he did turn back to the casket. "I will avenge you, my sweet Elizabeth. Next time I find you I promise I will not let him get in the way of our happiness," he affirmed, "we will be gods...and they will all suffer."

I was on the floor, the black gown lying next to me in a heap.

"Lizzy, are you all right?" it was Sallie. "I was just down the hall when I heard a loud bang."

"I'm fine, Sallie," I said as she helped me up, "just a fainting spell. I suppose I was overcome with sadness."

"It's to be expected on such a black day as today," she commented as she retrieved my gown from the floor and smoothed it out on the bed. "Though I'd wager you're going to look more like a princess than a widow in this fancy dress."

"Yes, I know what you mean. It was my mother's idea and as I have nothing else-"

"Oh no, Lizzy," Sallie broke in, "pardon me, but I had it from your sister's own lips that she thought it a grand idea to have this gown dyed for you. She told me as she brought it in, was her that convinced your mother. She said it represented your old life; now it's dyed it represented your new life," She paused, probably noticing the dark look on my face, and then added, "I'm sure she thought only of how lovely you would look in it, shining a little bit of light on this day."

I forced a smile as Sallie began helping me out of my corset from the night before, and said, "I'm sure you're right."

Sallie helped me into fresh undergarments as she soothed, "Sisters can be horrible, jealous things, but when you need someone to tell your secrets to they can't be matched."

I smiled, remembering how Emma and I had told secrets. We'd always been so different but we still found ways that made us closer to each other than to any other person on earth. Sallie continued helping me into the wretched, coal black dress and telling horror stories about her own sisters.

As she was expertly piling my hair up while I watched in the vanity I remembered my broach. "Sallie could you fetch my broach. I think I left it by the bed."

She halted the fussing of my hair to bring the broach to me, but I noticed her studying it and moving slower and slower back toward me. "This is a strange broach, Lizzy. May I ask where you got it?"

"It was a gift from Lady Sergison," I answered curiously, "Why do you say it's strange?"

"Well, I've seen many a mourning jewelry with many different designs, but that seems a strange choice of design. The moon there it represents death and rebirth. Not so strange a choice for mourning, but the serpent...Well, some people think it means eternal love, but there's some believe it simply means eternity. The combination of the two would mean something like eternal death. Doesn't exactly seem like a comforting thought, does it?"

I accepted the broach from her, looking more closely at the symbols. "No, it does not sound comforting at all."

A little less than half an hour later I descended the stairs into the main hall. I was still fuming that Emma had convinced my mother to have my gown dyed, and most likely for vindictive reasons. I guess I should have been grateful to have some other emotion in me other than sadness, but I felt a need to expose Emma's petty jealousy before it escalated to a point of no return. I had to side-step a few times as I made my way back toward the parlor as the house was all a commotion with the preparations for the day. After the burial the Sergisons were hosting an extravagantly large dinner party in the courtyard. The staff were rushing about not only preparing for the party, but for the burial procession as well.

"Oh, Lizzy, you do look handsome," my father commented walking toward me from the back of the house. "I have a surprise for you...before we leave. Come this way," he insisted, gesturing for me to follow him out the back.

I took his arm and let him lead me through the courtyard and then to the left, into the hedgerows. I looked at him anxiously, wondering if he knew I'd been in the hedgerows the night before, or perhaps he knew that Emma had been with a stranger. Was he going to reprimand me for wandering about at night? Was he going to question me about Emma being there...with a man? I was angry enough with her to tell him everything.

"Father, what is this all about?" I asked nervously.

He suppressed a smile, saying almost giddily, "You'll see, you'll see."

He led me right into the hedgerows. We snaked through the twists and turns until we came upon the statue of the little cherub. I started to tremble nervously as my father slowed his pace. I could now see where my candle had fallen and where I'd subsequently dropped the holder, and I waited for my father to point them out and question why they were there. Then I froze, my eyes falling to the nearly indiscernible gap in the hedge where a hand had shot through the night before. I was sure my father knew something had happened here, and was going to demand I tell him everything.

"Lizzy," my father called from behind me.

I turned to face him, preparing excuses, but instead I found myself speechless to see what was behind him. There on the direct opposite side of the gap, in an alcove I hadn't known was there in the dark, stood The Palladium. I stared at it speechless. It couldn't have been there the night before; I must have backed right into that alcove the night before to hide from the mysterious stranger Emma had been with.

"When did..." I stammered, staring with shocked eyes at my father, "when did you bring her here?"

My father furrowed his brows, obviously having expected a much happier response. "She is yours, if you remember correctly. I gifted her to you, and she belongs where ever you are."

"Yes, I remember, but-" I started to protest that The Palladium was meant to have been a wedding gift, and I was no longer getting married.

"It was always meant to be with you," my father interjected. "I may have found her, but she was really always yours. There is something special about this statue," my father explained, laying his hand on The Palladium's head. "I might even call it magical...Well, I really can't explain it, but it has always seemed as if it were bound to you."

I was a bit shocked by his words, so similar to what Dardanos had said. Did my father suspect that I had been Cassandra in a past life as well? Did he know the story of the cursed god? Did he think I needed the protection of Pallas with everything that was happening?

"Father, I have been having strange dreams," I began, testing the waters to see his reaction. "I'm so confused. I don't know what to believe."

He put his hand up gently to stop me. "I know what you would say, and we will talk about it, but first...let us get through this day. I promise, I will tell you all I know."

I nodded my head. Of course...not now. I would have to wait for answers...again. My father kissed me on the head and whispered to not be long before he went back to the house. I was alone again and now I had The Palladium to keep me company.

"Thank goodness you're here," I whispered, running my hand over Pallas's shoulder. "Everything has gone so horribly wrong. Emma is planning something..." I stopped, staring down angrily at my dress.

My dream flashed before my eyes...Dardanos weeping over a coffin. My strangely angled head resting above my unmoving body...wearing the same wretched dress I was now wearing. Was it a premonition? I had never dreamed a thing before it happened before, that is until Mrs. Gibson had awakened something inside of me. If Cassandra could see the future then perhaps so could I, after all, we shared the same soul. I cringed at the idea. If it was true that I shared the same gifts as Cassandra then one thing was for certain...death was coming. Could The Palladium protect me? Could this statue that had theoretically failed me twice before actually keep me safe from the ever encircling darkness?

❧16❧

I knew the hour was getting late and so I forced myself back to the house for the burial procession. The house was still a jumble of bodies pushing past one another to get everything ready. A lavishly long table had already been set up in the courtyard and was the focus of much of the fuss, but I could see even the house was being prepared to host a large number of visitors. Fresh flowers were being set out to mask the scent of death that had permeated the house. All of the mirrors and portraits were being covered with black cloth, a protection against Gabriel's soul being caught in the reflective surfaces or of him attaching to one of the portraits inhabitants and bringing them into death with him.

I peeked into the parlor to see who was already arrived, but except for the servants cleaning and rearranging the furniture there was no one. Even the casket had been removed. I rushed to the front door, worried I had lingered too long in the garden and had been left behind, but I found the whole of the funeral party standing about, waiting for something. I winced as I realized I was most likely what everyone was waiting for.

I could see the carriage carrying Gabriel's casket facing the gates, ready to leave. There were six black horses tied to the carriage, tapping restlessly at the ground and shaking the long black plumes that had been fastened to their heads. The carriage itself was strewn with more black plumes and amaranth, a plant with long, cascading, burgundy flowers that looked eerily like blood dripping over the edges. Within the open carriage the casket was inundated by deep crimson roses, so many in fact that the ground would be littered with them when the casket was removed. I knew the roses were a symbol of mourning, but the amaranth was trickier. I remembered it was also sometimes called love-lies-bleeding, due to its drooping flowers, and then it hit me...hopelessness. Lady Sergison had surely chosen them particularly and I worried for her, for the emptiness that Gabriel's death left in her life. Would she ever recover from such heartbreak? I told myself I must do my best to comfort her, to keep her from looming madness.

I turned away from the carriage, surveying the rest of the drive, and noticed that there were some forty to fifty people attending the procession. All of those pairs of eyes were focused on me. I froze as I realized there was no sound, all chatter had ceased. I felt as though I'd just walked in on two women gossiping about me, only it wasn't just two women, it was fifty men, women and children from the best houses in the village. My cheeks burned in embarrassment, knowing all these people in our society were curious about me, talking about me, maybe even making up stories about me. Lady Sergison stepped out of the mass and rushed to me, seeing my uneasiness.

"I'm so sorry, Lady Sergison, I had no idea it was time...no one told me-" I sputtered quietly in her ear as she hooked her arm through mine.

Lady Sergison just waved it away. "Nothing to apologize for, my dear. They only just finished loading the flowers onto the carriage. We still have a few minutes before we leave."

"Oh," I said meekly, lowering my head in front of all the prying eyes, and then I whispered, "Why is everyone staring? I hope I haven't embarrassed you in any way." I fumbled with the dyed black flowers of my dress, wondering if people were staring because of my somewhat ornate dress.

Lady Sergison's eyes darted back and forth as if she hadn't noticed and then turned back to me as if just realizing, "I'm sure there is a great interest in you now."

"What do you mean?" I asked shakily, adjusting my short cloak to cover my bare arm.

"Well, you were Gabriel's fiancée, and you are very beautiful, and...you've been named," she explained matter-of-factly, smiling strangely at people as we passed.

"Named?" I questioned, raising my eyebrows.

Lady Sergison pursed her lips as if she knew I was not going to like what she was going to say. "In the burial notice...and the invitations...it mentioned that you are named our heir. I didn't think it quite proper to announce it that way, but Lord Sergison insisted we must secure your position as our ward and heir as soon as possible. You understand how society can be, some might contest your claim even with the will once we're gone; we have to make it known that we acknowledge you now."

"Oh," was all I could say once more as I realized everyone was probably at that moment whispering about me and my future prospects, and perhaps how it might benefit them.

I walked with Lady Sergison to the front of the procession, just behind the carriage, along with Lord Sergison. Lord Sergison gave the sign to the carriage driver that we were ready, and I once again realized, despite what Lady Sergison had said, that they had been waiting for me. The Sergisons walked directly behind the slowly trundling carriage; a position that I would have occupied had Gabriel and I been married. As it was I walked just behind them, alone, in the place that should have been occupied by their children. The Sergisons wanted it to be known that I now took the place of their child as I was now their ward and heir. The procession wound down the tree-lined drive of Cuckfield Park and then down the lane. It was a rather short twenty minute walk to the neighboring Holy Trinity Church.

As I watched the lumbering carriage, shaking with the love-lies-bleeding over its edges I said quietly, "Peace, peace! he is not dead, he doth not sleep, / He hath awaken'd from the dream of life; / 'Tis we, who lost in stormy visions, keep / With phantoms an unprofitable strife, / And in mad trance, strike with our spirit's knife / Invulnerable nothings. *We* decay / Like corpses in a charnel; fear and grief / Convulse us and consume us day by day, / And cold hopes swarm like worms within our living clay."

"Shelley is a bit imprudent to be quoting today, don't you think, Lizzy?" My father whispered from behind me.

Lady Sergison turned, smiling strangely. "I quite like it myself. It reminds us how loathsome life can be. Surely the dead are the lucky ones."

I gave Lady Sergison a distressed look, but said nothing. I couldn't argue with her logic as I was feeling very nearly the same thing. I was grieved by Gabriel's death, but more than that the guilt of my feelings for Dardanos were consuming me. I thought how easy it would have been if I had died instead of being in this wretched position: mourning a man that had so many secrets I'm not sure I really ever knew him, and being secretly in love with a man that seemed to be pulling me down a dark path that I was willingly following.

I spent the rest of the funeral with my head down, avoiding the searching looks of strangers. The few times I did look up I found suggestive smiles from would-be wooers and calculating squints from well-to-do matriarchs. I cringed at the thought of how many visits I would have to endure from many of these attendees, looking to gain my favor in order to improve their place in society. Even as they looked down their noses at my social standing they were most likely calculating how to tie their family to me, and gain the prestige of being linked to Cuckfield Park. I smiled to myself as I thought about how shocked they would all be when I announced my engagement to Dardanos.

Thinking about Dardanos made me suddenly realize I hadn't seen him yet. I searched the crowds while we walked behind the carriage to the cemetery, but there were just too many people to find one among them. I thought, perhaps, Dardanos would come forward before or after the church service to be with the family, but he never did.

I listened listlessly during the church service. The words held no comfort, of heaven and hell, of belief in the father and son, and of Gabriel's constancy of faith. What about his constancy of secrets? What had he hidden from me, from everyone? Was it so terrible his soul would be denied entry into heaven? My tears fell heavy with thoughts of my sweet Gabriel being punished for deeds I knew nothing about.

Once the service was over Lady Sergison took my arm, choosing to walk with me out to the graveyard instead of with her husband which was customary. I didn't protest, though I saw a momentary look of surprise on Lord Sergison's face. We followed the pallbearers down the marbled aisle, past the gothic arches and seemingly endless mass of commiserating faces, and then to the right under one of the large arches leading to the massive wooden doors. The sunlight stung my eyes as we emerged, making our way to the graveyard which dominated the property surrounding the church.

We stood rigidly, Lady Sergison and I, staring as they lowered Gabriel's coffin into the ground. "I shall never see him again," Lady Sergison whispered just barely loud enough to hear.

I started at such a comment and tried to reassure her, "Surely you will see him again...in heaven. I know he will be waiting patiently for you."

Lady Sergison looked up and gave me a weak smile. "I know he will be in heaven waiting, but only death can bring one to heaven. I shall not take that bargain."

I swallowed hard, frightened by her words, but I tried to convince myself she was merely overly distraught. We watched in silence as the burial ceremony was complete, and the gravediggers took their places to start shoveling dirt. It was over, and somehow I had made it through the most trying part of the day. I attended Lady Sergison back to her carriage. Lord Sergison traveled in another carriage with a group of men, no doubt to drink without the disapproving eyes of any women. Lady Sergison did not seem to care about his absence; she didn't seem to care for his presence over the past few days either for that matter. It made me worry for them, for their marriage, and it made me wonder about my feelings for Dardanos. Would we one day act so coldly to one another? Would I ever even see him again?

"Lady Sergison, did Mr. Samothrace not attend today?" I asked as we rode back to the house in the open Landau carriage.

"Oh, no, dear, he had urgent business out of town today, but he did pledge to be back tonight...hopefully for dinner," Lady Sergison said as she waved to passersby. "He is such a thoughtful man. You know he has been to the house every night to sit by Gabriel and me."

"What?!" I exclaimed a little too loud.

Lady Sergison seemed to falter a moment as if she hadn't meant to say that, but explained, "Oh, yes, every night. He's so busy during the days...you understand, managing his affairs overseas and looking into investments here, but every night without fail he came to sit with me for a bit."

That was strange. Why hadn't Dardanos said anything? And why was he coming only at night? Did he still feel too guilty to be near me? I felt a pang of disappointment to think that Dardanos had made up an excuse for not coming to the burial because he didn't feel he could be near me. I knew it would have been strange to be so close to him, and to have to pretend there was nothing between us, but I still wished he had been there.

Now that I had the hope of seeing Dardanos later that night I floated through the day in another world. I didn't even slip

179

into anger when Emma commented on how beautiful I looked in my dress. I think I might have actually smiled and thanked her. Mostly I was at Lady Sergison's side as she gushed about how indispensable I was and how lovely it was going to be to have a girl in the house. It was rather an easy day for me as all I had to do was look respectfully sad and smile and nod whenever anyone spoke to me.

The dinner was pleasant enough; people laughed and cried and told stories about what a wonderful young man Gabriel was. Dinner was served in the courtyard and I felt a surge of relief when I sat at the large table that I would not have to avert my eyes from the ceiling of the dining room where the painting of Apollo looked down on all. The guilt that the cold glare of that painting produced in me would surely have made me break down in front of everyone. For some reason thinking about the painting brought to mind the man with the swirling blue eyes that had been in the hedgerows with Emma. Perhaps it was just the feeling of being watched that reminded me of him, but as I considered both the painting and the man I was sure that the painting had the same strange eyes. Those beautiful, many-hued, fire opals that glared down in fearsome knowing.

I pushed the thought of the painting and the man from my mind and tried to focus on the people speaking around me. Thankfully I was seated between Lady Sergison and my mother so that I wouldn't be forced into any conversations with any fortune hunters...or their mothers. I think Lady Sergison knew the position I was now in, and sot to shield me at least on this day. It was as if she knew instinctively that I was dreading the mere idea of being courted. I wondered if it was because she believed my heart to be too full of sorrow for Gabriel, or did she guess that I was in love with someone else? I still worried that either my father or the Sergisons had a suspicion about my feelings for Dardanos; especially because Lady Sergison always seemed to be able to guess my thoughts. Thinking about Dardanos brought back my feelings of disappointment that he had still not appeared. I feared that he had only told Lady Sergison he would attend later in the day to appease her and avoid offending her.

As dinner drew to an end Lord Sergison invited the men to join him in the billiard room to smoke and Lady Sergison invited the ladies back to the parlor for after dinner drinks and entertainment. I didn't follow. I felt a knot in my stomach at having to face all those proper ladies that would surely spend the evening gossiping, and most likely about me when I was out of earshot. While everyone left the table, splitting into their respective groups, I swiped a nearly full bottle of Claret and one of the decorative candelabras off the table and headed to the hedgerows. It was less frightening to think that I might run into the man with the swirling blue eyes than to face the ladies in the parlor. I did make sure no one was following me or watching me, though, as I drew long, unladylike swigs from the bottle. It was quite difficult to manage, holding the three branched candelabra in one hand, holding the wine bottle with the other, and gulping the liquid down as I walked through the maze. I nearly lit my dress on fire twice, but I pressed on wanting nothing more than to plop in front of The Palladium and get drunk.

Just past the little cherub statue I could make out a low shadow, across from The Palladium. Another statue perhaps? My heart thudded, considering that the man with the swirling blue eyes had come back, and was waiting for me. I walked on, the tingle of wine emboldening me. Who was he anyway to keep me from my statue? I would confront him, and find out why he had met with my sister. I carefully raised the candelabra up higher as I approached to better see what was before me, and found myself beaming like a child.

"General!" I shouted happily, running the rest of the way.

Now I could see why I had thought it was a statue. He was sitting on a stone bench, and I was fairly certain it hadn't been there before. I sat beside him, a little nervously as I was also certain the gap in the hedge was just above our heads.

He turned to me, his brilliant blue eyes beaming happily as he proclaimed, "A thing of beauty is a joy for ever: / Its lovliness increases; it will never / Pass into nothingness; but still will keep / A bower quiet for us, and a sleep..."

"Full of sweet dreams, and..." I bit my lip, my mind feeling a bit muddled from the wine. "Oh, I've forgotten the rest. Keats, is it not?" I asked, taking another inelegant drink from my bottle.

Dardanos laughed lightly. "Yes, it is Keats, and I am not surprised that you have forgotten. Was that bottle full when you started your walk?"

I ignored his question, giving him a playful smirk.

"So...this bench wasn't here earlier. Any idea how it came to be here now?" I asked, gesturing for him to set the candelabra down for me. (The corset and tight bodice did not allow for such easy movements as bending down.)

"I stole it," Dardanos said proudly, "for you."

I turned to him with a smirk. "Hmmm, you stole it?"

He forced a laugh, admitting, "Okay, I borrowed it...from another part of the grounds. I thought you would be pleased to have a place to sit when you are visiting your Palladium."

"Thank you," I whispered seriously.

"You don't have to thank me, it was noth-" he began.

"I don't mean for the bench," I interjected, staring at him longingly, "Thank you for being here...right now...with me."

I could see the astonishment in his eyes as his lips curved into a warm smile. Whatever was happening around us I felt I needed him near. I wanted him and needed him in a way I'd never felt for anyone before. I plunged forward, into his lips, dropping the bottle of wine onto the ground. I pushed my body as close to his as I could with the fabric of my skirt and bustle getting in the way. His mouth was cool as I forced my own warm-with-wine lips and tongue into it. He seemed surprised at first but was soon pushing himself back at me. His hands encircled my neck, his thumbs caressing all the way down to my chest, as he pulled me into his ever more passionate kiss.

Suddenly he held me back, putting his forehead to mine. "There are still many people about. Someone may happen upon us."

I strained against him, and pleaded, "I don't care. I don't care if anyone sees. I don't care who knows about us. I want you...I want all of you."

Again he seemed surprised, but I could see his body pulsing with excitement. He gave no resistance when I pushed at his jacket, sliding his arms out obediently. I began unbuttoning his white dress shirt, but found my fingers too clumsy in their excitement to get more than two undone. Instead I fought helplessly to undo the back of my bodice. Dardanos pulled me to my feet without a word and moved the candelabra into the alcove next to The Palladium. He then turned me gently so that my back was facing him, and while kissing my neck and back he undid the bodice of my gown, pushing the dress down to the ground. I stepped out of the center of the gown and removed the petticoats and bustle that had been beneath myself as I watched Dardanos carefully lay the gown out on the grass. He pulled it wide as if setting out a blanket for a picnic.

I stood there anxiously waiting for him to help me out of my corset and undergarments. Now that I'd gone this far I was starting to rethink my decision of how far I wanted to go with him; maybe I wasn't ready, maybe he would think me a crude, base woman afterward. I wasn't sure what to do next; I really hadn't thought past the ache I'd felt while kissing him, and now I could do nothing but wait because I couldn't undo my corset myself.

"Come here, darling one," he cooed from his place on the ground.

I obeyed, nervously crawling to sit beside him on the pitiful black gown. Again, he turned me away from him in order to unlace the back of the corset. He removed it, tossing it aside, then slid my simple white linen chemise over my head, and finally he pushed me to lay back so that he could slide my knickerbockers off. He ran his hands along the sides of my body, all the way down to my knees, before he stood and removed his garments.

I gasped. I don't know from excitement or fear, but it was the first time I'd ever seen a man nude. It certainly wasn't unpleasant. Looking at his pale, muscular body in the flickering candlelight ignited the want deep inside of me, and I felt certain my body would burst into flame if I had to wait any longer to touch him. Dardanos seemed to know my very thoughts as his lips curved into a devious smile.

He lowered himself down onto the ground at my feet and as if teasing me, slowly crawled his way up, pausing every so often to lick at my body. I didn't know what to expect, but he slowly, very slowly wound his way up to my breasts. I fought desperately to pull him up to my lips, but he lingered, pulling at my nipples with his tongue, using his hands in such a way that I had to stifle a scream. When he finally gave up his fervent tongue lashings on my body he moved to my mouth.

"You are all I have ever wanted," he pledged in the night.

Suddenly the cold heat of him was in me. I thought I would lose my will to breathe at his first thrust, but then the breath came back to me in one swift intake. I pulled him in, even as I felt the dull pain of first contact. I didn't care. The pain was only a moment; the ecstasy was endless. I grasped the folds of the accursed gown below me, almost relieved that it was being soiled and used as a vessel for my awakening. As Dardanos poured in and out of me I could feel the soft silk and velvet rubbing against my bare skin. I wanted him to push against me violently, ruining the dyed gown, perhaps destroying it with our love-making. I felt the breaking point, the cliff of intolerance looming, and as I clutched at Dardanos fervently he fell upon my neck and the pain and the pleasure of that moment were beyond compare or description. Suddenly the last lines of the Keats poem he had recited came flashing into my mind: *An endless fountain of immortal drink, / Pouring unto us from the heaven's brink.*

❧17❧

"Sister, you should be careful. Isis is always watching," a woman's voice echoed ahead of me where I could just make out the dull flicker of a candle.

"Nenet?" I questioned, unable to see her face, but recognizing the voice as one of the other priestesses.

She walked closer to me, filling the chamber with a pale yellow light, and I could just make out the shadow of her face. She wore a stern look of disapproval on her face, but I could see that she was also satisfied that she had caught me. Her usually bright blue eyes glared menacingly, though I couldn't understand where her ill-feeling for me came from. When I'd first arrived at the temple she had been quick to become my friend, and had even helped me to understand my visions. Lately, though, she had become distant, almost jealous.

"Amunet, the goddess will punish you for breaking your vow. You must not go to the prince again," Nenet stated harshly.

I shook my head unable to understand where her anger was coming from. She had been almost as excited as I had been when Setepamun had appeared at the temple, and she had even distracted the head priestess many times to allow Setepamun and me to spend hours alone in the library undisturbed. More than that she had been my closet friend and confidant; we shared everything about ourselves. Setepamun and I had even entrusted her with our plans to find Hecate's curse and become gods once more. Nenet had been helping us in our search up until recently when she'd suddenly become angry at everything I said.

"Nenet, you know that I love him. You know that I have pledged myself to him…forever," I beseeched her.

"What of your pledge to the goddess? You swore to never allow a man to touch you," she said in disgust, moving the candle closer to my face. "You have broken your vow many times over and she will punish you. I can no longer be part of your ruination. I have a destiny just as great and I will no longer stand in your shadow." With that she stomped off, leaving me alone in the darkness.

       I woke the next morning in my bed not really sure how I'd gotten there. I felt a dull ache in my head and between my thighs. As I twisted beneath my covers I realized I was naked. I opened my eyes and lifted the covers to convince myself I wasn't still dreaming. I was indeed nude, and to add to that I could see a few spots of blood on my crisp white sheets. I rolled over with a groan and found, strangely enough, a few specks of blood on my pillow as well. Feeling light-headed I forced myself out of bed.

       I went over to my vanity to inspect the origin of the blood on my pillow. I turned my face from side to side searching for a scratch or cut, perhaps some dried blood, but I discovered the blood was not from my face. On the left side of my throat were two small wounds, a scab of dried blood formed over both. My heart began pounding and my skin turned to ice. The marks looked like the same described to have been on both Mrs. Gibson and Gabriel. What could it mean?

       Suddenly a knock came at the door and before I could think it through I called out, "Come in!"

       As soon as the words escaped my lips I realized my error. I was sitting at my vanity completely naked with strange bloody marks on my neck. Sallie entered quickly, closing the door immediately behind her as if she were hiding from someone. She was carrying my black gown from the wash in her arms; probably rushing to return it as she knew I had no other black gown...save the one I'd defiled the night before. That thought made me scan the room hastily to see if I'd left the gown laying out where she'd see it, but I could see no trace of it. My head was so foggy; I couldn't even remember returning to my room let alone where I had put the wretched dress.

       "Lizzy!" Sallie exclaimed, and I waited for her to question my nudity, but instead she asked, "Are you all right? You look very ill."

       I turned back to the vanity and noticed I did look a bit paler than usual and my eyes were red and swollen. "I don't know," I confessed, "I feel a little weak this morning. I probably drank too much last night, and I didn't get much sleep."

       Sallie tossed the gown in a heap on the bed and fetched

my robe for me. As I put the robe on Sallie caught me by the shoulder and pushed my face to the side roughly.

"You've been marked," she declared ominously.

I shook my head desperately and sputtered, "I must have caught myself on a thorn or a branch as I walked in the garden last evening. I haven't been sleeping well and find an evening walk to be soothing."

"Lizzy, excuse me, but you did more than walk last evening," Sallie said flatly, lifting the gown from the bed. I could now see it was the gown Dardanos and I made love on the night before. "This was found in the hedgerows by the gardener, along with some of your under garments. Don't worry," she insisted, seeing the wide-eyed concern on my face, "I made up a story about dropping it as I took it to the wash, and I rushed it back here before anyone else could ask about it." She paused again, gulping nervously. "Lizzy, whatever man you met in the garden...I beg you...never see him again."

I was surprised by not only Sallie's loyalty but also her genuine concern for my reputation and safety. We had become fast friends since my arrival, but that friendship had only been a few days in length...and she was still a maid and I her mistress. I looked at her more like a friend or sister than a maid; in truth she was closer to me than my own sister lately. I wanted to tell her everything, but something made me hold back the complete truth.

I told her sadly, "You don't understand. I'm in love with this man. We plan to marry...after a respectful time has passed, of course."

As I spoke Sallie's eyes grew larger and larger, and she cried, "No, Lizzy, you mustn't! He's a demon! Only a demon leaves a mark like that!" She pointed to my neck.

I forced a laugh, though I was frightened by the mark myself. "Don't be silly. It was just a result of excited passion."

Sallie was shaking her head earnestly. "No, as I live and breathe; it's true. There's strange stories going about, Lizzy. You might not have heard the stories as they weren't about fine folk like your family and the Sergisons. There's been sightings of beasts pretending to be men, with unnaturally glowing eyes-"

"That's just nonsense," I cut in defensively, remembering the man in the garden with the swirling blue eye that had been illuminated though there hadn't been any light. "It's all just superstitious nonsense."

"That isn't all. They say there's men who hate the light, they only walk about at night. Only a demon would hate the light of day. Then there's the unexplainable deaths with marks like those on your neck. Lizzy, there've been at least a dozen deaths. They were mostly poor, depraved people, but they were all the same: marks on their necks and blood drained. It isn't your fault, Lizzy, I don't blame you. They're said to be devilishly cunning and charming. They have a kind of power to bewitch their victims."

"Who?" I asked, feeling the hairs prickle on my arms at Sallie's words.

"Vampires," she stated firmly, a look of terror on her face. "If it was a vampire seduced you, I beg you, you must never see him again." Then she dropped her voice to a whisper, "he'll steal your soul."

I wanted to laugh at her again, but I felt a strange foreboding. It wasn't possible; vampires didn't exist except in stories, but there had been rumors. My mother had overheard a lady at tea make mention of vampires, my sister seemed to have hinted at the possibility at dinner, my father and Lord Sergison had been suspiciously shocked when my mother had said the word vampire, and even Lady Sergison seemed to think that the marks on Mrs. Gibson's and Gabriel's necks were a significant clue to their deaths. Even though I had laughed at Sallie for being superstitious I had heard whispers among the servants of similar fears. I had heard them discuss the bizarre deaths, terror in their voices that some demon was hunting down poor folk like pheasant for the dinner table. There was even a saying I heard repeated several times a day by various servants: Demon eyes glowing in the night, death follows with stinging bite. Was this the curse from my visions? Was Dardanos a...No, I couldn't even consider it. It was too ridiculous to even imagine Dardanos was a vampire. Vampires weren't real, and even if they were they were hideous, demon-like creatures, not handsome, romantic gentlemen. They were evil...not considerate and gentle, and most telling they were unable to walk in daylight. I'd seen Dardanos during daylight hours many times....well, a few times at least. No...wait. I hadn't. Every time I'd ever seen him had been after the sun had set. I hadn't seen him once during the light of day.

"Damn!" I cursed to myself. "Sallie, you've actually got

me considering the possibility of such an absurd idea."

"I'm sure if you think on it you will discover clues that will hint at what I have been saying," Sallie pleaded. "I'm only worried about your safety. I would never forgive myself if I hadn't at least tried to help you...especially when I have the ability to do so."

I looked at her curiously and she seemed to drop her eyes as if she had not meant to say the last. "He is not a vampire, Sallie, I promise you."

"If you say so, Lizzy, but the signs are everywhere," she insisted, "the warning at the séance, the strange deaths, the peculiar men spotted about the village, even the cryptic flowers Lady Sergison has been choosing, and not to mention that broach."

"The broach?" I questioned incredulously.

Sallie grasped my shoulders. "I can't explain how I know, but I've heard of such symbols before. They are connected to vampires. Coincidentally when someone sees such a symbol or is given a token such as you have they are marked to be damned."

"Damned, because of a broach," I stated sarcastically, shaking my head.

"I don't know why, but the symbol of the serpent entwining the moon has been found among vampires. The very meaning of it, eternal death, is what a vampire is," Sallie argued.

I forced a laugh. "Sallie, if that were true then why hasn't Lady Sergison been turned into a vampire. She told me herself it was given to her long ago when her mother died."

"Then she is marked as well. Just because it hasn't happened yet doesn't mean it won't happen. Please, Lizzy, at least consider what I'm saying. I will do my best to protect you, but you must also be wary," Sallie pleaded.

I didn't want to agree with her, but I was nervously contemplating the facts when a knock came at the door. Sallie opened the door only enough to speak to the person on the other side; she explained that I was getting dressed. The door was pushed open and Emma forced her way in, past Sallie, knocking her back a few steps.

Emma's face was awash in tears as she glared at me. "You're not dressed?!"

I shot a look at Sallie, nodding to the armoire where my gowns were. "I was waiting for my mourning dress, but it seems the wash was never gotten to yesterday. Sallie, there should be a dark blue gown, that will have to do."

I could see Emma staring at my neck, a look of disgust on her face. "What are those marks on your neck?"

I put my hand defensively over the marks, shielding them from further scrutiny. "I...I...must have scratched it walking in the garden yesterday," I tried lying again.

Emma stomped over to me angrily and yanked my hand away. She examined the marks closely and then roughly grabbed my chin, turning my face side to side as she stared into my eyes. Without a word she threw back the curtains covering the window and forcefully grabbed my hand, yanking me toward the window. Sallie stared, bewildered, but when our eyes met I could see we had the same thought: Emma thought I'd been bitten by a vampire as well.

I shook her off, and pretended I had no idea what she was doing. "What is wrong with you?! Are you mad?! How dare you treat me so violently with no provocation and no explanation. I don't think your friend from the hedgerows would be happy to find out how you've treated me. I'm not supposed to get hurt, right? Or the deal is off?" I hadn't meant to reveal what I knew to her, but I was so angry it just seemed to explode from my mouth on its own.

Emma's face seemed to pale and she looked from me to Sallie before calmly stating, "We need to talk. There are things I must tell you. Meet me at The Palladium."

After she left I let out a loud sigh of relief. My head was now pounding in pain, no doubt from the copious amount of wine I had drunk the night before and an insufficient amount of sleep. I pushed my hand into my forehead to dull the pain as I motioned for Sallie to fetch my undergarments. Sallie didn't make any comment about what had just happened, but silently helped me dress. I was put at ease to find that the dress I had told Sallie to fetch from the armoire had a high collar and would completely hide the marks on my neck. I didn't want anyone else accusing me of being bitten by a vampire.

As Sallie was putting my hair up in a simple chignon she said quietly, "Remember, Lizzy, she is your sister. She's probably just worried about you."

"I wish it was that simple, Sallie, unfortunately the only person Emma is worried about is Emma," I commented tersely.

I went to The Palladium as soon as I was dressed. Emma was already waiting there, sitting on the stone bench Dardanos had relocated there for me. I walked up cautiously, but Emma seemed to be completely calm. She watched me approach with an unreadable look on her face. I wondered if she knew what happened here between Dardanos and me. Maybe she was worried about me, and merely wanted to warn me against behaving so imprudently. Still, I felt I was meeting a rival, perhaps not quite an enemy, but someone I needed to be wary of. I sat down beside her, refusing to be the first to speak.

Looking straight ahead she said simply, "What you heard the other night...I am trying to protect you. I've been pulled into something dangerous," she paused and turned to me, fixing me with her flooded eyes, "because of you."

"Me?!" I exclaimed in disbelief. "How could you blame me for something that is obviously a result of your improper behavior and frequent disappearing acts?"

Emma scowled at me before she answered calmly, "I was searching for answers to something, and what I found was that, once again, everything has to do with you."

"You mean Edward's death?" I remembered Emma admitting that she'd searched for answers to what had happened to Gabriel's elder brother. "You didn't believe the story they told either; that it was a robbery gone wrong? How could any of that be my fault? Even if there was a cover up involving Edward?"

"How did you know about-" she started, a look of surprise on her face. "Yes, when I found out I had been originally intended for Gabriel, not you, and before that I had been intended for Edward, I was inconsolable. I realized that fate had somehow twisted my life around and taken my only chance at happiness...and then gave it to you. If Edward had lived I would have married him, I would be mistress of Cuckfield Park, and you would owe any happy prospects in your life to me. I had this inexplicable desire to find out why my life had been ruined; why my future was stolen from me, and perhaps gain some kind of satisfaction in discovering what no one was able to." Again she paused to glare at me. "You just had to be so important, didn't you? You brought them here, they came because of you, and my fate was ruined as a result."

"I don't understand what you mean," I countered,

confused about what she was accusing me of.

"They came here trying to find you, but what they found instead was that your family was tied to a family of killers...vampire killers," she stated matter-of-factly.

There it was again, that word: vampire. "What are you saying? That somehow I attracted vampires here and they killed Edward?" I wanted to laugh in her face for not only suggesting vampires killed Edward but also for blaming me for his death. I wanted to laugh, but the hard look she gave me chilled me into silence.

"Vampires didn't kill Edward," Emma muttered contemptuously, "they made him an offer...an offer of immortality, and he accepted it. He was willing to join forces with a vampire to achieve the same goal; namely to destroy every vampire on earth."

"But, then...Edward is alive?" I asked hesitantly.

"You really are quite blind to what goes on around you," Emma reprimanded as if I were a witless child that didn't know any better. "Edward accepted The Immortal Fate, he became a vampire, but when your father is a vampire hunter that really is not the wisest choice."

"What are you saying? You don't mean...Lord Sergison..." I couldn't bring myself to say it. "He wouldn't...Emma, that is impossible. Lord Sergison loved Edward he could never have done such a thing."

Emma rolled her eyes to heaven and sneered, "The world is full of terrible things, wondrously terrible things...and they've come here to seek you out. In the meantime Edward was killed, Mrs. Gibson was killed, dear Gabriel was killed, and who knows how many nameless others; all because they got in the way of some plan involving you."

"Emma," I attempted softly, "what happened to Edward, truly?"

"Edward was beheaded...by Lord Sergi-"

"Emma!" I shouted reproachfully.

"If you want to hear the truth you mustn't always expect a happy ending. Lord Sergison and our very own father track down vampires and kill them. It is their important work which they are so keen for you to take over. It is the oath they have taken to rid this earth of vampires, and when Lord Sergison's eldest son allowed himself to be turned he was just another monster to be hunted."

I stared at her in horror, tears welling up in my eyes. It was such a fantastical story all reason told me it had to be a lie, a fabrication concocted by Emma to absolve herself of whatever wrong she'd done during her months of depravity. Unfortunately something deep inside of me believed it; deep down my soul was screaming, *this is it, this is the curse!* I jumped up and strode to The Palladium to rest my shaking hand onto her calming head. I started piecing together Emma's behavior and involvement thus far in everything that had happened, added to what I'd overheard the other night between her and the mysterious stranger.

I turned back to her abruptly and stated accusingly, "That's what you want, isn't it? The deal you made. You've been searching for a vampire to give you immortality."

Emma straightened, giving me an imperious look. "Yes, it is what I've been seeking. At first I had only sought to find the truth behind Edward's death, the man I was supposed to have married, but then I found strange stories. When I finally discovered what had happened to Edward I realized how silly my obsession had been; my pining for a man in love with my sister and then pining for the dead man I had been promised to. It all seemed so trivial when the prospect of living forever and all the power that comes along with it was out there just waiting to be discovered." She smiled somewhat manically to herself. "I did things that I shouldn't have, things that would take the breath from you if I spoke them aloud. I put myself into many dangerous situations with many unsavory people just for a whisper of how to find the path to my new obsession. Then he found me."

"Who?" I asked anxiously.

"The man you heard me with the other night. My inquiries had reached his ears and surprise of surprises he was very willing to make me an offer when he discovered I was your sister." There was that glaring look again.

"But why does he care about me? I don't even know who this man is," I argued, shaking my head.

"It isn't him that cares about you, it's his master, the one that turned him. It's him I've agreed to help in exchange for The Immortal Fate."

My heart pounded, recognizing the words The Immortal Fate from my vision, as I asked in a low whisper, "Who is his master? Who have you made a deal with?"

Emma's gaze softened, but she didn't answer my question. "All I have to do is watch out for you, keep you safe, and when the time comes explain everything to you so you will understand what must be done."

I turned away, hugging my arms to myself. "What do I need protection from?"

"There is another," Emma explained calmly, "another vampire. He is very-"

"Yes, yes, I heard this the other night," I interrupted, "the man you were with warned you."

"Lizzy, this powerful vampire," she confessed, sounding defeated, "he probably killed Gabriel."

"What?" the word barely escaped my lips as they trembled.

"Gabriel knew there was a vampire in town, that was why he left the night of your engagement," Emma said almost as if consoling me, "he was hunting this vampire, but he didn't discover him until a few nights later. There was nothing Gabriel could have done, this vampire is strong enough to kill other vampires. I was angry with you because I was told this vampire was here for you, but I knew that wasn't fair. I've been blaming you for so many things, but deep down I know none of it was within your control. It's just so hard to control my emotions when people we love are being killed...and Mother and Father..." she broke into sobs.

I dropped my hands, feeling everything in my body growing heavy with dread. "Emma," I pleaded in disbelief, "what about Mother and Father?"

She turned her blue eyes, now overflowing with tears, up to me. "They've been murdered. Marks on their necks, blood...gone." Suddenly she stood and pointed behind me and said simply, "The Palladium should never have been moved."

It would have hurt less if she had slapped me in the face; as it was I felt I'd been socked in the gut. I doubled over, clutching my middle as Emma stumbled away weeping. I tried to tell myself she was lying, just trying to hurt me, but I had seen the truth in her eyes. Not only that, but the way she had said it, not accusingly, but as if defeated, and none of her usual jealousy or malice. I needed to know how to stop this, how to get some kind of justice for my parents...for Gabriel. I thought about making my own deal.

"Who is this master you spoke of?! Who have you made a deal with?! What is his name?!" I demanded as Emma drew farther and farther away. "Emma, I must know! He must help us! I must speak to him! Who is the vampire you've made a deal with?!"

She turned back and shouted smugly, "Your very own beloved, Dardanos!"

❧18☙

I shut myself up in my room, the door locked against everyone. Lord and Lady Sergison both attempted to speak to me through the door, but I ignored their requests to let them in. Sallie knocked lightly at the door several times, pleading with me to give up my dark lover, and making me feel as if perhaps Emma had been right all along; maybe everything was my fault. So many had been murdered...and now my own parents, and I didn't even know why. Even Emma knocked at the door late in the day, sniffling loudly as she begged me to forgive her as I was all she had left. I wasn't even sure if I believed her; her recent behavior made me question if I ever really knew her for who she really was.

I despised myself that day. Why couldn't I have been like everyone else? Why didn't I spend more time worrying about fashions and hairstyles, gossiping at teas about who will marry who and the scandalous behavior of that one or the atrocious wardrobe of this one? If I had behaved like a proper lady perhaps Gabriel wouldn't have been interested in me, perhaps he would have married Emma as was planned. If I had at least behaved as was expected perhaps Gabriel wouldn't have hesitated for so long in asking for my hand; perhaps we would already have been married and he wouldn't be...But then if Emma was telling the truth Gabriel was a vampire hunter and along with being in constant peril, eventually Dardanos would have sought him out to aid him in his plans as he had sought out Edward.

My head hurt trying to connect the pieces of how fate had led to this moment. Dardanos had sought out the Sergisons because they were vampire hunters and he wanted to join forces with them to rid the world of vampires. While negotiating this plan of action with Edward it was somehow discovered that I, the reincarnation of both Cassandra and Amunet, was connected to the Sergisons. After Edward was supposedly killed by Lord Sergison Dardanos had to change his plans and find a new way of getting close to the Sergisons. In the meantime an ancient, all-too-powerful vampire was killing the people around me either because of my connection with Dardanos or because of who I was in the past. It still didn't make sense, and on top of all of that if I was to believe any of it then I would have to accept one intrinsic fact that I didn't want to. That vampires were real. That blood-sucking demons roamed the earth in the guise of humans. That Dardanos was...a vampire.

I drifted off to sleep with that thought on my mind and the words Amunet had said to Dardanos in my dream: *If it means being with you I would face an eternity cursed.*

"Amunet?" an accusing voice rang out behind me.

I turned, surprised by the cruelty in the voice. The man was standing near the opening of the room, sheathed in shadows. I put the scroll down that I had been transcribing and blinked the weariness out of my eyes to better see this stranger that seemed to not only know about me but was angry with me.

"I am Amunet," I announced flatly, pretending not to have noticed the angry tone, "who may I ask are you?"

The man stepped further into the room, allowing the candlelight to fall over his face. I gasped loudly and rose from my seat as I recognized the face.

The man smiled, seeing my reaction. "You know who I am I take it?"

I moved around to the other side of the table as I answered cautiously, "I know who you used to be."

"What?" the man asked in confusion, looking at me from beneath scrunched eyebrows. "Who is it that you think I am?"

I was hesitant to answer, but I couldn't lie, especially in the temple with the goddess watching me. "I have had visions of you. You were once the great sun god Apollo. You were also responsible for events which led to my death."

He stepped closer, the candlelight catching his startling blue eyes as he studied me. "How curious...you really do believe this nonsense about my brother having been a god in his past life?"

"How do you know..." I started to ask and then realized what he'd said. "Your brother?" I now noticed he was dressed in the lightweight linen of the upper class and wore gold jewelry on his hands and around his neck.

"Yes, I am Sethos" he said, smirking as he took a seat at the table as if he planned an extended visit. "I understand my brother has been here often, searching for answers. Now I see that his enthusiasm for the temple was not misplaced, "he stated, looking me up and down, "although I believe his search to be fruitless and unnecessary. I have come to find out what you have been telling him to keep him from his duties as prince, future ruler of Egypt."

I forced myself to sit down across from him, even as memories of the fear his face had produced in my visions threatened to overtake me. Sethos wasn't unpleasant to look at; it was quite the opposite; he was resplendent. He still held the unearthly beauty of Apollo in his features but his hair was no longer golden; it was black like his brothers. I wondered about his blue eyes, so strangely vibrant like his brothers, though not the same hue. Blue-eyed Egyptians were unheard of, even among the royals, but I reasoned that it must have had something to do with the remnants of their godly souls revealing themselves.

I finally tore my gaze from his disturbingly bright eyes and broke the uncomfortable silence. "Setepamun found me. Our fate brought us to each other. We have both experienced visions of the same events from the past and I believe it was no accident that we would find each other...again."

Sethos looked down as I spoke as if he found it uncomfortable to look at me. "Have you any proof that anything you have seen is true?"

"What would be sufficient proof?" I asked rhetorically. "I had visions which led me to this temple. I was not a priestess; I simply woke up one day and begged that my father send me here. I then had visions of your brother, though I had no idea that he was the prince, and then he arrived at this very temple, led by some inexplicable force to find proof that he was linked to the gods." I stopped, leaning down so that his eyes would meet mine. "I have even had visions of you."

"Me?" Sethos asked, the anger in his eyes fading to curiosity. "What have you seen?"

I gulped uncomfortably, not wanting to accuse him of Apollo's crimes, but if it would convince him that Setepamun and I were telling the truth then I had to try. "I have only seen glimpses of you from the past...your power, your cruelty, your obsession."

He seemed to soften his gaze even more as he realized, "You are afraid of me. Whatever you have seen, whomever you think I was in the past, I would not hurt you. I know that I came here with anger in my heart, but it was only because I feel I am losing my family. First I lost my father to some strange illness, then my mother seemed to contract the same illness that killed my father. She seems to not get worse, but she has not fully recovered either and it has been ten years. I fear she will not be long in this world and the fate of Egypt lies with my brother, but he has pulled away from me and his responsibilities."

I felt sorry for him; he seemed on the verge of tears. "I assure you your brother still has Egypt's future in mind. That is why our research is so important."

Sethos shook his head at a loss. "What is it that he thinks he will accomplish?"

I opened my mouth to answer, but hesitated a moment to think how best to explain. "I am not sure you can believe, you have not seen the visions, followed the path where fate has led, but I will try to explain for your brother's sake."

Suddenly Sethos reached across the table and pleaded, "Please, explain it to me. I need to know what has happened to my brother. You will help me, will you not?"

I nodded, touched by his concern for his brother. "I am sure you already know that your brother's search was to find an ancestral link between your family, the royal family, and the gods; that is what led him here. We have since pieced together our combined visions and researched the stories of the old gods and we have come to realize that Setepamun is not related to the gods; he actually was a god. His soul must have remembered and that is why he felt compelled to go on his quest. Our research has led us to believe that there was a great war among the gods, but there was nothing that we could find that specified who remained and who was destroyed. We believe most of the gods were incarnated as mortals, like yourself, and do not know what they once were.

"I did find a document which told the story of your brother's past life. He was a god named Dardanos and he was cursed by the sun god Apollo to walk the night, and should he step into the sunlight it would consume him. The document went on to explain a deal that Dardanos made with the goddess

Hecate. Dardanos wanted revenge on those that had caused the death of his beloved, Hecate's daughter Cassandra. I never got the chance to finish reading the story as the scroll disappeared the following morning, but we believe whatever power Hecate granted Dardanos is still being used. We believe this power can be passed from individual to individual...and it may be the key to making a man back into a god. Setepamun thinks your mother may have been given this power and is experiencing the transformation into a goddess. Setepamun wishes to become a god once more, restoring prosperity and order to Egypt, and then...recreating the world into one which will fear and love him. He wishes to restore the old ways, when people relied on the gods to watch over them, when people prayed to the gods for help, when people committed no crime for fear of punishment by the gods. He wants the world to be a beautiful paradise once more that can be enjoyed by all peoples without fear of one of their own hurting them."

Sethos's mouth hung open in shock and it took a moment before he responded, "That is not possible." He grabbed me roughly by the shoulders, forcing me to look into his brilliant, swirling blue eyes. "You must forget such things...about gods and monsters. Do you not see he has tricked you with his madness?"

I felt the glare of Apollo on me as Sethos stared intensely into my face, and I argued, "No, it is not madness. I had the visions before I even met your brother. We are linked, he and I."

"No!" He shouted, shaking me as if he could convince me in that way. "He is poison to you...poison to Egypt. I am here...I see what you could be. Your glory could resound through the ages."

I was trembling with the memory of his face from my visions. "What do you mean what I could be?" I asked hesitantly.

"You could be a queen," he whispered, his lips nearly grazing mine. "I could make you a queen."

"Setepamun does not wish to merely be king of Egypt," I responded boldly.

"And he never will be," Sethos answered coldly. "I have seen to that. I have saved you from his madness. I shall be king." Then he seemed to soften as he ran his fingers through my hair. "I want you by my side. I cannot explain it, but since I first saw you at the palace with my brother my heart has ached for you. I

200

cannot think of anything but you. Your face haunts me even
while I am awake. You understand, do you not? I want you more
than I desire to be king. There is an ache inside of me that can
only be suppressed by your love. I need you by my side."

I couldn't control the beating of my heart, but I was sure I
could see the cruel sheen of Apollo's greed in his eyes as I
countered, "No, Setepamun is my love. I would never betray
him. I have sworn myself to him. I will help him become the god
he once was."

Sethos seemed to falter, confused by my words and
started to stumble numbly toward the door as he grumbled, "I
will have you, or no one will. My brother is no god...and he
never will be. I have made certain of that."

"You should not speak of things you know not of,
Sethos," the voice was Setepamun.

My eyes shot to the open doorway, a chill running down
my back. Sethos froze in his tracks and stared in horror. I rose
from the table and slowly walked closer, feeling an indescribable
power emanating from Setepamun. His hair had a strange glint in
the candlelight, like smooth obsidian cascading over his
shoulders. Then his eyes shifted to me and I felt held in place.
No longer were his eyes the soft blue of a cloudless sky; they
were the clouds themselves. His eyes were so bright, the blue
was almost lost to them, but they weren't exactly white either.
They were cold, if cold were a color.

He'd done it. I knew, staring at his luminous features, he
had found Hecate's gift. I wanted to run to him, to embrace him,
but the stance his brother had taken and the glare he returned to
him gave me pause. I looked from one to the other, wondering if
I should say something to break the silence.

Sethos finally spoke, a threat in his voice, "What have
you done?"

Setepamun smiled cruelly, moving around his brother to
stand between us. "That is comical, little brother, when it was
you that drove a dagger through my chest."

I gasped and threw my hand on Setepamun's shoulder,
trying to turn him toward me. He simply raised his hand and
gave me a loving look as if to say he was fine.

Sethos took a step toward the door, pointing accusingly,
"You must be stopped. A man cannot become a god! You will
damn us all to punishment in the underworld!"

Faster than my eyes could follow Setepamun moved to where his brother stood and lifted him off of his feet by his throat. "You are wrong, brother. A man can become a god...and this man did," he sneered.

I walked to his side to better see his face, and was startled to see fierce fangs protruding from his snarling mouth. Setepamun saw me out of the corner of his eye and turned. When he saw the frightened alarm on my face he let go of Sethos, letting him drop to the floor. He looked at me, uncertainty in his eyes.

Sethos scrambled to his feet and backed up to the doorway as he shouted, "I will destroy you! I will find a way, Setepamun, and I will destroy you!"

Setepamun made no move to stop his brother, but simply said, "I am no longer Setepamun. I am Dardanos, the god reborn."

My eyes opened to complete darkness. It took me a moment of struggling to open my already open eyes to realize that I was awake and it was only night that prevented me from seeing anything. I had fallen asleep without lighting a candle. The result was a completely blinding darkness which made the transition from my dream world to the real world even more confusing. I fumbled among the contents of my bedside table for a few moments before I was able to feel the matchbox and candlestick, and then a few more moments before I was able to get the candle lit.

"Elizabeth, be still," a voice commanded from the shadows.

I grasped the candle and wheeled around in fear. If I hadn't just woken from a disorienting dream I might have screamed, but I was still slow to recover my senses. I stuck the candle out in front of me, searching the dark corners of the room, and discovered Dardanos sitting like a statue in a chair facing my bed.

"General...how long have you been sitting there?" I queried nervously.

He shifted, fixing those frozen eyes on me. "Not long. I did not want to wake you. You seemed to be dreaming and I thought it might be something important for you to see."

The dream came back to me, Emma's story came back to me, and I backed up a few paces. "I have heard strange things," I said shakily.

"Elizabeth, I can explain everything," Dardanos entreated softly.

"You're a vampire," I accused, my heart beating fiercely, backing away further.

The candlelight was now too far to see the features of his face, but he sighed loudly as if he had been afraid I would react this way. I didn't move; I didn't know what to do. I had wanted so much to have him near, to have his arms around me, but now that he was here I was scared. I feared that my visions had been right, I feared that Emma had told the truth, I feared that I was desperately in love with a vampire.

"Elizabeth," he began, rising slowly from the chair.

"Please," I whispered, holding my hand up to stop him, "I don't know if I want to rush into your arms...or scream in terror."

"Do not fear me," he said gently, and faster than my eyes could follow he moved across the room and caught me in his arms. "I love you; I would never hurt you."

Our lips were only inches from one another as I protested, "You're a monster."

His eyes looked at me pleadingly before he covered my mouth with his. I couldn't have moved even if I had wanted to, but at that moment I enjoyed the press of his lips and tongue against mine. I tried to push the thoughts away of why his skin felt cold as death or that a misplaced tongue might catch the point of his fangs. When he slid his hand along my neck I flinched, and he seemed to pull away guiltily.

"My parents are dead," I told him flatly.

He had his fist pressed to his lips before answering, "I know." He shook his head sadly. "I unwittingly led a deadly creature straight to you. It is my fault. I may not have drained them, but I am to blame for bringing the demon to this village. I should have been more careful. I should have made sure he was not following me. My need to be near you has made me careless, and you have had to pay the price. I am sorry."

I started to reach out to him, to reassure him that I didn't blame him for my parents' deaths, but I withdrew as my mind repeated the word: *vampire*. It was the same story Emma had told me: a powerful creature following Dardanos, drawn to me, had killed our parents and maybe even Mrs. Gibson and Gabriel. I stared at him hard, trying to decide if I truly believed what he was saying.

"I have something for you," Dardanos finally broke the silence, "a birthday present."

"Birthday?" I inquired confused, and then putting my hand to my head muttered, "I didn't even realize...It was completely out of my head. There's been too much death to think of such things."

I looked back at Dardanos to see him anxiously clutching a small box. My eyes shifted to his, searching his face for signs of his true feelings. Even with this unimaginable turn of events, Dardanos being a vampire, I still couldn't deny the pull he had over me. If he asked it of me I would probably have run away with him and left everything behind, but something inside warned me to be cautious.

Before Dardanos was able to offer me the little box in his hands I needed to assuage my uneasiness. "Did you have anything to do with Gabriel's death?" *I had had strange thoughts swirling through my head ever since I had considered that Dardanos might actually be a vampire, and those thoughts had whispered terrible things in my ear.*

Dardanos winced as if it pained him that I should ask such a question, and he shook his head sadly. "No...no I was not responsible for his death. The creature I spoke of...he attacked Gabriel. It could be argued that I was not entirely blameless as I led the creature right to the Sergisons, but it was not by my hand that he was killed."

"But why?! Why does this creature care about the Sergisons, or my parents, or me? Why would he go after Mrs. Gibson? Who is he?" I rattled off, nearly hysterical.

Dardanos gave me a pitiful look as he answered, "Sadly he only seeks vengeance on me. He knows who I am, or more accurately who I was. Unfortunately when I was a god I did something to anger him and he has sought me out ever since, trying to destroy me before I find a way to regain all of my past powers. He also knows of my connection to you and my need to have you by my side."

"So, what are you saying? Is he like you? He was a god and now he's a vampire?" I asked disbelievingly.

"He..." Dardanos pursed his lips as if he didn't want to

answer, but went on, "in all actuality...he still is a god."

"What?!" I asked in horror. "That is not possible." *How many times had I said that in the past week?*

Dardanos looked away as he explained, "He has not retained all of his godly powers; most had been stripped away before he was turned into a vampire, but his soul was never split from his body...as mine was...and yours, of course, more than once. He was a god that was punished; his powers were either diminished or completely taken, and he was forced to suffer for all eternity by having his liver torn out daily. I took pity on him. In my past life, after becoming the first vampire, I gave him The Immortal Fate, making him a vampire as well. In exchange for setting him free and giving him back some godly powers he agreed to help me in my revenge for Cassandra's death."

"Then why does he wish to destroy you? Shouldn't he be grateful for what you did for him?"

Still looking away Dardanos said simply, "I believe it is part of the reason he despises me; he blames me for the monster he has become, but more than that I cannot guess why he hates me so. There must have been something else that happened between us that I have never seen in a vision."

"Who is he?" I asked quietly.

"He was known as Prometheus," Dardanos answered.

"The giver of fire?" I asked in surprise.

"Yes, he was a great advocate for humanity, but he never liked taking sides among the gods and he was ultimately punished for it."

I raised my eyes upward wondering, "Was there truly a war?" I lowered my eyes to face Dardanos. "Did the gods destroy each other?"

"Yes," he said, pain etched on his face. "Sides were taken and the gods battled one another to the death. That was how my godly life ended, in battle, but not before I took Apollo's life. There were a small few that did not take sides, Prometheus among them. The ones that did not fight soon disappeared among the humans; their powers weakening over time until all they had left was their immortality. There are probably a few still out there somewhere, living like humans, keeping their heads down for fear of being discovered. Zeus was the only god that could not be destroyed. After the war he withdrew to Olympus, what you call heaven, surrounded only by the lesser immortals that are bound to that place. He stopped meddling in human affairs, watching instead, and allowing the lesser immortals short visits to Earth...but only by his permission."

"Why didn't Prometheus lose all of his powers then?" I countered.

Dardanos shook his head at a loss. "I do not know. The things I have learned were either through visions or what I gathered from humans that had come into contact with one of the immortals. Maybe he is something different because of the curse that is passed along in the blood. Maybe Zeus felt guilty for punishing Prometheus and so allowed him to retain certain powers. I do not know. All I do know is the cursed blood is the only path to attaining my place among the gods again...but I need you by my side." He fumbled with the box, opening it and turning it toward me. "You are part of me. I cannot go on without you."

I bent closer, shaking nervously at what I could see was a ring. A strange grayish-black ring in a silver filigree setting. It was hauntingly beautiful, but it made me think how everything in my life was turning dark, covered in shadows. I turned my gaze up to Dardanos, searching for the underlying reason for the ring.

"Marry me," he entreated, seeing the puzzled look on my face, "be mine, and I will be yours...forever."

"I...I..." I stuttered caught off-guard by the request. "I want to say yes, but...I fear it is too soon to make such plans. So much has happened in the last few weeks."

He smiled understandingly. "Of course," he said, removing the ring from the box and putting it on my right hand, "you need not give me an answer now. It was insensitive of me to ask it of you."

"Perhaps you should keep the ring until I give you an answer," I muttered, admiring the ring on my hand.

"No," he answered, laying his hand over mine, "it is my gift to you, for your birthday, with or without your answer. Do you like it? I heard that moonstone was your favorite."

"It's moonstone?" I asked in surprise, studying the ring more closely.

"Yes," he cleared his throat uncomfortably, "it is black moonstone. I thought you might already have a white moonstone ring."

I didn't comment, but it was obvious he knew Gabriel had

given me moonstone when he'd asked for my hand. Although I had worn the ring Gabriel had given me the past few days of mourning and the day of the funeral I hadn't worn it since I had given myself to Dardanos; it hadn't seemed right to continue wearing the symbol of our relationship when I was in love with another. Dardanos had been very careful not to bring Gabriel up, not to compare the ring he gave me to the one Gabriel had given me. Perhaps he worried my answer would be hampered by guilt, and it was...partly. It was also because I hadn't quite worked out how I would tell the Sergisons. They were now my official guardians according to the paperwork I had signed just days before, and I would need their permission to marry.

I wondered if Lord Sergison knew Dardanos was a vampire or if we would be able to keep it from him should we marry. I wondered if Lord Sergison was actually as fond of Dardanos as he had seemed to be. Perhaps he would be happy that I wished to marry someone that he believes to be distantly related to him, but what if Lord Sergison found out Dardanos was a vampire after we married? Would I be deprived of another husband? Had Lord Sergison actually murdered his own son because he was a vampire? If so, he would surely go after Dardanos should he find out.

Thoughts and scenarios rushed through my mind. All seemed to end tragically. I tried to imagine my life without Dardanos, taking over Cuckfield Park one day...alone. I could never love another and I could never marry a man I didn't love. My options were either to marry Dardanos and risk tragedy or spend the rest of my life alone and without love.

"I will marry you," I announced, almost surprising myself, as I shifted the black moonstone from my right hand to my left.

Dardanos practically leaped at me, embracing me and covering my face in kisses. We were both laughing, tears streaming down both our faces. It was something I couldn't deny; my life was tied to his...for better or for worse. A sound caused me to pull away suddenly.

"What was that?" I asked, listening intently for the sound again.

Dardanos had heard it as well and seemed frozen by shock. "It was a scream."

My heart thudded with dread as my eyes shot wide. I

pulled free of him, and grabbing the sconce at my bedside ran out of the room. Fear gripped me, but more than that a dreadful panic that more death was imminent. I rushed toward the scream that harkened danger, that most certainly called me toward doom, but I couldn't stop myself. I had lost so much in the past few days I shuttered to think what more could be taken from me, and that thought was more frightening than any creature in the night.

"No! Elizabeth! Do not go!" Dardanos called after me, his fearful voice echoing through the hall.

ℰ**19**ℭ

I ran down the hall, to the room a few doors down on the right. Emma's room. Dardanos followed close behind as I threw open the door. I moved close to the bed, my heart racing for what I might find, but the candle's light spilled over a frightened Emma. She was sitting up, clutching her blanket to her chin, a look of terror on her face. I felt relief to find her unharmed, but confused by what I'd heard. I was sure I'd heard a scream close by and as far as I knew no one else was staying in this hall.

"Emma, did you scream?" I asked brusquely.

Her face calmed, realizing it was only me, as she answered, "No, but I heard it as well. It seemed close by. I was afraid it was-"

She never got the chance to say what she thought it was. A series of loud bangs echoed down the hall cutting her off. We both halted at the sound, looking with widened eyes at one another.

"That sounded as if it were just down the hall," I said, rushing from the room in search of the disturbing sounds.

I was sure there were no other visitors sleeping in this hall. The only room that might have been occupied was Lord Sergison's study at the end of the hall going back toward the front of the house. I slowed my pace, terrified by what scene might await me in the study, terrified by what might still be in the study.

"What do you think it is Lizzy?" Emma whispered, just a pace behind me. "He wouldn't come here, would he?"

I stopped, startled by her whisper. I had been so focused on my pursuit of the noises that I hadn't noticed Emma following close behind. She put her hands on my shoulders as if using me as a shield should something jump out in front of us.

I shook my head at a loss, and looked to Dardanos. "Could it be him?"

"I do not know," Dardanos admitted, "if it were I should

feel his presence, but I do not perceive anything. I am not always able to feel the presence of another, especially if they have learned to cloak themselves, and he is very old. Surely he can hide himself from the minds of other vampires."

I decided to convince myself that Dardanos's inability to perceive another vampire close by meant that there wasn't one. What would I possibly do if it were this Prometheus he spoke of? What chance would any of us have of surviving should he attack? Dardanos took my hand encouragingly and walked beside me to the study. As we approached I could see the gas lamp was lit and the door was left wide open. I let go of Dardanos's hand and hurried through the open door more worried for Lord Sergison than for my own safety.

"No!" I cried, covering my eyes.

Dardanos and Emma ran in to see what had caused my scream. Emma let out an exclamation and Dardanos froze, saying nothing, but looking at me with heartbreaking concern. Lord Sergison was sprawled length-wise across his desk. Blood pooled all around his head, neck, and shoulders and dripped in a newly formed pool on the floor. His eyes were open, staring blankly at where I stood. My heart ached as I realized when we'd heard that scream not more than five or six minutes earlier that Lord Sergison had been alive. The loud bangs we had heard must have been made as Lord Sergison struggled against his attacker, mere moments ago, and yet no sign of the murderer.

"How could anyone have done this?" I demanded, tears streaming down my face. "And in minutes. We were just down the hall...we were so close."

Dardanos turned me away from Lord Sergison's battered body and put his arms around me. "He is more powerful than I can even explain. He did not drain Sergison, obviously, or there would not be so much blood, but he must be able to move at an unimaginable speed, even for a vampire."

Through sobs I asked, "Why wouldn't he drain him? Why kill him like this?"

Dardanos smoothed my hair as he answered, "It must have been out of revenge. Perhaps to avenge those Sergison had killed."

Another scream rang out. This one farther away...and female. My mind was numb with shock at seeing Lord Sergison so garishly murdered that the scream at first didn't register. Then

I thought it must be a servant seeing Lord Sergison's body, but when I turned there was no one behind us. I walked out into the hallway scanning both directions for the source of the scream when it came again.

"Oh, God!" I exclaimed, holding my clasped hands to my mouth. "Lady Sergison," I whispered in anguish as I took off at a run toward Lady Sergison's bedroom.

I turned right at the end of the hall, running past the main staircase to the door at the end. Dardanos kept by my side as I burst through the doors, hoping against hope that Lady Sergison was still alive. The room was empty as far as I could see. I swept my candle left and right looking for anything that would indicate someone had been there. I paused as my candle illuminated a large portrait on the wall facing the bed. The portrait was of Lady Sergison with her two sons. I stepped closer to better see Edward, the older brother that I had never met, and found I was looking at a death portrait. Edward's strangely ashen face held a stern look as his body was propped up by Lady Sergison's arm around his shoulders. Gabriel stood awkwardly behind, his hands on his mother's shoulders. Edward's neck and head seemed to have been stitched as if they'd been severed in two. I couldn't understand how, if he had been a vampire, he could have been killed.

I turned in confusion to Dardanos, "I thought he was a vampire. Aren't vampires supposed to live forever."

Dardanos looked at the painting curiously and answered, "He was a vampire, but he was also very weak. Vampires are vulnerable in their first month of immortality. They can be killed as easily as a human, and I suspect..." Dardanos said studying the painting closely, "that they removed all of his organs to be sure he could not regenerate. It was probably unnecessary. He was only a vampire for a night or two before he was discovered. Sergison could have easily killed him with nothing more than a sword or a gun."

"So it's true," I asked gulping in disbelief, "Lord Sergison killed Edward?"

Dardanos nodded. "I am afraid my sources have discovered it to be true. I would never have come here if I had known beforehand what lengths he would go to annihilate vampires. A man that would kill his own son cannot be negotiated with. I would never have been able to convince him that I wished to help him; his only thought would have been to destroy me"

I turned away from the painting, still unable to believe Lord Sergison had killed his own son, vampire or not. I continued in my search of the room, hoping to find a frightened Lady Sergison hiding in a dark corner, or perhaps shuttered in her dressing room. As the candle lit the bed my eyes passed quickly over it and continued scanning, but I suddenly realized what I'd seen and my heart caught in my throat. My eyes had seen what took my mind much longer to take in and process. I slowly passed the candlelight back over the bed as I held my breath.

"My God," I muttered numbly as I stared in heartbreaking shock.

Lady Sergison was not in bed. The cover and pillows were tossed about as if a struggle had taken place, but that was not what was so disturbing. The delicate white sheets and lacy pillow shams were covered in blood. When I say covered I don't mean spots here and there; I mean that the bed was soaked through. Only the outer edges of the sheets still retained their pristine color.

I stared in mute horror, unable to turn away. "She isn't here! Why would he take her?!"

"There!" Dardanos exclaimed, taking my candle to light the windowsill. "There is blood here. He must have taken her out the window."

I clambered to see for myself and sure enough there were great glistening globs of blood all over the window seat and sill. I leaned my head out of the large window to venture a look directly below. Though the moon was bright enough to see by there was nothing there to see. My heart sank as I cast my eyes over to the right, toward the pond.

I couldn't believe what I was seeing. A shadowed figure was trudging toward the pond with what looked like a body in its arms. I was so shaken I couldn't speak; I merely pointed my trembling finger. Dardanos bent his head out of the window to see what I was pointing to.

"Can you do what he did?" I asked, finding my will to speak, "Can you follow him out the window?"

Dardanos seemed to hesitate before answering, "Yes, I have the ability to fly. I can follow him for you if you-"

"No," I interrupted, "no, I want you to take me. I have to see where he's taking her. I need to see if she's…still alive."

He nodded his head, arguing no further. He sat on the broad ledge of the window and swung his legs out to dangle over the side. He gestured for me to do the same, holding me about the waist so I wouldn't fall.

"Put your arms around my neck," he instructed as he pulled me closer.

I wrapped my right arm around his neck and flung my left hand around to clasp my right arm. Dardanos's arms tightened around my waist even more just before he pushed off of the sill without warning. A scream stuck in my throat as I realized we weren't falling. We were hovering below the window sill and then slowly, very slowly descending to the ground.

I ignored my instinct to pepper Dardanos with questions as to how such a thing had been possible, even though I had been the one to suggest it. Instead, as soon as my feet felt solid ground beneath them I bid them to run hard in the direction I'd seen Lady Sergison being taken. Dardanos wasn't prepared for my quick departure, even with the unnatural speed he possessed it took him a few moments to catch me up. He scooped me up in his arms as we ran as if I were merely a flower being plucked from the ground; almost immediately we came within a few dozen paces of our prey.

The cloudless sky still illuminated the night enough to see more than just shadows at this close range. Dardanos stopped, lowering me gently to the ground, but I didn't move. I was unsure of what to do next. The demon was standing with his back to us, looking out over the large black pit of water. I worried if we approached any further he would simply take to the sky along with Lady Sergison's body and I would never know if she was still living, if she still could have been saved.

"Prometheus!" I shouted, thinking perhaps if I got him talking we might catch him off-guard.

"Elizabeth," Dardanos reprimanded in a harsh whisper. "I cannot protect you. He is far too strong."

Prometheus turned his head about slowly, those metallic eyes glinting strangely in the moonlight. His silvery eyes bored into me as a strange sadness swept across his features; I thought I saw his eyes flicker angrily at Dardanos and then back to me with something that almost looked like regret. It seemed time itself slowed as I attempted to scream no! He heaved the body out into the middle of the great pond and ascended into the air.

By the time I breathlessly reached the edge of the pond there was no trace of him or Lady Sergison's body. I sunk to my knees staring out over the inky pool. My insides turned to ice, and my heart beat angrily with each tear that fell. My anger was not for the evil demon that had entered my life or for Dardanos who had inadvertently led him here; my anger was directed at myself. I had allowed so much darkness to surround me, and it had consumed those closest to me. Why hadn't Prometheus just killed me? I was the one that was closest to Dardanos. Why was he taking everyone I cared for if his aim was to seek revenge on Dardanos? I thought there must have been more to the story; perhaps Dardanos really had no idea why Prometheus pursued him. Perhaps Prometheus was actually seeking revenge against me.

"I could try to find her," Dardanos whispered, scanning the surface of the pond.

"No," I said through tears, shaking my head, "she's gone. You saw the blood covering the sheets; she was dead before he even took her from her room."

Strangely my hand reached for the broach pinned at my neck. The mourning broach Lady Sergison had given me of the serpent entwined around the moon. I remembered what Sallie had said about it being a symbol that marked those that would be turned into vampires. I rubbed the broach watching hopelessly to see if Sallie was right, waiting to see if Lady Sergison would rise out of the water as some creature of the night. Moments passed like years, but I knew no matter how long I waited she wasn't coming back. I had lost her. Prometheus didn't turn his victims into what he was; he destroyed them, cruelly. I set the broach down at the bank of the pond as a kind of marker for Lady Sergison's watery grave. Her body would most likely never be found in the deep, murky depths of the pond.

"He didn't turn her," I stated lethargically. "Sallie was wrong. Lady Sergison is never coming back. I failed her."

"You have not failed anyone," Dardanos said brusquely, kneeling down and grabbing my shoulders to turn me to him. "I have rarely seen such loyalty or bravery, even among men. I confess I was uneasy to follow that evil creature, but you...you pursued at great risk to yourself at just the chance that your loved one was still alive. That is not failure; that is the action of a remarkable woman, a unique woman."

I knew he was trying to distract me from my feelings of guilt and impending depression, but I felt very far from remarkable. My family, through blood and through bonds of love, were dead. All I had left in the world was Emma, Dardanos, and Cuckfield Park.

That night was hellish. I asked Dardanos to leave as his presence would be difficult to explain. I returned to the manor house to find the entire staff roused in agitation, and a quick scan told me Emma was not among them. She seemed to have disappeared after we left Lord Sergison's study. As I walked into the chaos all eyes turned to me in stunned silence. I instructed one of the groomsmen to fetch the police, though what I was going to tell them I had no idea. I couldn't exactly tell them a vampire had swooped in and murdered Lord and Lady Sergison before flying off into the night. The truth of what had really happened would never be known and the murderer would never be caught, but I had to at least pretend the possibility existed. I had to at least attempt to want the killer found out even though if he were it would be certain death to whomever found him.

The servants huddled around me, asking me so many questions they all blended together and I couldn't understand any of them to answer. I finally convinced them to follow me into the dining hall, ignoring the looming glare of Apollo on the ceiling as it was the only room large enough to seat everyone. Once everyone was settled I explained that I believed a madman had broken in and murdered both Lord and Lady Sergison, carrying Lady Sergison out to the pond for some unknown reason and throwing her body where it might never be discovered. I told them that I had heard Lady Sergison's scream from outside and attempted to catch up with the madman, but he had had a significant head start.

I had to have a story to tell the police and this gave me the chance to practice what I would say, as long as I could keep my lies straight. All were shocked, but seemed to accept my story. All except Sallie. She quietly glared at me as if reprimanding me with her eyes. I could see by her harsh glare she believed it was a vampire, and most likely she thought it was the man I had met in the hedgerows. I knew I would have to tell her at least part of the truth to keep her from telling others her fears.

Then my night got even better.

Inspector Coghill, the man I had berated for his insensitive remarks regarding Mrs. Gibson's murder, was the officer in charge of the investigation. The man that I had completely insulted for his incompetence was the man that I now had to convince that there was a maniac on the loose that I had no description of running around Cuckfield killing people and draining them of blood. To say it didn't go well would be putting it lightly. By the end of our discussion I got the distinct impression that I was Inspector Coghill's top suspect. To make matters worse Emma had disappeared again making me look like an imbecile as I insisted she must be in her room, probably scared out of her wits as she had heard the screams as well. Of course when we both went to check on her she was not in her room as I'd guessed. Inspector Coghill commented that perhaps it had been more convenient to get rid of her, but I ignored him and instead pointed out that perhaps he should start a search for her, though I didn't believe Emma was in any danger. She had a habit of disappearing when she was needed.

Finally, around 6:00 AM the majority of the police officers left, taking Lord Sergison's body, and leaving me not arrested. A few constables were ordered to stay to protect us in case the madman reappeared, or as I thought was more likely, to keep an eye on me, the main suspect. The staff lined up around me where I'd collapsed in a large armchair. They looked at me, silently waiting. I gulped nervously not sure why they were staring at me so. I wondered if they blamed me for these strange occurrences. Were they going to torture me until I told them the truth?

"Should we clean up the study and Lady Sergison's room, Miss?" the head housekeeper asked.

I looked at their faces, stone cold from lack of sleep and felt a pang of pity for the people that would be assigned that task. "No, no," I muttered, "I believe we could all use some sleep. It can be taken care of later. Plus, Inspector Coghill hasn't given us leave to move anything yet."

Everyone nodded, trudging off groggily. I realized the staff hadn't been silently accusing me of anything; they had been looking to me for orders. I was the heir to Cuckfield Park. I was now their mistress.

I ignored the butterflies in my stomach at such a thought and stuttered, "Sallie, would you help me to my room before you retire?"

She didn't seem surprised and said simply, "Of course, Miss."

I closed the door to my bedroom after Sallie entered. I could see by the curt way she walked in she was furious, and I worried that she would alert the rest of the staff to her suspicions putting Dardanos and me into a dangerous predicament. I had decided I would have to tell her about Prometheus, to at least convince her it wasn't the man I was in love with. She didn't give me the chance.

"I told you he was a demon! I begged you to give him up!" she reprimanded, her blonde hair swishing behind her.

"No, Sallie, it wasn't him. There's another-" I tried to argue.

"He will pay. He will be punished for what he has done," she said darkly.

The look in her eyes scared me. "What do you mean?"

"The fiend chose the wrong family to attack. Let me just say we are prepared for such things. I can say no more. You will be protected, Lizzy, even if it is against your wishes. It's for the best." With that she left.

If I had been smart I would have taken Emma and Dardanos and convinced them to leave with me, but I was still too bound to societal rules and etiquette to abandon the servants and Cuckfield Park. I was still too in love with the place, even after the horrors it had seen, to leave it forever. There was still this dull ache that I could yet be happy there, married to Dardanos, and lovingly close to my sister once more. Unfortunately Emma never stopped to consider her own actions or exercise caution, and in this way she set my fate on a path I had never considered. A path that did indeed lead me away from the place that I so loved.

Later that evening I dined alone. Emma was still noticeably absent and I was beginning to worry, though I knew Prometheus had not taken her as I had seen him fly off into the night alone. Inspector Coghill's men were still stationed around the house, and two were assigned to stay with me, for my protection of course. I knew Coghill had ordered them to follow me on the off chance that I would give something away. The constables obviously thought it ridiculous that I should be suspected and were actually very friendly and concerned for my safety. I convinced them to allow me to walk in the hedgerows alone; I had neglected my Palladium for too long and she had some answering to do. As a protective statue she wasn't doing a very good job.

The constables stood at either end of the maze; I couldn't convince them to leave me completely alone, but at least I would see Pallas alone. I was wrong. Emma was sitting on the bench, staring at her hands and then grabbing her hair to examine it more closely, a manic smile on her face.

"Emma, you're all right!" I exclaimed, rushing to embrace her.

As soon as my arms touched her bare skin I cringed. Her skin was like ice. I pulled back from her, grabbing her by the shoulders to better inspect her in the lantern light. Her eyes glowed strangely and her hair seemed to catch any light around it, gleaming and seeming to move if you looked at it just right. I released her shoulders, shoving her slightly in anger, but she didn't move from my force.

"What have you done?" I demanded in disgust.

She either didn't notice my reaction or she didn't care as she answered giddily, "Isn't it amazing. Lizzy, can you believe how beautiful I am?"

"You were always beautiful," I argued. "You didn't have to do this. Was this what you wanted all along? The deal you made with Dardanos? I assume it was Dardanos that did this."

Emma smiled ecstatically at me, showing her newly formed fangs. "Yes, this is what I wanted. I have done everything that was asked of me and I have received my reward, but there is still one last thing I must do."

"And what is that?" I asked turning away as tears filled my eyes.

Emma took my hand gently. "Join us," she said passionately. "Let Dardanos turn you, become his forever. I know you love him, I know you want to be with him. Why not be with him forever?"

"Why hasn't he asked me himself?" I asked curtly.

She turned our clasped hands so that my hand faced up, displaying the black moonstone ring. "He has asked you; he just never got the chance to explain to you fully what being together would require of you."

I didn't answer but simply stared at the ring. The dark symbol of Dardanos's love. I had chosen this path when I let him in, when I gave myself to him, when I assented to be his wife. How else could I be with him if not to become what he is? Didn't I know that? Hadn't I suspected such a sacrifice would be necessary? For the first time since I'd met Dardanos I wished I were still marrying Gabriel. I wished I had never learned of this dark and dangerous world filled with devilish creatures. I wished I had been good enough to deserve Gabriel, and that I had never had visions whispering in my head of who I had been in my past lives.

Emma went on, "Lizzy, the world is full of dark, evil things; wouldn't you rather face them as their equal? Wouldn't you rather live your life without the fear of death?"

I didn't look up but muttered, "Vampires are demons. They're cursed…and they're killers."

Emma pushed off the bench so forcefully it was nearly knocked over with me on it. "You sound like an ignorant country maid. You know nothing of what being a vampire is," she spat and then turned back to kneel before me. "Vampires don't kill at random any more than humans do. Dardanos chooses victims from the dregs of society, usually going after humans that have harmed others. Don't you see; we can make the world better by diminishing the number of villains in this world." She stopped, seeing the shocked look on my face and sat beside me once more. "Lizzy, I am no demon. I know nothing of hell or the devil, but I do know that in a world of ants it is better to be a giant. Think about it: as women we have virtually no chance to be important or to have power. As vampires, though...the world could be ours to do what we like." Emma lowered her voice, taking my hand again. "Lizzy, whatever has been between us you are my sister and I love you and...I don't want to lose you. You're all I have left."

"Miss Cranford! Miss Cranford!" came the screams of one of the constables.

I stood in alarm. Something was wrong. I looked at

Emma but she seemed unfazed by the screaming.

"I'm here!" I called out.

Both constables reached me at the same time, approaching from opposite ends of the hedge maze.

Out of breath, the taller of the two, Burch was his name, panted, "Body...dead...found in the side garden." He waved his hand fervently. "Come...back to the house. We must get you inside."

I grabbed Emma's hand, introducing her quickly to the constables before letting them lead us back to the house. They seemed surprised by Emma's appearance; no doubt Inspector Coghill had told them of his suspicions that Emma was most likely dead and probably by my hand. Emma seemed reluctant to follow, but I tugged pleadingly on her hand.

"Is it known whose body was found?" I asked as we walked briskly out of the hedgerows.

"Yes, Miss," Burch called back to me, "It was one of the stable boys...white as ash with strange marks on his throat."

I shot Emma a worried glance. Had Prometheus returned so soon? Why had he come back to kill a stable boy? Had he simply gotten in the way, or did Prometheus plan on killing everyone at Cuckfield Park...one by one? Maybe Emma was right; maybe it was better to have the strength and power to fight back against such evil...rather than die helplessly. Emma didn't make any comment, but kept her head turned forward, a slight smile on her lips.

As we entered the house from the back I could see that the servants were nervously gathered in the main hall. The chatter was so loud it echoed down the hallway that we emerged out of. The servants were gathered around one of the constables that had stayed inside the house to keep watch. They were demanding the constable do something to stop all the murders. The constable stood in the middle of them putting his hands up to calm them, but nothing he said could even be heard over the outcries.

The two constables with me rushed to help, causing several servants to turn around, seeing Emma and me for the first time. I noticed Sallie eyeing Emma strangely and then whispering to two men beside her. The men scrutinized Emma, nodding as if they agreed with whatever Sallie had said. Did they know what Emma was? Did they suspect she was responsible for the deaths? I would have to get Sallie alone before she accused Emma of being a demon killer in front of everyone.

I pushed my way into the center of the servants and raised my voice, "Please, listen!" They fell silent. "I believe the man responsible for this is the very same responsible for the deaths of the Sergisons, my parents, Gabriel, Mrs. Gibson, and most likely countless others in the village. He is obviously an uncommonly strong and intelligent madman. We must all be on our guard until he is caught. I think it best to avoid being out of doors at night, especially alone."

"Well said, Miss Cranford," Constable Burch cut in, taking advantage of the silence.

I took the opportunity to slip away unnoticed, grabbing Emma's hand once more and pulling her along behind me. I yanked Emma all the way back to my room. I knew she had the strength to resist me if she wanted to, but she didn't even try. I was actually surprised that she came along so willingly.

After making sure no one could overhear us I closed the door. "Sallie knows," I warned in alarm.

Emma threw herself playfully onto my bed and laughed, "And? What do you think she can do, even if she does know?"

I looked at her infuriated by her carelessness. "I don't know. I'm just worried. She knows about vampires; she knew what the marks on my neck were, and she thinks my lover is the vampire that has been killing people. I tried to explain it wasn't him, that there is another vampire, but she wouldn't listen to what I was saying. She said the killer would be punished; as if she knew how vampires can be punished."

"Oh please, Lizzy," Emma scoffed as if bored, "your prim little maid probably meant some kind of superstitious damnation. Do you really think she believes in vampires? And even if she does how would she know that I'm one?"

"I don't know how she knows, but I could see it in her face. She knows what you are and she told others." I turned to her wringing my hands in agitation. "Why would she do that? Emma, I'm scared for you. What if-"

"Shhh," Emma comforted, rising off the bed to put her arms around me, "you don't have to worry about me. Lizzy, I am so unbelievably strong, you don't have to worry about anyone hurting me...and you don't have to worry about anyone hurting you either."

"What do you mean?" I asked hesitantly.

"Join us," Emma whispered, turning my face to hers. "Let Dardanos turn you, let him give you The Immortal Fate. Please consider it." Emma walked over to the window and threw it open. "If not for your own protection, consider it for me. I don't want to lose my sister, the only family I have left." With that she jumped through the window, landing on her feet on the ground below.

৪০**20**ওব

"You should have accepted my affections from the beginning. You wouldn't be in this terrible mess."

I was pushed up against something solid, like a wall, and the only thing I could see were the blue eyes staring back at me. Electric blue eyes that seemed to swirl and move with all the many shades of blue in the world. The most beautiful eyes I'd ever seen...and yet the most hateful to me. His breath was on my lips as he spoke and his hands were like vipers over my body, grasping roughly anywhere and everywhere that he chose.

"You will keep your promise?" A woman asked sternly from beside me.

"Yes, of course, Helen. You will receive your reward for unearthing Cassandra's treachery," Apollo answered in annoyance.

I turned my head slightly to see the beautiful woman my brother was in love with standing there smirking as if I deserved what was happening to me. "Did you really think I was going to let you outshine me in this war? This is *my* war…*my* moment, and I alone will reap the benefits of it." She came closer and whispered in my ear, "When all is said and done I will become a goddess and I will have Dardanos's love. He will be mine."

"Do you mind? I am busy here," Apollo spat in irritation, gesturing to my trembling body.

Helen raised her hands and said mockingly, "Of course, Lord Apollo, I will no longer delay your pleasure." I could hear the click of her shoes on the marble as she walked away, but she suddenly stopped and demanded, "Do not forget your promise!"

Apollo shouted in exasperation, "A god has no choice but to keep his promise! Once a vow is given it is recorded in the cosmos! Now leave us!" He ordered as he ran his hands over me once again, watching the horror it produced in my eyes.

"Apollo, please," I whimpered, struggling against the heat of his body.

He answered me by pushing his lips savagely against mine and tearing at the clasps that held my simple white tunic fastened over my shoulders, exposing my breasts.

"You see, I get what I want in the end, and now because of your treachery you will be punished. After I've had you...so will every man you come into contact with, and there is nothing Athena or your love can do to save you," he whispered harshly in my ear as he pulled the tatters of my tunic apart, letting it fall to the floor.

I fought to turn my head away from him and my eyes settled on a body lying motionless on the marble floor about twenty paces away. "Xanthós?" I cried.

"Yes, your pesky servant truly thought he could stop me. Poor, fool, he was so in love with you," Apollo drawled teasingly. "When he found out that Helen had been spying on you he tried to stop her from telling me the whole sordid story, but alas he was too late. I have to admit for a mere servant he was very brave and undeniably loyal, but he was mistaken to think I would allow a mortal to speak to me so."

Tears were streaming down my face for allowing Xanthós to get caught up in all this. I knew my fate was sealed, but I should have protected Xanthós better. I should have sent him away; I shouldn't have been so selfish to keep him near. I had known deep down that Xanthós felt something for me, though he was a eunuch and a servant, and yet I let myself believe his love was only that of a friend or a brother. What he thought he could do to stop Apollo I would never know, but I knew it was my fault that he had tried to do anything. I silently said a prayer that I might repay him in the next life for all he'd done for me.

"I never meant to disobey you," I said as calmly as I could muster. "It was not in my control. I fell in love. It was my fate," I argued, pushing at him to no avail.

As he forced himself into me he sneered, "Can you hear that? They've already taken the city. Troy is finished! All because of you and your love. I let the Greeks sneak in to take your precious Palladium. I gave them the idea to trick your father into opening the gates. None of this would have been possible without me. You chose your enemy poorly."

He pulled away abruptly causing me to fall in a heap on the floor. I felt broken and used...and dirty. When I looked up to

224

see what Apollo would do next I saw that I was in the temple. The sacred temple devoted to Athena, virgin goddess of wisdom and protector of women. Why had Athena allowed such an atrocity in her temple? Hadn't she received the prayer that I had carved into The Palladium? Had she abandoned me, abandoned Troy?

Apollo leaned down close to where I had fallen and said, "Here are some Greek warriors. Come to sack the temple no doubt. What a welcome prize you will be for them, their blood boiling with their victory. I'll be surprised if your body can withstand so much passion."

A moment later he vanished, leaving me alone and weak on the temple floor. I could hear the men screaming in triumph as they pounded up the temple steps. I pulled my body close, trembling in fear and disgust at what I knew would happen. I felt light-headed and confused as the first man grabbed me roughly, forcing his stinking sweat-soaked body over me.

"No!" I screamed, lashing out wildly in front of me.

"Elizabeth! Peace, it is only me," a man's voice soothed.

A moment passed as I sobbed into my hands and I listened as someone fumbled with items on the table next to the bed. Suddenly a candle was lit and I was staring at the bare-chested form of Dardanos.

"Are you all right?" he asked, smoothing back my moist hair. "What did you see?"

Still shaking from my dream I managed to say through sobs, "It was...horrible. Apollo...he...he raped me." I broke into louder sobs and tried to continue, "He left me to be raped by dozens of warriors...Greek warriors." I thought I could still feel the pungent sweat of the first warrior on my skin.

Dardanos pulled me close, wrapping his arms protectively around me. "I know...I know. I should have warned you. Some of the things Cassandra, and even Amunet, had to endure were painful...horrible...barbaric even."

I licked my dry lips and wiped at the warm tears still falling. "I remember wondering why Athena allowed me to be raped in the temple; why she hadn't answered my prayer. Where was she? Didn't she care anymore what happened to me?"

"She cared very much about what happened to you. That

is why she fought alongside me when the gods took sides. Unfortunately the godly war had already begun before Troy was taken, and Athena was preoccupied with battle. Apollo knew this and took advantage of her absence." He paused to run his fingers through my hair as he still embraced me. "I tried my best to keep Cassandra safe, but I could not always be there and Apollo made sure I was distracted by battle as well on that fateful day. I was unable to protect Cassandra and Amunet from the jealousy and greed of one single creature, but I will not make that mistake again. I will not lose you again."

I pulled back to look at his face, now wet with tears. "You won't lose me. I want to be with you...always."

"Do you mean..." he began, his eyes lighting happily.

"Yes," I answered, raising my hand to show I still wore the black moonstone ring he'd given me. "I told you I would marry you...how else can I honor my vows but to become what you are. I will do whatever you ask of me; I will become a vampire."

I wasn't sure I really wanted to become a vampire; it still seemed an unnatural and perhaps blasphemous thing to become, but I wanted to be with Dardanos. Also, ever since I'd seen Prometheus so much fear had grown inside me, causing me to wonder what other unknown evils were out there in the world. How could a mortal stand a chance if such terrible things existed and seemed to be drawn to her? I longed to possess the power to never feel fear again.

Dardanos began covering me with kisses. "You are wrong, it is I that will do whatever you ask of me. I am your slave."

I now noticed that Dardanos's body had been beneath the covers with me as if he'd been lying next to me as I slept. I felt a shiver of excitement thinking about his bare skin touching mine while I slept. It was only his torso that was bare, but it brought back the remembrance of his smooth muscles gliding over my expectant body in the hedgerows.

"There was a great commotion when I arrived," Dardanos said, calling me out of my daydream. "Police and servants were scouring the grounds and the house. Has something else happened?"

The events of the night had been completely erased from my mind after the hideous dream I'd had. "I had forgotten. Yes, there was another murder."

"Another murder?!" Dardanos exclaimed in surprise.

I nodded my head. "It was one of the stable boys. He was found by the pond with marks on his throat. The fiend must have meant to push his body into the pond, but either didn't realize he missed or was happened upon in the act of doing so," I reasoned, putting my hand to my head. "Then I had to put up with all the absurd questions from Inspector Coghill, basically accusing me beyond any evidence to the contrary. The constables kindly pointed out that they had been with me the entire day and there had been no time in which I could have done such a thing. It's all such a mess. I haven't even been able to mourn properly for my parents or the Sergisons because my emotions are so tangled up in fear of being the next victim."

"That is strange," Dardanos commented as if to himself, "Why would umm...Prometheus come back here just to kill a stable boy? Then for him to make such a fledgling mistake as to try to hide the body and fail?"

I studied him a moment and realized, "You don't think it was him?"

Dardanos seemed startled, "I cannot be certain, but...it does not seem like something he would do. He tends to be a bit more gruesome and much more precise."

The word fledgling echoed in my mind. "You turned Emma," I accused, forgetting about Prometheus for the moment.

"I did," he said simply. "I promised her many months ago that if she kept you safe I would give her the very thing she had been seeking. Plus," he said, cupping my cheek, "I thought you might want your sister with you if...if you decided to join me."

Dardanos leaned toward me, pulling me into his lips. I found myself ravenously consuming his mouth as I ran my hands over his smooth muscular chest. He gently pushed me back, continuing his salacious kisses all the while until we were lying side by side. He slipped his hand up under my thin nightdress, teasing the tender flesh beneath.

I suddenly pulled back from his lips, asking nervously, "Do you think it was Emma? Do you think Emma killed the stable boy?"

"Shhh," Dardanos lulled, running his fingers along my jaw, "that is not for you to worry about, but I hope it was not her. It would...complicate things for us."

"How so?" I questioned, trying to ignore the hand now caressing my thigh.

"There are certain, well, guidelines to abide if one is to live among humans. The first of which is to never feed on those close to you. If we are to remain at Cuckfield Park we cannot allow our own servants to suspect we are vampires. We must hunt far from our home to protect our secret," he explained.

"I'm frightened, General" I admitted shakily, "I'm frightened to change into such a thing. What if it changes me...my soul? What if I'm not me anymore?"

Dardanos paused in his attentions and reassured, "You have nothing to fear. I will be with you every step of the way. I love you as you are, and I would never do anything that would change who you are. When I gave Amunet The Immortal Fate she was still the same woman she had always been, perhaps I might admit she was even more beautiful and alluring."

I nodded my head, smiling weakly and asked, "Will it hurt?"

"I will not hurt you. Some say it is very much like love-making, a mix of bearable pain and unimaginable pleasure," he explained as he resumed his attentions beneath my nightdress.

I tried to ignore my anxiety and push aside my fears of the unknown. Instead I focused on Dardanos's hands running up and down my body, his lips nearly devouring mine, and the passion begging to be released. I fumbled with the button of his trousers, feeling foolish and inexperienced. Without a word Dardanos moved to undo his trousers and tug them off in one fluid motion. He slid his bare solid form over me, pulling roughly at my nightdress until it was deposited in a pile on the floor. His tongue moved to my breast, circling and biting playfully while his cool, strong fingers slipped between my legs, exciting my passion for him further.

I found myself gasping uncontrollably, digging my fingers into his back to pull him closer. He suddenly pushed inside of me, his unusually warm throbbing melting me like the last remaining snow patch on a warm spring day. I wrapped my legs around him, still trying to pull him closer as he moved once again to my lips.

Between vigorous kisses I managed to utter, "I'm ready."

Dardanos seemed surprised as he stopped everything he was doing, causing my eyes to go wide with frustration. Then realizing what I'd said he covered my face in kisses. He began pouring in and out of me once more, the fever inside of me rising to an almost unbearable point. Just before the moment I felt my very core about to break I felt a strange sensuous pinch at my neck.

In one glorious moment I was transported to a realm of utter ecstasy. Nothing else existed but the pleasure. I wasn't sure if it was the result of Dardanos's teeth at my neck or the culmination of our love-making, but I felt light and tipsy as if I'd drunk a few glasses of wine. I couldn't even say if my eyes were open or closed, but suddenly Dardanos pushed his wrist to my lips, the taste of metallic hitting my tongue.

Without considering what I should do I found myself latching onto his wrist, pulling the now warm blood into my mouth. I drank wantonly as images flashed in my mind. Images from Dardanos's life in Egypt to the very moment we were now sharing, flashing too quickly to really understand all that I was seeing. Without warning Dardanos yanked his wrist back. I think I actually gasped at the absence of the intoxicating liquid that had been flowing down my throat. It was strange how natural the want for blood was to me. I thought I would be disgusted by such things, but on the contrary I longed for it. I could feel the power of it coursing through my veins, and the strange sensation of everything inside of me slowing down.

Dardanos collapsed beside me, pressing his lips to my ear, "You are mine now...forever."

ஐ21ଔ

"You will need to feed properly once the marks I left at your neck heal," Dardanos explained, still lying naked beside me. "Once the marks heal your transformation will be complete and your hunger will become unbearable."

"I'm scared," I whispered horrified, "How can I do such a thing? How can I take a life to feed my hunger? It's murder. Surely our souls will be damned for all time."

Dardanos rolled on his side to face me, and I noticed for the first time how much clearer everything looked in the dim candlelight. My eyes felt no strain and the near crispness of every object surprised me. Now I understood how Dardanos had been able to direct me so easily during the séance and how he had effortlessly led me to the pond in the dark. It was obviously one of the advantages of being a vampire to be able to see in near darkness, perhaps even in complete darkness once I had completely turned.

"I will teach you everything you need to know, and we will choose our prey from those least deserving of life. You would be surprised how many there are. I believe we do a great service to humanity, eliminating some of the deranged and dangerous from society."

I nodded my head nervously, remembering Emma had said something similar, but I still wasn't sure if I could even take the life of a vicious killer. Wouldn't there be sin in my soul for such an act? Was I a demon? Would I be punished one day for my evil deeds? Did I already have sin in my soul from my past lives? I tried to push the thought away. I would face it when it came, and instead I draped my arm across Dardanos's firm chest. I thought perhaps I would fall back to sleep wrapped in his arms, but sleep would not come. There were too many thoughts rushing through my mind and added to that I felt no weariness in my body. I felt none of the drowsy fatigue I had the first time we'd made love, nor did the act of giving and taking blood cause me any weakness. I felt I could stay awake forever.

"Did you hear that?" Dardanos asked, sitting up abruptly in bed and then jumping from the bed to retrieve his clothing.

"What is it?" I asked, straining to hear what he had. "I don't hear anything."

Dardanos continued buttoning his shirt as he shook his head. "I am not sure. I hear a commotion, somewhere far off, perhaps at the edge of the grounds. Stay here," he instructed, quickly kissing my cheek. "I can get close without being detected. It may only be a squabble between a couple of drunk servants. I will not be long."

I sat there, heart pounding in trepidation. Something was wrong. Something was happening out on the grounds; I could feel it. I still could hear nothing out of the ordinary, but I could feel some kind of malicious energy pushing toward me, warning me. I sprang from bed and got to work with the arduous task of dressing myself. I managed to pull my corset somewhat tight over my chemise, but struggled to tie it at the back. After securing two underskirts and a bustle I stepped into one of the few black skirts I had, and slipped my arms into a black and gray button-up bodice. I once again chose a bodice with a high collar to hide the tell-tale marks on my neck. I was just brushing out my long burgundy hair when Dardanos thundered clumsily into the room.

"We must leave," he announced darkly.

"What happened? What did you find?" I demanded, seeing more keenly the worry in his eyes with my new vision.

"There has been another murder. One of the lady's maids, Sallie I believe was the name-"

"Sallie?!" I exclaimed, "Why would Prometheus kill Sallie?!"

"The servants do not believe it is the murderous madman that you told them about, and I am inclined to agree," Dardanos replied flatly.

I looked down, knowing what he was hinting at, but still demanded, "What do you mean?"

"The servants seem to be under the assumption that not only is your sister a vampire, but that she is a murderer. If I ventured to guess I would say that Lord Sergison not only revealed his secret life as a vampire hunter to several of the servants, but may have actually trained many of them to aid him.

I had not foreseen such a possibility."

I ran my fingers across my forehead, circling my eyes in disbelief. "I told Emma that I thought Sallie knew what she was. I told her that there could be trouble for her. It's my fault she killed Sallie. I shouldn't have said anything. I must have frightened her into thinking she had no choice but to get rid of Sallie." I shook my head. "Poor Sallie."

Dardanos knelt down in front of me where I sat at my vanity and enclosed my hands in his. "It is not your fault for warning your sister. Perhaps I should have kept better watch over her, made sure she understood the repercussions of such actions."

"Where is she?!" I asked apprehensively. "I don't care what she has done; she's my sister. We have to find her. We have to make sure the hunters don't go after her."

"I did not see any sign of her," Dardanos said sadly, "but we do not have time to find her. If any of the servants have truly been trained to be hunters they will know immediately what we are when they see us, and staying here during daylight hours would only put us in further danger."

"You're frightened?" I asked in surprise. "I would have thought you to be afraid of nothing."

"I am afraid," he admitted slowly, catching me in his arms, "of losing you. I am strong; I can overpower many men, but I fear what might happen should you be attacked. I will not bring you into a potentially harmful situation. I need you."

I kissed him lightly but argued determinately, "I will not leave without at least looking for Emma. If time is our issue then we should not be standing here arguing about what is to be done. I must look for her...then we can leave."

Dardanos didn't argue this time; he simply nodded and gestured toward the door. We first went to Emma's room on the very unlikely chance that she would simply be there waiting, unaware of the commotion going on outside. Naturally it couldn't be so easy. Emma was not in her room, and as far as I could tell and Dardanos could sense no other vampire was in the house.

"Let's check the gardens," I suggested.

Still we found nothing, not even the group of servants that Dardanos had seen earlier. I was about to give up and tell him that we could leave when a shriek split through the air like a bolt of lightning. The sound was so loud and so terrible it sent a shiver through my body. I was sure it hadn't come from a human. Dardanos seemed to freeze uncomfortably as well, a look of dread spreading across his face.

"An animal perhaps?" I questioned uneasily, looking out into the near visible darkness.

"I cannot be sure, but..." he began and then turning and taking my hand he warned, "we may have just found your sister."

"No!" I screamed, shaking off his hand and running in the direction of the scream.

Dardanos was at my side in a moment and caught me around the waist to stop me. "We must not be seen. Come, I will take you to her...quietly," he insisted, opening his arms for me to hold onto him.

Once I had my arms securely fastened around his neck he shot into the air. As soon as we were above the trees I could see a strange light coming from the edge of the property. Dardanos headed toward the strange flickering light that seemed so out of place in all of that quiet darkness. I tried to focus with my vampiric eyes, but there were just too many trees on the edge of the property to make out what it was.

Dardanos set us down in a thick patch of trees in which we could stay hidden. We moved slowly through the trees until we came to a gap filled with the ghostly light of a blazing bonfire, hissing and screeching like a wild animal. I stared at the large group of servants gathered about the fire, holding various weapons all aimed at the fire. I didn't understand what they were doing, some kind of ritual perhaps?

Then another spine-chilling shriek rang out, now deafeningly loud. My eyes shot to the center of the bonfire. There I could see a large wooden post or perhaps a tree with its top cut off.

"Oh God!" I exclaimed in a hushed whisper as I moved to rush forward toward the fire.

Dardanos caught my hand. "We cannot save her."

My eyes burned with tears as I watched Emma barely moving in the heart of the bonfire, her clothing a mass of flames. She was somehow restrained against the wood post I had noticed earlier. I refused to leave, even as I knew there was nothing I could do for her. I needed to look at her until there was nothing left to look at. Through the sting of my tears I watched as first her curly black hair was incinerated, leaving her a sickly singed creature, and then slowly her skin began to catch fire, creating great patches of exposed bone and sinew. She had stopped shrieking; I hoped she had completely lost consciousness and could no longer feel anything. I thought it would go on like that for hours, a slow, agonizing deterioration of her body, but there was a sudden flare-up around her and everything that she once was fell into an ashen heap in the tortuous flames.

I whispered in empty sorrow, "She's dead; and all which die / To their first elements resolve; / And we were mutual elements to us, / And made of one another. / My body then doth hers involve, / And those things whereof I consist hereby / In me abundant grow, and burdenous, / And nourish not, but smother."

I knew the poem was about a man mourning a woman, but it felt as if part of me had died with my sister. My mind filled with memories of clasped hands and secrets that we would never tell another soul, of laughing at one another's jokes and drying each other's tears, and of all the silly whispers of what our lives would be like when we were grown. It felt as though everything we ever shared, everything we'd ever felt were now my burdens to carry. The very memory of her was my burden to carry for the rest of my long, immortal life.

"We should go before they see us," Dardanos said, turning as if to go back the way we'd come.

I stood there numb, staring at the now diminishing fire. Before I knew what I was doing my feet were moving out of the protective shadows of the trees toward the bonfire. Longing to fall at the edge of my sister's ashes, to mourn her properly as I had been unable to mourn my parents and the Sergisons. I wanted to reach into the now dying flames, not caring if they singed the skin from my hand, and take what was left of Emma into my hands. No one noticed me approaching; I was still quite a distance from the dimming light of the bonfire. Suddenly I felt something pushed up against my temple.

"I knew you were involved in all this," came the superior voice of Inspector Coghill.

I turned slightly to the left to look at him and the gun he had pushed against my head. As I turned he seemed to see something in me that caused him to gasp.

"I know what you are," he whispered, a touch of fear in his voice, "you're a vampire, a bloodsucking demon."

"I am no demon and I haven't sucked anyone's blood...yet," I protested, though I felt a strange sensation to lunge at him.

"Leave her alone. She has done nothing wrong," Dardanos commanded from behind me.

Inspector Coghill was careful not to move the gun as he turned to see who was speaking. "Who are you, sir?" he demanded.

In answer Dardanos said, "If you are looking for monsters you should be rounding up the men around that bonfire. They have just burned an innocent woman to death."

"Hardly innocent, sir," Inspector Coghill said, laughing, "she was caught draining the life from her last victim and is suspected of many more deaths."

I could smell the fear and righteousness coming off of him as if they were merely flavorings of his blood, and I longed to taste them. I wanted to draw every emotion and secret from his all too close veins. I could feel the pulse of those veins beating against my lips though I stood at arm's length from him. I felt a strange dizziness, a drunken haze that pulled me toward him. My mouth was reflexively opening as if I could catch tastes of him on the air. For a moment I wasn't even sure who I was; I only knew there was blood so close I could touch it with my fingertips.

"It is a shame, Miss Cranford, such a lovely woman as yourself being bitten. We'll have to rekindle the bonfire for you," Inspector Coghill said cruelly.

"You are not going to do any such thing," Dardanos stated taking a step closer.

Inspector Coghill seemed to feel Dardanos getting near and turned his head abruptly to explain, "Sir, you don't know what is going on here. Cuckfield is being overrun with-"

The distraction was all it took for me to push the gun aside and thrust myself at Inspector Coghill's throat, knocking him over in the process. He had been so focused on Dardanos he didn't even notice I had moved until I was lying on top of him ripping fiercely at the great throbbing vein in his neck. It was a horrific animalistic attack, but I couldn't control myself. I clawed and tore at him, anything that would release the addictive substance hidden just below the surface. The blood rushed past my tongue and down my throat bringing a kind of pleasure and peace I thought impossible. For a moment I was reminded of the finest wine, but it was more than just the tipsy feeling, more than the rich, sweet taste. It was as if I were taking in a delightfully euphoric elixir; one that offered me peace and contentment along with strength and knowledge.

Inspector Coghill's short life passed before my eyes. His days as an average, scrawny child picked on by his schoolmates to the over-proud man he was now. Much of his life was ordinary, he seemed to have always been just average his whole life, and it had twisted him. As a man with a vast deal of authority he took pride in bullying others, from the sergeants and constables beneath him to the petty thieves just trying to survive on the street. I saw him taking bribes from struggling shop owners and blackmailing prostitutes into his bed where he abused them unmercifully.

I felt Dardanos's hand on my shoulder and suddenly he was pulling me away. I was so shocked by Inspector Coghill's cruelty that I couldn't focus on what was happening. I heard distant yells, most likely the men around the bonfire finally noticing us, and then I was being picked up by Dardanos. Moments later we were in the air, skimming the clouds. I buried my face into Dardanos's chest disgusted at what I'd just done and dreading when I would have to do it again.

"Where are we?" I whispered, still shaking from everything that had happened at Cuckfield Park.

"We are safe," Dardanos answered, wiping at my face with a wet cloth, "we are in Romania."

"Romania!" I exclaimed, sitting up on the bed that Dardanos had set me on. "We couldn't possibly be in Romania. How long was I asleep?"

"You were not asleep," Dardanos said, a small smile on his lips. "It was only a little over an hour to get here. I have the ability to fly, and my abilities allow me to fly quite fast."

"Romania..." I muttered to myself, looking around the vast stone room I was in.

The room had few furnishings for how large it was, but was well lit with massive metal braziers on the walls and an equally impressive fireplace set against the wall opposite the bed. The bed I was sitting on was the largest I had ever seen with broad posts on all four corners that resembled roman columns.

The wall at the head of the bed was covered with a dull-colored tapestry depicting a wide expanse of clouds upon which were gathered men and women of exquisite beauty in various poses holding various items. From their clothing and the items they held I could see that they were meant to represent Greek gods.

There was an ornately painted wood armoire on the wall to my left and an alcove to the right with two seats facing each other and a leaded glass window made up of many colored glass circles between the seats. The bed was on a level raised above the rest of the room; a few paces from the foot of the bed were three stone stairs leading down to a sitting area. Directly across from the bed and the small set of stairs was a massive gothic-style stone fireplace with decorative shapes carved into it and two carved ravens holding what looked to be a single ring in each of their mouths facing each other. Surrounding the impressive fireplace were two carved wood and cushioned chairs and a stunning crimson sofa, also made of a decadently carved wood. The furniture seemed out of place in the cold, dull, and primitive expanse of the room; they looked like they would have been more at home in a palace in England. I noticed as I faced the great fireplace and sitting area that the door to the room, a wooden monstrosity which angled into a point at the top, was to the left and another, larger window was to the right.

"Is this a castle?" I asked, remembering my few visits to similar looking places in England, though none of them had seemed so darkly somber and yet so hauntingly lovely.

"Yes," Dardanos answered, looking at me as if he could read my thoughts. "I acquired it from the Sergison's ancestors. They fled Romania to escape Christian persecution and because they were known vampire hunters, highly renowned in their time. When the Turks took over belief in vampires was frowned upon, and hunting vampires was considered not only ridiculous but a waste of the Sultan's resources."

"So you really aren't related to the Sergisons as you said?" I asked, though I had guessed long ago that he couldn't have been related to them if everything else he'd told me about his life was true.

"That was an unfortunate lie I thought was necessary to gain Lord Sergison's trust," he explained, "I am in no way related to the Sergisons, but I did suggest that the Hunyadis, their Romanian ancestors, go to England. They were planning to go east but I convinced them England was the new home of Christianity."

"In the end perhaps England was not the answer for them," I muttered to myself, thinking of the once great family that was no more.

"Elizabeth," Dardanos cooed, holding me about the shoulders so I would look at him, "Fate finds us all...no matter where we hide. The Sergisons and their ancestors lived happily and prosperously for over two hundred years. I, above anyone, feel guilt and responsibility for what happened to their great family. I, who pointed them to England, a place rife with vampires, and it was I that sought them out all these years later. I led them to their end just as surely as I unwittingly led the damnable creature that killed them to their very doorstep."

ᘒ22ᙅ

That morning, a few hours before sunrise, I learned the other intrinsic part of being a vampire. Hiding from sunlight. Dardanos pulled the heavy, dark gray embroidered drapes over both windows, shrouding the entire room in darkness save the one candle still lit. I found it strange that, although I had yet to feel tired or weary, I was suddenly having trouble keeping my eyes open. I felt an indescribable pull from inside of me to simply collapse.

"Something's wrong. I feel I'm going to faint. My body feels so heavy," I muttered groggily, struggling to unbutton the neck of my dress to feel the marks that Dardanos had left there.

Dardanos coaxed me to lie down and inspected my neck. "They have healed completely. There is nothing to worry about; everything is as it should be. One as young as yourself will feel the pull of sleep before the sun has even risen. As time goes on you will be able to stay awake longer and wake earlier. Do not be frightened; daytime is not our natural time. We live in the night. Do not fight it. Close your eyes and relax. You will be perfectly safe here. This is my home, and those that serve me are loyal to the death. No harm will come to us here."

I closed my eyes as Dardanos suggested, though I really had no choice. My eyes were closing on their own, pulling shut as if a switch inside of me had been flipped. I struggled to stay awake, to stay conscious, but something deep down was pulling me. It felt as though there were a deep, dark pit in the center of my being and it was pulling me down into it. There was a great spiraling universe of quiet oblivion devouring me, and I had no choice but to give in to it. The last thought I had was a dread of what visions my vampiric mind would induce.

A loud bang came at the door, echoing through the cavernous room. It was probably a result of the horrifying scene I'd witnessed at Cuckfield, but I actually leaped defensively from the bed. My first thought was that the servants had tracked us down and were going to burst through the door any moment. Of course, then I realized that was impossible if we were truly in Romania; humans couldn't possible travel so far so quickly.

"Come in," Dardanos called, calmly rising from the sofa in front of the great blazing fire.

He turned, holding his hand up to calm me, and gave a reassuring smile. I looked around the room, remembering passing out on the bed after Dardanos had assured me the overwhelming pull of sleep was perfectly natural. A quick glance at the windows showed that it was still night, or more accurately a day had passed in which I had slept, and this must have been the following night. It had been a full day since Emma's death at Cuckfield.

"Domn," a man addressed Dardanos as he entered the room, and then noticing me bowed slightly. "Mr. Cavanaugh is waiting for you in the Knight's Hall. He has news of Cuckfield."

"Excellent, I will see him straightaway," Dardanos answered excitedly.

After the man left I approached Dardanos and asked in surprise, "Cuckfield?"

"Yes, I have a man assisting me, looking out for my interests. I hope he will have found some good news for us," he explained, smoothing down his hair and retying it with the black ribbon he always wore.

"But..." I began confused, "how could he have gotten here so quickly?"

Dardanos seemed uncomfortable at my questions but answered at last, "He is a vampire as well. He has committed himself to my cause, and his help has been invaluable to me."

I nodded my head in acceptance and started walking toward the door. "Well, I guess we shouldn't keep him waiting then."

"Elizabeth," Dardanos called, a look of pity on his face, "I do not want you to come with me. This man has been very important in my plans, but I do not completely trust him. I worry...I worry that he might try to hurt you."

I walked back to where he still stood, studying his face,

"Why would he hurt me? He doesn't even know me."

Dardanos pursed his lips in thought and said simply, "I do not know that he would. I am only speculating that it is a possibility. He can be...unpredictable. Please understand I only wish to keep you safe, not keep things from you. I will tell you everything when I get back." He kissed my lips briskly and turned away to leave.

"Domn!" I called before he walked out the door. When he turned I asked playfully, "What does it mean?"

Dardanos seemed embarrassed as he answered, "It has several meanings: sir, lord, king...master. My men call me Domn out of respect, not because I demand it of them."

I smiled warmly at his simple humility, adding, "I'll always think of that first day we met when you told me that you had once been a general. It suits you better, I think, than master." I paused, looking down thoughtfully, and then gave him one last loving look. "I'll see you soon, General."

As he closed the door I could see a broad smile appearing on his lips, and I thought that I almost caught the faint sound of his heart beat, pumping the blood of his last victim through his body. I couldn't be sure if my abilities allowed me to hear such a thing, but as I stood there alone in a strange room in a strange land it comforted me to think I could still affect him so.

I walked past the sitting area of the lower level of the room to the window, to look out over the landscape of my new dwelling. The tall window had three clasps: one at the bottom, one at the center, and one near the top, holding the shutter-like window panes closed. I undid the clasps, reaching up on tip-toe to undo the top, and swung the panes inward. There was just enough room for me to step through the window frame and lean out of the windowed turret onto a small stone balcony.

The moon was not full and bright, but I was still able to see better than I should have been able to. My vampiric eyes looked out on a scene that could have been illuminated by the setting sun. I could see the rolling hills of the countryside and the various trees and flowering plants in bloom as if caught in a warm orange glow. I knew it was because of the change that had taken place in my body, that this would be commonplace to me after a while, but right then I couldn't tear my eyes away from the scene in front of me. It was like a vision from a hazy dream. Everything looked cloaked in magic, too mystically beautiful to be real, and yet it made me sad. It was a strange land and I was a strange creature in it, and everything was drenched in darkness like the starless night sky had switched places with the earth.

I whispered to the empty night, "The moon, their mistress, had expir'd before; / The winds were wither'd in the stagnant air, / And the clouds perish'd; Darkness had no need / Of aid from them—She was the Universe."

A door shut behind me, waking me from my daze. I turned abruptly, a sudden feeling of confusion for where I was flooding me. I let out a great sigh of relief at the sight of Dardanos smiling as he walked toward me. How much time had passed? It had only felt like a few moments, barely enough time for him to walk down the hall let alone to another part of the castle.

"Was he not there?" I asked, sure he hadn't been gone long enough to have had a conversation with anyone.

"I spoke with him," Dardanos replied excitedly, ignoring my confusion, "things may not be as grim as we had thought."

"How so?" I asked methodically still caught in my haze.

"My assistant informs me that an investigation is being conducted to find out what happened last night. Your Inspector Coghill was found by another officer on the grounds and apparently there is some concern as to what happened to you. There has not even been a hint of a whisper that it was you that killed Coghill...nor that you are a vampire. The general consensus is that you were the latest victim of the madman you told everyone about. They still hold out hope that you have only been abducted and a ransom will be sought."

"Did they find Emma's body?" I questioned, casting my eyes down.

"No, not her body," he answered, "but someone was able to identify a piece of her dress that had not completely burned. We should be able to use this to our advantage."

I scrunched my eyebrows not understanding what he meant. "Use what to our advantage? We've been driven from our home by vampire hunters; we can't simply go back and hope they won't attack us as well."

Dardanos took hold of my hands and explained, "We can bend the circumstances of what happened last night to explain why we fled, and at the same time secure ourselves as the rightful owners of Cuckfield Park."

"Oh," I replied shakily, remembering the horror of the night before, "I don't think I could return there. They murdered Emma. Surely they will come after us...and...they will know what we are!"

"No, no, my dear Elizabeth," he soothed, taking me in his arms, "I would not suggest we return so soon. The murderers must be sorted out...and I must discover all of the hunters. Those willing to follow me in absolute obedience will join us in our great plans. First, we must see your lawyers to stake our claim and announce me as your husband."

"But...we aren't married-" I began to protest.

"That is easily fixed. I have a loyal friend in England that will get us the documents we need to show to the lawyers. That will be our reason for fleeing from Cuckfield so secretly...to elope quietly to avoid it being announced so soon after your fiancé's death. Then, of course, we heard about the vicious attack on your sister and the inspector and were scared to return. Once the lawyers are convinced of our marriage and add me to your property I will be able to take care of everything in regards to Cuckfield Park. Then once it is safe to return we will have our happily ever after."

I gulped nervously, not sure if I quite agreed with pretending to be married, but the idea that I might one day return to Cuckfield Park gave me hope. "Are you going to go to the police about what they did to Emma?"

"No," he answered gravely, "I do not want the police involved. I will take care of the threat at Cuckfield."

"How?" I asked before considering and then realized in a whisper, "oh...you mean to kill them all."

Dardanos cupped my face in his hands. "Do not look at me that way. I know everything is new to you and it will take time for you to fully understand what it means to be a vampire. There is no justice for us when we are wronged; we must make our own justice. We live by different rules. It is necessary to ensure our own safety."

I stared into his cold blue eyes, seeing for the first time how much sadness they held. "I understand more than I like to admit. I suppose I'm not ready to let go of everything I've ever known. I'm not ready to blur the lines between good and evil."

"I know, my love," he soothed, kissing me between each

word, "You expect too much of yourself. It has only been one night since I gave you The Immortal fate, you must give yourself time to lose the bonds of human restriction. Remember you are no longer human and are no longer bound by human laws."

I nodded and turned back to the window to change the subject, "It's very beautiful here. Perhaps we could go explore. I'll have to learn the area if we are to stay for an extended period."

"There is nothing I would love more," he answered hesitantly.

I turned back to him and asked in disbelief, "You're leaving, aren't you?"

"I must, before too much time passes," he explained, turning his palms open in defeat, "I must track down all of the hunters before they flee Cuckfield. If we are to be safe there I must make sure I find them all."

"I could go with you. I could help you," I protested.

Dardanos's face lit with a stern fire. "No! I will not risk your protection. You must stay here, where you will be safe." He softened his gaze, cupping my cheek in his hand. "I understand you wish to be of use, but I will have help. There is no reason to put you in jeopardy."

"But..." I whispered nervously, "what if I get hungry?"

Dardanos took my hands in his and raised them to his lips. "My men will assist you with everything you need."

"They're human," I remarked, feeling uneasy about being surrounded by humans after what I'd seen a group of them do when they had discovered my sister was a vampire, or what I had done to Inspector Coghill almost against my own will because of my hunger.

"You will be safe with them," he promised, "They know what we are and they are loyal to me. They are the beginning of my great army."

"Army?" I questioned nervously, wondering what else he had yet to tell me.

"Yes, they are part of my plans," he began. "I had hoped to offer the men I have trained to Lord Sergison that we could combine our efforts to end the vampire epidemic."

I scrutinized him and asked "What of us? Who are we to condemn others to death for being what we are? When we are the last vampires shall we be forced to destroy ourselves?"

"When we are the last of our kind...we will be gods. The only gods this world will have ever seen," he said, taking hold of my shoulders firmly. "It will be as it should be; we will bring back order and give humans something to believe in again."

I remembered my visions of Amunet. She and Dardanos had been seeking a way to become gods. Amunet's explanation to Sethos had been clear. She believed it possible; she believed she and Dardanos would one day become gods and rule the world. Amunet seemed to think it was what was best for the earth: Dardanos becoming an all-powerful god that would strike fear and devotion into the hearts of mortals, and Amunet at his side to rule with temperance and mercy. The words she had pledged echoed in my mind, *if it means being with you I would face an eternity cursed.*

"I...umm," I sputtered at a loss. "I don't know what to say. I've seen the visions, and I know what you and Amunet were trying to achieve, but that seems an impossible goal. If I really am her I no longer feel the surety of such a goal. I'm not even sure if I would want to be worshiped."

He cupped his hands around my face and said low, "You are already worshiped."

I smiled weakly at the sentiment but argued, "You know what I mean. Having so much power doesn't seem right. I don't want to be feared."

"No one need fear you. You will be the balance to my severity. You will be loved and adored...prayed to by all for your gentility and wisdom and grace."

"I don't know," I answered, shaking my head, "I've never really been comfortable with too much attention. All I really want is to be with you...at Cuckfield Park."

"Do not think on it, my love. I will take care of everything," he coaxed, kissing me on the forehead. "I will not be long. I hope to sort out the men that killed your sister in a night or two. My assistant is to acquire the paperwork we need to prove we are married and make an appointment for us to meet with your lawyers. Then he will meet me back here in two days."

"Mr. Cavanaugh?" I asked, interrupting him. "The man that you fear may try to hurt me?"

"I only said he is unpredictable and you mean too much to me to risk him doing something potentially harmful. I have complete faith in his competency; he has been of immense help to me thus far," Dardanos attempted to convince. "That being said I have already instructed my men that Mr. Cavanaugh is not to bother you; he is to wait for my return. If everything goes according to plan we should be back at Cuckfield Park within the month."

My eyes teared up and I jumped into his arms. "Do you really believe we'll return so soon?"

His face lit with delight at my excitement as he replied, "If everything goes as it should...and I will do my best to see that it does. Now I must go, as much as I wish I did not have to, but you will be well looked after. Remember...you must not feed on those closest to us. You do not need to leave the castle; my men will bring you blood."

My heart beat wildly, "But...where will they get-"

He cut me off, "Do not worry. They will bring you someone undeserving of life, and they will dispose of the body. These are things you will eventually need to learn, but we are pressed for time. I promise when I return I will venture to teach you all you will need to know."

I felt tears falling over my cheeks, feeling trapped in the life I had chosen for myself. I loved Dardanos and I wanted to be with him, but how many would have to die for us to be together? How many lives was Dardanos willing to end to see his grand scheme reality? How long could I stand to watch people die around us in order to help create this new world in which he and I were the only all-powerful beings in existence?

I had seen the visions of Cassandra and Amunet. I knew Dardanos's ambitions. I had known before I agreed to be with him that he had this great desire to change the world, to become someone of importance, but I had convinced myself that the talk of being a god was simply a metaphor for wanting power and influence. I thought that he relished the idea that I would take over Cuckfield Park for the simple reason that he would then be master of it, not that he wished to take over the duties of killing vampires from Lord Sergison. It was time to stop lying to myself and accept that the things Dardanos had told me had been meant literally, and that all of my visions were real. I was the tragic princess. I was the doomed priestess. I was the woman that had fallen in love with a god and changed the whole course of mankind, and it now seemed I was heading down a path that would once again change the very fate of the entire world.

⊱23⊰

The hour after Dardanos left I felt a significant emptiness inside of me. My life was so connected to his now that his absence left me feeling that a part of myself had left with him. The emptiness I felt was less to do with my unwavering love for him and more to do with the ever consuming feeling I was losing my sense of self. Everything I was now seemed tied to his likes and dislikes, to his dreams and goals. I now relied so much on Dardanos that without him I feared facing the world. I feared what I had become, and I feared what I might do without him near to keep me in check.

I paced the large room, comparing the cold, harsh enclosure to Cuckfield Park's warm, inviting rooms. It wasn't an ugly room. In fact I thought it was quite beautiful with its sparse furniture and bright splashes of color against the dull gray stone of the walls, floor, and ceiling, but it wasn't where I wanted to be. I wanted to be back at Cuckfield, with the hunters and perhaps even the entire staff gone, and that longing caused me to look at my new dwelling with dissatisfaction.

A knock at the door caused me to pause in my frustrated pacing.

I waited a moment before I answered, nervous it was one of the humans come to check on me, "Yes?"

The man I had seen earlier entered, face hardened and stern like a warriors. "Doamnă, my name is Codrin. I have been instructed to serve you. Are you hungry? Shall I fetch you blood?"

I was so unprepared for the question I simply stared at him. He was dark from head to foot: dark close-cut hair, dark eyes, dark mustache and trim beard, dark complexion, dark clothing. I guessed he was no more than thirty; his features were hardened but youthful, and his body was firm as if he spent much of his time keeping it active. Probably training in Dardanos's army; the army that Dardanos had failed to mention before. Codrin's eyes seemed to shift uncomfortably when I didn't answer him, as if he felt he had looked at me for too long.

"Doamnă?" he repeated stiffly, "Shall I fetch you blood?"

This time I forced myself to answer, "No, that won't be necessary, thank you."

Codrin's face didn't change, but as he pulled at his stiff, gray, military style shirt-coat he warned, "You must feed eventually. You put us all at risk going too long without blood."

"How do I put you at risk?" I questioned, setting my jaw stubbornly, and wishing for nothing more than to be left alone.

"The longer you go without blood the stronger your hunger will become. Wait too long and the hunger will become a creature in itself, taking control of you until you quench its thirst." He took a slow, studious step toward me, perhaps looking for signs of my hunger. "Once the hunger is your master you will drain anyone and everyone until it is satisfied. You would kill your own mother, sister, child, your lover without thinking twice; the blood is all that would matter, not from where it came."

I couldn't meet his dark eyes, feeling their accusation. "You must think me a monster."

Codrin softened, giving a shake of his head and a tight-lipped smile. "I did not mean to give that impression. I do not think you are a monster. I have been with the domn many, many years and he has taught me all he knows about vampires. I am merely helping to teach you what I can in his absence."

I nodded my head to show that I understood, but I really didn't want to learn about being a vampire from this stern, humorless human. I wasn't even sure that I wanted to know about being a vampire at all. What I wanted more than anything was to be alone, to wallow in sorrow over every bad thing that had happened over the past few weeks. I needed The Palladium; I needed to hear the soundless whispers that I had as a child, guiding me and telling me everything would turn out all right. My heart sunk as I recalled that seeing my statue was an impossibility. She was still standing in the hedgerows at Cuckfield Park, an empty stone bench her only companion.

"I should very much like to walk outside. Are there gardens?" I asked, glancing sadly toward the window.

"The domn instructed me to keep you in the castle. He worried that your inexperience could get you into trouble. If you'd like you may explore the castle," Codrin explained flatly.

I suddenly felt more like a prisoner than the mistress of the castle. "I won't leave the grounds. I simply need to be outside; it calms me. Please," I pleaded, trying to fill my eyes with pitiful tears.

I could see he was considering it, and then he sighed, "Very well, but stay on the property. If you leave and the domn finds out that I let you he will kill me. My death will be on your conscience."

I stared at him a moment in shock. If he hadn't been so serious I might have thought it a joke. "Really?"

"Really," he stated matter-of-factly as if he were merely telling me it was dark outside or that we were in a castle. "I know my place. If anything happens to you while you're in my care I will be punished...and there is only one punishment for such a thing."

I felt a tinge of guilt to put him in such a position, but I needed to be outside. I needed to feel the breeze, the trees, the earth beneath my feet. "I will stay on the grounds, I promise. I won't do anything that would cause you to be punished."

"Very well," he huffed, rubbing at his beard, "I'll show you the way."

I followed him down a corridor, cold and undecorated, until we were walking in a covered parapet with open arches along one side. The parapet led to a set of stairs which first led down to the right to a small platform, and then led down to the left. Only the first half of the stairs were covered; once I stepped off the center platform there were no walls or roof closing me in. I stepped off the bottom stair into the cool, fresh night air, and closing my eyes I breathed deep the sweet fragrant breeze. When my eyes opened I was disappointed to see I wasn't exactly outside; I was in an inner courtyard, surrounded on all sides by castle walls.

"Will you be able to find your way back?" Codrin asked from behind me a few steps up.

I had forgotten he was still there. "Yes, I'll be fine"

He nodded and added, "If you have any difficulties there are men patrolling the castle; they will help you. Try not to attack any of them."

I ignored his comment, and walked further into the courtyard. I couldn't understand why Codrin had been so hesitant to allow me outside. The courtyard seemed to be completely closed in save for two open archways that were almost directly across from one another. The courtyard itself looked to be at the center of the castle as it was surrounded on all sides by the dull gray stone of the castle. There wasn't much to see in the courtyard, a scant patch of grass, a bench or two, and an uneven path of stone slabs.

I ventured through one of the arches, hoping there might be a decorative garden on the other side, but instead I seemed to be at the entrance of the castle. I found myself staring through the wooden slats of a portcullis. I pushed my face up to the crisscrossed slats to see what was beyond, but all that was visible was a long, wooden bridge perhaps six people wide. Even with my improved night vision I could make out little more than the rolling hills and a small village beyond. I walked back to the courtyard, crossing almost directly to the other side. The door just opposite had a crest above the door with the same image of a raven as I'd seen on the fireplace in my room, and above that was an ornate stone cross. I assumed the room beyond must have been a chapel, most castles had one, but I wasn't interested in seeing it right then. I continued to the right of the door and discovered the other open archway just beneath the staircase I had walked down.

This time there was no medieval barricade to stop me, but I still had not found what I wanted. I walked out into an open area between two of the high castle towers, one of which I thought might be where my room was. There was a large, circular raised area which I thought might have been a fountain or decorative pond, but as I peered into it I could only guess that it must have been a well at one time. It was a strange place for a well but then I guess it would have been convenient to not have to leave the safe confines of the castle to get water. I put my hands on the cold stone slabs to look down into its unfathomable depths and a shudder coursed through my body. A well should not have caused such uneasiness, but I could have sworn I'd heard fervent whispering as I leaned over the side. When I was finally able to pull my eyes away from the gaping hole I saw that there were three stone steps leading up to another parapet walkway on the outer wall of the castle protected by battlements.

I was disappointed once more to discover that the walkway didn't lead into a garden either; the walkway simply circled the outer castle walls, obviously a strategic place for archers or cannons to shoot at enemies. Leaning over the edge to see if I might see a way to get out into the grounds I was surprised to see just how far up I was. There were probably a good five levels below me where the castle met land, but it wasn't flat land; it was steeply sloping land covered in vines and brush.

I looked to the left and could just see the end of the wooden bridge I'd seen through the portcullis, a stream rushing beneath it and cascading over rocks creating small waterfalls. To the right was another smaller wooden bridge which led to a stone wall that encircled the castle and its steep overgrown grounds. It was apparent that this castle had been built for one purpose: to keep people out. The steep hills and narrow bridges would have made it impossible for an attacking army to get very far before they were taken down by soldiers within the castle. Now I understood why it seemed so different from Cuckfield Park and even other castles I'd visited; most homes were designed for the comforts of its inhabitants, showing off their wealth and status, but Corvin castle had been built with the sole purpose of protecting its inhabitants and making it near impossible to invade. It was still beautiful in its simple necessity, but now I knew why it felt so cold, so sad, and so grim; it had obviously seen more than its share of death.

I was lost in thought, imagining an army struggling to climb the steep hill below, when I heard a voice behind me, "Intimidating isn't it?"

I spun around, a chill running through me as I thought I recognized the voice. There stood the man with the swirling blue eyes, resplendent in his trim navy blue suit, his dark hair slicked back loosely. I thought being a vampire would allow me to lose some of my fear, but I was paralyzed by it. Not only did I still feel the uneasiness from my encounter with him in the garden, but I also remembered the loathsome fear he'd induced in my visions.

"You...you..." I sputtered, moving backward until my back was up against the battlement.

"Please," he said, raising his hands, "I never meant to scare you. If I had known it was you in the hedgerow I would never have attempted to grab you. Well, I might have grabbed you, but it would have been for completely different reasons," he joked and then insisted, "Please believe me...I would never harm you."

I shut my eyes tightly, thinking I must surely be experiencing another vision, but when I opened my eyes the man was still standing there with angelic eyes pleading and hands clasped as if begging me to believe him. I knew it must have been a trick. It reminded me of the painting of Apollo slaying Python; everyone believed Apollo was the hero, the golden angel come to the rescue, but I'd always seen him as a fraud. He had always seemed a devious charlatan that used his beauty to get what he wanted.

"How...why...if Dardanos finds you here he will destroy you," I managed to get out, clutching the wall behind me defensively.

"But," he looked at me in confusion, "I'm here because of Dardanos. I'm assisting him."

"You're lying!" I snapped, clutching at the collar of my dress, feeling exposed. "He would never have anything to do with you. Not after the things you've done to him in the past...and to me."

The man shook his head and his swirling blue eyes clouded in confusion. "You must have me confused with someone. I have never done anything truly horrible to Dardanos...unless you count disobedience, but really he knew my behaviors before he turned me; I think it might actually have been the reason he turned-"

"Turned you?!" I interrupted in disbelief.

"Yes, he gave me The Immortal Fate," the man stated simply and then added in disappointment, "Has he never spoken of me?"

"No, never," I answered in a whisper, still eyeing him suspiciously.

"May I ask then why you think I've done you wrong? We've never met except that night in the hedgerow which I already apologized for and you said yourself you've never even been told about me. Surely, my existence is not so encompassing that I've managed to have influence over your life without my knowledge," he joked, winking at me.

"I've seen you," I muttered, my eyes filling with tears as I envisioned my last dream of him, "in visions...in dreams. Don't pretend you don't know who you are. The dreams I've had..."

252

He studied my stricken face and remarked, "It must have been a nightmare. I still don't see how I've done you wrong; most women would consider dreams of me a gift."

I couldn't tell if he was still joking, but he did seem very full of himself so he might have been completely serious. "These weren't just dreams; they were visions. They were memories from my soul...from my past life."

"Hold on," he said, putting his hands up, "this is getting a bit too metaphysical. Do you mean you literally saw things from another lifetime?"

"Are you pretending to be ignorant on purpose?" I asked harshly.

"I don't mean to sound ignorant, but I have absolutely no idea what you're talking about," the man admitted, shaking his head, "but you do look quite sumptuous talking about it."

I glared at him in disgust. "I'm talking about our past lives in which you were Dardanos's enemy and the cause of my deaths. The things that you did…" My lip trembled involuntarily. "So much death…so many died because of your greed. Now you make jokes as if none of it mattered. You may pretend all you like, but I know who you really are," I said darkly.

He seemed to find my words amusing and grinned at me as he asked dramatically, "And who am I...really?"

"Apollo," I answered with as much hatred as I could put into one word.

☙24❧

"Apollo?!" he exclaimed with a loud laugh, "Well that is an impressive name. Do you mean *the* Apollo, charming sun-god extraordinaire? My, but I do wish I could remember that, but I know nothing of past lives such as yourself. I'm only me...Alexander Cavanaugh," he announced with a flourish of his hand as he bowed.

I recognized the name as the one that Codrin had announced to Dardanos the night before. He was the man that had brought news of Cuckfield, but I couldn't understand why Dardanos would be allied with him: the reincarnated Apollo. He was our greatest enemy, and yet he was helping us? Maybe it wasn't a trick; maybe he really had no clue as to who he had been. I stared into his hypnotic blue eyes which had always seemed so hateful to me, but now seemed merely rakish and jovial.

"Well, you've certainly retained *his* ego, but...you have no idea what I'm talking about? You've never been awoken?" I asked, studying his cheerful countenance.

He took a step toward me and said seductively, "I believe I'm awake right now, though, you do look like a dream."

I opened my mouth to answer him back, but couldn't find the words to express my discomfort at his ridiculous remark. "It's something...umm...a medium told me," I stuttered nervously, ignoring his last comment. "Your soul must be triggered to awake in order to see into your past. A gifted psychic opened a door within me allowing me to see visions and have memories of my past lives. Your soul has never been awoken."

"Ah, well, I suppose you have me there," Alexander answered playfully, pointing at me, "I have never been to a medium or psychic, but...I would *love* to hear about your experience. Would you allow me to walk with you?"

I felt the uncomfortable tingle of my visions once again as I looked at him, but though his face and eyes were the same as

Apollo's and he looked identical to Sethos with his black hair there was none of the malevolence of either. The smiling face waiting for my answer seemed to lack the cruelty I had seen in Apollo and even in Sethos. I thought he had the look of a man that was used to getting his own way, not through authority or fear, but through his unmistakable beauty. I wanted to refuse him just for the fact that he seemed so confident that he could persuade me to change my mind, his self-assurance so blatant that it was almost infuriating, but the ease of his manners and the honest need to enthrall induced me to give him a chance.

"Very well, Mr. Cavanaugh," I huffed, pretending unsuccessfully to not be affected by his appearance.

"Please," he said low, taking hold of my hand and wrapping it around his arm, "call me Alexander. After all I hope that we shall be great friends, and great friends call each other by their given names. I shall call you..."

"Elizabeth?" I prompted, assuming that he didn't know my name.

"No, no, that's too stuffy. I may look like a proper gentleman, but I don't go in for all of that tediously pompous behavior," Alexander joked, crossing his arms as if to better study me.

I shook my head in exasperation. "Elizabeth is too stuffy, but Alexander isn't?"

"Hmm," he said, putting his fist to his mouth. "You're right. You should give me a nickname if we're going to be great friends."

I rolled my eyes to heaven, but humored him. "How about Alex?"

"No, no, that's too common. Look at me! Do I look common to you?" He questioned spiritedly, gesturing to himself.

"All right…" I huffed. "Al?" I could see by the horrified look on his face that he thought that was even worse. "Why don't you just tell me what to call you then," I demanded, but the pleading look in his eyes caused me to make another attempt at pleasing him. "Lex…how about Lex?"

He grabbed my hands and raised them to his lips. "That's it! Perfect! I knew we were going to be the best of friends. Now, I am going to call you…" he trailed off, studying my face closely.

I looked away, feeling uncomfortable at how freely he

stared. "My father called me Lizzy," I offered.

"Lizzy, yes, I like that," he said softly and then added, "Though, I do much prefer little queen. If you don't mind, that is?"

I gulped nervously, inquiring, "Why did you call me that? You said that the night in the hedgerows."

Lex bit his lip, and I tried my best to not think about how his lips would taste as he responded, "I don't know. Honestly...I didn't even think about it. It just came into my head when I looked at you. I suppose I thought you something grand like a princess or a queen. Perhaps I should have called you goddess instead," he jested, raising his eyebrows.

"No!" I exclaimed automatically, and then realizing how foolish I sounded I said, "I'm no goddess. I'm just...Elizabeth Cranford, an ordinary woman."

"You mean an ordinary vampire," Lex corrected me, smirking.

"Right," I admitted.

I smiled to hide the discomfort I felt at being referred to as a goddess. I wasn't sure what he knew of Dardanos's plans. Perhaps he had been teasing me because he knew Dardanos wanted me to become a goddess once he was a god. I wondered also if his automatic reaction of calling me little queen might have something to do with our past lives. I had never heard the pet name before, but perhaps that was how Apollo had seen Cassandra or even how Sethos had seen Amunet. Cassandra, after all, had been a princess and Amunet had been an object of Sethos' desires along with becoming king.

"Where shall we go then? I am yours to command," Lex stated softly, hooking his arm through mine.

My cheeks warmed once again as I answered, "I had hoped to walk the grounds. There doesn't seem to be any gardens here, but I would like to at least feel the ground beneath my feet."

"And so you shall, little queen," Lex announced grandly.

He took hold of me tightly and with a playful wag of his eyebrows he jumped over the side of the battlements. I was still so surprised by the ability of vampires to fly that I screamed in absolute terror, and buried my head in Lex's shoulder.

"How's this?" he asked with a little chuckle and an obvious delight in my clinging so inappropriately to him.

I pulled away, embarrassed to realize we were already on the ground. We were standing near the little waterfall, which was larger than it had looked from above. The wooden bridge was just in front of us and so high up it made me remember this place was more fortress than castle. I turned away from the waterfall and saw a rough path a little way up the hill. The area near the stream wasn't quite as steep as the land up past the path, as if someone at some time had enjoyed walking here by the water and had worn a path with their frequent footsteps.

Without a word I made my way up to the path, and could hear the light crunch of footsteps behind me. "He doesn't want me around you, you know," I stated flatly when Lex had caught up to me.

"Who?" he asked automatically, and then realized, "Oh, you mean Dardanos. Well, I can understand that; most men feel uncomfortable by my charm and beauty."

I laughed out loud, but stopped as I saw the serious look on his face. "I thought you were joking. You have a very high opinion of yourself."

"Can you blame me?" he asked teasingly as he flashed his boyish smile.

I tried to glare at him, but it was difficult to not be taken in by his rare giddiness for life. Instead I turned away from him, taking in the overgrown stream bank and the occasional glint of tiny white flowers among the brush. We continued on in silence a few moments and though I knew nothing of Alexander Cavanaugh I felt grateful for his company. It made me think of Emma. If she were alive she would be keeping me company while Dardanos was away. Emma, who had been driven away by the intrigue that I hadn't even known was surrounding me. Emma, who had felt so trampled over that she sought refuge in the impossible notion that she might live forever. Emma, who had been burned alive a mere night after becoming a vampire, after convincing me to become a vampire. *It's always about you*, I heard her accusing voice whisper on the wind.

"What is it?" Lex asked softly.

I turned to him unsure what he meant and shook my head. "I didn't say anything."

He pointed to my face. "You're crying," he said, wiping at my cheek.

"Oh," I replied, putting my fingers to my eyes. "I was just

thinking about my sister...she died...cruelly."

"I know," he admitted, "I'm sorry."

"I forgot...you knew her," I commented, remembering that night in the hedgerows, and then I lightly pointed out, "You weren't very kind to her that night."

"I know," Lex answered uneasily.

"But, you did say some very nice things about me," I added, smiling shyly, hoping he didn't think I was angry at him for his treatment of Emma.

He looked down as we walked, finally saying, "I felt I had to make it clear to Emma that I didn't have feelings for her, nor would I ever. I don't wish to anger you or upset you by saying unkind things about your sister, but I must tell you the truth. Emma was desperate for affection and attention...obsessive even. She wanted so much for Dardanos to want her the way that he wanted you, but when Dardanos told her plainly that was not to be she shifted her affections to me. Then I made it clear to her that she would never have my heart...for it belonged to another."

I felt an ache in my heart for Emma. Why had she been so obsessive? "That must have broken her heart," I said sadly, but not wanting Lex to feel badly I added, "I'm sure in time she understood that your heart belonged to another and it would be wrong to try to change your affections."

Suddenly Lex took hold of my hand, causing me to stop and turn to him. "She didn't understand," he said desperately, his beautiful swirling eyes misting over. "She didn't understand why yet another man had fallen in love with her sister."

I could hear my own heart pounding in my ears as I said in a hushed voice, "You shouldn't say such things."

"I know I shouldn't," he answered passionately, catching me in his arms, "but I cannot deny my heart, and I cannot lie to you. It may seem strange to you that I should be in love with you; you didn't even know I existed before tonight. I've been following you for quite a long time, watching you, making sure you stayed safe. It was part of my duties to watch over you...I couldn't help but fall in love with you."

I knew I should protest. I should remind him I was in love with Dardanos and he with me. I should have asked him to leave and never come back. I thought the memory of Apollo's unwanted desire would cause me to react in disgust. Instead I stood there in shock, transfixed by his earnest eyes as he leaned in and put his petal-soft lips to mine.

My mind finally woke from its hibernation and screamed at me to do something. I pulled away from Lex and pushed him angrily, not because he had stolen a kiss from me, but because I had let him...I had enjoyed it. I took off at a run, trying to escape him before I let anything else happen. I ran with no idea where I was going. I wasn't even sure if there was an entrance back into the castle from where I was.

Suddenly I felt a whoosh of air from behind and I was being lifted off of the ground. I wanted to protest, to fight him, but before a word was able to leave my mouth Lex had landed on the small stone balcony of my bedroom, my body still pressed against his.

"I assume this is where you had hoped to retreat to," he whispered provokingly, still holding me tightly.

"How did you know...how could you know this was my room?" I demanded, trying to lightly pull away from him.

He let me go, flashing his charming smile. "I told you it has been my mission to watch you the past few years..." He shrugged almost bashfully as he explained, "I guess I had become so accustomed to seeing you that I just continued to watch. I saw you as I left the castle last night, leaning on the balcony, staring off into the distance...I could feel your loneliness. You can't imagine how much it hurt me to see you so desolate and not be able to do anything about it. More than that, as I stared at you wanting to be near you, wanting to comfort you, my heart tore in two as I realized you didn't even know I existed."

I turned away from him and walked into the room, putting my hands on the back of one of the chairs to steady myself. "You know that these feelings you have for me aren't real. They're all a result of the connection our souls had in another life," I explained hurriedly, not sure if I even believed what I was telling him. "I never returned Apollo's love, nor Sethos' love, and your soul probably remembers that longing...longing for something you never acquired. That is all."

Lex walked around to the other side of the chair and threw himself unceremoniously onto the sofa. "I see what you're trying to do, and truly I would love to believe I was an irresistible, ravishing, golden-god, but I really don't believe in past lives or the immortality of the soul-"

"But," I cut in, exasperated, "you're a vampire! By definition your soul *is* immortal."

"Not so," he countered, holding up his finger, "my body is immortal...until someone finds a way to destroy it, but my soul? My soul is only tethered to my immortal body. My soul will fade into nothingness once my body is no more."

"How could you say such a thing?!" I protested, moving around the chair to sit in it. "How could you think that any of God's creations were so finite?"

He was leaning back lazily, his right ankle propped over his left knee as he shrugged, "Honestly, I don't believe either which way. I have never seen nor heard anything to prove or disprove the immortality or even the existence of the soul. I simple wanted to talk with you more," he mused, twisting his lips into a seductive grin.

I licked my lips and turned away, fighting the curving of my mouth. "You purposely provoked an argument with me so that I wouldn't throw you out of my room?"

"It worked didn't it?" he boasted, his blue eyes twinkling. "I rather like arguing with you."

I stood up with a huff, "It would probably be better if you left. Dardanos would be angry if he knew you had spent time with me. He told me himself he wished to keep you away from me, and now I understand why."

"Because I'm devilishly handsome," Lex asked playfully, raising his eyebrows, "and you wouldn't be able to resist me?"

"No!" I said too loudly, and then calming I sat down beside him on the sofa. "He said you can be unpredictable...and from what I've seen I must say I agree."

He sat up, giving me a serious look. "You know, some people find unpredictability irresistible. It lends a bit of excitement to life. Like racing a horse at breakneck speed through the rain, or..." he leaned over and pecked my lips quickly. "...or kissing a stranger on the lips."

I primly set my hands in my lap, pretending to not be affected by his kiss, and looked down. "I would rather have stability in my life."

"Oh," he answered smartly, "you mean like having your entire family murdered, being lied to by your dead fiancé, and having to flee your home as peasants burn your sister to death?"

My eyes burned with anger as I spat back, "Unpredictability aside, you are potentially dangerous to me. Whether you believe in an immortal soul or not Dardanos and I have seen what you are capable of, and more than once it has resulted in my death."

"I'm sorry," Lex said sincerely, "I didn't mean to upset you, and I know Dardanos only wishes for your happiness. Sometimes I let my cynicism take over. Please forgive me and please...please don't send me away. I don't know what I did in the past, but I'll apologize for it, and I promise I would never do anything to bring you harm. Just let me be your friend. At least allow me that one happiness."

"I...I don't..." I knew I should tell him no, but the hopeful look in his eyes gave me pause. "I'll have to discuss it with Dardanos. I won't keep things from him. If you truly wish to be my friend it will be done honestly, not behind Dardanos's back...and no more kissing."

"I can live with that. Well, not the no kissing, but I suppose I'll suffer through," Lex said, lying back on the sofa once again, "that is if Dardanos doesn't go berserk when he finds out I was here with you when I was supposed to be running errands for him and kills me."

"Was that supposed to be a joke?" I asked, frowning at him.

"Yes...and no. Dardanos takes loyalty very seriously. If he views my visit to you as disloyal he wouldn't hesitate to destroy me. Why," he questioned, wagging his eyebrows at me as he continued, "are you worried about me?"

I huffed, "I might be concerned if you weren't so frustrating. *AND* you're wrong about Dardanos; he's practical, not cruel. He has already told me how valuable your help has been to him; I doubt he would just kill you with no thought of everything you've done for him."

Lex sat up and leaned toward me to whisper, "You really don't know Dardanos very well, do you?"

"I know him well enough to know he doesn't behave like a mindless beast, devouring everything in his path," I argued, feeling a strange wave of weakness come over me.

Lex didn't seem to notice how much effort I was exerting in order to just continue sitting up as he laughed lightly, "Right...so basically you're saying you really don't know him very well. I may be wrong, I've only known him about one hundred years, but he has always been driven by an almost manic single-minded goal. I have seen what happens to those that threaten to interrupt his plans. You...you are irreplaceable to him, but me...well, I know where I stand. I know he keeps many things from me, and yet he trusts me with his most important tasks…"

I heard what he had said, but it sounded so far away. I felt a strange haziness as if I'd had too much wine. My eyes seemed to be misting over and though I could see Lex's mouth was still moving it sounded like a murmur from another room. Lex stopped talking and looked at me in confusion as his mouth moved, making the shape of my name. Each blink of my eyes seemed to drain me until I could no longer hold myself up. My body pitched forward heavily and Lex moved to catch me.

Everything was dim, but I could hear Alexander mumbling something; all I could understand was one word, "...blood..."

With what little strength I had left I forced two words from my mouth, "Blood...yes."

☙25☙

Images were flooding my mind of people being murdered, soldiers laughing and drinking, women being beaten and taken advantage of. Was I this horrible person? What made me so cruel; wasn't I supposed to protect people? I had a vague remembrance of a beautiful man with opulent blue eyes and strong, full lips, but the memory was so dim I thought it must have been a dream. A woman fought against me. I had her pushed up against a wall, struggling to pull my gun from its holster. I fumbled drunkenly, causing the gun to go off, shooting the woman in the chest. I had my way with her anyway. My eyes shot open in repulsion. I was confused as to when I had closed them and discovered my mouth was locked against a wrist. The arguing in the background became louder as my body grew stronger from the blood I was ingesting.

"You are not supposed to be here!" Codrin yelled.

"If I hadn't been here you and your men would have found yourselves in quite a predicament," came the calm reply from Lex.

I let go of the wrist hanging over the side of the sofa, having drained the man, and looked at my victim. The man was lying on the sofa dressed like the soldiers I had seen in my vision and I realized I had once more seen images through the blood of someone's life. The line between who he was and who I was seemed to have blurred as I drank from him, making me feel for a few moments that I was him. I shivered at the twisted thoughts that had swirled in my head. Looking up at the dead body lying there, remembering the images from his life, I wondered if perhaps Dardanos was correct: perhaps there were many that were undeserving of life.

The arguing continued as Lex pointed defensively at Codrin. "I did you a favor. If I hadn't been here you or one of your men would have been her snack, and you know Dardanos would not have given your death a second thought. Leave

Dardanos to me; I'll explain why I was here." I could see Codrin considering what Lex had said as Lex smiled warmly and put his hand on Codrin's shoulder. "He should not have left her here...with only mortals to look after her. She's a newborn; she needs guidance. I know you are very capable of fighting vampires, but you and I both know if you even laid one finger on her to defend yourself you'd be dead before you got one word of explanation out. It's an unfair thing to ask of a mortal."

Codrin nodded, his iciness melting under Lex's charm. "You are right, of course, but I have my orders. I must do as I am told."

Lex narrowed his eyes and smiled thinly in understanding as he soothed, "I know, my friend. Leave it to me. I'm to meet Dardanos tonight; I will explain everything and I will convince him that this should never happen again."

"You would do that?" Codrin asked in disbelief.

"Of course," Lex tossed off, "I would hate to see such loyal, well trained men killed because a fledgling vampire was not properly educated. I will explain to Dardanos that the girl needs guidance...from a vampire. You and your men should not be risked."

"Thank you, my friend," Codrin gushed, the first hint of a smile on his face. "Shall we bring more blood?" he asked, nodding toward me. "Will she be all right now?"

Lex put his arm around Codrin and began leading him toward the door. "She will be fine. I will see to her; I need not leave for a few hours yet. Think on it no more. I will sort everything out."

Once Codrin left the room Lex came to me to help me off the floor. I had been sitting on the floor leaning against the sofa, drinking the blood of the soldier lying on the sofa. I turned my eyes away from the white-gray face staring blankly up at me, a look of horror on its face. I closed my eyes in disgust, feeling sullied by the blood of this wretch coursing through my veins.

I forced my eyes to light upon Lex and his boyish grin. "How did you do that?"

Lex scrunched his eyebrows and asked, "Do what?"

I gestured toward the door. "How did you talk Codrin into letting you stay? How did you get him to smile?" I asked in amazement.

Lex looked down, smiling almost bashfully. "Oh, that,

well...it's...I guess you could say it's one of my powers."

"Your power is talking people into things?" I questioned, raising an eyebrow.

"I like to call it charm," Lex said slyly, reaching out a hand to roll the body of the dead officer off the couch, and offering the seat to me. "But yes, you could say I'm very good at convincing mortals that I'm completely wonderful and they should listen to me," he explained,

My mouth turned down and I shook my head to indicate I didn't want to sit. "And what about immortals?" I asked suspiciously, worried that my hesitation to tell him to leave could have been because he had some power over me.

"It's possible," Lex admitted with a shrug, "but it's more difficult. Every power takes a great deal of effort and concentration. To use a power on an immortal takes even more concentration...especially if they're powerful."

"So you can charm, as you call it, an immortal?" I asked defensively.

He shifted uneasily from one foot to the other as he realized what I was asking. "Yes, I have done it, but it is indescribably difficult, and I swear I never used it on you."

"You swear?" I demanded, crossing my arms in front of me.

"Yes, I swear it...on my soul," he pleaded, putting his hand over his chest.

I almost laughed out loud. "I thought you didn't know if you had a soul. You can't swear on something you don't believe in," I mused.

"But you believe in it," he said, his eyes swirling with sincerity, "and I believe in you...that is enough to bind me to my promise."

I turned my head from side to side, studying him. "I can't tell if you're being serious or if you're making fun of me."

"I would never!" he exclaimed in mock indignation. "Now...how are you feeling?"

"Better," I admitted, shaking my head at my own stupidity. "Thank god you were here. I didn't listen. Codrin told me I needed to feed, but I was so disgusted with the thought I told him I didn't need blood. What if I had..."

Lex put his hand under my chin to lift my eyes to his. "Don't regret what might have been. You're fine...Codrin is fine...the other men are fine," he soothed, and then giving me a bright smile he announced, "I have a poem to recite to you. Well, it isn't mine, but I heard you liked poetry and when I saw you on your balcony last night it brought it to my mind. Perhaps you know it: I heard the trailing garments of the Night / Sweep through her marble halls! / I saw her sable skirts all fringed with light / From the celestial walls! / I felt her presence, by its spell of might, / Stoop o'er me from above; / The calm, majestic presence of the Night, / As of the one I love."

"Longfellow," I answered, feeling thankful for Lex's presence, but also somewhat confused about why I allowed him to stay.

Lex beamed with pride, and teasingly added, "Makes you wonder if the old boy had a vampire lover, doesn't it?"

I rolled my eyes and answered, "Just because a lady wears black and appears at night does not automatically make her a vampire."

A knock at the door startled me; I was still feeling a bit unsettled from my loss of control. "Who is it?" I shakily asked.

Codrin's stern voice answered, "It is I, Doamnă. I have brought two men with me to remove the body."

My eyes shot to the decaying soldier now lying on the floor. "Come in!" I called out, repulsed at what I had done and what I'd seen.

I walked away from the sitting area as they entered. I stared out the balcony window, my back to the men, feeling like a monster. I didn't want to meet their probing eyes; no matter how common such things might be to them I knew their thoughts were probably filled with fear and disgust for me. Lex walked the three men back to the door, making them laugh stiffly at some lewd joke about death.

"They're gone, little queen," Lex's voice lilted across my hair, and then stepping to the side he leaned against the wall to the right of the window so that he was facing me. "You're wrong, you know? The lady in the poem is a vampire," he explained seriously, "because she's you. They're all you. Every poem, every song, every painting, every whisper on the wind of love...it will always be you."

My heart beat wildly with the fresh blood in my veins as I admitted sadly, "I think I'm cursed, Lex."

Lex sat with me for hours, waiting for me to feel the pull of my day-sleep, and telling me about his life in Ireland before Dardanos had turned him. As I had expected he had been born into a wealthy family, living a life of privilege in which he was spoiled not only by a limitless fortune but adored for his uncommon beauty. He had always gotten everything he had ever wanted...from everyone. That is until his parents chose a bride for him, a woman with not only a fortune to match his own but also a title. He refused to marry her believing his parents would give into him like they always did. On this one point, though, they would not be moved, and so Lex ran away in rebellion.

That was when he met Dardanos. Stumbling down the street on his way to yet another tavern with friends he shared rooms with. Dardanos struck up a conversation with them, and invited them back to his large home with the promise of all the wine they could drink. Lex and his friends spent a week at Dardanos's massive house. They would sleep until late in the day, go out drinking late into the night, and Dardanos would invite musicians and women back to the house to entertain them. On the sixth or seventh night, after Lex's friends had passed out from too much wine Dardanos made Lex an offer. Dardanos offered Lex The Immortal Fate, and though he left it entirely up to Lex to decide if he wanted it or not he had made sure Lex consumed enough wine before he offered it.

"Of course I accepted. I could barely see straight...I thought I was dreaming. You know that feeling you have in dreams like anything is possible? I felt like that. When Dardanos asked if I'd like to live forever it only made sense to me to say yes. How could I turn down such an offer?" he asked rhetorically, raising his hands with a dramatic flair.

I nodded my head in understanding and asked quietly, "Do you ever regret it? What you've become?"

"No, never," Lex uttered resolutely, "I feel I was always meant to become this. I can't imagine ever having to watch myself grow old...growing older until my body finally gives out. No, I was meant to be young and beautiful forever."

"I envy you. I feel I have nothing but regret. I love Dardanos and I know that becoming this...this thing was the only way to be with him, but it's as if every decision I've made recently has only brought misery and guilt. I wish I could feel no regret at allowing myself to be turned; I wish I could be like you...no regrets," I explained softly.

Lex smiled weakly and admitted, "There is one thing I feel bad about. I'm sorry that my friends had to die. They weren't bad fellows; they simply made a poor choice in befriending me."

"Dardanos killed them? Why?" I asked surprised.

Lex's eyes met mine as he answered, "We...*we* killed them. The hunger came over me while they were still passed out from the wine. One of them tried to escape as I was draining my second victim. Dardanos went after him to protect our secret. I don't blame Dardanos for their deaths; it was my own inability to control the hunger which killed them."

We were quiet a moment before I inquired, "Did Dardanos ever tell you why he chose to give you The Immortal Fate? There must have been a reason he chose you over your friends."

Lex shrugged innocently, "I never asked. I always assumed it was because it was what I wanted, even before I knew vampires existed I wanted to live forever, and Dardanos had somehow been able to hear that secret wish though I'd never spoken it aloud. That...and he probably felt impelled to preserve such rare beauty."

"Just when I think you're going to say something thought provoking you ruin it with your vanity," I pointed out, a smirk on my lips. "But Dardanos never gave you a reason? He never mentioned that you reminded him of someone?"

Lex shook his head, a look of puzzlement on his face. "You mean because you think I was Apollo? You think he chose me because I had been a god?"

I didn't answer him, because I honestly didn't think Dardanos would give him The Immortal Fate knowing that he had been Apollo in his past life; if anything I would have expected Dardanos to have killed him on the spot. Instead he had made him a vampire, and I couldn't understand why Dardanos hadn't explained to Lex that he was not only the god Apollo in a past life but also Dardanos's brother Sethos. I now knew why Dardanos had tried to keep me from Lex: he feared the remembrance of our souls. He feared that Lex's soul would remember the bitter jealousy felt by both Apollo and Sethos which had resulted in my past deaths. What I couldn't understand was why he would choose to give someone he feared immortality? Why would he entrust such a person with his most confidential plans?

"What are you thinking?" Lex asked, leaning toward me intimately.

"Nothing, I just...I just don't understand a few things, but I plan to bring it up with Dardanos." I explained, biting my lip. "Are you truly going to tell him you were here with me? Are you going to ask to assist in my...education, as you called it?"

"I plan to," he said, grabbing my hand joyfully, "with your permission of course."

"Yes, I would like for you to tell him that we met. It will make it easier when I start asking him questions about you."

"So you do find me interesting?" Lex teased, raising his eyebrows playfully.

"Yes," I stated flatly and then quickly added, "but it has nothing to do with your appearance. It has to do with your past lives. Knowing what I know about your past lives makes it completely illogical that you're standing before me as a vampire. All reason dictates that a meeting with Dardanos should have resulted in your death. Obviously there must be a reason that I can't see, and I don't like being kept in the dark about things that have direct bearing on my life. I think Dardanos has gotten too used to everyone obeying him without question. If he wishes to have my trust as he claims to trust me then he cannot keep such things for me. I must have truth...or this life is no more than an illusion."

The following night Dardanos returned. I was a little surprised by his early return, even with what had happened the night before. After his insistence that he need find all the hunters before they disappeared I was sure he would be delayed at least a few days. I could see as he rushed into the room, tossing what appeared to be a blanket over one of the chairs carelessly, that he was worried. Lex had obviously kept his promise to tell Dardanos that we'd met, and that he'd helped me with the hunger. The only thing I didn't know as Dardanos practically ran to my side in front of the fire was if he was concerned that I had blacked out from the hunger or if he was concerned that I'd spent time with Lex.

"General," I said brightly, ignoring the worry on his face,

"you didn't have to return so soon because of me. I was foolish to put off feeding; Codrin even warned me, but I didn't listen. I'm fine now."

Dardanos threw himself onto the sofa beside me, grasping my hand. "You saw him?!"

"You mean Alexander?" I asked, trying to keep my voice steady. "Yes, I met him. I don't know what I would have done without him. Thank god he happened to show up; I might have killed one of your men...or several of them."

Dardanos looked down, a sigh of relief escaping his lips. "He did not scare you?"

"At first I was frightened. I was confused as to why he was here. I recognized him, of course-"

"Did you tell him?!" Dardanos demanded.

I could see the anxiety in Dardanos's eyes as I answered cautiously, "I told him I recognized him as Apollo. I assumed he was like us and knew about his past lives."

Dardanos nodded as I spoke and then calmly asked, "What did he say? Did you tell him anything else?"

I felt uneasy thinking about all of the secrets that Dardanos was keeping, but this was exactly what I had wished to speak to him about so I forced myself to go on, "He didn't believe me. My opinion is that he thinks everything is a joke." I paused seeing the smirk on Dardanos's lips. "I did tell him that he had been responsible for my death...twice, but I didn't tell him that he had been your brother in his most recent past life. When I discovered that he had no idea what I was talking about I assumed there was a reason you hadn't told him and I refrained from revealing anything else."

Dardanos stood abruptly and paced in front of me. "Good, good," he muttered.

"Why are you keeping these things from him?" I ventured to ask quietly. "You trust him to help you, but you've kept many things from him."

Dardanos stopped pacing and sat beside me, taking a long calming breath. "I fear triggering his memories by telling him about his past. That was my main reason for trying to keep you away from him. I thought if anything could trigger his memory it would be his obsession with you."

"But it didn't," I pointed out, feeling more confident with my questioning, "his soul has not been awakened. He has absolutely no hint of who he was, or who we were. You have nothing to fear from him."

"Perhaps," Dardanos answered lightly, tapping his fist against his mouth. "I prefer to be cautious, nothing is ever absolute."

I pursed my lips and put my hands in his. "Why did you turn him if you think he's so dangerous to us?"

"I turned him because I believed him to be dangerous to me," he sighed. "I had a theory that once one receives The Immortal Fate their soul can never be awakened. Of course, if it had already been awakened there is no way to erase those memories. I made the mistake once of turning someone before making sure that their soul remembered who she had been in the past. No matter what I tried I could not wake her memories."

"What happened to her?" I asked, wondering if I really wanted to know.

Dardanos looked down guiltily. "She was killed. I could not save her."

"Oh," I muttered. "So you believe Lex's soul will never be awakened now that he is a vampire?"

Dardanos nodded and looking up asked, "How many visions have you had since I turned you?"

I shrugged, thinking back over the past few nights. "I don't know...I guess I've had...about..." I scrunched my eyebrows. "I don't think I've had one vision. At least I can't remember any."

"Nor have I...since I was turned in 245 A.D.; nor did Amunet in the few short nights that she spent as a vampire. It seems the cursed blood does not allow visions. Once the blood flows through your body all chance of discovering more about a past life is gone."

I felt a little relieved that I would never have to suffer through another disturbing vision or suffer the imminent confusion afterward. I did, however, wonder about the woman he had turned that was unable to learn who she had been in her past life. Who was she? What link did she have to Dardanos? Did someone really kill her, and if so did Dardanos really try to save her? Did he think she was another incarnation of Cassandra and Amunet?

"What is it?" Dardanos asked after a moment.

I blinked at him before realizing I had been glaring at the

fire. "I was just considering what you were saying. If you're correct then Lex poses no threat...to either of us."

"He asked to aid in your...training when I am away. He said you need someone to watch over you, especially now in these early days," Dardanos said as if he had no opinion either way.

I still wasn't sure how I felt about Lex; he was an interesting specimen, but his declaration of love made me uneasy. "I was glad he was here when my hunger took over. I don't think I could have lived with the guilt if I had fed on one of your men. Plus...I don't feel comfortable around humans, and this place begins to feel like a prison with no one to talk to."

Dardanos nodded understandingly, a look of guilt on his face. "I am sorry I had to bring you here; it was never my plan to take you away from Cuckfield. I had hoped we would reside immediately at Cuckfield Park once we were married. I never took into account the possibility that Lord Sergison had trained his servants as vampire hunters. I should have been more thorough. I know this place is not an ideal home for you; in truth it is little more than a fortress." He paused staring at the fire thoughtfully. "I will be gone quite often over the next month. I actually must return to Cuckfield this night to conclude my search for the hunters before I lose track of them. I only returned to make sure you were all right. I wish I did not have to leave you, but I must tend to things if we are ever to return to Cuckfield, and it is too dangerous there right now for you to go with me."

"I could help you. Now that I'm a vampire I'm much stronger," I offered hopefully.

Dardanos gave me a sad look and brushed my cheek. "You are still in your first moon." He had said something similar when we had been searching for Lady Sergison but he repeated, "A vampire is as vulnerable as a human in the first month that they are turned. You may have special abilities, but you can still be killed by quite common means. I am afraid you are not truly immortal until you have been a vampire for one full month, and I will not risk you getting hurt while you are so vulnerable."

"I see," I answered sadly, rising to look out the balcony.

"Lex is in Cuckfield tonight, keeping up the search for the hunters, but he should be able to return tomorrow night," Dardanos stated, moving to put his arms around me. "I want you to be happy and I will do anything to make you so, even if I do not particularly like it."

I smiled appreciatively. "Thank you. I feel better that another vampire will be here in case...well, in case I can't control myself."

"You tell me if he does anything strange...or...stranger than usual for him. If he makes you feel uncomfortable at all, or he does something that makes you think he is remembering Apollo or Sethos you must tell me at once."

"I will. I wouldn't have praised his conduct if I had felt uncomfortable around him." It wasn't the complete truth, but my curiosity for Alexander Cavanaugh was stronger than my uneasiness about him.

"I almost forgot, I brought you some things," Dardanos whispered excitedly in my ear.

I turned to see him pulling an object from his inside pocket. A book. A small, green, linen book. I couldn't help but smile at the little copy of *The Moonstone* that I had left behind in Cuckfield. I took it from him gratefully.

"I have not had time to finish reading the story so I thought perhaps you could tell me what happens," Dardanos offered softly.

"Yes," I answered distractedly, thumbing the spine of the book, and thinking about Gabriel. "I was at a very interesting part where the true thief is about to be named, and it has already proven not to be who I thought it was. Thank you," I said, kissing him lightly on the cheek.

Dardanos smiled brightly and as if just remembering stated, "I have something else for you. Something very special."

He walked back to the sitting area and lifted the bulky blanket that I'd seen him toss so dismissively onto the chair when he'd arrived. I looked at it curiously, wondering why he would have brought me a blanket. I walked closer and realized it was the blanket from my room at Cuckfield Park. I smiled at his thoughtfulness, though I felt no real attachment to the blanket, but then I saw that he was unwrapping something from within the blanket.

"I wrapped it in the blanket from your room in order to protect it on the flight over," Dardanos explained as he unraveled his prize from the jumble of cloth.

A low gasp escaped my lips as I gazed upon the gift

Dardanos had brought for me. It was the accursed dress that my mother had dyed black for Gabriel's funeral. Dardanos held it up, a look of adoration on his face. I could see that for him the dress represented the culmination of our love. That night in the hedgerows was arguably the night that I gave myself, mind and body, to Dardanos, but I didn't associate any of that with the horrid dress.

Dardanos seemed unaware of my repulsion at seeing the dress again as he continued his narrative, "I ventured back to your room and saw your dress laid out on the bed. It must have just been brought back from the laundry...as if someone knew I would be arriving to fetch it."

Or someone reasoned that my dead body would be found any day and I would need a proper dress to be buried in so they might as well just launder the one I had lying around.

Dardanos walked closer, holding out the dress to me. I hesitated, remembering the last time I had touched the dress and the disturbing vision it had produced; a vision of myself in a coffin, my head strangely out of alignment with my body. If Dardanos was correct in his theory I didn't have to worry about visions now that I was a vampire. The cursed blood that coursed through my veins would prevent such things, at least it would prevent me from seeing anything from the past, but what if my vision had been of the future? As the reincarnated Cassandra did I have her gift of seeing into the future? Did my future end with me wearing the wretched funeral dress, the symbol of how dark and twisted my life had become?

"Are you not pleased?" Dardanos asked, waking me from my thoughts.

I softened my glare and lied, "Oh yes, very pleased. I'm surprised that's all." How could I explain my irrational hatred and fear of an article of clothing to him when he had obviously taken great joy at the idea of returning the dress to me?

"Will you wear it?" He asked hopefully.

I closed my eyes a moment to gulp down my disgust and replied, "Yes, if it makes you happy."

"I must speak with Codrin before I leave," Dardanos explained holding the dress out to me. "I'll be back soon."

I reached for the dress, bracing myself for any dark images it might induce. When nothing happened I smiled in relief and let out a loud sigh. Dardanos gave me a puzzled look, but said nothing before he left. I tried to convince myself that I shouldn't let silly things like the dress bother me; after all I was an immortal now and such things were trivial. Still, I couldn't shake the idea that the inky gown was a sign. A sign of death and darkness that seemed to be following me.

ꙮ26ꙮ

I changed into the funeral gown as I had agreed to do. I spent the long minutes waiting for Dardanos telling myself the dress was just a dress, nothing more. It didn't represent anything. It wasn't an omen; it wasn't a sign; it was just a dress. Finally I put my discomfort aside to find a mirror. It had been days since I had looked at my reflection and I was sure the result was probably not pleasant. I remembered seeing Dardanos check his appearance a few times in a half-length mirror on the inside door of the armoire.

My face was somewhat smudged with dirt and my hair was in desperate need of a brush, though not so bad as it should have been. I remembered Codrin bringing in a pitcher of water earlier and a large bowl. I had thought it strange, as vampires didn't require water to drink, but now I could see he must have been hinting that I needed a wash. After washing up a bit I ran my fingers through my hair which surprisingly worked to tame my unruly, tangled curls. Dardanos walked in as I was attempting to finish styling my long, burgundy hair so that it didn't look like such a wild mess.

"I should have thought to bring you grooming items," Dardanos said as he wrapped his arms around me. "As you can see I am unaccustomed to having a woman around."

I smiled weakly. "It isn't as if we had known we were coming here. It wasn't exactly a planned escape. How could you have known those men would attack in such a way? The last thing on my mind were toiletries."

"Still, I shall have things sent for you," he stated before turning me to face him. "Not that you need any of it...you are mesmerizing."

He put his lips to mine, pushing against my mouth wantonly. I felt the heat rising in him, his recent feeding bringing a blush to his cheeks and a firmness to his entire body. I found myself softening expectantly against him; the scent of blood on him as enticing as his muscular frame. He lifted me easily into his arms, still running his tongue along mine, and carried me to the bed.

As he placed me gently on the bed and began removing my gown I felt the cold tendrils of hunger lapping at my insides. I tried to push the strange tipsy feeling away, the same feeling I had felt the night before when I'd blacked out. I didn't want to ruin this moment with Dardanos, our first real chance for intimacy in nights. Dardanos was just pulling his shirt off, moving to undo his pants when my vision blurred and my hands shot out for him.

I was trying to focus on Dardanos, focus on the room, and force the animalistic hunger back. I opened my eyes, a moment of clarity washing over me, and I found Dardanos was staring up at me. I was straddled atop him on the bed, my hands pressed into his shoulders as if to hold him down, as if I had the power to hold him down. I looked at him in confusion, not sure exactly how we'd gotten into this position, but I could see a sly smile spreading across his lips.

He was enjoying this, and I had to admit I found it surprisingly exciting. Although I wouldn't say I was prudish I did live in a world where women were taught to suppress their passions. I had never hidden my pleasure from either Gabriel or Dardanos, but I had never initiated any kind of passion. I had always let Gabriel, and even Dardanos, induce any acts of intimacy, but now I felt the call of blood urging me on in uncharacteristic boldness.

I pushed my nails gently into Dardanos's chest, dragging them downward toward his navel and leaving thin paths of blood behind. I dizzily fell to my hands lapping at the blood before the wounds healed. It tasted of metallic sweetness, and a low cry escaped my lips as I realized the wounds had already healed.

"Come here," Dardanos whispered, holding out his arms.

I crawled up to his neck where he had made a small scratch with his nail, tempting me with the irresistible dot of blood. I licked at it, but it had already begun to heal; I would have to use my teeth to break open the tantalizing drink that awaited. The hunger didn't allow me to hesitate, to worry that I would hurt him. I punched my fangs through his skin forcefully.

At the moment his blood rushed down my throat I felt his teeth in my neck. I braced for the images of his life to start playing in my head, but they never appeared. Instead I felt a strange weightlessness as if I were floating. I looked about me and could make out a meadow of low grass and wild flowers, a stream winding its way through as the water coming off the distant snow covered mountains rushed past. The light was soft as if looking through a gossamer veil.

"Where am I?" I asked aloud, my voice echoing in the strange space.

"We are everywhere," Dardanos answered, though I couldn't see him.

"Why can't I see you?" I wondered dreamily and then looking down added, "Why can't I see my body?"

"Gods do not need bodies," he said plainly.

"Gods? But we're not gods...we're vampires, or was that a dream?" I asked confused.

"This is only a taste of what being a god would be. We can be anywhere...be anything. This is our realm, our...heaven, if that is what you prefer to call it. It was created with our minds, our bodies, our souls...through the circular transference of our blood."

I was only half listening as I attempted to reach out toward a flower to see if it was indeed real. Even without being able to see my body I still felt I was a tangible substance, and I was sure I could still touch things, perhaps even grab them. Instead of plucking the flower I found myself drifting closer and closer to it...no, drifting into it. I was the flower. I could feel my shape around me, the breeze lightly rustling my petals, bugs crawling past my roots, and a pulse like a heartbeat radiating through me.

"Can you feel it?" Dardanos's voice boomed from somewhere above, "Can you feel the connectedness? This is the way we were meant to be...a part of everything and everyone, able to go where and when we choose. Bound to everything, but bound by nothing."

I understood now his great desire to be a god. The freedom of being...without any restriction. It was something I never knew I desired until I felt it for myself. Perhaps his goal to become a god wasn't so hard to understand after all. I was about to tell him so when the world began to fade. There was a great tremor and then darkness. I tried to focus on the hazy realm; I tried to bring back the flower. I wanted to be that flower forever.

I had never felt so whole, so content, but it was gone. I opened my eyes to candle and firelight.

"What was that?" I asked dreamily, rolling over to lie next to Dardanos.

Dardanos turned on his side to face me, propped up on one elbow. "That is what the world would be like for us when we are gods. Intoxicating is it not?"

"Yes..." I answered thoughtfully, "but how was that possible?"

"I do not know. It only works when two feed at the same time. I do not know if it has to do with the blood cycling through two bodies or if it is because of who we are. I have only ever tried it with you and Amunet. It may be that we can achieve it because we were once gods."

"But I was never a god," I argued, running my fingers over my skin to make sure I was still real.

"Cassandra was the daughter of a goddess...that made her part god. I do not even know if that matters. I have never tested it with another vampire that I knew was not once a god."

I stared at the ceiling only half listening. "It was incredible. I could have stayed there forever." I turned my head hearing rustling to see Dardanos getting dressed. "Are you leaving?"

"I have to. I have already stayed longer than I had intended," he explained, walking around the bed to take me in his arms. "Remember, Alexander will be back tomorrow night. Tell me if he does anything that makes you uncomfortable...and promise me you will not discuss anything more about our past lives. Though I am sure it is not possible; I do not want to take any chances. I do not want him to remember...I do not want him to wake up."

I kept my promise to Dardanos and never mentioned another word about our past lives to Lex. Any time that Lex brought it up I would remind him that I had made a promise and I intended to keep it. He would just shrug his shoulders as if he really wasn't interested anyway.

Three weeks had gone by at Corvin Castle and I was spending most of my time with Lex; I actually saw him more than I saw Dardanos. It was nearly a month since I'd been turned into a vampire, but it seemed our stay in Romania was going to be extended well beyond what Dardanos had thought. My claim on Cuckfield Park was not as simple as we had hoped, and there was not even a guess at how long it would take to gain our home.

When we had arrived at the law firm with our marriage papers and to begin the legal acquisition of the estate we were informed that Lady Sergison's family had decided to challenge the will. I was still responsible for the running and upkeep of Cuckfield Park, which was where Dardanos spent most of his time taking over matters as my husband, but we were not permitted to reside at the estate until matters had been settled with Lady Sergison's family. After the gruesome way Lord and Lady Sergison died Lady Sergison's relatives seemed to harbor suspicions about Dardanos and me. There was an investigation being mounted at their expense to look into the murders. They were even challenging our marriage papers, causing me to think that they were more worried I had been manipulated by Dardanos and that he was simply trying to gain the property dishonestly through me than that they thought we had any connection to the Sergisons' deaths. Besides the disappointment of not being able to return to Cuckfield Park I was also denied the papers that my father assured me would come into my possession should both he and Lord Sergison die. I was eager to find what secrets they contained, but they too were tied to the Estate and so would only be given to me once I had been proved rightful heir.

If Dardanos wasn't arguing with lawyers or arranging things for Cuckfield Park then he was hunting vampires in the area or seeking out recruits for his army. The amassing of an army of vampire killers made me very uneasy, but Dardanos would only answer my fears by saying that it was an intrinsic step in his plans. I discovered early on that he was also keeping his army a secret from Lex, and even the plan to eventually eliminate all vampires had been kept secret. I didn't tell Lex, but the more time we spent together the guiltier I felt for keeping so much from him. Lex seemed to hide nothing; he was open and honest in a way I'd never experienced. Although I didn't share Dardanos's secrets with him I didn't hesitate to share all of myself: my childhood, my beliefs, my fears. I felt as if I'd been forced to hold everything in for so long that I had no choice but to let it all flow out, and Lex was the only one around to hear it.

During these long absences by Dardanos Lex was teaching me what I needed to know about being a vampire. I could focus on sounds as far away as the village, I could leap great distances, and I could read some mortals' thoughts. I could sense presences before I saw them and Lex had even taught me to charm people, though I wasn't nearly as good at it as he was. Our nights were usually spent in distant towns where I could practice these skills without fear of someone recognizing me as the new mistress of Corvin Castle. Just being able to be out of the castle, walking a lonely street beside Lex was enough to forget my uncertainty about Dardanos and my longing to go home.

One evening while we were walking toward the little stream that ran alongside the castle, as had become our custom, Lex gave me a sly smile.

"What is it?" I asked expectantly, now so familiar with his looks to know he was excited about something.

His swirling blue eyes flashed with mirth but he just shook his head. "You'll see."

I couldn't guess at what he was hiding. A joke? A surprise? A test of some kind? Then the hill evened out before us and I could see what he'd done.

"The Palladium," I whispered in surprise. "You brought her here...for me?"

Lex's smile broadened so wide it almost lit the night. "Are you pleased? I noticed when I watched you at Cuckfield Park that you seemed very much attached to this statue. I thought it might bring you some comfort while you're away from your home."

I stepped onto the grassy area of the hill and sat down, facing The Palladium. "I'm very pleased. The Palladium used to sit in my own garden before it was moved to Cuckfield Park. I've loved it since I was a child." I turned to Lex who was staring at me with penetrating eyes. "Thank you."

Lex didn't take his eyes from me, but moved this way and that as if looking at me from every angle. I was about to reprimand him for staring, but before I could he jumped in front of me with his hands making a square around me, as if he were putting me into a frame. I was so astonished I didn't know what to reprimand him about: being rude or being unbalanced.

"You're even more beautiful than Rossetti's women," he announced, still moving around to look at me.

"Rossetti?" I inquired, pushing my hair behind my shoulders.

"You've never heard of Dante Gabriel Rossetti?!" Lex exclaimed, throwing his hands up in the air dramatically. "Painter, poet...lover of women."

"Oh, that Rossetti," I said, laughing at his false indignation. "I don't know if I'd even say I compared; his women were quite beautiful. So beautiful in fact I wouldn't be surprised if he hadn't exaggerated their beauty."

"You don't know what true beauty is," Lex stated, pointing an accusing finger at me. "As for exaggeration, I can tell you plainly his ladies *were* that beautiful."

I gave him a skeptical look. "And how would you know that?"

"Because I," he proclaimed, putting his outstretched fingers to his chest, "was a friend of Rossetti's. We had great laughs...until he started having bouts of depression, but even then he was still quite amusing. He had wombats."

"Wombats?" I snickered. "What does that have to do with his women?"

"Nothing," Lex answered seriously, "they were just terribly funny to watch. My point is that I saw many of his models, and they were breathtaking. Honestly, it was a challenge to not steal them from him, but I reasoned that he needed them more than I did."

"That was so thoughtful of you," I said sarcastically.

"I know," he conceded and then cried, "Oh, you'll like this: I looked and saw your heart / In the shadow of your eyes, / As a seeker sees the gold / In the shadow of the stream; / And I said, "Ah me! what art / Should win the immortal prize, / Whose want must make life cold / And Heaven a hollow dream?"

I smiled appreciatively. "Yes, it's lovely. Rossetti?"

"Yes, I helped him with that one," Alexander stated so seriously I wasn't sure if it was a joke.

I cocked my head to the side and teased, "Are you going to tell me it's about a vampire?"

"Of course it is," he said and resumed his curious staring, moving side to side. "I've got it! Let me paint you?!"

I laughed uneasily, "Are you asking me or telling me?"

He stopped in his tracks and said seriously, "I very much would like to paint you. Would you give me permission? Or would you like me to beg on my hands and knees? Shall I recite more poetry? What would it take for you to say yes?"

The blood from my most recent victim was rising to my cheeks as I blushed. "Why would you want to paint me?" I asked shyly, and then added jokingly, "Do you even know how to paint?"

"Of course, I know how to paint. You could probably paint if you tried. Anyway I want to paint you because you're beautiful and I want to capture that beauty. If Rossetti were still alive he would die of envy. Plus, I can stare at you for hours on end while I capture every detail of you, and you can't yell at me for it," Lex reasoned, sounding more like a child than a nearly hundred year old vampire.

"Oh, very well," I huffed, in mock indignation, and then added, "At least it will pass the time." In all honesty I was flattered by Lex's attentions and I found myself wanting to be in his company more and more, but I would never admit it to him.

I posed on the hillside for two nights, under the overly attentive eye of Lex, and waited patiently on the third night for him to finish the details. He wouldn't let me see it until it was done which annoyed me a bit because I had only agreed to the painting in order to see the process. I was interested in how he went about creating the painting; his comment that I might be able to do such a thing buzzing in my head, but he was adamant that I not see the painting until it was finished.

Finally Lex threw down his brush with a flourish and declared, "It is done!"

I started to rise from where I had been lying watching the stars, but he raised his hands to halt my advance and instead I merely sat up staring at him. He made me wait as he rearranged all of the candles we'd brought out into a small cluster so as to completely illuminate the painting, though I was sure my vampiric eyes were strong enough now to see quite well in the semi-darkness. He made a grand fuss of making me close my eyes as he turned the painting to face me, and then took painfully slow steps toward the candles just in front of me.

He dramatically called out, "Now!"

If I had been standing I probably would have fallen to my

knees. I put my hand to my mouth to muffle my sobs. Lex hadn't only painted me walking down the hill, the castle behind me; he had also painted Emma. We were walking down the hillside hand in hand; the castle behind us watching like a grim demon. The beautiful blending of grays and purples in the cloudy night sky lighting up behind the daunting fortress. I wished it were brighter, perhaps with sun peeking through the clouds, but that would only make it further from the truth. Seeing Emma standing beside me was all the fairytale I could bear; that we were both cloaked in fading light, though dispiriting, seemed appropriate. There was no more light in my life...save perhaps Lex.

"Well? What do you think?" Lex asked expectantly.

"It's...it's glorious," I struggled to say without choking up.

As Lex set the canvas back on the easel I ran to him. He seemed surprised when I kissed him quickly on the mouth.

"I guess you do like it," he said playfully, smiling that boyish grin.

"I didn't expect to ever see her again," I explained, moving closer to inspect the painting. "You've caught her perfectly. How were you able to remember such detail?"

Lex shrugged dismissively. "A vampire's memory," he said tapping his temple, "once you see something it's there forever; like one of those photographs that are becoming so popular. You can pluck it from your mind to look at any time you like."

"But..." I began, turning to him puzzled, "then why did you need me to pose for you?"

Lex snickered to himself and flashed his swirling blue eyes mischievously. "I didn't need you to pose. I know your every feature by heart, but it gave me leave to stare at you for three nights without any reservation from you."

I shook my head at his audacity, but couldn't help smiling. "Well, whatever your method I am very pleased with the outcome. I'll have it hung in my room."

Lex carried the painting back to my room, pausing momentarily for Codrin to admire his skill. I still found it annoying that Lex was able to melt the icy sternness Codrin showed to everyone else. I did notice Codrin's eyes examining me curiously as he looked from the painting to me, and giving me an approving look he commented that I seemed to be meant to be painted. Lex placed the painting on the mantle above the fireplace until it could be hung.

"I forgot I brought you a gift," Lex spouted excitedly, squeezing my arm gently. "I left it on your bed."

"A gift? For what?" I asked unable to hide my pleasure as I dashed up the steps to the upper level of the room.

Lex walked a little nearer, but didn't climb the steps. "We've been spending so much time together...I thought...well, I thought...I suppose I couldn't help but think of you when I saw it. You're always on my mind," he admitted sadly.

I found a large box lying on the bed, but I hesitated to open it, knowing that I couldn't return Lex's feelings. I had made a promise to Dardanos, and I intended to keep that promise no matter how inattentive he'd been lately or how obsessed he'd become to get Cuckfield Park back. I hesitated, thinking that accepting this gift from Lex was like accepting his feelings, encouraging them even.

Lex seemed to sense my reluctance to open the box and prompted, "I didn't mean to worry you. I only thought it suited you, and I thought it would make you smile. That's all."

I gave him a sad smile, knowing that he was trying to hide his feelings for my sake, and I ventured to open the box to set him at ease. "Oh, Lex. It is lovely," I exclaimed removing a dark moss green, silk gown.

"Would you...wear it...for me?" he asked hopefully, his swirling blue eyes lighting.

I nodded my head, feeling uneasy, but wanting to please him all the same. "You'll have to leave the room that I might change."

Lex seemed to breathe a sigh of relief. Perhaps he had worried I wouldn't accept his gift. It was so unlike him to be unsure of himself, to be nervous and uncertain of how others felt about him. He left the room immediately, a small smile on his lips. Once I completed the arduous task of removing my gown and undergarments, save for my corset and one petty coat which was all I thought would fit beneath the thin silk gown, I turned to the mirror in the armoire to make sure I'd fastened everything correctly. It was a stunning example of regency fashion: slim silhouette, gold sash around an empire waist, golden embroidery along the hem and conservatively flowing train, low puckered neckline, and delicate puffed sleeves.

"There are not words to describe your beauty," Lex gushed from the door.

I turned, surprised he had entered without knocking. "Where ever did you find it? A gown such as this hasn't been in fashion for quite some time."

"I have my sources," he bantered, and then frowning asked, "You do like it?"

"Of course, how could I not," I assured him, walking down the steps, and approaching the fireplace once more to focus my attention on the painting. "I feel you know me in a way no one else on earth does," I admitted wistfully.

Lex didn't answer, but sat soundlessly on the sofa behind me. I turned to see him with his head down and his hands clasped between his knees. My heart sunk to see him so disheartened and to think that I had caused it. I sat down beside him, nervously wondering how I might cheer him to his usual facetious self.

"I'm worried. I know he is keeping many things from me," Lex stated in a faraway voice, "I'm worried that what I don't know not only puts me in danger, but you as well."

I was caught off-guard by Lex's comment, thinking his sudden seriousness had to do with his unrequited feelings for me. "What are you talking about?"

"Dardanos," he said not looking up, "I know he's keeping things from me, and I worry for your safety. If you knew the things he's done, the things he's capable of…"

I felt my heartbeat quickening with the guilt of all I knew, but I didn't know how much I should say. "There are things, obviously you're aware, that he is keeping from you. There are things that he has asked me not to tell you. I assure you these things in no way put me in danger."

"Would you tell me…if you thought I was in danger? Would you break your promise to Dardanos to protect me?" He asked in agitation, running his fingers through his perfectly smooth black hair.

"I…I don't know," I stuttered. "I wish I could tell you everything I know now, but I want to believe Dardanos has a good reason for not revealing everything. Sometimes I worry what his plans could do to the world." I paused and turned my concerned eyes to his. "I worry what his plans might mean to you, but I don't know how to go against him. The promise I've made to him spans more than just my lifetime."

Lex turned his eyes back to the painting as if contemplating something. "If I told you one of my secrets would you keep it from Dardanos?"

I gulped, wanting to tell him yes, wanting to learn something more to unravel the mystery of Lex. "I hold too many secrets as it is; I don't know if I could bear any more."

"Then I will tell you anyway, and hope that you will keep it for my sake," he said matter-of-factly, his eyes still fixed on the painting as if he would lose his nerve if he faced me.

I hung my head guiltily. "Why would you do that? Why trust me when you know what Dardanos and I are to each other?"

"Because," he whispered forlornly, "I love you, and I believe in your absolute goodness. I believe that you would never intentionally cause harm to anyone. I believe that your feelings for me are at least strong enough to wish me to continue living; even if that meant keeping something from your vampire husband," Lex spat the last disdainfully before adding, "I want you to know what is going on around you. I want you to be kept out of harm's way should things get...complicated."

I put my hands on either side of his face and made him turn to look at me. "Who would want to hurt me?"

"Not you," he confessed.

"Dardanos? Who would want to hurt him? Lex, is he in danger right now?" I demanded.

"He's not in immediate danger...it has to do with my secret," he admitted, searching my eyes. "I know I shouldn't tell you. You're too close to him, you care too much for him, but I must. If anything happened to you and I hadn't at least warned you I could never forgive myself."

I dropped my hands from his face. "Lex, you're scaring me. Please tell me what has you so worried."

"I was sent here...well, not here exactly, but to get close to Dardanos. Vampires all over the world are organized into covens called councils. It's like a vampire government. Each council watches over their own territory, keeping vampires in check and making sure humans don't find out about us. Sometimes there is a threat so great that all of the councils combine their efforts to end that threat. My council asked that I use my past dealings with Dardanos to get close to him, and ascertain if he is a threat to our kind. My elders believe he may be dangerous not only to vampires but to humans as well. I've been sent to find out what he is planning, and to find out if he is too dangerous to be ignored by the councils any longer. Two of the councils, besides my own, are concerned that Dardanos is planning something so destructive and terrible that we will have to invoke the power of all of The Councils of the Eternal to stop him."

"You're a spy?" I asked in dismay, twisting the silk of my gown at my lap in agitation.

"I suppose you could say that," he admitted casually, "but it is the responsibility of the councils to protect our secrets, to keep the balance between vampires and humans, and it is my responsibility as a council member to do what my elders ask of me."

I turned away from him to hide the tears forming in my eyes. "You used me," I accused, a quiver in my voice. "You've been pretending to be in love with me this whole time just to get close to me, to convince me to let something slip!"

"No!" Lex exclaimed, falling to his knees in front of me and pleading, "No, I never used you. Everything I've ever said to you has been the truth. I didn't get close to you in order to get close to him. I got close to you because I do love you and I'm worried you've gotten yourself in the middle of something dangerous. Do you think I want to find out Dardanos has some dreadful plan that would put us all at risk? No! I hope Malika is wrong. I hope Dardanos is simply ambitious and nothing will come of my investigation. Dardanos and I may have had our share of disagreements and trust issues, but he is still my maker and I wish no harm to him."

I kept my head turned away from his mesmerizing eyes and asked angrily, "Who is Malika?"

Lex sighed as if he hadn't meant to say that name. "She's one of my elders, one of the leaders of my council, and...she gave Dardanos The Immortal Fate."

"That doesn't make sense. Why would his own mother have him followed, and investigated? To discover if he's a danger...presumably to punish him to death?" I demanded.

Lex was shaking his head vigorously as if everything I was saying was wrong. "She isn't his mother. Well, I guess you could say she's his vampire mother, but it's different than a human mother."

I narrowed my eyes at him and realized, "You don't

know. She sent you on a mission and didn't even tell you the whole story." I paused, shaking my head. "I had visions of the time when Dardanos was given The Immortal Fate. His mother, the queen of Egypt, turned him to save his life. His brother tried to kill him, and his mother gave him The Immortal Fate to save him, and you...you-" I caught myself before I said anymore.

"What about me?" he asked curiously, seeing the accusation in my eyes.

I shook my head, looking down. "I can say no more, but if your elder is indeed the woman that made Dardanos a vampire then she is also his mortal mother."

"It's possible, I suppose, but unimportant. All of the elders are among the oldest of our kind, and most are very secretive about their origins. If she is his mother and the one that turned him then she obviously knows him better than anyone else on earth," Lex reasoned. "Knowing Malika is his mother makes me more uneasy about Dardanos's plans, not less. She must have a reason to be suspicious of him."

We were quiet a moment as I considered everything I knew, and finally I came to the conclusion, "I wish to see Malika. Would you take me to her? Could I speak to her about all of this?"

I could see Lex was not comfortable with the idea; he obviously didn't want to agree so I promised, "I will keep your secret if you take me to her, but you must swear to never tell Dardanos that I went to see her. There are things I promised to never discuss with you, but if Malika is who I think she is she already knows most of it anyway and *she* never made a promise to Dardanos to keep things from you. We can both learn what we want without breaking our vows."

❧27❧

Lex gave me no assurances that he could take me to see Malika. Instead he made it clear that he would have to obtain permission from not only Malika but from the council that they were staying with to bring me into one of their safe-houses. I was sure when he told Malika who I had been in my past life that she would want to meet me as well, and that Lex was merely trying to discourage me from getting even more mixed up in the issues between the councils and Dardanos. Despite his obvious worry Lex returned to the castle to fetch me the very next night; it seems Malika was curious to see if it was true, if I really was the reincarnated Amunet. I could tell Lex was unsettled by Malika's acceptance of my request. He must have thought she was going to refuse, but as she hadn't he seemed nervous about why she wanted to see me. He also didn't seem to like the idea that I knew more about his elder than he did.

"You are spectacular," he commented lightly as I was just finishing putting my hair up. "Wouldn't you rather go somewhere where your beauty will be appreciated? I could take you to the theater, to the opera, dancing. Anywhere you like; anywhere in the world. It's a shame that you're so ravishingly dressed just to go to a vampire safe-house."

I gave him a stern look and countered, "I only wore this gown because I have so few gowns, and I already had it on, and we're in a rush."

"I'm not in a rush," he answered quickly. "I can wait for you to change," he said, plopping down on the sofa and picking up *The Moonstone* which was sitting next to him as if he meant to read for the rest of the night.

"I'm not going to change my mind Lex," I huffed sternly, taking the book out of his hands. "I have to see Malika."

"Very well," Alexander said standing up reluctantly and producing a handkerchief from his pocket. "I have to take precautions,"

"I thought you trusted me?" I questioned, raising an eyebrow.

"I trust you," he whispered in my ear as he moved to tie the cloth behind my head. "It's Malika and the council that don't trust you," he explained gently sweeping his hand under my hair, letting his fingers slide across the back of my neck.

I felt a tingle of excitement spark down my spine, but I forced myself to ignore it. "Well, that isn't exactly comforting, but I understand. It must seem very strange that the would-be wife of someone they consider dangerous wishes to speak to them. It's only natural they should be overly cautious."

"You're not his wife, would-be or otherwise. The councils are simply cautious of outsiders. Are you sure you want to do this?" Lex's lips were inches from mine, the breath of each word playing across my lips, "I'm frightened for you. There are too many secrets...too much I'm in the dark about."

"I know, Lex," I answered back in a whisper, trying not to disturb the sparse distance between us. "I'm trying to piece everything together, as much for you as for myself."

He ran his thumb across my lower lip, and I could feel the heat of his stare on me. "I feel my hands have been tied behind my back. How can I keep you safe when I don't know what it is I'm keeping you safe from? What if I am delivering you into the hands of your enemy?"

"Do you think Malika wishes to harm me?" I asked, furrowing my brow with worry.

"I would normally say no, but I feel the world has been turned on its side. I know too little of everyone's past to be certain of anything," he admitted, playing distractedly with my hair.

I knew he was right. I knew little of Malika and her experience with Amunet. For all I knew she may have blamed Amunet for taking her son away just as Sethos had seemed to think. I didn't even know much about Dardanos's relationship with her. In my visions he had been concerned by her sickness and she had saved him from death, but that didn't mean there wasn't any kind of dissension between them. After all, Malika hadn't even punished her younger son for trying to murder his brother, and she had accepted the reincarnation of her younger son into her council.

My thoughts were faraway when I felt Lex's lips on mine. His hands were behind my head, pulling me into an ever deeper kiss. I put my hand on his chest as if I were going to push him away, but I couldn't. I let him run his hands along my body, feeling the heat building inside of me. I had a momentary thought of trying the circular feeding that Dardanos and I had done to find out if Lex and I could create an alternate realm as well, but I pushed the thought away.

"Perhaps we should go," I struggled to say, pushing Lex back slightly. "You will try to protect me, won't you?" I asked, a fleeting moment of uncertainty hitting me.

"I will. I swear it...on my soul," he answered softly before grabbing me about the waist.

The flight was surprisingly short, remembering how long it had taken Dardanos to fly from England to Romania I asked, "I thought you said your council's safe-house was in America?"

"It is," Lex answered, letting me go to stand on the ground, "We haven't gone to America. I can't tell you where we are, only that it isn't my council, nor my safe-house. Malika and I are guests here."

"Of course, I forgot you said you were staying with another council." I stumbled up a few steps, being pulled along by Lex who had failed to mention they were there. "I only asked because of how quickly we'd gotten here," I commented as Lex rapped loudly on a door.

Lex ignored my comment and hurriedly explained, "Council members tend to be very suspicious of outsiders, especially those not affiliated with any council. You shouldn't have to speak to anyone other than Malika, but be warned this council is very old, very traditional, and they are not particularly happy that the wife of a potential enemy is here for a visit. Watch what you say."

"I'm not really his wife, remember?" I pointed out, though I suppose it wasn't important at the time.

The door creaked open noisily, and although I still had my blindfold on I could tell it was an exceptionally large door. "I see you've brought her," a gruff male voice grumbled a few feet in front of me. "Well, bring her in. Malika is in the library waiting."

"Charming as ever, Grigore," Lex said sarcastically, leading me into the house. "I suppose it goes without saying that we should make ourselves at home."

In reply all I heard was an angry huff, and the click of shoes walking swiftly away.

"Watch what I say, hmmm? I think if one of us were going to offend the old, traditional council it wouldn't be me," I stated half kidding.

"Yes, yes, come along," was all Lex said.

Lex led me on, still blindfolded, and I could tell by the click of my own boots that the floor must have been made of stone. It sounded very similar to the floors at Corvin castle and I wondered if this too were a castle. I felt eyes on me as we walked through a large open area. I was sure at least a few council members were eyeing me cautiously, deciding if I was a threat or not. I tried to reach out with my mind to see if I could feel their individual presences, but I could feel nothing. There was either no one there or they were much more powerful than me.

"Just down this hall," Lex finally said. "Let me open the door. Once we're inside I'll remove the blindfold."

As the door shut behind me I felt hands undoing the knot of the blindfold, but it was not Lex standing before me removing the blindfold. A tall, regal woman with dark hair and features had pulled the blindfold from my eyes, an unreadable expression on her face as she studied me.

"I am Malika," the woman announced, reminding me that she had once been a queen, "and you, my dear, must be the reincarnated Amunet. I did not know her, but I caught a glimpse of her once in the palace."

"You know about that?" I blurted out, surprised. "Then you must know about Lex…I mean Alexander; who he was I mean?"

"Of course," she purred matter-of-factly, "and no, I never told him that he was once my son."

"But why? Why keep him so close and never tell him the truth?" I questioned curiously.

Malika gestured to a round polished wood table further into the library for us to sit. "The past is a funny thing. It may be filled with horrors, and yet the few moments of happiness still burn bright in your memory. On one hand you wish you could dig up everything you ever loved, but on the other hand you know most of the time it is best to let dead things decay into nothingness. I loved both of my sons, naturally, and I could never side with one over the other; even when Sethos," she said the name and gestured toward Lex, "tried to kill Setepamun."

"Wait," Lex broke in hastily, "are you saying all this nonsense about past lives is true? I was..." he sighed, "I was your son? Wait..." Lex interjected, holding his hands up, "that means I was a prince." His face lit up momentarily with a boyish grin.

Malika's face remained calm as she turned to Lex. "Yes, you were my younger son, Sethos, brother of the future king of Egypt, but that was never to be. Your brother Setepamun knew he was different; he was obsessed with becoming a god, and I, in my delusions of being an immortal queen, encouraged him to follow his quest. I believed I could rule Egypt as a vampire while the future king spent his time traveling our kingdom searching for something that did not exist."

"But he was right. He was a god once and there may be a way for him to be one again," I argued, not meaning to say so much.

If what I'd said surprised Malika she didn't show it. "I know what he believed. I did not think it possible; even after he told me about your visions; even after he told me the tale of the cursed god. I did not believe in coincidence, and yet I would not let myself believe that the very blood that had given me immortality was that of the cursed god. "

"Who is the cursed god? What tale?" Lex demanded at a loss, his usual mischievous smile replaced by clenched teeth.

I looked at him and could see he hadn't expected any of this. He had probably only given in to my request because he'd thought Malika would deny everything. Instead he was faced with the idea that fate ran much deeper in his life than he had ever believed. He must have realized how much his past life, something he didn't even believe in, had influenced his present one. Had he not been Dardanos's brother in his past life Dardanos would never have given him The Immortal Fate, and if he hadn't been Malika's son he might not have become a council member. Even the devotion and love he felt for me could arguably be an echo of Apollo's jealous obsession with Cassandra or Sethos' inexplicable desire for Amunet.

I decided to break my promise to Dardanos. As much as

it pained me to go back on my word I couldn't bear to keep Lex in the dark any longer. I told him the story of the cursed god. I told him everything I'd seen in my visions, and I made sure he understood the part he had played in everything. Malika only nodded her head patiently as I spoke as if she had already known everything, but when I described the monster that had killed all my loved ones Malika stirred.

"A vampire turned during the Trojan war? I did not think our kind went back so far," she said meditatively. "I know of one that is believed to be the oldest of our kind, but I don't believe he is that old and he certainly does not call himself Prometheus."

Lex cut in, "I heard Dardanos speak of Prometheus as well. He warned me that there was an unbelievably powerful vampire near and that he might seek revenge on him by going after Lizzy. I never saw him, but I did see the destruction he left behind."

"I saw him," I interrupted. "Dardanos and I both saw him. I know I'm not as strong as either of you, but I could feel the power coming from him just as I feel it coming from you," I stated, gesturing to Malika. "It may not mean anything, but what I feel from you is nothing compared to what I felt coming from him. It made me feel like an insect in his presence."

"Is it possible?" Lex asked, addressing Malika, "Is it possible this all-powerful vampire was once the god Prometheus?"

Malika shook her head at a loss. "I do not know. There was a time when I would have said it was not possible, but I have seen many extraordinary things and so I cannot discount anything...no matter how incredible it may seem."

While Malika and Lex sat in quiet contemplation I took the opportunity to ask what I'd come to find out, "Are you planning to kill Dardanos?"

For the first time Malika seemed surprised as she answered, "I do not wish to harm my son...but he has dangerous ideas. Ideas I had hoped would have faded over the centuries. All I wish to do is keep our kind hidden as we have always been, and keep humanity from being devastated by us. If my son's plans do not put those two things in jeopardy I am satisfied that he is not a threat."

"And if his plans do put your kind and humans at risk?" I asked shakily.

Malika put her hand over mine as she corrected, "*Our* kind. You are one of us now, and our ability to blend in among humans is as much an asset to you as to us. If my son is planning to risk such things then I must find a way to end my son's life," she responded simply, her dark eyes steady.

Lex waited until we were outside the safe-house before he spoke, "You know what he's planning, don't you?"

I was once again blindfolded, but I could tell by his voice that he was shaken by what he'd just heard. "Yes, I know his plans, but they are nothing to worry about," I lied, trying to convince myself more than him.

Lex pulled me close once more and took to the sky. "Then they are not as dangerous as Malika thinks?"

I pursed my lips. What could I say? Dardanos's plans were dangerous, but they seemed so far away, so unlikely to ever come to fruition. I still didn't really believe in everything Dardanos spoke of, even after all I'd seen for myself. My rational mind had been lying to me, telling me that the seemingly impossible schemes Dardanos hoped to achieve were just that...impossible, and therefore not dangerous.

"They are dangerous," Lex guessed when I didn't answer.

It was difficult to gauge how worried he was without seeing his face so I decided to play it safe. "His plans may be dangerous, but I don't believe he will ever achieve them. They are far too grandiose to fulfill. It would take several lifetimes, perhaps several centuries."

"He has already had several lifetimes and several centuries, and he yet has all the time in the world," Lex pointed out.

"Yes, but he also has me," I countered. "Relationships take time as well."

He scoffed, "Oh yes, I see how much time he spends on your *relationship*."

We had thankfully touched down on solid ground, because without thinking I shoved Lex as hard as I could. The unexpected shift in balance caused Lex to misstep, and I ended up stumbling a few feet before being able to regain my balance. I tore the blindfold from my eyes and threw it at him.

"You know nothing of our relationship!" I screamed, noticing for the first time that we were back in my room in

Corvin castle. "Everything he has done, everything he has ever done, has been for me!"

"Really?! Then where is he, Lizzy?! Why did he agree to let someone he doesn't even trust keep you company?! Why didn't he send me to Cuckfield so that he could stay here with you?!" Lex shouted, following me to the sitting area.

I wheeled around angrily to face him. "That's just it! He doesn't trust you! What he is doing in Cuckfield is far too important to entrust to you!"

"But he trusts me with you? His grand prize?!" Lex shook his head in frustration and grabbed my arm roughly. "Don't you see?! He has stuck you in this fortress, and locked you away from the world! You're like the Lady of Shalott, sitting up in your desolate tower, watching from your window until he comes to break your curse…when he's ready to allow you to live again."

I shook loose of his hold and spat, "And I suppose that would make you Sir Lancelot, tempting me from my tower...and to my death?"

"I'm not trying to tempt you," his voice faltered, "I couldn't help falling in love with you, and I cannot help worrying about you. You're feelings for me or lack of feelings for me will never change my concern for your welfare."

"Dardanos would never let anything happen to me," I argued. "I am everything to him, and I'm beginning to think your presence here is a mistake!"

Lex opened his mouth as if he were about to shout again, but instead he said calmly, "Little queen, don't you see? You were just an item for him to acquire in his process to fulfill his goals, an item on his list to check off. Now he has you he's on to the next item on his list, his next secret ingredient. I've seen him do it before. He obsesses over something until he has it, and then he tucks it away somewhere safe until he has use for it. He isn't concerned about what you're doing right now or who you're doing it with, because he doesn't need you right now. When he does need you he knows right where to find you, because it's right where he put you. I don't know what he has planned, but you…" he paused shaking his head again, "you are merely a playing piece in his game."

✢28✢

It hurt to hear Lex say such things, mostly because deep down I felt they were true, but in my anger I wouldn't let him have the last word. "I'm not a playing piece...you are! You do everything he asks and yet you have no idea what he's planning. No, it's you that is just a playing piece and I," I emphasized pointing to myself, "I am the game."

Lex grabbed me roughly about the shoulders. "You are not his goal, Lizzy! You and I both know that! You are simply a means to achieve the next step. He may have loved Cassandra once upon a time and maybe he loved Amunet before he was given The Immortal Fate, but something has twisted in him. I don't think he's even capable of love. Not real love. The kind of love that makes you sacrifice yourself for another. Lizzy...it isn't real."

My anger melted away as my fears washed over me. I put my hand over my mouth, tears bursting uncontrollably forth. I felt more helpless than I ever had in my life, even more so than when my loved ones were being murdered around me. It didn't matter that I was immortal, powerful, or that I could live any way I chose even though I was a woman; I felt trapped. I loved Dardanos, but was it possible he only loved me as much as he needed me? What would he do if I refused to help him? Or tried to stop him?

"I love him still, Lex. Even knowing he wishes to destroy every vampire and enslave humans...I still love him." The words left my mouth like poison on my tongue; I hated that I'd said any of it aloud.

Lex's fingertips dug deeper into my arms. "Is that his plan?! How does he hope to accomplish this?!" he demanded, shaking me.

I put my hands to my mouth and shook my head vigorously. *Why had I told him that?* "I can't tell you! I should never have told you anything! Oh God, I shouldn't have said a word."

"Lizzy, how can you protect him when you know he is planning to murder so many?! And for what?! Some mad thought that he could take over the earth...force humans to obey him out of fear?!" Lex demanded.

"I don't know!" I countered through my tears, "I don't know any more what to think. In the beginning it was only about the love we'd been denied in the past, and then he started revealing his plans for revenge, but it's more than just revenge. He believes he deserves to be a god, that his fate was stolen from him, and this is the only way to set things right. He truly believes he can make the world better: end hunger and poverty, stop senseless violence, wars, and petty crimes, give people something to believe in, something to fear."

Lex dropped his hands from my shoulders, "You sound as crazy as him...taking over the world and making everyone worship you. Is that what you really want?"

"No! It isn't what I want at all, but maybe I can get him to change his mind. Maybe he will give it up once he sees how happy we could be at Cuckfield Park," I entreated foolishly.

Lex didn't answer, which I knew was kind of him because I heard how naïve it sounded as the words left my lips. Lex dropped dejectedly onto the sofa, his arms resting on his thighs. He stared at the fire in uncharacteristic seriousness, and I felt as though I had held up a mirror to reflect my ignorance back at me. I knew in my heart Dardanos was dangerous. I knew I would never dissuade him from his course. I knew if I remained with him my life would be a worthless shell of eternity, spent in regret and secret longing.

"I don't know what to do, Lex," I said softly, sitting beside him.

"Nor do I," he admitted, his eyes glazed over. "I meant what I told you; I wish no harm to come to Dardanos, but what can be done...he plans to annihilate so many. I cannot ignore the planned murder of all vampires nor the countless human victims." He paused and turned abruptly to me. "Am I to assume that I too will be among those destroyed?"

I gulped unable to look him in the eye. "I don't know," I muttered. "I believe he has told me more than he has shared with anyone else, but even so he has kept many aspects of his plan from me. I only just learned that he's trying to amass an army."

"An army?" Lex asked in disbelief.

"That's why he wished to combine forces with the Sergisons. He wanted them to help him train an army to kill vampires on a large scale. He said the men he has at Corvin castle are the beginnings of that army, and he's tracking down the servants that killed my sister to force them to join him. There are things he has kept about our pasts as well, but I don't know why. He never told me that my sister and Gabriel had both been important in our past lives; they helped to shape our fates as much as you did, and yet he never once mentioned them."

"And you?" Lex asked his eyes looking glassy as if filling with tears. "What part do you have to play in this grand future?"

"The future he has painted for me is being the benevolent counterpart to his harsh and fearsome godly rule," I admitted, looking down in shame. "He wishes to make me a goddess that I might rule beside him."

"And he truly believes he can become a god once more?" Lex asked sadly.

"Yes, and..." I felt I was betraying Dardanos by revealing so much, but now that I had repeated it aloud it sounded so sinister, "I believe he can achieve the transformation. I have seen a glimpse of it...he is so close."

Lex nodded solemnly. "He has promised it to you. Is that why you're so loyal to him? The promise of becoming an all-powerful goddess?"

"How could you think that of me?" I asked in outrage, grabbing at the folds of my moss green gown in distress. "I don't wish for omniscient power...I didn't even wish for immortality, but I don't know how to stop what he has put into motion."

"Oh, darling, my little queen, I didn't mean to put any of the blame on you," Lex gushed, taking me in his arms. "I told you that I love you, and I will devise an answer to the problem...to all of our problems," he said, smoothing back my hair. "I will not let you be trapped in his dreams of grandeur."

Before I could stop myself I exploded in a torrent of tears, my body shaking violently with the emotion I was trying to hold back. Lex kissed my lips lightly, reassuring me that he was there, but he didn't stop. He pushed closer, wrapped his arms around my back, and pulled me toward him as he closed his mouth possessively over mine. I didn't stop him, not even when his hands delved down the front of my corset, not even when he kissed hungrily at the tops of my breasts. Far from stopping him I was actually kissing him back and running my hands over his clothed body. I wondered once again if we fed on one another at the same time if we would experience our own version of heaven together, but I quickly banished the thought from my mind. I knew what I needed to do to keep things from getting worse.

Lex paused in his loving attentions to whisper, "Come away with me. Leave this place...leave Dardanos, let me love you, show you the world. We can go anywhere and everywhere you've ever dreamed of going. I'll do everything you ask of me...just please come with me. Leave him."

I pulled away from him, wanting so much to accept, but I had already decided what I would do. "I can't. I have such strong feelings for you, Lex...I might even say I love you, but I must stay. And...you must go. Don't you see? If I stay I can stop him from carrying out his plans."

"Lizzy, that's madness; you can't stop him. He's too powerful!" Lex protested.

I cupped his cheek in my hand. "I don't mean to fight him...I mean to persuade him. Hinder his plans whenever I see them becoming dangerous. I mean to use his love for me to keep him from harming anyone. If I can't stop him completely then at least I can slow him down...perhaps delay the inevitable for a few centuries."

Lex grasped my hand away from his cheek and kissed it. "I know you think his love for you is stronger than his ambitions, but I have known him a long time. He is very single-minded and he puts his next goal above everything else. I'm not saying he doesn't still love you in his way...I'm saying that if you get in his way he will put you somewhere where you can't get in his way...until he finds need of you once more."

"I've made up my mind, Lex!" I shouted angrily, standing and moving away from him. "If I do nothing Malika may decide he is too dangerous, but if I can convince him to stop or at least slow down his plans then no one will get hurt."

"Little queen," Lex pleaded, moving toward me.

"No," I said, holding out my hand to stop him. "This is the only way. I want you to leave and never come back. I will tell Dardanos that we argued and you said you would help us no longer. Then I will get to work convincing him that he needs to take a break from all this god nonsense. We will go to Cuckfield Park and live as husband and wife...for as long as we can."

"It's a dream, Lizzy. He'll never give up his pursuit," Lex said in anguish.

"Leave that to me," I stated boldly, "this is how it must be. Go, please, for my sake, and never come back. Please...let me do this. I could never live in the world knowing he was out there, and possibly hurting others...when I might have stopped him. You can't understand, part of what he has become is because of me, because of Cassandra and Amunet. It may seem unfair, but I bear some of the responsibility for his actions and I need to at least try to make things right. Perhaps one day it won't be so, but for now I must stay with him. I must try to have some influence over him...for the sake of every living thing. Please...go!"

Lex looked at me at a loss for what to say, but finally agreed, "Very well, I'll go, but I will check on you from time to time...from a distance if I must. I will not leave you to face him without some kind of precautions. I'll be out there, listening, waiting for you to call my name." He kissed my hand once more, giving me a look of hopelessness. "I swear it...on my soul."

I broke down the moment Lex left, falling to the floor and weeping until the front of my dress was speckled with damp spots where the tears had fallen. I felt as if I'd banished my only friend, my only chance for real happiness. I hoped Dardanos would stay away at least a few more nights to give me time to get over my despair, and to fortify myself to the choice I'd made to stay with him. I knew it was going to be difficult to do what I hoped to do; I wasn't even convinced that I did have the power to sway Dardanos's mind to do what I wanted of him. My life was now going to be theater: pretending, lying, and using myself as a kind of bait to dissuade Dardanos from his plans.

My eyes hovered sadly over the beautiful moss green gown Lex had given me. Seeing the wet spots and streaks of my tears in the dark green silk woke me to the reality that I would have to get rid of the gown. I would never be able to lie to Dardanos about where I'd gotten the gown, and he would surely find it strange that I should wear something given to me by someone I now claimed to hate. I couldn't force myself to get up, though. I sat motionless on the floor, tears falling at random, until I felt the unmistakable pull of morning. Before the day took

complete hold and forced me into my coma-like sleep I quickly
changed out of the gown Lex had given me and back into the
cursed, dyed gown. I knew it would please Dardanos to see me
wearing the dress should he return the following night, and I
hoped to see him in the best of moods to begin my pleas to settle
quietly at Cuckfield Park and put off his ambitions for a while.

The following night I awoke alone. Dardanos had still not
returned, though he would have been able to have risen hours
ago. I pulled out the moss green gown from where I'd stuffed it
in the armoire, and set off to a nearby village. I tore the gown to
shreds and tossed it into the river before entering the village; it
was probably not necessary, but I had to be certain Dardanos
would never find it and know it had been mine. I continued on to
the village and hunted alone for the first time since I'd been a
vampire. Although I had now done it a few dozen times it felt
strange to not see Lex's smiling face as I drained my victim.
With no one to keep me company in the quiet little village I
grudgingly made my way back to the castle.

I felt empty as I hop-scotched great distances back to the
castle. I still didn't possess the ability to fly, but I could quickly
cover large expanses by leaping. Lex had assured me there were
many things vampires couldn't do in their first month, flying
being one of them, but over time I might develop the skill. My
last great leap brought me over the stone wall that ran along the
left side of the castle, and I decided to follow the little worn path
down to the stream to where The Palladium stood. If I couldn't
talk to Lex at least I still had Pallas. Perhaps tonight she would
whisper to me as I had imagined she had when I was a child.

I should have felt nothing but the warming effects of the
blood coursing through my veins, but instead I felt ice trickling
beneath the surface of my skin. I froze, and though vampires did
not technically feel such bodily fluctuations: a chill ran through
me. Standing at the end of the path where my Palladium should
have been was the creature that had destroyed everything that
had been dear to me.

"Prometheus," I half growled, rage filling me where I
thought there would be fear.

He gave me a weak smile, as if he hadn't murdered my
whole family, and with a strange laugh he said, "No one has
called me that for a long time."

"But that is who you are, isn't it?" I demanded, taking a

tentative step toward him.

"Yes, I am Prometheus, or at least I was...as difficult as that may be to believe, but that is not why I am here." He drummed his fingers together, waiting for me to agree to listen to him.

As much as I wished at that moment that I could shoot fire from my hands and burn this audacious monster on the spot I was, unfortunately, weak, even for a vampire. "Why have you taken The Palladium?"

Prometheus seemed surprised by my question, and narrowed his strange silvery eyes. "I have not taken anything. I was not aware you had The Palladium."

"But…" I began, gesturing to the spot where he stood, "It should be right there. It was there last night, and now it isn't. Surely you don't think I'm so ignorant that I wouldn't suspect it was you."

This time Prometheus shook his head sternly. "I have not taken your statue. I have been waiting here for you for nearly an hour, and there was no statue when I arrived. It seems someone else has decided to take your Palladium, but I am not here to discuss your statue."

I knew he was telling the truth; something in those cold, metallic eyes expressed a kind of strength that seemed to say: *there is no reason for me to lie; you can do nothing to me if you don't like the truth*. The mystery of who had taken The Palladium burned inside of me. If not Prometheus then who, and why? Had Dardanos come back while I was gone and taken it to Cuckfield Park? Had Lex, in anger, taken it to get back at me for not choosing to be with him?

Finally I realized Prometheus was still watching me; quietly waiting for me to acknowledge him. "Very well, what are you here for?" I asked, trying to sound braver than I felt.

"I am here to warn you," he said, a look of genuine concern on his face.

This seemed wrong. Why wasn't he attacking me? Why wasn't he at least threatening me? I stared at him, trying to get an idea of what he was up to, but the only thing I could see was great sadness.

"What do you want to warn me about?" I asked, moving even closer with curiosity.

His strange silver eyes flashed as he lamented, "I want to

warn you not to make the same mistake I made. Do not make a deal with Dardanos, do not allow him to have power over you."

"The only deal I have made with Dardanos is to love him," I answered hotly, folding my arms, and giving him a superior look.

"Ah, well, love can be a dangerous thing, my girl," he remarked sagely, "as dangerous as hatred and vengeance, and all three...well, that is the most dangerous of all. I know Dardanos has told you about your past, perhaps you have even been awakened. I know he has tried to convince you that the two of you were fated to be together, but that life was stolen from you both. Cassandra was an unusually honest and lovely woman; Dardanos had a fair heart and was a natural leader, but sometimes two good people can cause chaos in the world."

I wanted to slap his face, but I restrained myself by balling my hands into fists. "Are you saying that just by the two of us being together we cause bad things to happen?"

He shook his head gently. "I am saying your loyalty to Dardanos fuels his ambition, and unfortunately he is driven by love, hatred, and vengeance. I am sure he has not shared the extent of his plans with you or you would not show him such loyalty. I myself cannot repeat these plans as I am bound by an ancient promise which hinders me from going against Dardanos's wishes."

"Convenient," I retorted smugly. "You just expect me to believe you that Dardanos is an evil man, but you can't tell me any specifics. And I should just trust you, because you've proven yourself to be a trustworthy kind of guy."

"I know you are angry with me and at least on that I may illuminate you on Dardanos's true nature. The same ancient promise that I spoke of before binds me to Dardanos and I must do as he asks. He is the reason your family is dead-"

"What!?" I shouted before he got another word out.

"Please," he said gently, raising his hands as if to ask for calm, "let me explain. You already know that you were part of his plan from the beginning; he needs you by his side just as he needed Cassandra. Unfortunately, just after he started watching you you fell in love with the other part of his plan, the young Sergison. As the time drew closer when he would have to enact his plan, just before your twentieth birthday, of course-"

"Wait, why just before my twentieth birthday?" I

interrupted.

Prometheus gave me an agitated look as if he didn't have time to explain everything. "Cassandra was twenty when she was poisoned, the girl Amunet had just turned twenty when he'd turned her; the other two didn't work. He decided it must be like a formula; everything must happen at the right time, in the right circumstances."

"What other two?" I questioned, feeling an uneasiness inside as I moved even closer to him.

He sighed and clipped me under the chin. "That is a story for another time; perhaps next time we meet I will tell it to you. The story I must tell you now involves the order to kill the psychic, your fiancé, and his family. I did not attack them of my own accord...I had no wish to kill anyone. I was given the command by Dardanos. He wanted everyone out of the way. The psychic knew too much about your pasts and he worried what she might tell you. Your fiancé he wanted killed because he did not want to take the chance that you would choose a life with him over Dardanos. He also knew it would be easier to get Cuckfield Park and Lord Sergison's hunters with the Sergisons out of the way."

My eyes welled up as I denied what he was saying. "No, you're lying. He would never have them killed. He wanted to work with Lord Sergison...he didn't even know Lord Sergison had hunters."

Prometheus put his hands on my shoulders comfortingly. "He knew. Dardanos has been planning this for a very, very long time. All of it was part of his plan."

I held back my tears as I spat sarcastically, "And my family? I suppose you're going to tell me that he had you kill them as well?"

"Yes, he had them killed" he answered patiently, "but not by me-"

"And Emma," I cut him off, not really paying attention to what he'd said, "the hunters killed my sister. If he knew there were hunters he would have protected her; he would have made sure she wasn't put in harm's way."

"That was no accident: your sister's death. He told your sister she should choose her victims from among the servants; he told her that they were as much to blame for the Sergison boys' deaths as myself and Lord Sergison. He knew eventually the hunters that Lord Sergison had trained would come for her. He was the one that suggested your sister kill that maid to protect his secret. When Emma told him the maid might be connected to the hunters he told her to kill the maid; he knew the hunters would go after Emma for killing one of their own. It allowed Dardanos to easily identify all of the hunters, and it allowed him to get someone out of the way that had wronged him."

I stared into his silver eyes and argued, "Who? Sallie…or Emma? Emma never wronged him. He had no reason to have her killed. He told me he turned her for me, so that I wouldn't lose my sister; he wouldn't turn around and try to get her killed. You're making all of this up."

Prometheus brushed the hair back off my shoulder, looking off into the distance as if lost in thought. "You must have seen her, you must have recognized her. It was not Emma he wanted vengeance from, it was who she used to be...in her past. The beautiful woman whose need for attention caused the greatest war that the cosmos has ever seen. Her jealousy of Cassandra and her desire for Dardanos led to Dardanos's curse and Cassandra's punishments...not to mention the rivalry she incited among the gods, pitting them against one another. And the priestess in Egypt. When she realized she could not have Dardanos's love, that his loyalty to you was unwavering she went to his brother and revealed all your plans and even helped Sethos to try to kill Setepamun. Dardanos may love you, but his thirst for vengeance and power far exceeds his capacity for love," Prometheus explained sadly. "I, of all beings on Earth, should know. He only set me free to help him bring his plans of vengeance to fruition. I am bound by the universe, by the oath that I gave during my imprisonment, to obey Dardanos. My will belongs to him, and he uses me monstrously to get what he wants."

I stared at his silver eyes, now seeming more hopeless than fearsome, and I thought of one more thing that didn't make sense. "You said you didn't kill my family, someone else did. Who?"

Prometheus regarded me a moment as if wondering if he should tell me, but finally admitted, "Dardanos gave the order, but it was Emma that carried out that task. Dardanos knew her desire to become immortal and he used it to force her to do something that would be torturous to her. Surprisingly she didn't hesitate in the slightest, and she made sure Dardanos knew how unimportant they were to her compared with him. Your sister's need to be wanted and important has always been her greatest weakness, and Dardanos knew this. It was the same when she lived as Helen of Troy and the same when she was the priestess Nenet; her soul craves the attention only the gods ever received."

I said nothing while he spoke, but kept shaking my head as if everything he said was a lie, but I knew yet again that he had no reason to lie. I held back the tears trying to force their way out. Emma killed our parents? No, it wasn't possible. Prometheus must have been mistaken if he wasn't lying. Maybe he was only repeating what he'd been told to say, but I could see the forsaken look in his eyes wishing it was all a lie. He took no pleasure in telling me any of this, and yet he had defied Dardanos to warn me of what I was facing. How could I hope to control such a man as Dardanos? A man that had Mrs. Gibson, the Sergisons, my parents, and even my sister murdered. A man that had the beginnings of a great vampire hunting army at his beck and call. A man that had the last living god (besides Zeus) doing his bidding.

Prometheus turned as if he were leaving, but suddenly stopped. "She wanted you to have this," he said, placing something small in my hands, and giving me a weak smile.

I looked down and saw the broach Lady Sergison had given me, the one I had left beside the pond the night she had been murdered. "How did you know-" I began to ask, but as I looked up I saw that Prometheus had already taken to the sky.

☙29❧

After Prometheus left I crumbled to the ground in front of the spot where The Palladium should have been. The fact that it had been moved without my knowledge barely registered any more, but I did momentarily wonder if it had been taken for a reason. I stared at the bare ground where The Palladium had been, despairing over the prison I had willingly built for myself. I wanted to believe everything Prometheus had said was a lie. I wanted to believe Dardanos was the loving and honorable man I had fallen in love with. I wanted to believe I was more than just Dardanos's pawn, but everything I'd been told seemed to point to just the reverse. How could I hope to impede his plans? How could I make any difference when it seemed Dardanos had already calculated every possibility?

"Lex," I called halfheartedly, and then wiping my eyes I forced myself to scream out as loud as my vampiric voice would allow, "Lex! Help me! Please!"

I'm not sure what I expected. I guess I really thought Lex's love for me would keep him close. I listened intently to any hint of him swooping in to my rescue, but the night was strangely silent. I pinned the broach Prometheus had brought back to me to the front of my dress, and lay down in the prickly grass, feeling as though my vision of seeing myself dead in a coffin had come true. Now it seemed obvious to me as to why my head had seemed at a strange angle to my body in the vision; I had lost it. I had lost my head. I had closed my eyes and ignored my reasoning, letting my heart rule over my mind. Now I was hopelessly in love with a man that was using me to destroy the world as I knew it. A man that, if I were to believe Prometheus, had destroyed everyone dear to me.

"Little queen?" Lex's voice lilted into my thoughts.

I opened my eyes believing it to be a dream, but there he was, standing over me, a look of worry on his face. I was so

surprised to see him that I didn't move, only stared at him
waiting for him to disappear.

"What happened? Are you hurt?" Lex asked anxiously,
dropping to his knees beside me.

I was so relieved he was there that I bolted up to embrace
him, and managed to knock him backwards as I tumbled on top
of him.

He wrapped his arms around me and chuckled, "I guess
you're happy to see me?"

I laughed at first, but my relief soon turned to tears. "He
told me all of these horrible things, and now I don't know what
I'm going to do. I've made a terrible mistake. I should have been
terrified of him, but I was so angry at what he'd done...but he
didn't do it, or at least he was forced to do it. If what he told me
is true..." I trailed off, shaking my head and added, "then I've
made a deal with the devil."

"Who are you talking about? Who told you horrible
things?" Lex asked still beneath me.

"Prometheus."

Lex didn't make a move to push me away; instead he held
me tighter to himself. "He was here?! What did he say? Did he
hurt you?!"

I shook my head, my nose nearly touching his. "He was
surprisingly kind. He said he came here to warn me. He said
whatever plans Dardanos has revealed to me his true plans are
far worse, and he said...he said..." I gulped down the emotion
rising in me. "He said Dardanos had ordered him to kill Mrs.
Gibson and the Sergisons, and Emma...he said Emma killed our
parents."

"Do you believe him?" Lex asked simply.

"Yes, I do," I whispered sadly, my hair spilling forward
to make a veil around us, "I wish I didn't, but I could feel the
truth coming from him. I've known all along that Dardanos was
keeping things from me; I just didn't know it was so many things.
So many horrible things."

Lex brushed my hair to the side, and smiled playfully.
"So...are you ready to run away with me yet?"

"Not just yet," I said softly. "I need to speak with Malika
again, find out what we can do to stop Dardanos. If we even can
stop him."

Lex shifted his eyes away from mine. "Are you willing to

kill him to stop him?"

"No," I gulped nervously, "I could never kill him, but...I won't stand against anyone if that's what must be done to prevent the unimaginable destruction that he has planned."

"I didn't mean you personally."

"I know...you meant if it's our only option would I agree that it must be done." I paused, resting my forehead against Lex's shoulder. "I still love him; God forgive me, but I do. I can't deny that our souls are connected, but I could never live with myself if I allowed him to murder countless humans and vampires all for the purpose of having unwavering devotion from those left alive. He has taken everything from me...he's left me alone in the world, and yet he claims to love me. I'm frightened of what he'll do next."

Lex rolled to the side, still holding on to me so that he ended up on top of me. "You're not alone in the world. I'm here, and I will do whatever you ask of me; I will stand by whatever decision you make. I swear it...on my soul."

I smiled halfheartedly and lamented, "Someone has taken The Palladium as well. I'm sure it wasn't Prometheus, but I can't imagine-"

"I have it," Lex admitted, wincing, "I wasn't going to keep it. I only took it for Malika and the council to examine. They were interested in how it has played a role in all of this. I was going to bring it back later tonight. I had hoped to return it without you having missed it. I know how much it means to you; I would never take something away that would cause you such sadness."

I leaned up slightly until our lips softly touched. Lex fell upon me instantly, pushing back forcefully. As much as my body craved his touch and my mouth craved his blood I pushed him away. It was selfish of me to accept his love while my heart was breaking for another.

"We should go," I said quietly. "There are…plans that need to be made."

"Of course," he said, kissing me quickly and pulling me to my feet.

This time Lex didn't bother to blindfold me, not that it mattered because I had no idea what direction we were going anyway. The only thing I was fairly certain of was that we were still in Romania, or close to it. In the short distance we had traveled the mountains never seemed to get any closer or further away. I couldn't make out any signs to give me a clue as to where we were, and as we descended to the ground Lex got us as close to the safe-house as possible so I had no chance of seeing the nearby village. I did discover I was correct in my assumption that the safe-house was a castle, though not as large or daunting as Corvin castle.

"What is she doing here?" A young man with dark hair and eyes demanded after opening the door for us. "You were not given permission to bring her back!"

Lex didn't seem surprised by the outburst, but just walked in patting the man's shoulder as he quipped, "Give it a rest, Grigore. Nobody is going to burst in here and try to take over this rotting corpse of a castle."

I wanted to apologize for my intrusion and Lex's rudeness, but Lex pulled me after him so quickly I could barely keep up. He seemed too impatient to stop and ask someone where Malika was and instead decided to rush from room to room with inhuman speed, dragging me dazedly behind. We found Malika once again in the library, reading on one of the sofas.

When she realized it was Lex and me that had entered she threw down her book and jumped to her feet. "What has happened? Are you in danger?"

I opened my mouth to answer but Lex cut me off, "She saw Prometheus!"

"Prometheus?" she asked Lex in surprise and then turned to me, "Then it is true? He does exist?"

I could see Lex was anxious to answer once again but I quickly explained, "Yes, at least he claims to be *the* Prometheus, the titan that gave humans fire. Whether he is or not I could tell he is unimaginably powerful."

"How did you escape?" Malika asked.

This time I couldn't stop Lex from speaking first, "He didn't attack her; he was there to warn her."

Malika gave me a puzzled look. I told her in detail everything that had passed between Prometheus and me. I hoped that something might sound familiar to her; that she might have some insight as to how her son would have such a powerful ally, but she remained silent and thoughtful throughout my narrative.

"I wish we knew who this Prometheus was," Malika commented a few moments after I had finished. "Perhaps he could assist us, tell us more about this god that my son believes himself to be and how he plans to attain his godliness once more."

"I am afraid that is quite impossible...you see he must do anything I ask of him," boomed a familiar voice from behind us.

The three of us seemed to realize at the same moment who it was as our eyes widened looking from face to face and then whipping around toward the door. Dardanos stood there calmly, staring at us with a cruel smile on his lips. He seemed to avoid looking at me as if I weren't really there, or perhaps it wasn't my fault that I was there. I wanted to run to him, to explain everything, to give him the chance to deny all that Prometheus had told me, but the vicious look on his face gave me pause. This was the man that had every person close to me killed.

"Hello, Mother," he addressed Malika with a scowl, "I see you have met my wife."

"She's not your wife," Lex spat through gritted teeth.

"Dardanos," I said, stepping forward tentatively, "I asked to meet her. I forced Alexander to bring me to see her. There were too many secrets. I needed to find out for myself what was going on." I kept my voice steady, trying to keep the accusation out of my voice until I knew how Dardanos would react.

Lex put his hand on my arm to stop me from going any closer to Dardanos. "You haven't been entirely truthful with Lizzy, have you? Is it because your true plans are so revolting that she would never stay with you if she knew the truth?"

Dardanos gave Lex a narrow smile and his eyes seemed to frost over. "I can see that you know all about keeping the truth from those that you claim are close to you," Dardanos sneered, flashing his cold eyes toward Malika.

Malika stepped forward. "Setepamun, my son, Alexander is not to blame for keeping things from you. He honestly had no idea who he was or who I was. He was merely following orders."

"I do not go by that name...as you are well aware," Dardanos growled dangerously, balling his hands into fists.

"Of course, forgive me, old habits," Malika explained smoothly.

I shook off Lex's hand and took another step toward

Dardanos, no longer able to keep my anger at bay, remembering Prometheus's words. "Why are you here?"

Dardanos's cold eyes dropped as he admitted, "I followed you. I heard you call out to Alexander and I worried you were in danger, but when I arrived you were...you had just pulled away from a kiss."

I could see the hurt in his face and I again fought the urge to rush to him, my heart torn between my love for him and my hate of what he had done and planned to do. "I never meant to hurt you," I stated coolly, "but I can't be part of something that will result in so many deaths. I didn't know how to tell you. I guess I hoped you would just forget about everything to be with me. I've been so confused about my feelings...and so lonely. You were never there; you left me. I was never enough for you, and you…you…" I cried out in disgust, "…you murdered everyone I loved! How could you think I would never find out?! How could you think I would forgive you for inflicting such malicious suffering?!"

"I don't understand. You are supposed to want what I want. You are supposed to love me...no matter what," he protested as if these were rules written down somewhere.

"I do love you," I countered, "but now that love is mixed with hatred. What you've done to me is something I would never think to do to my worst enemy. I loved you; I agreed to marry you; I became what you are to be with you, but I cannot condone the killing of countless people for the sake of your dream. If you truly love me you will leave this bloodthirsty vengeance behind and live a quiet life with me at Cuckfield Park. I'll put my anger aside for what you've done if you promise to come back to England with me and live as my husband. We'll live as mortal husband and wife for as long as we can without drawing attention to ourselves." It was the plan I had told to Lex and now I would see if Dardanos would even consider it.

"You would have me give up my rightful place as a god to lead a meaningless life pretending to be human?" Dardanos asked in disgust.

I looked at him sadly, seeing he would never even entertain the idea, and I muttered sadly, "Yes...it's all I have ever wanted. Since the day I knew I loved you all I wanted was for us to be together, to share our life, preferably at Cuckfield, but we could go anywhere…anywhere in the world as long as we're together."

Dardanos regarded me a moment and then seemed to remember that Lex and Malika were still there. "I will never give up my goal," he snarled at them.

Malika stated flatly, "Then you will die...to protect the world from your madness."

Dardanos was shaking his head slowly and hissed, "I will be a god and I will wipe every last vampire off of this earth. I was going to hunt you down last, out of respect, Mother, but I suppose it is just as well if you are first. Don't worry, your deceitful son will follow soon behind you."

I looked from Dardanos to Malika in fear. Although I had said I would not stand in their way if they decided Dardanos had to die now I couldn't imagine watching him being destroyed right before my eyes. If I had fed as I should have my heart would have been beating out of my chest in anticipation of who would strike first. Lex seemed to be as shocked as I was, because not only had he kept quiet but his eyes too darted back and forth between Dardanos and Malika. He finally looked to me with a look I'd never seen in his eyes: fear. It wasn't fear for himself, but fear for me. He seemed to be calculating that I was the most likely to be hurt or killed as I had not been a vampire for a full month.

The strike happened so quickly it only looked like a blur to me. One moment Dardanos and Malika were at least twenty paces apart and the next moment Malika had crashed backward into a bookshelf and Dardanos was standing where she had been. I was so in shock I didn't know what to do, but suddenly Lex grabbed me and pulled me back as Malika rushed at Dardanos. As the two grappled, Malika flying into Dardanos and knocking him into the opposite wall, the door opened. Several vampires rushed into the room with weapons ranging from swords to lit torches.

"I'm going to get you out of here," Lex said fearfully, taking in the mayhem around us. "You haven't even made it past your first moon. You can still be killed as easily as a human."

He started pushing me toward the door when multiple screams stopped us in our tracks. We turned in terror to see (or rather I should say I assume it was what happened as it happened faster than I could see) Dardanos moving from vampire to vampire, draining them in moments. Three of them fell to the ground and turned a strange grey color; the other four seemed to only be weakened, but they were unable to even stand.

"That's not possible," I whispered in shock to Lex, "I thought vampires were immortal."

Lex put his arms around me protectively and answered, "We can still be killed. Those three were young, maybe only a few years as vampires, and Dardanos...well, he's more powerful than any I've seen."

Before I could ask another question Dardanos turned toward us, the murderous glare in his eyes made me fear not only for Lex's life but for my own. Dardanos turned into a blur as he advanced on us. Lex and I took shelter in each other's arms waiting for his attack, but it never came. Instead Dardanos let out a howl of pain.

Lex and I pulled away from each other confused. Malika was standing in front of us withdrawing a sword from Dardanos's middle. My eyes filled with tears, tears of pity at seeing Dardanos hurt and tears of relief that he hadn't attacked us, but I could see the wound was only a mild annoyance for him. His hand flew out like a whip across Malika's face, knocking her back a few paces. While Malika stumbled in surprise I saw Dardanos's eyes alight on a sword one of the dead vampires had dropped. I broke free of Lex to intercept the sword before Dardanos could reach it. Our hands locked on the sword at the same time and we stood with the sword held up between us. I thought it strange that Dardanos didn't use his immeasurable strength to take the sword from me; it would have been only too easy, but he was distracted by something behind me. His eyes flickered frantically behind me and Lex called out to Malika in horror. A rush of dread went through me as I turned in slow motion to see what was happening.

Malika had not seen me run past her to retrieve the sword before Dardanos could get it; she had been so stunned by Dardanos's strength she had been recovering from being knocked back so forcefully. In the moments that Dardanos and I grabbed for the sword Malika counteracted the blow Dardanos had dealt her by swinging her sword wide in an attempt to sever Dardanos's head from his body. The only problem: I was standing in front of Dardanos. It was only a second or two that our eyes met and I could see the dread on Malika's face as she realized there was no chance of redirecting the sword's aim.

There was nothing I could do. I closed my eyes and hoped I was strong enough to survive such an attack, but I knew this was it. I hadn't been a vampire for a month yet; I was still as vulnerable as a human to such an attack. My vision of lying in a coffin with my head askew had no figurative meaning; it hadn't represented the loss of my reasoning. It had been a very literal vision of my future, a future in which I literally lost my head…a future in which I was dead.

A NIGHT IN THE UN-LIFE...

"No! Malika!" Lillian screamed, throwing her hands out to block the sword.

"Lilly, it's okay! You're safe," Lex soothed, grasping Lillian's outstretched arms. "It was just a dream."

Lillian's eyes shifted from Lex, sitting beside her on the couch, to Ben, standing behind Lex smiling in relief.

"Ben!" Lillian exclaimed, jumping up and knocking Lex to the floor to embrace her father.

"Gee, I see where I stand in your affections," Lex said in mock indignation from the floor.

Lillian laughed and flung herself into Lex's arms on the floor. "Of course I'm happy to see you as well." Lillian's laughter turned to tears as she gushed, "I've been searching for you...for all of you, for years, and Ben..." Lillian turned to Ben. "The last time I had seen you you'd been stabbed with a necro-aim sword. I was so scared you were..."

Ben knelt down and took Lillian's hands. "I'm fine. Lex took me to safety and Malika healed me with her blood, but you? We saw you in the bonfire; how could you have survived that?"

Lillian shrugged and grimaced. "I'm not really sure. I stayed in the fire for a long time and it didn't so much as singe my hair; it only weakened me. I did drink from a very powerful vampire before we went to Cuckfield Park. His name was Vasile. His blood must have saved me. He told me it would make me as powerful as Dardanos."

Ben's green eyes were lit with pride. "I knew you were still alive; I knew you had to be. You're so much stronger than any of us thought, and I don't just mean because you drank from Vasile. Dallen knew you must still be alive as well."

"Dallen?" Lillian questioned, hope in her bright green eyes. "Where is he? How is he? I knew he would escape."

Ben gave Lex a stern look and explained, "We saw him on the roof as we were escaping. Lex grabbed him and we took him to safety. He fought us the whole way. He said we had to go back for you, even when we told him we saw you go into the fire and never come out. If he had been strong enough to travel he would have turned right back around and marched back onto Dardanos's property. He would be with us now, but, well," Ben paused and looked at Lex again. "Well, there were disagreements and he decided to stay with Vasile's coven for a while."

"You found them? I searched the North for Vasile, but I couldn't find his safe house. Where are they?"

Lex answered glumly, "Quebec. Dismal place."

"So they did go to Canada," Lillian said to herself. "Let's go. I must see Vasile; he's kept secrets that have hindered us from the beginning… and I…want to see Dallen."

"We'll take you there, I promise," Ben said, "but first there's something we want you to see." He got up, retrieving what looked like a book from a side table and handed it to Lillian.

Lillian opened to the first page and read aloud, "I would like to relate an account of the extraordinary discoveries I have unearthed. I was a prince in ancient times. You will not have heard my name or that of my mother's," Lillian paused and looked from Lex to Ben, "What is this?"

Ben answered, "It's an account of his life...Dardanos's. It seems he kept a journal detailing his life as an Egyptian prince, how he became a vampire, and how he set upon his current path."

"Where did you find this?" Lillian inquired, turning the book over in her hands.

Lex gestured toward the window facing the great estate in the distance. "We searched the manor house where he turned you. We thought we might find some clue as to where he might be, but instead we found that journal. It was only by chance we stopped here to search the manor house; we happened to be close by and thought it as a good a place as any to look for any hint of Dardanos or his army. While we were searching the house I felt the pull of a very powerful vampire nearby."

Lillian's eyebrows knitted as she asked, "Was it Dardanos?"

Lex and Ben both laughed out loud, but it was Lex that answered, "It was you. Your presence is strong enough to scare most vampires away, but we too thought it might be Dardanos.

We figured we should check it out, see if we could at least find out where he's hiding himself. Instead we found you passed out on the stairs as if you had begun crawling up just as you passed out."

Lillian shook her head unable to remember crawling up the stairs, but her eyes fell back to the journal. "I don't need to read this. I know all about Dardanos, his life as a prince, and his plans. I saw it all."

Lex propped himself up on his knees. "What do you mean you saw it?"

Lillian gave Lex a long sympathetic look. "I had a dream, or a vision, or a memory...I don't know what to call it." Lillian pursed her lips before saying low, "I am Elizabeth Cranford...or at least I was. I experienced what happened to her, to me, just before she became a vampire until her death. I have memories of her, of being her, and even some of being other women even further back in time. I was Cassandra of Troy and a priestess in Egypt name Amunet. I remember them all as if I were them yesterday, especially Elizabeth. I almost feel like I'm still her and this is the dream."

Lex was stunned to silence as he stared at Lillian, searching her eyes for the truth. "Then you know–"

"I know everything," Lillian cut in lightly, "at least I know everything Elizabeth knew." Lillian placed her hand over Lex's. "I know you were in love with her. I can't imagine how much it must have hurt you to look at me every day...and see her. I know that Malika killed me, and I know it was an accident; she was trying to kill Dardanos. I know that Dallen and Rachel have also played significant parts in my past, and you were once a god. I also know where Dardanos came from and what led him to his grand scheme. It was me, or more accurately Cassandra of Troy, which I guess is me as well. The cruelty inflicted on her caused Dardanos to beg Hecate for the power to defeat his enemies. She gave him The Immoral Fate: the power to devour his enemies, mortal and immortal. And the priestess Amunet, me, she enlightened the reincarnated Dardanos as to who he was and agreed to help him to become a god once again. Everything truly is my fault...from the very beginning."

Ben knelt down, pushing the hair back from Lillian's face. "I know why you might think that; we read the journal, but you can't blame yourself for something that was set into motion thousands of years ago by two men fighting for the affections of the same woman."

Lillian nodded her head, but noticed Lex still looking down. "Lex, what is it? Is it me? Are you upset with me?"

"No," Lex muttered, the beginning of a sob hanging onto the end of his word. "Now you know what happened. You know that Malika caused your death; you know that I failed you. I'm so frightened I'll fail again. Lilly, how can you ever forgive me...I'm not strong enough to protect you. I've spent the last hundred years convincing the oldest of our kind to share their blood with me just so that I would be strong enough to face Dardanos again, but it's still not enough. Somehow he is always just a little stronger."

"Lex, I don't blame you or Malika for what happened. You did your best to warn me and I didn't listen until it was too late." Lillian paused, looking down and smiled softly. "I should have accepted your offer to run away with you, but even then fate would have found us. It's something Dardanos told me once: fate finds us all...no matter where we hide. Eventually we would have had to face fate. And I know Malika was trying to protect us from Dardanos...she didn't mean to hit me. I saw it in her eyes just before I died. There is nothing to forgive," Lillian said, putting her hands on either side of Lex's face. "And you don't need to be strong enough to protect me. No one needs to worry about being strong enough to protect me, because I intend being strong enough to protect us all. If my soul truly is connected to Cassandra, Amunet, and Elizabeth, these remarkably strong women, then it's time I accepted the responsibility of setting things right. It was my greed, my need for love and unwillingness to give it up, that caused the fate of the world to become so twisted. Sometimes the best way to win a war is to give up."

Also Available
By J.M. Merillo

The Immortal Fate: Lillian's Story

Immortal Dreams: Poetry by Lillian Gray
(Companion book to The Immortal Fate)

J.M. Merillo

was born in Medina, NY. She fell in love
with writing poetry at the age of ten and soon
after found a passion for creating stories. J.M.
spent her childhood moving every few years
to a new place, continuing to write to cope
with the constant upheavals. *The Immortal
Fate: Lillian's Story* is her first novel. She
also wrote a book of poetry titled *Immortal
Dreams: Poetry by Lillian Gray* as a companion
book the *The Immortal Fate.*

J.M. lives in Florida with her husband and two
children.

For more information visit:
www.facebook.com/authorjmmerillo
www.twitter.com/jmmerillo
www.jmmerillo.wordpress.com

www.ingramcontent.com/pod-product-compliance
Lightning Source LLC
Chambersburg PA
CBHW080837250626
47160CB00009B/2963